DARKEST FLAME

DONNA GRANT

St. Martin's Paperbacks

This is a work of fiction. All of the characters, organizations, and events portrayed in this novel are either products of the author's imagination or are used fictitiously.

DARKEST FLAME

Copyright © 2014 by Donna Grant.
Excerpt from *Fire Rising* copyright © 2014 by Donna Grant.

For information address St. Martin's Press, 175 Fifth Avenue, New York, NY 10010.

ISBN: 978-1-250-04136-4

Printed in the United States of America

St. Martin's Paperbacks edition / May 2014

St. Martin's Paperbacks are published by St. Martin's Press, 175 Fifth Avenue, New York, NY 10010.

10 9 8 7 6 5 4 3 2 1

Praise for the Dark Warrior novels by
DONNA GRANT

MIDNIGHT'S KISS

5 Stars TOP PICK! "[Grant] blends ancient gods, love, desire, and evil-doers into a world you will want to revisit over and over again."   —*Night Owl Reviews*

5 Blue Ribbons! "This story is one you will remember long after the last page is read. A definite keeper!"
                                                                —*Romance Junkies*

4 Stars! "The world of the Immortal Warriors is a thoroughly engaging one, blending powerful ancient gods, fiery desire, and touchingly human love, which readers will surely want to revisit."   —*RT Book Reviews*

4 Feathers! "*Midnight's Kiss* is a game changer—one that will set the rest of the series in motion."
                                                                —*Under the Covers*

MIDNIGHT'S CAPTIVE

5 Blue Ribbons! "Packed with originality, imagination, humor, Scotland, Highlanders, magic, surprising plot twists, intrigue, sizzling sensuality, suspense, tender romance, and true love, this story has something for everyone."   —*Romance Junkies*

4 1/2 Stars! "Grant has crafted a chemistry between her wounded alpha and surprisingly capable heroine that will, no doubt, enthrall series fans and newcomers alike."
                                                                —*RT Book Reviews*

MIDNIGHT'S WARRIOR

4 Stars! "Super storyteller Grant returns with…A rich variety of previous protagonists adds a wonderful familiarity to the books" —*RT Books Reviews*

5 Stars! "Ms. Grant brings together two people who are afraid to fall in love and then ignites sparks between them." —*Single Title Reviews*

MIDNIGHT'S SEDUCTION

"Sizzling love scenes and engaging characters fill the pages of this fast-paced and immersive novel." —*Publishers Weekly*

4 Stars! "Grant again proves that she is a stellar writer and a force to be reckoned with." —*RT Book Reviews*

5 Blue Ribbons! "A deliciously sexy, adventuresome paranormal romance that will keep you glued to the pages…" —*Romance Junkies*

5 Stars! "Ms. Grant mixes adventure, magic and sweet love to create the perfect romance story." —*Single Title Reviews*

MIDNIGHT'S LOVER

"Paranormal elements and scorching romance are cleverly intertwined in this tale of a damaged hero and resilient heroine." —*Publishers Weekly*

5 Blue Ribbons! "An exciting, adventure-packed tale, *Midnight's Lover* is a story that captivates you from the very first page." —*Romance Junkies*

5 Stars! "Ms. Grant weaves a sweet love story into a story filled with action, adventure and the exploration of personal pain." —*Single Title Reviews*

4 Stars! "It's good vs. evil Druid in the next installment of Grant's Dark Warrior series. The stakes get higher as discerning one's true loyalties becomes harder. Grant's compelling characters and the continued presence of previous protagonists are key reasons why these books are so gripping. Another exciting and thrilling chapter!" —*RT Book Reviews*

4.5 Stars Top Pick! "This is one series you'll want to make sure to read from the start…they just keep getting better…mmmm! A must read for sure!" —*Night Owl Reviews*

4.5 Feathers! "If you're looking for an author who brings heat and heart in one tightly-written package, then Donna Grant will be a gift that makes your jaw drop. You don't want to miss *Midnight's Lover*." —*Under the Covers Book Blog*

4 Blue Ribbons! "Ms. Grant wields her pen with a lot of skill. Her consuming stories and relatable characters never fail to grab my attention. Her latest book, *Midnight's Lover*, is a wonderful example of what a good romance should be about, passion, love and plenty of action." —*Romance Junkies Reviews*

To Mom –
For all the joys of being your daughter!

ACKNOWLEDGMENTS

So much goes into getting a book ready, and I couldn't do it without my fabulous editor, Monique Patterson, and everyone at SMP who was involved. Y'all rock!

To my amazing agent, Louise Fury, who keeps me on my toes. Hats off to my team – Melissa Bradley, Stephanie Dalvit, and Leah Suttle. Words can't say how much I adore y'all.

A special thanks to my family for the never-ending support.

And to my husband, Steve. For . . . well, everything! I love you, Sexy!

CHAPTER
ONE

Dreagan Land
April 20th

The night was dark and tranquil as Denae slid against an oak and waited for her partner, Matt, to catch up. They had jumped from a slow-moving van under the cover of darkness two nights earlier.

While she had only her knife—and two more no one knew about—Matt had been given a Glock. He had tried to keep it hidden, but Denae had seen it just the same.

An owl hooted nearby and crickets sang loudly in the stillness. Wind rustled the leaves as it swept through the branches of the trees. The moon played peekaboo with dense clouds that moved like dark giants swiftly across the sky.

A perfect night for spying.

"What are you waiting for?" Matt whispered irritably as he moved around her and took the lead.

Denae adjusted the pack on her back and watched Matt through her night-vision goggles. He was such a prick. Not once in all her time at MI5 had she questioned orders. But she found herself doing so now.

MI5 protected the UK, its citizens, and its interests on its own soil as well as overseas, against threats to national security. Denae had done her research on Dreagan Industries, as she did with any target she was given. Dreagan had been making whisky for as long as there were records, and besides the fact that the file was anorexic, there was nothing about Dreagan that would prompt MI5 to take a closer look.

Yet here she was.

It made sense with her photographic memory that they would send her with Matt, but . . . there was more going on. Spies rarely trusted anyone—especially other spies.

There were factions within divisions of MI5 that were kept secret, or as secret as it could be in a building full of spooks. That wasn't what was disturbing. It was the fact that there was a deeper Black Ops level section she had only caught whispers of after being put on this mission that sent her mind into overdrive.

Denae had become paranoid and suspicious once she learned it was that secret division that gave the order to infiltrate Dreagan. She became even more suspicious after she found two bugs in her flat as well as a tracking device on her car.

Even so, opting out of the mission wasn't a possibility. So here she was, in the dead of night with a partner she couldn't stand.

Denae kept low and followed Matt through the thick underbrush of ferns. Ever since she had crossed the border onto Dreagan land she'd had an odd feeling prickling the back of her neck. Almost as if they had broken more than just the law by trespassing.

And it left her on edge and tense.

Not a good mix with her suspicions—and her dislike of Matt the Prick.

There were consequences for breaking rules. What

would be the price if they were caught? Then again, they were MI5 agents. They wouldn't get caught.

She and Matt had a few hours to reach the spot designated on the GPS she carried. In two days they had crossed just over twenty thousand acres. They moved quickly and quietly, resting sparingly.

"How close, Lacroix?" Matt asked once she reached him.

He didn't wait for her to answer before he rushed to the next tree. Denae ran by him without stopping. Matt had never particularly warmed to her, and though she had worked with him before without incident, he hadn't been happy when she was assigned to this mission.

Matt had voiced his displeasure loud and clear for the entire department to hear. Denae hadn't cared—at least outwardly she had portrayed that sentiment. What she did care about was that it was just the two of them. More teams should have been sent to different parts of Dreagan's border to make sure nothing was missed. There were so many mistakes being made that she couldn't help but wonder why Dreagan was a target.

Her apprehension kicked up a notch. Vague statements of "You'll know what it is we're searching for when you see it," combined with the clandestine faction giving the order, mingled with nonexistent proof that anyone at Dreagan was doing anything wrong made her anxious and tense.

Denae bit back a grunt when Matt spitefully slammed into her shoulder. She cut him a look. "Three clicks," she bit out.

Matt was the golden boy of MI5. She had earned her position after years of hard work, but Matt had climbed the ranks easily—too easily. Her annoyance was also due to the fact Matt had been given private orders beyond the ones they had been given together. And it left her with a weight in her stomach.

When MI5 became secretive with their agents, people died. Was that what this was about? Had Matt been dispatched to assassinate someone? Denae hadn't gotten that order, and though she loved her work, the only time she had taken a life was in self-defense.

She paused at the threshold of the thick forest, which protected them as the trees turned to a sea of grass that stretched endlessly from one end of the valley to another and majestic mountains rose up on either side.

Denae took the lead since she had the GPS device. She kept as close to the mountain as she could, her eyes darting around, waiting for an attack she felt was imminent.

Frank, her superior, stated the people of Dreagan were dangerous, but she had been given no specifics on how they could be. Nor had her look into Dreagan shown anything.

Frank had said Dreagan and its people were private because they were hiding something. What exactly that was she hadn't been told either. She was just supposed to know it when she saw it.

Denae glanced over her shoulder as she ran. Had Matt been told? Did he know what made the people of Dreagan—all of them—so important that MI5 was sent?

Her musing was cut short when they approached the designated spot. Denae slowed to a walk and pointed to the pool of water that rippled as a gust of wind blew past. "That's it."

"Good," Matt said and jerked off his night-vision goggles before shrugging out of his pack.

Denae did the same and stepped out of her black utility pants and removed her black jacket. Beneath, she wore a solid black wetsuit. She had just taken out the small tank, mask, and fins when Matt stared at her with an unreadable look.

She felt his censoring gaze and slowly counted to ten. "I know you don't like me, but get over it. And remember the feeling is more than mutual."

"I understood your use when you were undercover at the universities, but I can't believe they sent you on this important mission."

"Why? Am I not good enough?" she asked as she put on her fins.

He was silent for several seconds. "You do well enough, I suppose."

Denae frowned and looked at him. "Wow. I guess that's as close to a compliment as I'll get from you."

"You should've stayed in America and joined the CIA or FBI instead of being lured to MI5. There are others with photographic memories."

"So, it's because I'm American."

"You'll regret ever joining MI5," he said cryptically and jumped into the water.

It wasn't the first time a colleague had made mention of her being American, but none had ever come close to threatening her as Matt just had. She would prove that she was put on this mission because she deserved it.

Denae slipped the tank onto her back, fit the mask over her face, and put the regulator into her mouth before she plunged into the deep pool. Thanks to the weights on her belt, she sank quickly.

Swimming had always come easy, and she used her skill and speed to cut through the water. Small lights on either side of their masks lit the way through the pitch-black water.

Huge rocks jutted from the floor beneath. The closer they got to the mountain, the thicker the boulders became until they were weaving through them.

Denae effortlessly caught up to Matt. She was swimming past him when he reached out and pulled her regulator out of her mouth. With a twist of her body, she turned to see what he was about when she spotted the knife in his hand.

In an instant, he cut the straps to her tank. It fell out of sight into the water below before she could grab it. Denae immediately went on the defensive. She kicked out her foot and hit him squarely in the chin.

Matt jerked backward, giving her enough time to turn and slip through the narrow slit where water gushed from the mountain to fill the pool.

Her lungs burned. She focused on cutting through the water as fluidly as a fish, just as her father had taught her. The retort of the gun was loud in the water. Denae turned her head and saw Matt firing his Glock, the bullets narrowly missing her. She had to get on land and gain the upper hand.

Twice she nearly bumped into rocks. She spent the precious few seconds and bent her leg to her chest, where she pulled out a glow stick stashed in a pocket on her leg and cracked it.

Bright green light flared. Denae let out a few bubbles of air and started swimming. There was no doubt Matt had tried to kill her. Since she didn't know how long the tunnel was before it opened up inside the mountain, he could very well get his wish.

Death by drowning. She should've expected as much since it was how her sister died.

Denae refused to think about Renee and that life-altering day as she kicked harder with her legs. Matt was still behind her, and if she was going to come out of this with any chance at living, she had to reach the surface before he did.

With the water so dark, she wouldn't know when the tunnel opened up without feeling it. Denae moved as close to the top of the tunnel as she could. The water rushing the other way made her progression slower—and her body shake from the need for air.

Denae squeezed her eyes closed for a second to focus. When she opened them, she powered forward even as she caught a glimpse of Matt's mask lights cutting through the water.

She let out another few bubbles of air and wondered if

this was how Renee had felt when she drowned. It had been years since Denae had thought of that fateful day that changed her family's life forever—and guilt remained her constant companion.

With her thoughts churning, it took her a moment to realize the roof of the tunnel was no longer above her. Denae pointed the glow stick upward and saw only water.

She kicked hard and propelled herself up. When she broke the surface, she gasped in air before she sank beneath the water again. Denae wasted no time swimming to the edge. She tossed the glow stick onto the floor of the cave and quickly jumped out of the water.

Matt was right behind her before she had time to kick off both her fins. His, she noticed as he stood glaring, had been removed in the water. They circled each other around the glow stick while she managed to kick off the last fin.

Matt's smile was sinister as he shrugged off his tank. "I should've known you'd be a fast swimmer."

"Was it always your plan to kill me in the water?"

"Not kill you, Denae, just wound you."

She frowned. "Wound me. Why? So you get all the glory of this mission?"

"You are a stupid one."

"Enlighten me then, or get on with the fight."

Matt lunged, the knife in his hand aimed for her leg. Denae blocked his thrust with the side of her arm and punched him in the jaw with her other fist.

He spun and thrust his foot out, trying to trip her, but she jumped and kicked, landing a foot directly in his chest.

"You're bait," he said with a sneer as he stumbled a few steps back.

A fission of dread made her heart skip a beat. Bait. There was only one reason for bait, and it never ended well. "Since I'm such an idiot, explain it to me."

The excitement in Matt's eyes said it all. "Your mission

in all of this was to die so we could reveal just who those at Dreagan really are."

Just as she expected. "You'll wound me because you suspect those at Dreagan will kill me once they discover me."

"Something like that," Matt said with a snort of laughter. "We need to catch those at Dreagan. Your death will ensure that. Those here at Dreagan will never know they killed an MI5 agent."

"But my death will give MI5 the reason to investigate Dreagan," she finished.

Denae was appalled. Not just because they wanted to kill her—and "they" meaning everyone in her division had planned this—but because those at Dreagan were being set up.

There was no need for her to reply. Matt had his mission, but Denae wasn't going to go down easily. She feinted with a left jab and kicked Matt against the side of his head with her right foot.

He hissed and lunged for her again. This time she wasn't able to block him and felt the sting of pain as the blade slid through her wetsuit and into her skin on her left side.

Denae hit Matt's arm, which held the blade, so it pulled the weapon out of her. She then elbowed him in the throat as she was turning. He landed a foot at the back of her knee sending her to the ground.

She tucked and rolled, and when she came to her feet, she had her knife in her hand. No one liked to spar with her when it came to knives because she was so good. Now that she had her weapon, she had a chance.

"Know your death will free the world," Matt said as he attacked once more.

CHAPTER
TWO

Kellan kept utterly still in his corner. The sound of water sloshing against stone woke him instantly. He opened one eye to see the normally glass-like surface rippling violently as he caught sight of a human emerging from the water.

He barely had time to register it was a heavily breathing woman before a second joined her—this one male.

Kellan shifted his head to get a better look. It had been many centuries since he'd seen a human, and quite frankly, he could go through eternity without seeing another. How he despised them.

He didn't like his sleep being disturbed either. Yet, he knew Constantine wouldn't be happy if he made himself known in his dragon form and ate the two intruders . . . as tempting as that might be.

His only other option would be to shift into human form and confront them. And that was too distasteful to even consider.

Kellan stayed in his spot and watched as the two circled each other. *Nothing's changed. Humans are always fighting.*

No matter how many centuries passed, no matter what

country he visited, they were all the same. Selfish, belligerent, arrogant, greedy bastards.

Not that he cared how many humans killed each other. The more dead meant they were that much closer to the dragons returning home. It was because of the humans that dragons no longer ruled the realm.

It was humans who had begun the war.

But it had been dragons who ended it.

The humans were talking. Kellan listened to their exchange with interest. He thought back to the many times Con had visited him while he slept, and realized it had been many, many, *many* centuries since he last woke.

Con's visits every few decades kept those dragons who wished to sleep away centuries—or millennia—up to date on the world so when they awoke they were more or less knowledgeable about the times. So it wasn't difficult for Kellan to make out what the humans were saying.

The male disliked the female according to the way disdain dripped from his voice. Surprisingly, the female didn't cower. She fought back, moving quickly—for a mortal—and striking the male deftly and accurately. None of her punches or kicks went astray.

Kellan smelled blood. It had been a long time since that scent assaulted him. It made him think of the last time he had walked among humans—and why he had chosen to sleep.

There was a grunt from the pair. The male had a broken nose and a cut lip, but the scent Kellan held was strong, too strong for such paltry wounds.

His dragon eyes locked on the female, and he caught sight of her left arm held protectively against her side. Blood ran thick and fast down her leg to drip upon the stones.

In a whirl, the female came up with a weapon of her own.

Kellan's interest sharpened when the male said he

wanted to wound the female. It wasn't hard to guess she was to lure the dragons.

He inwardly snorted. Stupid humans. They all thought dragons base creatures who wanted to eat everything in sight or char it. How could he and the other Dragon Kings have fallen so far?

They used to rule the skies, the seas, and the earth. Every dragon of every color had called earth home. They had reigned supreme.

And for Kellan and the other Dragon Kings, it had been their right to rule their dragons, keeping everyone in line. That's not to say there weren't battles, but with one word from a Dragon King, all fighting would cease.

How Kellan longed for the days of old. He missed his dragons, and he missed being able to take to the skies whenever he wanted. It was one of the many reasons he decided to sleep away the time. He couldn't look upon the earth and humans without wanting to kill them all.

Kellan was impressed with the female, even though he hated to admit it. She was a valiant fighter, and though she was wounded, she was winning.

She moved in a lightning-quick spin before she kicked her opponent to the ground. Then she landed on top of him and sunk her blade into his heart.

Just like that, the battle was over.

The female had lost too much blood, however. She couldn't swim back out, and she didn't know her way through the caves of the mountain to seek help.

The only one that could help her was Kellan. And that wasn't going to happen. There would be hell to pay with Con, but Kellan had ceased to care long ago.

He wouldn't return to sleep until she had breathed her last though. Kellan expected her to fall over and die, or try to find her way out.

Instead, she kicked the male away and leaned back against a boulder before pulling some sticks from a pocket on the leg of her skin-tight suit. She bent them, and with a slight *pop*, green light shone around her.

She set those aside and took another small pack from a pocket next to her ankle on her other leg. Her breathing was harsh, and sweat coated her skin.

"Shit," she murmured and swallowed audibly.

Her accent wasn't Scots or British. Kellan went through all the dialects Con had played for him over the centuries in his mind until he reached American.

Could that be why the Brit hadn't cared for her? It was a silly reason, but then again, humans rarely made sense.

Kellan forgot about accents as the female reached behind her and grabbed something. There was a zipping noise before her black suit loosened.

With a grunt she pulled her right arm out of the black material before carefully extracting her left. She pushed the thick fabric down, giving Kellan a view of a small top that held her breasts. A bathing suit, he recalled.

Her chest heaved as she tried to breathe through the pain and her skin grew pale. Once more she took the small black parcel she pulled from the pocket of her leg and opened it. She grabbed a white packet and tore it open using her teeth. She briefly closed her eyes before pouring the tiny granules over her wound.

A gasp passed her lips as she jerked from the contact. Kellan had never had much to say about humans, but he had to give the female credit. Her hands were coated with blood, her arms shook, she was weak, and it was dark, yet she never gave up.

His interest was piqued when he saw her pull out a curved needle and thread. With her wound on her left side, she had to twist to see it, yet she managed to get several stitches done before she slowly fell unconscious.

For long minutes, Kellan stared at her. The female was slumped to her side, her breathing low and irregular. He knew that a fever could soon overtake her.

If it were up to him, he would forget her. She'd die—as all mortals did. Then Kellan remembered why he had chosen to sleep. He had made a vow once, a promise he had broken because of his hatred of humans.

Con could have ended his life, but he had allowed Kellan his sleep. He seriously doubted Con would give him another pass. Constantine was the King of Dragon Kings. He was the ultimate law—though that never stopped any other Dragon King from doing what he had to do.

Con took their duty of protecting humans seriously. If it had been up to Kellan, he'd have wiped the world of mortals long ago. They were an infection that stained everything. Look what they had done to dragons.

Everything known about dragons was nothing more than a myth, feared and fantasized into something that wasn't even close to resembling what life as a dragon really was.

Kellan vividly remembered standing after a battle with the humans to find his beloved Bronzes littered upon the ground. The bronze dragons were the Bringers of Justice.

While Kellan had ordered them to protect the humans, the humans had in turn killed them. A betrayal that even now, thousands of millennia later, Kellan couldn't forgive.

Because even though dragons were supposed to defend mankind, mankind had never wanted their protection. The mortals had sought early on to betray the very beings that had ruled the land first.

But Kellan hadn't been the only one betrayed. Ulrik, King of Silvers, had been deceived by a human female— and then by the rest of the Dragon Kings.

Kellan squeezed his eyes closed as he thought of that day. If he'd known what would become of his Bronzes, he'd have sided with Ulrik.

In the end, the dragons had been the ones to lose everything. Con had sent them to another realm.

And the Kings remained behind.

What good were they though? The few times Kellan woke from his sleep and faced the world, he found his brethren hidden away in plain sight, waiting until cover of darkness or a storm to dare to take to the skies.

Flying was their right, their privilege, and even that had been taken away. Because of humans.

Hours ticked by while he mused over his hatred of man, but still the female didn't so much as twitch. Kellan would have no choice but to bring her to Con, because he didn't trust himself to try and see to her wound.

Hatred didn't so easily dissipate through the centuries.

He wasn't ready to wake from his sleep, but with the two humans invading his mountain, Con would want to investigate. Kellan also found himself curious at the intrusion.

Using the telepathic ability between all Dragon Kings, Kellan called out Con's name, knowing his friend would arrive quickly. With barely a thought, Kellan shifted into human form. He rotated his arms and shook out his legs. There were no clothes for him to don because he'd had no intention of waking for many more millennia.

He walked naked to the woman and squatted beside her. Kellan didn't have the power to heal her as Con did. The bleeding had slowed, but it hadn't stopped.

Kellan shifted the woman onto her back, noting how hot her skin was to the touch. His body, however, responded instantly to the softness of the female, and it infuriated him. His body needed release, but it wouldn't be by this woman.

Promptly ignoring his thickening cock and the soft curves of the female's breast, Kellan picked up the needle she had been using and finished stitching the wound.

The male had managed to miss any of her vital organs, but the wound was long and deep. As delicate as humans were, Kellan knew Con was needed if she was to live. The choice of whether she died or not would be Con's.

Once Kellan finished, he bit the thread with his teeth and tied it off before lifting the woman into his arms. The feel of her curves reminded him of the yearning for a release clawing at him. He had to see to it. It wasn't because of this particular female in his arms. It had just been too long.

Kellan told himself that once more for good measure before he strode from his cave.

Many of his fellow Dragon Kings had taken human females as lovers. Kellan had had several before his Bronzes were killed. Afterward, he took a female only when he could stand it no more.

It was unfortunate that his body demanded such release. He glanced down at the woman in his arms. She was thin, but her muscles were finely honed. Her dark hair was held back away from her face in a knot so he had no idea how long it was.

Kellan barely looked at her face. There was no need. He never planned to see her again once he deposited her at Con's feet, even though Kellan admired her courage and tenacity. That's all she would get from him.

That's all he could give.

It was much more than he had given a human in thousands of years.

Kellan navigated the corridors of his mountain easily until he came to the entrance. Just as he expected, Con, along with Rhys and Kiril, stood waiting for him.

Con's face was grim, his blond hair wet from the rain that drenched the world outside. "I knew it had to be something important for you to call to me. Who is she?"

"I doona know, and I doona care," Kellan said as he tried to hand her over to Con.

Instead, Con clasped his hands behind his back, clearly refusing to touch her, and inhaled deeply. "You found her wounded?"

Of course Con would think he had hurt her. Kellan didn't blame him, not after what sent him to sleep in the first place.

"Nay. She located my cave," Kellan bit out as he tried to keep his anger in check. He didn't want to hold the female any longer or smell her scent or feel her curves. "Take her so I can return to my sleep."

Rhys raked a hand through his long, dark hair before wiping the rain from his face. "Most of the other Kings have been awake for months. Did you no' hear Con's call to arms several months ago?"

"If I did, would I have remained asleep?" Kellan asked, a brow lifted as he stared flatly at Rhys.

"This isna the first time our borders have been breached," Con said before Rhys could respond. "I need you to take a few days and return with me to the manor. After we have this woman settled and her memory wiped, you can resume your sleep, old friend."

Kellan didn't bother arguing. He didn't like hearing Dreagan's borders had been crossed, and if Con issued a call to arms, then it must have been important. "Fine. But someone take her."

Kiril's green eyes danced with humor as he turned away. "You look as if you've got her in hand. She's nicely formed too. Are you tempted?"

The woman's head turned, bringing her cheek against Kellan's shoulder. Her fever raged, reminding him why he'd called Con in the first place.

"She's fevered," Kellan said, his gaze locked on Con as he ignored Kiril's question.

Con said not a word as he closed the distance between them and laid a hand on the female's forehead. "Aye. I'm anxious to know what happened to her."

"There's another in my cave. They fought, and the female killed him."

"No' good news." Con frowned. "In that case, I think it might be better if our visitor isna completely healed until we have more information from her."

He didn't care what Con did as long as he took the woman. Kellan didn't want to be responsible for her anymore. He'd done his duty and brought her to Constantine. That should be enough.

It had to be enough.

As Con used his magic and healed the woman enough so that her fever vanished, Kellan looked over the King of Kings. Con wore black slacks and a white dress shirt with the cuffs unbuttoned and rolled up to his elbows. Con's blond hair was shorter than last time, but his black eyes still saw everything.

Kellan then glanced at Rhys and Kiril who stood at the entrance of the mountain with their backs to them. Each wore jeans and boots. While Rhys donned a thin, dark olive-green sweater, Kiril wore a simple white tee.

"That should do it," Con said and stepped back. "It's a good thing I had Kiril drive with this storm."

Rhys chuckled. "His driving has improved enough in the six months he's been awake that he's no longer hitting sheep."

"I only hit the one, damn you," Kiril said testily and shoved Rhys.

Con walked between them, and once he was past, Rhys's arm swung wide and lightly punched Kiril in the jaw before he ran into the storm. Kiril gave a shout and followed.

Kellan looked toward the outside world he wanted no part of, to the woman in his arms. The sooner he got her to the manor, the sooner he could return to his cave and to sleep.

Yet, somehow, deep in his soul, he knew as soon as he left the mountain, his life would change forever.

Kellan walked to the opening and looked through the curtain of rain to find his friends waiting for him in a black vehicle that read "Range Rover" across the front.

He met Con's patient gaze before he stepped out of his mountain.

CHAPTER
THREE

Denae slowly came awake, but kept her eyes closed. Even without looking around she knew she was no longer in the dark mountain by the clean smell and light hitting her eyelids. Who had found her? And where had they taken her?

After what Matt had divulged, she couldn't return to MI5. They would kill her one way or another for the information she now knew about the setup of Dreagan and MI5's interest. She could inform those at Dreagan, if they believed her. Yet, where could she go afterward? The agency would easily track her down.

There was movement around her and a chair squeaked as someone rose to their feet. When the door opened a second later, a male voice spoke in low tones to someone else in the room.

"How is she?"

"The same," said a deep, gravelly voice close to her. It sounded as if the man hadn't used it in a long time.

"She's been sleeping for twelve hours."

"I know." The irritation and annoyance practically dripped from his voice.

He didn't want her there, whoever *he* was. The other man who came into the room seemed genuinely worried about her, however. If she was lucky, maybe he wasn't part of MI5.

"Let me know the moment there's change," said the first man before the door closed behind him.

The floor creaked as the irritated man walked around her bed. "You can open your eyes now."

For a split second, Denae thought of staying as she was, but the man knew she was awake. Why pretend? She opened her eyes and found herself looking at a chair covered in a navy-and-red plaid. The chair the man had been sitting in, she mused.

It was close to the bed, giving him access to tend to her? Or to keep watch?

Probably the latter.

Denae turned her head to get a look at the room and found him standing with his back to her as he gazed out the large window opposite her bed. His hair hung down the middle of his back in thick, loose, caramel waves.

He kept shifting his shoulders as if the deep orange tee was confining when it shaped his shoulders, arms, and back to perfection.

His arms hung loose by his sides, but his fingers gripped the windowsill, telling her that being in the room was the last place he wanted to be.

Her gaze lingered on his wide, thick shoulders that tapered to narrow hips. Slung low on those hips was a pair of dark denim jeans, which hugged his bum nicely.

As much as she was enjoying the view, her mission had been compromised. If she survived long enough to leave Dreagan—because there was no doubt that's exactly where she was—she wouldn't be alive long enough to pack her bags and get on the first flight back to Texas.

"Are you in pain?" he asked.

Denae tentatively tested her left side before she carefully pulled herself up against the headboard. "It's minimal."

The silence lengthened until she thought he'd fallen asleep standing up. Suddenly he turned to face her, and her breath locked in her lungs. Her mouth went dry and her heart pounded.

The man before her was as beautiful as a god, as blinding in his anger as the sun. And she couldn't look away.

His caramel-colored hair was parted on the side and hung in those same waves around a face sculpted from granite. He had high cheekbones and hollow checks that gave way to a hard jawline and square chin. His lips were wide and seductively full. His eyes, a startling celadon, held her captive in his intense, almost cruel gaze.

Somehow she pulled away from his eyes and looked down to his chest, which was just as impressive as his back. The tee molded to the thick sinew of his arms and chest.

He was a man who took action, a man who suffered no fools. A man who wouldn't rest until he had all the answers he wanted.

"Who are you?" he demanded.

She was drawn once more into his pale green eyes. "My name is Denae Lacroix."

"Well, hello, Denae," said a voice from the doorway.

Her head snapped to the door to find a tall, commanding man with surfer-boy blond hair and eyes as black as pitch. He was tall and broad of shoulder, and she had a feeling his dress clothes hid a body corded with muscle.

He stood confidently, his control over the house obvious. He was the leader, the one who would determine if she lived or died.

Behind him was a woman holding a tray of food.

How had Denae not known someone was at the door? The hinges popped when it opened. She was usually more aware of her surroundings than that.

She glanced to the man by the window, but he had already looked away. As if he couldn't stand the sight of her.

Disappointment settled uncomfortably in her belly. She'd been so drawn to him that the world had simply vanished. It had never happened before, and in her line of work, that could get her killed.

And obviously the attraction was one-sided.

"Do you know where you are?" the man from the doorway asked as he walked into the room.

The woman *tsk*ed and hurried to Denae, placing the tray across her legs. "Con, please. She's injured and most likely starving."

"She trespassed."

This came from the man at the window. How Denae wished she knew his name. Even when she was looking at the others, she couldn't completely pull her attention from him.

"Hi," said the woman with a bright smile and coffee-colored eyes. "I'm Cassie. I wasn't sure what you'd like, so I brought a little of everything."

Denae couldn't help but return her smile. "You're American."

"Yep. From Arizona actually. You?"

"South Texas."

Cassie's eyes widened as she pushed her brunette hair over her shoulder. "We'll have to catch up later."

"I'd like that." And Denae meant it. She hadn't thought she would miss the States, but after being gone for so long, she did. She cleared her throat to settle herself and looked at the man Cassie had called Con. "Yes, I know where I am. I'm on Dreagan."

"We'll get to the why of that in a moment," he said and settled himself into a slender chair near the window that looked too dainty to hold someone of his size.

He sat as if he were relaxed, but he reminded Denae of a caged lion just waiting for a reason to attack. And when the attack came, it would be quick.

And lethal.

"My name is Constantine. Have you heard of me?"

She glanced at the other man. Again. "Only in reports. I know nothing else."

"Reports?" asked the unknown man, his gaze flickering briefly to her.

Con leaned forward in the chair and motioned to the second man. "This is Kellan, Denae. He's the one . . . who found you."

Con's pause was deliberate, but she didn't understand its meaning. Her gaze returned to Kellan to find he had once more turned to look out the window, dismissing her as irrelevant.

Damn, but he was gorgeous. Even if the thought of being in the same room with her annoyed him.

"Who sent you?" Con asked.

Denae lifted the glass of water from the tray and drained the entire contents before she bit off a piece of toast, chewed, and swallowed. That little bit helped to ease the hunger gnawing at her. "I wish it was as simple as telling you."

"You're safe here," Cassie said.

Denae smiled sadly and stared at the tray of food, her appetite suddenly gone. "I was betrayed."

"By who?" Cassie urged.

What difference did it make if they knew? They could have let her die. Instead, they brought her back and tended to her wound. Was it a ruse, though? She had been well and truly betrayed by MI5. Denae no longer knew who to trust, but her odds were on those at Dreagan at the moment.

In all her missions, with all the insight she'd gained from people, she had learned one hard lesson—the only one she could trust was herself.

She lifted her gaze to Con. "If I tell you, can you get me out of the country under a different name?"

"You want to disappear?" he asked, intrigued.

"Yes. If I can get out of the country, I'll make sure I'm never found."

Cassie sank into the chair beside the bed. "And if they find you?"

"They'll kill me. It's what Matt tried to do. I was bait."

"Bait," Con repeated slowly, his brow furrowed. "Tell me who sent you."

"MI5." Denae almost expected MI5 operatives to bust the door down at the mere mention of their name. They did claim to know everything that was going on.

Con surged to his feet and paced the room in silence. For the first time Denae actually noticed the room and not just Kellan.

The bedroom was spacious, with the large window in front of the bed and two narrower ones on either side letting in an abundance of light. The walls were painted a muted steel blue with eggshell-colored crown molding so large and intricate that it boggled her mind.

The floors were dark hardwood with rugs of varying sizes and colors placed throughout. A fireplace with a white marble mantel was on her right.

A cream comforter accented with navy piping around the edges lay across the mattress of the four-poster bed. Next to the bed was a small table with an antique-looking clock and an array of yellow daffodils and white tulips.

The window dressings were the same cream as the comforter with navy sheers pushed aside to let in the light. A picture of a sunset over a loch filled one wall, while an ornately framed oval mirror graced another, and a collection of small square pictures of what could only be described as Scottish life filled another.

It was a gender-neutral room, and she found the colors soothing. She had never been partial to floral prints or pastels.

"Why has MI5 focused on us?" Con asked as he stopped at the foot of her bed.

She looked into his black eyes noting the barely suppressed anger and shrugged. "My orders were to use my photographic memory to record what was in the cave."

"What were you looking for?" Kellan asked.

Denae glanced at Kellan before looking at the bed. "My superior said I would know it when I saw it."

Con's frown deepened. "That's all you were told?"

"Yes," she answered. "On the swim to the cave, Matt tried to cut me before shooting at me. At the surface we fought. He said that once you found me wounded, you would kill me, never knowing I was MI5."

"And giving MI5 ammunition to come after us," Con finished with a mumbled curse as he dropped his chin to his chest.

"Why do you work for them?" Cassie asked.

Denae carefully shifted against the pillows and hid a wince as her stitches pulled. "I was recruited mainly because of my photographic memory. It was when I considered joining the Navy and took the tests that people from the FBI and CIA tried to acquire me. I didn't know what I wanted to do. Before I could make a decision, an MI5 agent contacted me. It was a change of scenery that I needed, so I accepted."

"You left everyone behind for a change of scenery?"

Denae looked at the floor as the old pain, an ache that always hit her right in the middle of her chest when she least expected it, slammed into her. "There was no one to leave. The real reason is that they had me working undercover at the universities for stalkers, rapists, and for those thought to want to bring down the UK. I brought those scumbags to justice."

She licked her lips and looked up to find Kellan watching her with those celadon eyes of his, devoid of emotion. Some would consider him cold, callous. She thought him indifferent, as if he watched the world and wasn't really a part of it.

How she wished she could have adopted such a life after her father died. Instead, she'd been rudderless, going wherever life took her—and it hadn't always been good.

"How long have you been in MI5?" Con asked, thankfully pulling her out of her thoughts.

"Seven years. I was a sophomore in college when I took their offer. I worked for them while they paid me to attend the universities undercover. It worked great since I was American and no one suspected I worked for the British government."

"And from there?"

"I worked my way up like anyone does." She swallowed, trying not to notice how she couldn't get her heart rate down as long as Kellan was staring at her. "I was making progress. I didn't expect to be a field agent forever, but until I could find where I fit elsewhere in MI5, it was a great starting point."

Con took his seat again. "Tell me about your latest mission."

Denae ran a finger over the back of the knuckles on her left hand. She'd worn gloves that kept her skin from breaking when she'd hit Matt, but her knuckles were still sore.

"I was chosen with Matt. He was lead operative, the favorite of the bigwigs at MI5. No one was more surprised than me when I picked to pair with him. Two days later we were dropped off in the middle of the night on the edge of Dreagan."

"Dropped off?" Cassie repeated. "How did you cross?"

Con's jaw clenched. "More importantly, where were you dropped off?"

"We were at your southeast border about twenty miles west from the village. As for how we crossed, we were on foot. For two days, Matt and I followed the coordinates we'd been given."

Con had been sitting passively while she spoke, but as soon as she mentioned coordinates, fury filled the room.

Denae glanced at Cassie to see worry lines bracket her mouth. Denae's gaze swiveled to Kellan to see even he was startled by her revelation.

"I don't know where the coordinates came from," she hurried to add.

Cassie scooted to the edge of the chair and looked at her with expectation as she asked, "Can you find out?"

Denae slowly shook her head. "Matt wasn't given that information either. The coordinates led us to a small pool outside of a mountain. Beneath that pool is an outlet. We followed that through until we reached inside the mountain and a cave."

"And that's all the mission was?" Con asked. "To get inside Dreagan so you could be betrayed and used as bait?"

"I don't know what the real goal was. Matt's mission was to leave me behind so I would be killed by you. I was told we were to do reconnaissance on everyone at Dreagan after we found whatever was in that cave."

"Reconnaissance on us? Why?" Cassie asked, startled.

"Too many secrets here, I guess." Denae shrugged. "I wasn't told."

Kellan snorted with scathing hostility. "And you didna ask."

"It's my job to do the mission, whatever that may be. I'm protecting the people of the UK."

Con sliced his hand through the air. "Get back to your story. What happened once you reached the cave?"

"As I already told you, while in the water, Matt tried to kill me. I wasn't ready to die or be used as bait, and I was angry at being betrayed. Only one of us was going to come out of the attack alive. I made sure it was me."

"There's more," Kellan said.

Denae opened her mouth to say there wasn't when she remembered Matt's words. "Matt did say that the world would know who you were and be freed."

Cassie rose and turned her back to the bed as she whispered, "Oh, God."

"But you won the fight," Con said. "You killed him. Why should I believe what you say? He's the one who could be bait. We're mostly men here. Would it no' serve your purpose if we were to rescue you instead of a male?"

Denae wasn't surprised by Con's words. "I've nothing to offer as proof. I don't want to know whatever it is MI5 is trying to uncover. They sent me here to die. If I return to them, I've failed in the mission and I know too much. They'll kill me. If I leave and try to travel anywhere under my own name, I'll befall some accident that will take my life."

Con rose, a small, calculating smile on his lips. "So, Denae Lacroix. Your life is in our hands, aye?"

"Yes," she said, though it pained her to do so.

"Good. Considering I believe you, I'll allow you to leave under a new name, but until that happens, you're going to give me everything you know about MI5 and who is working there."

As if she had a choice. She needed to leave Dreagan—and the country—and her best chance was by cooperating. "Deal."

Con opened the door, and Cassie walked out ahead of him leaving her alone with Kellan. He walked with slow, measured steps to the bed, and her heartbeat accelerated at his nearness. Not because she felt threatened, but because he intrigued her, fascinated her.

Transfixed her.

He paused beside the bed and leaned down. Denae was as still as stone as his head lowered. Her lips parted in anticipation of his kiss.

His hands gripped the tray and lifted it from her lap. Then he turned on his heel and left the room, the door closing softly behind him.

"Great, Denae. Thinking you're going to get a kiss from a man who can't stand to look at you."

She had better things to worry about, like how she was going to evade MI5 and MI6 for the rest of her life. But even through all of that, she couldn't stop thinking of celadon eyes and caramel-colored hair.

CHAPTER FOUR

Kellan pulled the door shut behind him with his foot as he walked from the room. He wasn't sure what prompted him to get that close to Denae again.

Denae. It was a beautiful, refined name that rolled off his tongue with ease. As much as he hated to admit it, it suited the woman who bore it.

He had seen for himself how well trained she was, but even with her defensive moves and confidence, she was all woman. And he hated how he noticed that.

Noticing was nothing compared to recalling the feel of her body in his arms. The entire car ride back to Dreagan he'd held her against him.

Her warmth, her clean smell still hadn't left him. Nor was he able to push aside the enticement her amazing body offered.

And her face. Kellan nearly groaned aloud as he thought of her whisky-colored eyes that pierced his very soul.

Her heart-shaped face was captivating, her kissably plump lips tantalizing. How he kept his hands from running over her cheekbones and delicate jawline, he'd never know. Even her coppery-brown eyebrows tempted him as they arched over her eyes.

She was, he hated to admit, breathtakingly beautiful. There was a fragility about her that warred with the strength he had witnessed.

Denae was an enigma, an irresistible morsel he did *not* want to take a bite of.

Kellan walked to where Cassie stood with the others and stopped in front of her, the tray he held nearly hitting her before she grabbed it. He waited for his body to respond to Cassie as it had to Denae, but to his chagrin, nothing happened.

"You better have a damn good reason for being so close to my mate," Hal stated, ice dripping from each word.

Kellan turned his gaze to Hal and lifted a brow. "If you doona want men around her, perhaps you should've thought twice before living here where she's surrounded by Dragon Kings."

"Enough," Con said before Hal could respond.

Kellan looked back at Cassie. "She willna eat now. Give the woman another thirty minutes and then bring her a new tray. I suspect she'll eat then."

"Why won't she eat now?" Cassie asked, her brow furrowed as she took the tray.

"Because she's scared," Con answered. "That much was obvious. What isna so clear is if she's frightened of us or MI5."

Cassie glanced at the door to Denae's room and frowned. "She was given coordinates to Kellan's cave. Is someone betraying us?"

"No' someone here," Hal said as he put a comforting arm around her.

Con sighed loudly. "It's Ulrik. We just have to figure out how he's doing it."

"He's no' been on Dreagan in thousands of millennia," Kellan said. "How do you figure it's him?"

"Who else would it be? Besides, the layout hasna changed," Hal said.

Cassie looked up at Hal, love shining in her gaze. "How quickly you all forget. We don't know if it was Ulrik leading the plot through PureGems. It could be someone else."

"Nay," Con stated emphatically. "It can be no one else, Cassie. Ulrik is the only Dragon King who isna on this land. He's the only one with a grudge against us, the only one who would benefit from seeing us destroyed."

Kellan listened intently. There were goings on that he had no idea about. Despite his desire to return to his cave and resume his sleep, it might be prudent if he stayed awake long enough to ensure whoever was causing this mischief was taken care of. Even if it was Ulrik.

It had been a shock for Kellan to learn that Hal had taken a mate, but Kellan had been stunned to discover Guy and Banan had as well.

Had none of them learned from the duplicity and treachery of humans? Had what happened to Ulrik with his woman faded from their memories?

Memories of his last dealings with humans tried to surface, but Kellan quickly pushed them aside. If he thought of that day, he might as well let his fury take him again. Then where would that leave all of them?

"PureGems?" Kellan repeated.

Con nodded. "Aye. I need to catch you up on some things. Follow me."

Kellan gave a nod to Cassie and Hal as he walked behind Con to his office. So much had changed at Dreagan Manor, and yet so much remained the same.

The same dragon pictures still hung about the place, though in different areas. Dragons could still be found in everything from the carved banister to table legs to metal dragons protruding from the walls holding the lights.

As much as it soothed him to see the familiar things, it amazed Kellan how much humans had advanced. Through Con's visits to his cave, Kellan had learned of every war, electrical invention, plane, vehicle, and weapon. He'd learned of clothing and speech, and world powers.

None of it put the mortals in a good light.

Once inside Con's office, Kellan sat in one of the over-stuffed chairs situated in front of Con's large desk where dragons were carved in unique—and sometimes—almost invisible ways.

"You've no' said much," Con said as he sank into his chair. "You've been asleep for a verra long time, my friend."

"I'd prefer to have remained that way."

"You really didna hear my call?"

Kellan shook his head. "You know I wouldna have ignored it had I heard you."

"Most of the others awoke," Con said as he picked up a pen and twirled it in his fingers. "That's another story I need to tell you. We're now allies with the Warriors."

Kellan was astounded by the news, and he didn't hide it. "I suppose there's a good reason for that."

"There is. I'll tell you all about how Cassie, Elena, and Jane came to be mated with Hal, Guy, and Banan. That will lead into why the Warriors know of us and how we came to go to battle with them."

This was getting more and more interesting. Kellan was almost happy he was awake to hear these stories. For so long the Dragon Kings had watched the Warriors, but Con had been adamant about keeping away from them. Something drastic must have happened to change his mind.

"Before I get to all of that, I need something from you."

Somehow Kellan wasn't surprised. "You've no' changed."

"Nay, I suppose I have no'." Con's nostrils flared as he drew in a deep breath. "I need you to keep an eye on Denae. Find out all you can about MI5, her involvement, and if she's lying. Gain her trust by any means necessary."

"I'd rather no'." The words came out harshly, but Kellan was so averse to spending any more time with Denae, that the mere mention of her name caused his hackles to rise.

It was Con's turn to lift his brows in disbelief. "You'd rather no'?"

"I didna stutter."

"Care to explain?"

Kellan shifted, hating how the clothes confined him. It was because he had spent so long sleeping that his body had forgotten what it was like to be in human form and wear clothing. "I doona want to chance a repeat of . . . the last time I was awake."

"You willna," Con said as if he were the one making that decision. "Need I remind you that it was your cave they had the coordinates to? You saw them fight. You heard their words. No' me, no' anyone else. You, Kellan. It has to be you who gains her trust."

"I doona like her."

"You doona like any humans. I understand and respect that, however, there are three females mated to your brethren."

Kellan gripped the arms of the chair to rein in his growing ire. "You think I'll harm them?"

"Nay. I'm merely pointing out a fact. I may no' have wanted Cassie, Elena, or Jane at Dreagan or mated to Dragon Kings, but there is no denying the love between all three couples. Be nice to the females. I doona want infighting. We've enough to deal with."

"You doona have to worry about the mated females. I'll be courteous to them."

Con leaned forward until his forearms were braced on the desk. "There are other humans about, Kellan. We hire many of them to work at Dreagan in various tasks."

Surrounded by humans. It was enough to send Kellan back to his cave that instant. Then he remembered the threat to all the Dragon Kings, and he knew it would be awhile before he returned to his cave and the peaceful sleep he longed for.

"Will that be a problem?" Con asked, his black eyes piercing him.

Kellan met Con's gaze. "If they doona betray me, then there willna be a problem."

"Fair enough. Now, about Denae."

Kellan rose to his feet and walked around the office. He needed to move, to work the tingling of his limbs out. His gaze clashed with Con's sword hanging on the wall. Each Dragon King was marked with a tattoo, but they were also gifted with a sword.

"I'll share all I know about what I witnessed with Denae and her partner, but I think it wise that I stay away from her."

"I disagree," Con said.

Kellan faced him and narrowed his gaze on the King of Kings. "What are you up to, Constantine?"

"I'm trying to protect Dreagan and everyone who calls it home. I want to know why your cave in particular was targeted, and you're the best one to discover the reason."

Kellan wasn't buying it for a minute. Con would do anything to protect Dreagan and the Dragon Kings, but there was more to his request.

"Fine," Con said and threw down the pen. "I think you need some interaction with humans to help curb your hatred. No' all of them are bad, Kellan."

"That I doona believe. I saw for myself, remember."

"That was a verra long time ago."

Kellan walked until he stood behind Con's desk, looking out one of the windows to the green valley below and the white dots of sheep. "There will always be hatred in my heart for the humans. They butchered my Bronzes who were there to protect them. They betrayed Ulrik, thereby betraying every one of us."

"Did killing that human wash away the pain?"

He ignored Con and said, "It's because of them I no longer have any Bronzes to rule."

"None of us have dragons to rule," Con said quietly. "We all feel the loss of them."

Kellan had been so lost in his own misery that he had forgotten that small detail. He wasn't the only Dragon King who had been betrayed. Or the only one feeling the loss of the dragons.

Con wasn't asking a lot. In fact, despite Kellan being the one who kept the history of the dragons, Con had allowed him to sleep away almost thirteen centuries.

"I'm no' the Dragon King I used to be," Kellan told him. "I'm no longer as patient or forgiving. I doona know how to be merciful or lenient anymore. If that's what you want with Denae, then I highly suggest you ask another."

There was a beat of silence before Con said, "I want you, Kellan. I wouldna have asked if I didna think you were up to the task."

Kellan clasped his hands behind his back. "I have to warn you, I have a particular distaste for Denae. Gaining her trust willna be easy since she'll know how I abhor her."

"I think you'll manage."

It was the smile in Con's words that had Kellan turning to his friend. At the wide grin on Con's lips, Kellan groaned. "What?"

"Do you think I didna see how you didna like touching her?"

"Aye, because I doona *like* her."

Con nodded, the smile still in place. "How long has it been since you've relieved your body?"

"You know the answer to that," Kellan bit out. "I'll remedy that as soon as I can."

"I saw Denae watching you."

"She was watching everyone. Her position is precarious, and she knows it."

Con leaned back in his chair. "Would it be so bad to get close to Denae?"

"Aye."

"Hmm. So you're no' attracted to her?"

Kellan walked to the door as he said, "Nay."

"No' even a little?"

"No' even a drop," he stated as he walked from Con's office.

It wasn't until Kellan was in the hallway that he considered exactly what Con was asking him to do. Get close to Denae. How was Kellan going to pull that off when he could barely stand to be in the vicinity of the female?

"For the dragons," Kellan murmured.

Just as Con had sacrificed so much, and the other Dragon Kings had hidden in order to preserve who they were, Kellan could do no less.

Con would do anything, say anything to guarantee Dreagan and the Dragon Kings lived on. Kellan would set aside his hatred to gain Denae's secrets.

But if he learned she had betrayed him and the other Kings in any way, he would kill her.

CHAPTER
FIVE

Denae gripped the sink in an effort to combat the pain of getting out of the bed and making her way to the bathroom. When the pain was under control, she lifted the pale yellow tee to examine her wound.

A large strip of gauze covered it. She peeled back the gauze and stared dumbfounded at the wound in the mirror.

"Is something wrong?"

At the sound of the deep, sensual voice, Denae spun around, forgetting her wound in her surprise. The pain struck instantly and caused her to gasp and try to grab for anything to stay upright.

She found herself in Kellan's arms as he held her gently but securely. Denae gripped his strong arms while she absorbed the heat radiating off him. She looked up and was snagged in his celadon gaze, his lashes so thick and black they would have looked feminine on anyone else.

Her body responded instantly to his touch. Her blood pounded through her while a slow, steady heat settled between her legs. Denae couldn't explain the irresistible and seductive attraction she felt for Kellan. It was there, as if it had always been and was just waiting for her to meet him.

As beautiful as his eye were, there were no emotions

there. It was like a bucket of ice water thrown on her. Denae pushed away from him, trying to ignore the rigid muscles of his chest beneath her palms as she did.

"You can leave now," she said as she faced the mirror
once more.

"You're pale."

Denae gripped the sink again. "Yep. That tends to happen when a person is wounded and loses a lot of blood."

"You should be feeling better."

She lifted her gaze to look at him through the mirror.
His words, combined with the way her wound looked as if
it was a week old instead of just a few hours, made her
scowl at him. "What did y'all do to me?"

Denae cringed as she finished. It had taken meticulous
work on her part to eradicate all Texas twang from her
speech, especially the *y'all*s.

"We tended to you."

She turned to face him, making sure to move slowly so
as not to pull her side. "What else did you do? I know how
deep that wound was. I know I was bleeding badly."

"The cave was dark," he said and leaned a shoulder
against the door frame before he crossed his arms over his
chest.

It caused his shirt to stretch even tighter over the thick
sinew. Denae had to look away. Damn him for looking
good enough to lick from head to toe. "You just happened
to be in the cave?"

"It is my cave."

Her eyes snapped to him as she frowned. "*Your* cave?
What does that mean exactly?"

"If I hadna been there, you'd be dead."

"I think it would've been better for everyone if that
were the case." Denae faced the sink again and turned on
the faucet. She splashed water onto her face, suddenly exhausted to the marrow of her bones.

She dried her face and spotted a brush. Without thinking,

she unpinned her hair and let it fall around her. It was still damp in places as she ran the brush through it.

Denae caught Kellan watching her hand as she moved the brush through her thick hair. Something flickered in his eyes, some nameless emotion that caused her to pause.

When she did, his eyes jerked to hers and the coldness returned. For several tense seconds, they simply stared at each other. He made her edgy, as if there was an undercurrent of something primal and sexual she couldn't grasp.

Denae wished she knew how to use her body as some agents did. Seduction wasn't one of her skill sets, and it hadn't been cultivated at MI5. If only she had paid closer attention to the agents who went undercover using their bodies, she might know what was happening to her now.

She returned the brush to its place and fidgeted, suddenly unsure of herself. The only time she felt such . . . restlessness was in Kellan's presence.

Was he doing it to her on purpose? If so, it was a great tactic because it was working to perfection. Double damn him.

"Do I make you uncomfortable?" he asked.

She refused to make eye contact with him again, even through the mirror. "Isn't that what you want?"

"Why would you think that?"

"Why are you in my room?"

"Is that no' obvious?"

Denae shook her head and gave a rueful laugh. "I've already said I would tell you all I know of MI5's plans regarding Dreagan. I don't need someone watching over me. I doubt I could escape even if I was up for it."

"You got onto our land and into my cave without us knowing."

"I think we got lucky," she said and started for the doorway, making sure to look anywhere but at him.

Just as she thought he might step out of her way, he

blocked it, forcing her to look at him. "What were you searching for?"

"Anything. Everything. As I told you, they said I would know it when I saw it. That's all I was told. When I asked why Dreagan was targeted, I was told there was suspicion. Matt knew more."

"And you killed him."

"It was kill or be killed," she said through clenched teeth.

Her strength was waning fast. As if sensing it, Kellan moved out of the way and she walked the few steps to the bed and gingerly sat down.

"Cassie brought you pain medication," Kellan said as he sat in the chair Con had vacated earlier.

Denae bit back a wince as she had to twist to get both legs onto the bed. "I have a high tolerance for pain."

"You mean you doona trust what's in the medicine."

"Something like that. I'm sure you understand."

To her surprise, there was a softening of his lips as if he had almost smiled. "Aye. It could be you're just obstinate."

"I don't enjoy pain," she said and pulled the covers over her bare legs. The shorts she wore had ridden up, exposing almost everything.

She might have left off the covers had she thought Kellan was interested, but his aloofness said it all. If only she could convince her own body that he wasn't worth the time, she might feel more in control of things.

"If you doona enjoy pain then take the medicine."

"Fine. I'll take the damn meds."

One caramel brow lifted. "You're easily riled. No' something I expected from an MI5 agent."

"Yeah, well, you seem to bring it out in me." As soon as the words left her mouth, Denae wanted them back. "Look, I'm tired, hurting, and angry over the betrayal of an organization and country that I've been protecting. I'm not myself."

"Actually, you're more yourself now than at any other time."

"Which is why you want to interrogate me now." She leaned her head against the headboard and got comfortable. "Shoot."

For a split second, she saw the confusion on his face before her word registered. "Can we no' just sit and talk?"

"You've not been talking. You've been antagonizing me."

"That's where you're wrong. I came in to see how you were doing."

Denae sighed. It was draining trying to talk to Kellan. It was almost as if they were dueling, except with words instead of swords. And she was losing badly.

"Why not send Cassie? I know you don't want to be in here with me."

"Cassie is busy tending to her husband."

Denae smiled then, feeling as if she had gained a small victory. "Ah, but you don't deny not wanting to be here."

"I doona deny it."

"I'm sorry." And she meant it. "It's never fun to be stuck with a job you don't want."

He didn't respond, and Denae found she couldn't keep her eyes open as the minutes ticked by.

She was drifting off to sleep when he said, "What is MI5 looking for on Dreagan?"

"I wasn't told," she repeated and yawned while her eyes remained shut. "I thought I was coming to do reconnaissance. It wasn't until Matt told me I was bait that I knew there was another mission. Why was I bait though? And why did I need to be wounded? Did they think some animal was going to attack me?"

"There could've been something in the cave with you."

Denae cracked open her eyes. "It's your cave. You said so. What was in there?"

"Me."

"You?" She couldn't get her sleepy mind around what he was saying. "You were there? You saw me and Matt fight?"

He gave a single nod of his head.

That brought Denae instantly awake. "How long did you let me bleed?"

"You're alive, are you no'?"

"That's not what I asked." She swallowed past the dismay in her throat. "You actually had to decide to save me or not. What kind of person are you?"

"No' like anyone you know."

"Obviously," she said, not bothering to hide her anger. "You're as bad as Matt. He used me, and I almost wasn't worth saving in your eyes. What has this world come to?"

He stretched out his legs and crossed his feet at the ankles. "I've been asking myself that for years. Aye, I admit to debating whether to help you. The fact is, I did."

"Do you regret it?" She waited tensely for him to answer, wondering why she put herself in such positions to continually get hurt.

"That depends on what you can tell us about MI5."

"Are you asking me now?"

"Nay."

Denae slid down on the bed until she was flat. "Do you plan to remain here all night then?"

"We wouldna want you thinking you could escape, now would we?"

Denae looked up at the ceiling. "Where would I go? For the moment, Dreagan is the safest place for me."

"As long as you cooperate and we doona believe you're lying, then you will be protected here."

"Can you really get me out of the country?"

"There is much we can do."

She grunted. "Maybe that's why MI5 is interested in you. I saw the file on Dreagan. It holds just a few slips of paper. So thin it didn't make sense for us to be sent in."

"How big are the files you normally see?"

She held up a hand and spaced her index finger and thumb apart. "About three inches or so. Before any mission is set, information is gathered on everyone and everything connected to whatever is being watched. From there, the mission is determined and several teams are sent in."

"I thought you said it was just you and Matt?"

Denae put a hand beneath her head to see Kellan. "It was just the two of us. That was another red flag for me, but then I thought other teams might have been sent in that we didn't know about."

"No one else has been located."

He said it with such certainty that it made her wonder if MI5 had been right to want more information on Dreagan and its people.

"Dreagan consists of over sixty thousand acres. There is no way you could cover all of it in the time since I was brought here unless you have advanced military equipment."

Kellan simply returned her stare, refusing to admit or say anything.

"You do, don't you?" she asked and sat up again too quickly, causing her side to pull and her to grimace. "Did you steal it? MI5 will stop at nothing to have that equipment returned."

Kellan leaned forward in the chair. "Did you ever stop to think there are more ways of doing something than a human's tiny mind could comprehend?"

Denae was left with her mouth hanging open as Kellan rose and walked out of her room, leaving her with his question running through her mind.

And no answer in sight.

CHAPTER
SIX

Somewhere in Scotland . . .

The dungeon was dark, as was the entire crumbling castle. As if that would make him anxious. He'd asked for the meeting to continue to cultivate a union that had not existed for well over ten millennia.

The Dragon Kings had made a crucial mistake in alienating the Fae. An error he wasn't going to repeat. He knew a secret about the Fae the Kings had been desperate to keep quiet.

He was taking things a step further and aligning himself with the deadliest Fae—the Dark Ones. These were the Fae who didn't hesitate to use their considerable power for anything—and everything—they wanted.

"You've kept me waiting," he said into the darkness.

He wasn't alone. He hadn't been alone since the moment he stepped across the old drawbridge. The Fae were everywhere. Two stood not a foot from him.

Not that he was scared. The Dark Ones had their own way of doing things, and they were still learning to trust him.

"Because I wanted them to," said the raspy voice of the

Darks' leader, Taraeth. An unearthly blue light suddenly filled the dungeon area. "Why did you call this meeting?"

"The plan to infiltrate Dreagan has run into a problem."

Taraeth's lip lifted in a sneer, his red eyes glowing. "We know. The human failed in his quest. The female is now in the hands of the Dragon Kings."

"Do you think they'll trust her?" he asked. "Of course they won't. They'll get all the information out of her they can, and then they'll let her go."

"She'll have seen them."

He shrugged. "Perhaps, but I don't think so. They will be careful. Once the woman has been released, I'll make sure MI5 is there to take her. The Kings will be keeping watch. They'll come to her aid. That's where you come in."

Taraeth's smile was cold and calculating. "You'll let me have a Dragon King?"

"Take as many as you can capture, and use them as you see fit."

Taraeth considered the new plan for several minutes before he folded his arms over his chest. "There is just one I want."

He nodded. "Ah, yes. Kellan. Why him?"

"None of your concern. What happens if this plan goes awry?"

"It won't," he stated. "I know the Kings. I know how they think. They'll play right into our hands."

Taraeth gave a nod, and the next instant the blue light was gone. And so were the Dark Fae.

He walked from the dungeon and back through the ruins of the castle, over the drawbridge to his car. He slid into the driver's side and started the car before pointing it in the direction of Perth.

Banan stared at the group of sheep being herded into the pen to be sheared. Ever since he had been told an MI5 agent was being held in the manor, he hadn't wanted to believe it.

It had been Henry North, an MI5 agent they had called on a couple of times, who helped him track the men responsible for kidnapping Jane in London.

The sound of approaching footsteps was drowned out by the bleating of the sheep, but Banan heard it just the same.

"It might be time to give Henry a call," Constantine said as he walked up.

Banan glanced over to find Con had traded his slacks and dress shirt for a white tee, faded jeans, and boots. "No' your usual attire."

"I couldna very well walk out in the mud and gunk in my customary clothes, now, could I?" Con stated in annoyance.

Banan closed one gate as that pen was filled, and then quickly opened another gate. "I doona want to hear what Henry has to say."

"You might. Jane said he's now taken to calling her since you willna answer your mobile."

Banan leaned upon the fence. "I like Henry, Con. Every time we've asked him for something he has always come through."

"What makes you think now will be any different?"

"Why didna he tell us?" Banan asked as he turned his head to Con. "Why did he no' warn us?"

Con shrugged. "He might no' have known. You know how different departments keep secrets from the others in the spy world."

He had a point, but the churning in Banan's gut told him that if Henry had betrayed them, there would be retribution.

"Call him," Con urged. "If Henry did betray us, do you really think he'd keep trying to call?"

"Aye. He might no' know what we are, but he knows we're powerful."

Con leaned over the fence and patted one of the fat sheep as it darted by. "If you doona call him, I'll invite him to Dreagan. Your choice."

Banan looked into Con's eyes and saw the truth of his words. A gust of wind passed through the valley, ruffling Con's blond hair. Banan turned away and rubbed his hand over his short, dark hair.

"Fine," he said and pulled out his mobile phone.

There were ten missed calls from Henry and three messages. Banan didn't bother to listen to the messages as he dialed Henry's number.

Henry answered on the first ring. "Banan."

"Tell me you didna know."

"I didn't," the Brit said hastily. "I swear. I only found out because I heard about two missing agents. When I learned what department they were from, I discovered their covert mission to Dreagan."

Banan closed his eyes. "I want to believe you."

"Then do. I called as soon as I found out. Jane wouldn't tell me anything. I can be at Dreagan in a few hours."

"Why would you come here?"

"Because I know you won't believe a word I say over the phone. You'll need to see me."

Banan turned around and faced Con. He knew Con could hear the entire conversation. "Why does it matter what I think?"

"I spend my life lying and blending in so that I'm not seen. I couldn't be picked out of a crowd of one, Banan. I'm good at my job, but there are times I want to be seen. You and the others from Dreagan see me. I'm not a ghost to you."

"Your decision," Con told Banan.

Banan closed the second gate before moving to another set of holding pens. "Will you be tracked here?"

"No. Nor are they listening in on this mobile. They don't know about this number. I'll be there tomorrow. Early."

"One of the agents is dead," Banan told him. "The second agent killed him when he attacked her."

Henry let out a long sigh. "This is so fucked up. We'll get it straightened out."

"We can handle it. The female claims she was betrayed by your organization. She willna trust you."

"She doesn't even need to know I'm there. I know the department she was working for. They've been known to leave agents hanging out to dry as well as having factions within their department go after each other. Keep her safe. They'll be coming for her."

Banan hung up the phone and pocketed it. "We've been so lucky in staying hidden all these centuries. Why do I get the feeling that's all about to end?"

"If it does, it does," Con said. "We'll follow our dragons to their realm and live with them once more."

"What about us protecting the humans?"

"Once they learn we're dragons they'll hunt us ceaselessly. Look at what they've done to Loch Ness just because someone claimed to see something in the water. That something just happened to be one of us. They've combed Loch Ness endlessly, and they willna give up even though they've no' found anything. What do you think they'll do when they discover we can shift into dragons?"

Banan squeezed his eyes shut. "No amount of hiding will help us then. There isna any place on this planet we can go."

"Nay, there isna. We'll have to leave or face war once more. I doona want the Kings divided again."

"We could scatter. Asking Jane to leave her realm will be difficult. If we're no' here, they'll have a hard time knowing who is a Dragon King."

Con looked out over the land. "They'll find out. They always do. You know we can no' leave for long. If we are no' here with our magic, the Silvers will wake and kill the humans. Those Silvers are the largest of Ulrik's dragons.

We have to keep them sleeping since they wouldna leave with the others after Ulrik's command."

"It willna be long until we're hunted. I'm no' sure I could bring up any pity for what the Silvers would do to the humans."

"And what would Jane think?"

Banan winced as he thought of his human wife who had become his mate a few months earlier. "She's one of us now. She would understand."

"I doubt it," Constantine said as he walked away.

Banan motioned to the shearers to get started as he moved to the next pen and opened it. For so long anonymity had been theirs. And they had taken it for granted.

It was one thing for Banan to be on the run hiding from the humans hunting him. It was quite another to take Jane with him. Leaving her wasn't an option either.

As his mate, she was now as much a part of Dreagan, despite that she couldn't shift. They were connected, joined in more ways than just their love and their vows. She would live as long as he did, and die when he did. Since he could only die by the hand of another Dragon King, she could, in effect, live forever.

Could they leave the realm? Part of Banan wanted to depart this instant. To see his Blues again was something he dreamed of often. Then he thought of Jane and knew she would follow him anywhere, but would she be happy?

Con walked into the still house and breathed in the many aromas involved in the process of making their renowned whisky. With the copper stills going, the place was loud, and it helped to mask the thoughts running through his head.

Banan was right. They would be discovered soon. It all hinged on just how soon was soon?

It was Con's job to keep the Kings safe and Dreagan a haven for them. How had it gotten so messed up? It would be easy to blame the women who were mated to his Kings, but Con knew they had no part in it.

No, the blame lay with whoever was pulling the strings behind the scenes. First it was PureGems and their attempt to discover something when they came in under the pretense of "caving."

It was only by following that lead, with Elena and Jane's help, that the Kings learned PureGems was just a cover, that there was someone else masterminding it. Jane had spoken to the man, but she never saw his face.

In his gut, Con knew Ulrik was a part of it—if not the one behind it all.

For centuries Con had waited for Ulrik to take his revenge, but he assumed Ulrik would target just him—not all of the Dragon Kings.

Con had done the right thing in killing Ulrik's woman those hundreds of thousands of years ago. She had betrayed Ulrik and the Kings. As King of Kings, it was Con's duty to take action.

He thought he could talk to Ulrik and make him see there had been no other choice. But Ulrik had spiraled out of control.

Con walked up the stairs to the platform to overlook the workers. He leaned his hands upon the rail. Ulrik had done the one thing they were forbidden to do—he had taken his Silvers and waged war on the humans.

It didn't matter that the humans were killing dragons. It was the Dragon Kings who were meant to keep the peace between both dragons and humans.

Con had failed in that.

Ulrik had been beyond talking to, leaving Con with only one choice again. He had stripped Ulrik of his right to shift into dragon form and had taken his sword. Con then bound Ulrik's magic so he couldn't communicate with his Silvers.

The rest of the Kings trapped a few Silvers to hide them

in one of the mountains where Dreagan was created. Ulrik was left to walk through life immortal, with no other benefits of a Dragon King.

The confrontation between him and Ulrik was coming. He had been expecting it for a while now. His onetime best friend, the one he had called brother above all else, was now his enemy.

Ulrik craved revenge.

Con would give it to him.

CHAPTER
SEVEN

Kellan wasn't sure why he returned to Denae's bedroom long after she had fallen asleep. He had stood guard outside her door for hours afterward, going over their conversation.

As dawn came, he entered her room expecting her to wake. Instead, he found her in the throes of a dream, and not a good one by the way she jerked and cried out.

Kellan went to her, ready to wake her, when she went still. He halted, then retraced his steps and took the same seat as the night before, not wanting to disturb her.

As hard as he tried to look away, his gaze was drawn to the long length of her thick brown hair that was streaked with copper as it flowed over her pillow.

When she had taken down her hair the night before and he had seen it fall around her in a curtain, Kellan had the urge to run his fingers through it. It was longer than he had expected, falling midway down her back, glossy and straight.

Rays of sunlight streamed through the windows. Once Denae had eaten, Kellan would begin to pull information from her. Con wanted him to use any means necessary.

Kellan hoped it wouldn't come to that. Being close to

her was a test he didn't want to put himself through. There hadn't been time for him to find a willing bed partner in the few hours since he had woken, but he needed to do it soon.

Things were getting drastic if Denae tempted him as she did. Even now, when he saw her leg peek out of the covers, he had the insane need to run his fingers along her skin, to push the blanket away so he could see more of her.

Kellan was jerked out of his musings by a distressed moan. Once more Denae was caught in a dream. She became tangled in the sheets, her words garbled so he didn't understand them.

"Renee!" she screamed and then her eyes flew open.

He remained still, not wanting to spook her.

After a moment, Denae let out a breath as her face crumpled. She covered her face with her hands, but no sobs could be heard, and there didn't seem to be any tears. Then she slowly sat up and ran a hand through her long tresses, moving the strands so that they hung to one side.

Her hand lifted and reached for the bottle of medicine. Kellan knew there was some drug called codeine in the pills that would diminish the pain. Yet, Denae's hand hovered over the bottle for several seconds, shaking, before she dropped her hand to her leg.

Suddenly her head lifted and she looked at him. Kellan didn't say anything, mostly because he wasn't sure what he should say. Obviously Denae was struggling with pain, and there had to be a good reason for her not to take the pills.

"Do you often have nightmares?"

She drew in a shaky breath. "They return when I'm stressed."

Kellan watched her closely as he asked, "Who's Renee?"

"My sister." Denae's eyes slid closed as she swallowed. "She died because of me."

When her eyes opened, Kellan held her gaze, waiting for her to continue. He hadn't expected her to open up, but now that she had, he wanted to know why she blamed herself for her sister's death.

"Renee was just a year older, and we were close. She had been dating an older boy in secret from my parents. Everything was going well until it suddenly wasn't. She suggested we go to the beach one afternoon where she told me she called things off with the guy but he wouldn't leave her alone."

He remained still as Denae lightly placed her hand over her wound and took a deep breath.

"I thought she was joking. I had no idea the guy had turned into a stalker and followed us. She was such a strong swimmer, stronger than I was. But when she wouldn't take him back, he drowned her. I can still hear her screaming my name while I stood in line for ice cream."

"How old were you?"

She blinked as if pulling herself out of her memories. "Fourteen."

"Where were your parents?"

"They were walking along the beach."

He couldn't believe he was about to comfort her—a mortal. Kellan looked into her eyes and said, "It's no more their fault than it is yours."

"Perhaps," she replied in a whisper.

"Would you like some food?" he asked to break the silence.

Her shoulders sagged as if a great weight had been lifted. "That would be nice."

"I'll see it done." Kellan stood and walked to the door. He paused as he opened it. "You may no' like to hear this, but you're weak. If you need help, doona be foolish and no' ask for it."

"You want me to ask you?" she asked with suspicion.

He looked into her whisky-colored eyes and wished to hell she didn't look so good rumpled from sleep, as if she had spent a night being made love to.

His need was great, and she was looking more tempting and alluring the more he was around her. It had to be just his body's need for release and nothing more. Kellan fisted his hand as he imagined sliding it through the cool locks of her hair so he could hold her head as he plundered her mouth in a savage kiss.

"Me or someone else," he said after he cleared his throat. "I can have Cassie come up if you like."

"I'll manage on my own."

She was as stubborn as they came. Despite trying to look away, he couldn't stop his gaze from sliding up her long, lean legs as she stood, or from watching the way the shorts stopped just short of him seeing the delectable bottom curve of her ass.

His gaze continued up to the shirt that hung loose, hiding her hips and waist from him, but there was no hiding the soft bounce of her breasts or the way her nipples were puckered and pushing against the fabric.

With his body already in need, his cock was hard and aching in an instant. The overwhelming, devastating craving to relieve his need was magnified tenfold just by looking at Denae.

Long slim fingers grabbed ahold of the bathroom door, and her whisky gaze turned to him. "I didn't lie last night. I can take a lot of pain. You can leave me alone for a little while."

Damn if his body wasn't fighting him to go to her. It was infuriating, even if he knew it was just the fact that she was a female in close proximity to a man who desperately needed to ease his body. He didn't want to be attracted to her, no matter what the reasoning.

Kellan left the room and shut the door behind him before the head between his legs ruled him instead of the head atop his body.

"How is she?" Rhys asked as he ascended the last few stairs to the second-floor landing.

Kellan couldn't get the image of her breasts swaying beneath her shirt out of his head. How easy it would be to rip that flimsy shirt in half and feast his eyes upon her.

He also couldn't stop thinking of her story about Renee. There had been true remorse and guilt in her eyes. The pain of her sister's death haunted her.

"Kellan?"

He inwardly shook himself and looked at Rhys. "She's hungry. I need to get her a tray of food."

Rhys narrowed his aqua eyes on him. "Let Kiril bring her the food. I think I should drive you to Inverness."

"Con wants me to get close to her." Though Kellan wanted to be anywhere but there. A ride to Inverness sounded great, especially because it would get him farther from Denae, but also because he could find a willing woman to slake his lust on.

"Does Con know you're barely holding it together?"

Kellan briefly squeezed his eyes shut. "I suspect he does. I also suspect he's doing it on purpose because I've been asleep so long." Kellan didn't bother to say the third reason, the main reason he had decided to sleep—the one only Con knew.

"He can be an arse," Rhys stated flatly. "I wouldna put either past him. None of us begrudged you your sleep. Return now. I'll see to Denae."

Without a doubt Rhys would do exactly as he claimed. It was Kellan's way out of all of it. Con might be the King of Kings, but that didn't mean he controlled the Dragon Kings.

So if Rhys was giving him the excuse to leave as he wanted, why then wasn't Kellan taking it?

All of a sudden, the image of Denae's hand shaking over the medicine bottle flashed in his mind. There was much the female was hiding. It could be something to harm the Kings, in which case Kellan couldn't return to his sleep.

At least that was what he told himself.

"No' yet," he said to Rhys. "I want to get to the bottom of all of this."

"Has Con filled you in on everything?"

"Last night," Kellan said. "It's quite a story how the women came to be mated with Hal, Guy, and Banan. The Silvers really moved?"

Rhys nodded woodenly. "We've still no' uncovered how or why."

"And the Warriors." Kellan had soaked up all the information on the Warriors and Druids of MacLeod Castle and their many battles with the evil Druids, or *droughs*. "Con actually told the Warriors what we are. And he fought beside them."

Rhys smiled widely as he stuffed his hands into the front pockets of his jeans. "Kellan, it felt wonderful to fight again. Besides, Charon and Phelan are good men. You'd like them, I think."

"So much has changed."

"And so much hasna," Rhys said softly. "We still wait until nightfall to take to the skies. Sometimes if the storm is intense enough we can fly during the day. We're no' free."

Kellan scratched at his chin and felt the whiskers growing. "We've no' been free since the humans arrived, my friend."

"I've missed you. I know it was your hatred of the mortals that kept you sleeping so long, but it's good to have you back."

His words eased Kellan somewhat and he forced his lips into some semblance of a smile. "It's good to see you again, too. Doona tell Con, but I've missed walking around this place."

Rhys laughed loudly. "Anything to put a knot in Con's knickers."

Kellan found himself freely grinning. Rhys never failed

to irritate Con one way or another. "How many of us are awake now?"

"About a third. Most took one look around and returned to their caves. The others are a bit more curious. We took turns through the centuries keeping up your work, but since we're no' official Keepers of the History, it might no' be all there."

At the mention of the history of the Dragon Kings, Kellan pushed away from the door and started for the stairs. As Keeper, he didn't need to be at an event to record it. It showed in his head much like the movies that were so popular. They continued even while he slept away the centuries. All he had to do was record them now.

At one time being Keeper of the History had been something Kellan had been proud of. That wasn't the case anymore. He turned his mind away from then when he heard something hit the shower wall. "Listen in case Denae falls. She's stubborn."

It took ten minutes for Kellan to find Cassie downstairs and then make his way back to Denae. As he neared her room, he found the door cracked with Rhys nowhere in sight.

Then he heard Denae's laugh and Rhys's voice. Kellan pushed the door open to find the pair at the window looking out.

"The sheep are climbing over each other," Denae said in awe as she laughed.

Rhys leaned a forearm against the wall. "They tend to do that sometimes. The sheepdogs run along their backs, especially when the sheep are penned as they are now."

"The sheep aren't being slaughtered, are they?"

Rhys's laugh was long and deep. "Nay, lass. They're being sheared."

"But you do slaughter them here," she said as she turned her head to him.

"A few. Mostly we sell them. They're loaded onto a truck and shipped off."

"Will you bring them all in? I see some far off in the distance that look like little white specks."

Rhys turned his head and spotted Kellan. "Aye," he answered Denae. "I think my time here is done."

"Done?" she asked and turned to see where he was looking.

As soon as her gaze locked with his, Kellan felt his blood heat. Her hair was still loose, beckoning him to touch it—to touch her.

Rhys cleared his throat into the silence. "Uh, Kellan, I told her I'd go see about finding her some clothes. She's no' comfortable walking around in . . ." Rhys pointed to the shorts and shirt on her body. "Well . . . that."

Kellan didn't understand why not. She hadn't said a word yesterday or earlier about wanting something else to change into. As it was, he wanted out of his shirt, jeans, and boots.

He wanted to be in the clouds, floating upon the currents and looking at the world from high above. He wanted his hands in Denae's hair, her body beneath him.

He wanted inside her.

Kellan looked away from her to Rhys. "That's a good idea. I'll go see about it."

"Already on it," Rhys said and hurried out of the room.

Kellan looked at the empty doorway long after Rhys walked out. There was no way he could begin to interrogate Denae until he had his body under control. That much was obviously—painfully—clear.

"Now it's my turn to ask if I make you uncomfortable," she said.

"Nay." It was all he could get out. And he prayed she stayed away from him. He wasn't sure how much restraint he could maintain if she came near him.

"Dreagan is a beautiful place. I've tasted the whisky as well. It's no wonder y'all have done so well."

He regarded her, comprehending that she was going somewhere with her talk. "But?"

"But . . . I get the feeling there is much more to this place. Take you, for example."

"What about me?" He shouldn't engage her in such a manner, but he was curious how she saw him.

She licked her lips, bringing his attention to their fullness, their plumpness that begged to be kissed. "You're different. When I look in your eyes, it's almost as if . . . as if I'm looking back in time."

Kellan knew he couldn't allow her to go on. He had to turn the tables on her, to get her to talk about anything but how she saw him. It was too dangerous for her—and for him.

He decided to repeat the questions already put to her. Perhaps he would learn something different, because there had to be more. He didn't want her to be a woman in need of assistance. He wasn't sure how much longer he could ignore her sweet curves.

Admitting that, even to himself, infuriated him. She was a human. He must remember what they had done to him and his bronze dragons.

"What did you and Matt really think you were going to find here? What did Matt believe would come out once he had you wounded and used as bait?"

CHAPTER
EIGHT

Denae wasn't fooled. Kellan changed the subject because something she said hit a chord. She refused to look away from his celadon gaze as he challenged her with his words.

"I got the feeling Matt was expecting something to come out." She closed her eyes and thought back to the cave. Denae had been intent on staying alive, but her training and her photographic memory let her catch every detail. "The way he said I was bait. It's almost as if . . ."

Her eyes flew open as a thread of disquiet wound through her.

"As if what?" Kellan pushed.

"As if Matt was expecting an animal. He wanted me bloodied, hurt so that I couldn't escape or move. The only reason for that would be if there was some kind of being and he wanted to get its attention."

Kellan looked away, a muscle in his jaw jumping as he clenched his teeth. "What was Matt's plan when this 'thing' he was trying to see arrived?"

"I don't know."

"Guess," he said tightly.

Kellan might be so damned gorgeous that she couldn't think straight, but he was infuriating as well. She allowed herself to glare at him a second before she considered the cave and what Matt might have been waiting for, plus their gear and weapons. "I would have returned to the water. The air tanks had more than enough oxygen to make several trips back and forth."

"Does MI5 no' need more than just one agent's eyewitness account?"

Denae nodded slowly and leaned against the wooden footboard of the bed. "They would've wanted definitive proof. Matt must have had some sort of device on him to take a picture or recording."

"And you expect me to believe you had no idea what you came to Dreagan for?"

"I'm cooperating, but no, I don't have any proof that would tell you I was the one who was betrayed. They wanted me dead. I was expendable, dispensable. The UK might not be my country, but I took an oath to protect it."

"MI5, however, didna take an oath to protect you, did they?"

How she hated that he was right. "No. I could say the same of any intelligence agency in any country. I knew if I was ever caught during a mission that I was on my own. This was different. I was set up, my own people turning on me."

"It's no' a good feeling, is it?"

The way he said it, the fury-laced words and bone-deep resentment told her that something similar had been done to him. "The feeling is enough to change someone forever," she said and watched him closely.

"More than you know," he murmured before he took a deep breath. "What else can you tell me about what MI5 knew concerning Dreagan?"

At that moment, Rhys returned, smiling. "I got you some clothes. Cassie pointed out that you might not want anything too constricting near your injury, so she gave me some of these."

Denae watched as Rhys held up a pair of black yoga pants. "Those will do nicely. Thank you, Rhys."

"My pleasure." He handed her the clothes with a wink.

She laughed at his flirting, because she knew it was harmless. Rhys was one of those guys who would flirt with any woman up to the time he found one who captured his heart—if he ever allowed that to happen.

At Kellan's odd look, Denae slowly made her way into the bathroom to change. She was elated to find a cami that had a built-in bra. Denae stripped out of her bottoms first.

Whoever had undressed her had removed her wetsuit and bathing suit she'd worn beneath, and then put her in a pair of bright pink cotton panties.

Denae turned on the sink faucets and grabbed a washcloth. She might not be able to get her stitches wet in the shower, but she was going to bathe.

"Need some help?" Rhys asked her through the door.

"Bugger off," Kellan said. "We were talking."

Their words became muted, and even when she turned off the water she still couldn't hear them. A moment later she heard Rhys leave the room.

Denae found the soap and began to bathe as best she could. "This place holds many secrets," she said, raising her voice so Kellan could hear her.

"Every place holds secrets."

She thought of the beach house her family owned, of that terrible day years ago, and knew he was right. "Will Con really let me go? Or will he turn me over to MI5?"

"MI5 came after us," Kellan said, his voice hard and unforgiving. "As long as you hold up your end of the bargain, we'll keep ours."

"There's a catch," she said as she dried off and began to dress. When she was finished, she opened the bathroom door to find Kellan sitting in his usual chair. "There's always a catch."

"And what do you think the catch is this time?"

"I don't know yet. There is something about Dreagan I can't put my finger on. It's a beautiful place with secrets, although, as you pointed out, there are many of those. There is still something different about this place. And you."

Kellan ran a hand through his long hair and shrugged. "We make whisky and raise sheep and cattle. No' anything to worry MI5 about."

"You were in the cave." The realization hit her out of the blue. How could she have forgotten that he'd said she was in his cave?

One caramel eyebrow lifted. "I've said it was my cave."

"But you were in it. How else would you know I was there?"

"It was luck that had me walking those caves and finding you. That is all."

Denae sank onto the chair near the bed and pulled her hair over one shoulder to braid it. She had thought another piece of the puzzle had been found, but Kellan had a believable answer to every question or statement she had.

"What would happen if both you and Matt had died and I hadna found you?"

"I suppose MI5 would have sent another team in, but more likely several teams. They would've guessed that whatever we'd been sent here to find had killed us."

"So you admit to being sent to find something?" he pressed.

Denae rolled her eyes as she finished her braid and tied it off. "For the third time, yes. I don't know what it was however."

"Did you no' have communication with MI5?"

"No. We were going in blind. MI5 didn't want anything traced back to them."

Kellan gave her a sardonic look. "And two agents wouldna lead us back to them?"

"We had nothing on us to suggest we worked for MI5. We could have been anyone. The only reason you know who we worked for is because I told you. MI5 has spies everywhere. You might think you're keeping me hidden, but I can guarantee they know I'm alive."

He sat forward, his gaze fixed, direct. "And we've guaranteed your safety as long as you cooperate."

"Which is what I'm doing," she said, exasperated. It was hard to stay irked when Denae didn't know if Kellan's anger was directed at her or something else.

He made sure to keep his distance from her. If she got too close, he would move away. It was subtle, but obvious.

"You said MI5 had a file on Dreagan," Kellan said, putting the conversation back on track. "What was in it?"

"Next to nothing. There were maybe twenty pages, tops."

"Anyone's picture? Any names?"

"Con's. His name, but not a picture. There was a picture of a woman with blond hair and green eyes. It said she worked for PureGems both in the US and UK."

Kellan's chin dropped to his chest. "That would be Elena. She's now married to Guy and living here. What else did they say about her?"

"They had a question mark by her name."

His head lifted, and the grim set of his features said that her words weren't what he wanted to hear. "A question mark? Why?"

"It could mean anything. For instance, it could be that they don't know if she's alive or dead, or if she's still in the country or not."

"Or if she's a part of whatever is going on at Dreagan, aye?"

Denae clasped her hands in front of her. "That is another possibility."

"Any other names or pictures in the file?"

"No, which is what really struck me as odd and very unlike MI5. When I questioned it, I was quickly put in my place and told my job was to complete the mission I was given."

Kellan rose to face the window, putting his back to her. The tan pullover he wore was just as fitted as the shirt from the previous day, and just as before, he looked uncomfortable in it. Though he didn't shift his shoulders as much.

Denae scooted back in the chair. "I wasn't given long to look at the file, but from what I could see, it was mostly pictures of Dreagan taken from a satellite."

"What did the pictures show?" he asked as he turned his head in profile to her.

"All of Dreagan. In every season. Nothing seemed out of the ordinary to me, but I did notice some of the mountains were marked as well as certain spots. Your cave was one of those."

When he didn't reply, she pushed her braid from her shoulder. Kellan stood as still as a statue. He was troubled by what she had divulged, the emotion evident in his gaze and rugged features.

"I can tell you some ways they'll come at y'all," she said. "Come at you," she corrected. "But I need something in return."

"You're alive," he bit out, turning his head slightly to the side. "We're keeping you alive. That should be enough."

It was more than anyone else would give her, but it still wasn't enough. "Will you give me proof that I'll leave here alive and with a new identity?"

"I could, but it might be a lie."

"I know."

He slowly turned to face her, his brow furrowed in a frown. "You would trust me?"

"As much as anyone in my position can. I don't fully trust you, just as you don't really trust me. You hold my life in your hands. I'm at your mercy."

"Con has given his word. That is all the proof you need."

Denae knew by the set of Kellan's jaw that she wouldn't get any more from him. It was a gamble she was taking in telling them everything she knew. They could easily kill her and dump her body, claiming neither she nor Matt ever made it to the cave.

Or they could get her a new identity and help her get out of the country to live as normal a life as anyone could on the run.

"I shouldn't tell you," she said. "I took an oath that I take very seriously."

Kellan leaned one shoulder against the wall. "They used you."

"Just as you're doing."

"Aye, lass, but we willna be trying to kill you when it's all finished."

Denae couldn't believe how far she had tumbled from her path. "I know I shouldn't tell you, but for some reason I can't even begin to explain, I want to."

And she did. Was it Dreagan? Was it Kellan?

Either way, she wanted to help them because she liked Dreagan, with its beauty and mysterious secrets. And because of Kellan.

Despite trying, she was fascinated by his chilly green gaze, enticed by his wide lips, and lured in by his hard body.

It was a hell of a position to be in, but somehow she knew that it wasn't just chance that Kellan had found her in his cave or that he was the one questioning her.

Their paths would continue into the future. Denae just didn't know for how long.

CHAPTER NINE

Kellan was about ready to rip off Denae's oversized shirt with its wide collar that kept hanging off one shoulder, giving him a tantalizing view of her supple skin.

He remained against the wall while he kept a tight leash on the desire raging out of control, its burn singeing him from the inside out. Damn, but why did Denae have to be so tempting?

"If you would rather I get Con so you can tell him, I will." Kellan prayed she took him up on his offer so he could have a few minutes alone to get ahold of himself.

Her head cocked to the side, and the long braid fell over her bare shoulder. It was almost too much. Kellan bit back a groan before it passed his lips.

Instead of rebuking him, she set about telling him all the different ways MI5 could be—and would be—watching Dreagan. Once she finished with that, she went on to explain how MI5 could infiltrate Dreagan without any of them knowing it.

By the time she was through, Kellan had even more reasons to hate humans. He pushed away from the wall and opened the door. When he spotted Con standing in the hallway, Kellan knew Constantine had heard everything.

Con gave him a nod before he walked into the room. "It's time."

Kellan glanced at Denae before he turned to Con. Alarm sizzled along his skin. He gave a firm shake of his head. "I doona think that's a good idea."

"It's only fair. She has, after all, shared her secret. Even before she's known ours."

Kellan wasn't sure what bothered him the most. That they were going to tell—as well as show—Denae what they were, or that right before they released her, Guy was going to wipe her memories of anything to do with Dreagan.

She would forget him, forget that her eyes would track him around the room and look at him as if he held the answers to everything.

But he would never forget the heat of her gaze or the pure seduction that she exhibited.

"I don't want to know," Denae was quick to say.

Kellan looked to the chair where she sat. She was stoic, but he sensed the thread of fear running through her. It was due to her training that she realized what kind of position she was in.

"If you tell me, you'll kill me," she told Con. "I don't want to know. I don't want to see. I don't want to hear."

Con merely smiled, though it didn't reach his eyes. "Come, Miss Lacroix. Do you really believe we'll harm you?"

"Without a doubt. You've gone to a great deal of trouble to keep your identities secret."

Constantine opened the door all the way. "We willna kill you. There are other methods. I've a gift, something that will prove we keep our word."

Kellan took a step toward Denae, not sure if it was to help her or Con. Con's curious look stopped him in his tracks. What the hell was wrong with him? Surely he hadn't been about to step between Con and Denae to protect her? The thought shook him to his core.

He hated humans, even beautiful ones.

Whisky eyes lifted to his, and Kellan gave her a nod of encouragement. It's all he would give her. He couldn't chance getting any closer. She had no idea how a boxy shirt that kept one shoulder bared set his blood afire.

"Show me your wound," Con bade her.

Once more Denae glanced at Kellan before she did as Con asked, lifting the cami and oversized shirts together so the square of gauze could be seen.

Kellan hadn't seen the injury since he'd finished stitching it. It had been Cassie who had cleaned and bandaged the wound.

"You were verra lucky your partner didna hit anything major," Con said as he squatted beside the chair and reached for the bandage.

Denae pulled away. "What are you doing?"

"I'm going to look at your wound."

Kellan turned the other way, unsure at the sudden prickle of irritation growing within him. Con wanted him to develop a connection with Denae, and he had, apparently.

Fuck!

"I don't know," Denae said.

The sound of movement caused Kellan to look over his shoulder to see Denae had risen and moved near him. Her face was pale and she wasn't able to hide the pain from her quick movements.

Without thinking, Kellan took hold of her arm to steady her. "Con willna hurt you."

"Perhaps you should remove her bandage, Kellan," Con said as he stood.

Kellan looked down into Denae's eyes. She was too close, their bodies touching. His desire flared, lust riding him hard as he started to pull her closer. Her eyes searched his face. And she again lifted her shirt, this time for him.

His hand brushed over the warm skin of her stomach

and he felt it quiver. Her sharp inhale confirmed that she wasn't immune to his touch.

It was Con's watchful stare that returned sanity to Kellan's mind, if not his body. He did his best to ignore the swell of her breast so near as he gently removed the gauze.

But his cock wasn't so obedient. It was hard and aching, straining to get next to Denae. Kellan inhaled deeply, breathing in Denae's clean, wholesome scent.

In the light of day, Kellan could see the five-inch gash and the uneven stitches she had started before he took over. The skin around the injury was pink, signaling that it was healing.

He looked back at Denae's face to find that somehow their bodies had moved closer together. They were so near all he had to do was bend down to kiss her.

"This willna hurt," Con stated as he came up beside them.

Denae's hands gripped Kellan when Con put his hand near her wound. In the next instant, Con's magic filled the room. As she watched, the gash healed and the stitches dropped to the ground.

Her eyes widened as she looked from Kellan to Con. "What did you just do?"

"I healed you, Miss Lacroix," Con said arrogantly. "It's one of our secrets here."

"You all can do that?"

Kellan shook his head. "That is Con's power."

"Power?" She squeezed her eyes closed while still clutching him. "I don't understand."

"Let us show you," Con urged.

Kellan waited for her to open her eyes. When she did, the uncertainty there confounded him. In battle, she had been sure of herself. Even while lying in a bed wounded, her confidence had been unshakable.

If seeing a wound healed disturbed her, could she handle seeing them shift into dragon form?

"Con, I'm no' sure it's such a good idea," Kellan said.

"You don't think I can handle it?" Denae asked him, squaring her shoulders.

Kellan sighed. "Nay."

She stepped back, releasing him, and turned to Con. "Show me."

Con walked to the window and waited for her to stand beside him. "Kellan? Do you want to do the honors, or should I ask one of the others?"

"Sod off."

Con chuckled and faced the window. "Look to the sky, Denae."

A second later, Kellan caught a glimpse of deep red scales. Guy.

Denae took one step back, her hand over her mouth, before she moved closer to the window, watching how Guy soared through the air and clouds. Her face held a dose of disbelief, a dollop of confusion, a touch of fear, and a trace of excitement.

Kellan wondered which would win out. He had seen humans terrified of them, while others hadn't been able to get close enough.

Denae was practical, realistic. She would probably never fully accept what she was seeing.

"Dragons," Denae whispered, fear making her voice shake. "That was a dragon. A very large dragon."

Con turned from the window and walked to the door, his eyes briefly locking with Kellan's. "That's right, Miss Lacroix. Now you know our secret."

Kellan watched Con leave the room. Con was leaving him to answer any of Denae's questions, as if that would make her trust him more—or make him forget about the life he took.

His head swung around to Denae. She was watching Guy with wide, bright eyes. One hand was on the window as she strained her head to follow his path. She looked like she was enjoying the show Guy put on.

But he knew how duplicitous humans could be.

"It's frighteningly beautiful," Denae said. "Is it the only one here? Is that what I was bait for?" She looked over her shoulder at him. "Will he eat me?"

"Nay. Aye. Nay."

She faced him, her eyes shining with wonder. "That was amazing. It never entered my mind that dragons could exist. There's been no video, no blogs, nothing about Dreagan."

"We like our privacy."

"That's what MI5 must be after. The world can't know you have a dragon. Wait." She blinked and then frowned. "You said nay to my first question. That means . . ."

"There are more."

She took several breaths as she contemplated him. "Con asked you to do the honors. Are you . . . are you a dragon?"

He could lie. She would never know. But for some reason, it wasn't the lie that crossed his lips. "Aye."

"You can turn into that?" she asked and pointed out the window.

"I can."

"And your cave? You were there, weren't you? You were in . . . dragon form?"

He nodded slowly.

"I was bait for you," she said and sank onto the bed, a shell-shocked expression falling over her. "Bait for a *dragon*. And MI5 knew. How did they know you were dragons?"

"Dragon Kings, actually," he corrected her.

Her brows lifted high on her forehead. "Dragon Kings. What does that mean?"

"Dragons have been in this realm since the beginning of time. Every size, every color ruled the sky, the land, and the waters. Each class of dragon had a King."

Her lips softened as she said, "You."

"The dragons with the most magic, the most skill and intelligence were chosen as the King to their group."

"And yours is?"

"I'm King to the Bronzes."

She rubbed her hands together, her coloring beginning to return. "Where are all the dragons? Are they hidden in the mountains?"

Kellan looked at the mountains out the window. "I wish. They're gone. Sent away because humans arrived in this realm."

"I . . . I don't understand," she said hesitantly.

"The Dragon Kings were charged with keeping the peace between dragons and humans. For a while it worked, but a human woman betrayed one of the Kings, Ulrik, and started the war. The dragons— and Kings—were divided on whether to protect the humans or kill them. Con united us."

"Why Con?"

"Because he is the King of Kings. He is King to the Golds, but he earned the right to reign over all dragons."

She licked her lips and nodded. "Okay. So he united you. Did that stop the war?"

"Nay. The humans were bent on killing. The bronze dragons were the Bringers of Justice. I charged them with watching over a village while I fought off other humans. The humans turned on my dragons and killed them, and because I had charged the Bronzes to protect humans, they did no' defend themselves."

"Oh, God," she murmured. "I thought it was just me you don't like, but it's humans in general. Now I understand."

He took a step toward her. "You can no' begin to fathom the depth of my hatred. I tried to live with it, and I managed to for centuries. But there was one last betrayal done to me."

Denae instinctively knew that Kellan had retaliated. "What did you do?"

"I took his life after he raped and murdered a girl he promised he would see safely home. After that I couldna look at another mortal."

So much of Kellan was beginning to make sense now. Who knew someone so gorgeous and with such amazing power would suffer so? "And your dragons? Where are they?" she asked to change the subject.

"We had no choice but to send our dragons to another realm," he continued. "Once they were safe, we hid on Dreagan. It wasna difficult to keep the humans off our territory. We faded into legend and then into myth. And then we were forgotten."

"Apparently not," she said as she rubbed her hands on her thighs. "Someone knows what you are, and they want you exposed. It all makes sense now. The nearly empty file, the secret mission, Matt using me as bait. They were trying to get a glimpse of you to tell the world." She swallowed hard. "The world can't know. Do you know what they would do?"

"Verra much so. Why do you think we've taken such steps to remain behind the scenes?"

"I don't think it's going to be enough. Now I know. What were y'all thinking, showing me?"

"To gain your trust, but doona worry. You willna be able to tell anyone anything. We will wipe your memories of anything to do with Dreagan."

"Wipe my . . ." She trailed off as she looked at him in exasperation. That quickly faded as she sighed loudly. "That's probably for the best. Besides, MI5 will keep coming until it gets what it wants."

"They can try."

Denae rose and walked to him. "Stop being stubborn. I'm trying to help. Y'all can't remain here. You must leave."

"We've called Dreagan home for thousands upon thousands of years. We willna leave."

She twisted her lips as she regarded him with narrowed eyes. "Can you fight them?"

"There's no need."

"Obviously you don't know MI5."

One side of his lips lifted in a smile. "We can no' be killed. The only being who can kill us is another Dragon King."

"Well. That certainly changes things."

CHAPTER
TEN

Denae rubbed her hand over the spot where her wound used to be. It was a little sensitive, but all the pain was gone. As wonderful and mind-boggling as Con's little trick was, it was nothing compared to the dragon flying around Dreagan.

"Only a Dragon King can kill a Dragon King," she repeated. "I think MI5 should know that. If they do, they might back off."

"Do you really believe that?"

She sighed and shook her head. "No. They would then try to turn one of the Kings against the rest of you."

Kellan gave a loud snort. "That wouldna happen. No' after all we've been through."

"You trust them implicitly?"

"Aye."

The idea of that baffled her. "You're lucky, you know. They teach you, as a spy, never to trust anyone. But you have to trust the people on your team. I was the one who got burned this time."

"You learned a lesson."

"That I did. I really can't trust anyone." Not even Kellan or anyone at Dreagan, as much as she wished she could.

Con healed her as a show of good faith. That was a load of shit, and she knew it. Just as sharing their secret was due to her telling them about MI5.

"So how will it come?"

For a second, confusion marred Kellan's features. "What do you mean?"

"My death? How will it come? Poison in my food? A knife in my back? Or maybe as a snack for a dragon?"

"Con said we wouldna kill you. We'll wipe your memories."

She shrugged and stood to look out the window again. "I'm not stupid. You've kept your secret from everyone. Why tell me? Someone suspected of being the enemy? The only logical conclusion is that I'm to be killed."

"It's true we're no' sure if we can trust you. You've helped your position by giving us information on MI5 and their interest in us."

"But?" she prodded.

"There is no but," Kellan said.

Denae laughed and turned to look at him. "Then when can I leave?"

"If I know Con, he's already working on getting you a new identity."

"It better be good, because MI5 will be looking for me everywhere." She realized that she would need to alter her appearance, if she could trust that she would be leaving. She had no choice but to keep thinking that. As if they could wipe her memories. Then again, Con had healed her right before her very eyes. "I'll need scissors and some hair color."

Kellan folded his arms over his chest, a small frown forming. "For what?"

"I need to change how I look."

"By cutting your hair?" he asked incredulously.

She pulled at the end of her braid. "It's just hair. It'll grow back."

"There willna be a need for you to take such action," Kellan said as he turned on his heel and walked out.

Denae shook her head after he left. Kellan was certainly enigmatic. If she didn't know better, she would think he didn't want her to cut her hair.

"It's just hair," she repeated, though she didn't want to cut it either. Her father had always loved her hair long. He used to gripe every time she cut it.

Now that she was healed, Denae found it difficult to stay in her room. She wanted to explore Dreagan, and possibly get a closer look at a dragon.

She wanted a closer look at Kellan. Just what did he look like as a dragon? And was she brave enough to find out?

Rhi sat back on her chaise longue and surveyed her newly painted fingers and toes. The light-up-the-night shade of glistening coral—named Bright Lights-Big Color—was going to look great with her new dress, and the black-and-silver stripes were a great accent.

No one knew of her little hideaway, not even her queen. It was where she came to get away, a place she didn't have to share with any of the other Fae.

And the best part—the Dragon Kings would never be able to find it.

"Jessie really outdid herself this time," Rhi said to herself about her nail tech.

Rhi laid her head back and closed her eyes. There was nothing for her to do. She could look in on Phelan and Aisley, but she had just spied on them the week before. It wouldn't be long now before her queen wanted Phelan and Aisley to visit for more than an hour.

Until then, Rhi was going to leave the couple alone to enjoy themselves. A huge weight had been lifted off the shoulders of all those from MacLeod Castle with the death of Jason Wallace—a *drough,* or evil Druid, who had been trying to kill the Warriors and Druids.

She wished she could tell Phelan and the other Warriors that peace would enter their lives, but she couldn't. Because there was a disturbance in the air that wouldn't shake loose. And it was pointing directly at Dreagan.

For weeks, Rhi refused to even think about the interfering, inflexible, mulish Dragon Kings. After all that had happened between the Kings and the Fae, Rhi knew better than to get involved.

But there was a history there, one that no matter how much Rhi wanted to forget—she couldn't.

"I'll go see the Kings for *him*. Only him."

She closed her eyes as she thought of their all-too-brief affair. How exciting it had been, how glorious.

How incredible.

He had said it was because they were supposed to be enemies, not lovers. But Rhi knew it was because . . .

She couldn't even think it, because if she did, she would splinter into a million pieces all over again. It didn't matter what happened in the middle or how happy they were. All that mattered was that he left.

And she had found her hideaway.

For months Rhi hadn't left her refuge. Not even when her queen called to her, pleading for her to return. Not even when those pleas turned into demands.

A Fae wasn't supposed to have a broken heart for a Dragon King.

It wasn't that Rhi was embarrassed because she had given in to the temptation for a King. She didn't want to hear the other Fae bashing the Dragon Kings as they always did. When she finally did return to court, someone had begun a tirade on the Kings, and her lover's name was mentioned.

Rhi would have killed the Fae who dared to slander him if it hadn't been for her queen, Usaeil. Even now, hundreds and hundreds of years later, Rhi still pined for him.

Did he still feel their fiery passion?

She wished she could believe that, but since he hadn't tried to contact her, the truth was staring her in the face.

"Why then should I tell the Kings what I suspect?" she asked herself.

Rhi sat up and shifted her legs over the side of the chaise. Other Fae would ignore the urgings, but she couldn't. Just as she hadn't been able to stop from helping Phelan when he needed it.

She had a duty as Queen's Guard to follow her instincts. Because even though it might lead to the Kings, that meant whatever was in the air was liable to affect every magical being. Including the Fae.

"But I hate the Kings," she murmured.

It was a mutual loathing, one that grew as time went on. And with both sides being immortal, things were only going to get worse.

Rhi stood and walked onto the porch as the sun sparkled off her metal wind chimes. It was a beautiful day that was about to be ruined with a visit to Dreagan.

With a long sigh and a wistful look at her beautiful coral dress, Rhi let her sanctuary disappear as she thought of Dreagan.

Banan drove up in his BMW 640i just as Henry North descended the train with dozens of other people. Banan stopped the car and put it in park while Henry nonchalantly made his way to him.

It wasn't until Henry was inside the car and the train departing that Banan looked at him.

"What do you know?"

Henry's hazel eyes met his. "You still don't trust me."

"At this point we can no' afford to trust anyone."

"I understand." Henry sighed and looked out the windshield. "Coming here will most likely cost me my job."

"Then you shouldna have come."

Henry cut him a look, and proceeded as if he hadn't

heard. "It took some digging, but I learned that Matt Dorsey and Denae Lacroix were sent on a highly secret mission to Dreagan put together by their boss, Frank. I gather it's Denae you have?"

Banan lowered his head once in a nod.

"Good. No one cared for Matt, so his passing won't be missed. Denae, however, was rumored to be on her way up. She's very well liked, despite her being American and working for MI5. I'm not sure why she was sent on this mission."

"Were both Matt and Denae told what they were sent to Dreagan for?"

Henry ran a hand through his short, nondescript, brown hair. "It took me calling in all the favors I've accumulated over my fifteen-year career, but I can tell you that Denae was meant to be killed during the mission. Matt would report her death as an attack by men at Dreagan, and then MI5 would swarm in. That's when they expected everyone at Dreagan to attack them, though Frank was unclear in his reports how you would go about the assault."

Banan started the car and gripped the steering wheel tightly. He mulled over what Henry had told him as he started driving.

"I'll do whatever it takes for you to trust me," Henry said into the silence.

"Why does it matter?"

"Because no one at Dreagan has ever let me down. I can't say the same of anyone else. In my business, you learn quickly who you can trust and who you need to watch. You men from Dreagan have never told me something you didn't follow through on. Your word is your bond."

Banan felt like an arse for questioning Henry's allegiance. "Someone is after us, Henry. Or rather, they want to expose a secret we have."

"We all have secrets."

"Perhaps. Matt told Denae she was meant to be bait.

The wound he gave her was meant to draw out a predator, not to kill."

Henry scrubbed a hand down his face. "Someone did mention the word bait, but I was told she was meant to be killed when all was said and done. They think both are dead. You say a predator?"

"Aye."

"None of this is making sense."

But it did to Banan. Denae was meant to be bloodied to draw out Kellan in dragon form, and then MI5 was hoping to witness a dragon killing Denae so they would have the excuse to come onto their land.

"MI5 is coming to Dreagan," Banan stated.

Henry's face was set in hard lines as he looked at Banan. "Yes, my friend, they are. They expect to find two dead agents. Whoever sent Denae won't be happy she's alive and Matt is dead."

"Denae willna be there."

Henry's lips twisted. "There is nowhere she can go that they won't find her. She'll be better off turning herself in. I can try to protect her, get her to the higher-ups who want to see her career move forward."

Banan glanced at him as he turned onto another road and sped up. "Do you believe your superiors can keep her alive?"

"No."

That one word sealed Denae's fate. Banan pressed the accelerator and sped down the narrow road. "When will MI5 come?"

"They'll be on their way now. They've never stopped watching Dreagan."

"They'll know you're helping us."

Henry smiled. "Yes, they will."

For the first time in days, Banan grinned. "I'm glad I helped you out in that bar fight years ago."

"Me too," Henry said. "I'd be dead now if you hadn't stopped that fifth guy I never saw from using that knife."

"I knew someone worthy of friendship when I saw it."

"I'll not let you down now," Henry vowed.

Banan knew he wouldn't. He just hoped he hadn't set Henry on a course that would take his life.

CHAPTER
ELEVEN

Rhi knew the shit was about to hit the fan. It had been eons since a Fae—any Fae—dared to step onto Dreagan. There was no need for the Kings to use magic to ban the Fae. The treaty signed by the Light and Dark Fae promised they'd never venture onto Dreagan unless they wanted the Fae Wars to start again and the Kings to kill them all. It was enough to keep the Fae out.

Or it usually was. When it came to annoying Con, Rhi never backed down. Besides, what she had to tell him was enough for him to hold off declaring war against the Light.

She hesitated for a moment as to whether to return to her cottage and forget about alerting the Kings, or letting them know what she felt. It wouldn't be just the Kings affected, but the entire realm.

Rhi was veiled when she popped into Con's office and saw a group of Kings, including Con, talking. She remained veiled because they also had a human with them. It went against the "rules" set up between the Kings and Fae for her to be veiled and listen to their conversations. But she didn't much care.

For several minutes she eavesdropped as the human

spoke about MI5 and how they would arrive at Dreagan. Rhi found the information particularly interesting, mostly because she noticed how upset Con was by how still he sat.

She found an empty chair and arranged herself so that her legs were dangling over the arms of the chair. Once she was comfortable, she dropped the veil.

"We need to get Denae out now," Kellan said.

Rhi's brows rose when she spotted Kellan. It had been ages upon ages since he had last woken. And then to hear him talking about a female? Things had certainly gone pear-shaped at Dreagan.

Suddenly Con's black eyes shifted to her. For several seconds they stared wordlessly at each other. No one else in the room knew she was there. Rhi waved her fingers mockingly at Con and swung her feet, which were sporting the newest Ralph Lauren boots in saddle-brown leather.

"We've a visitor, gentlemen," Con said with an exaggerated sigh, anger dripping from his voice.

Kellan's head jerked around to her, and to Rhi's surprise, one side of his mouth lifted in a grin. "Cheeky, Rhi. Even for you."

"It's been awhile, Kell. Nice to see you up and about," she said with a wink.

Banan merely shook his head while the mortal's mouth hung open. Banan had to reach over and physically close it. Rhi gave the human a dazzling smile.

"What are you doing here, Rhiannon?" Con asked.

Her smile slipped. He knew how much she hated to be called by her full name. Her eyes swiveled to him, and she glared.

"And inside Dreagan," Rhys said with a chuckle. "Are you trying to start a war?"

Rhi shifted until she was sitting correctly in the chair. "I'm trying to divert one, actually."

"You helping us?" Kiril asked in surprise.

She glanced at Rhys and then Kiril. "Actually, now that you mention it, I don't have to help." Rhi was just about to dash out when Kellan said her name. She paused and looked into his light green eyes. "What?" she asked in exasperation.

"You came for a reason," Kellan said. "What is it?"

Rhi felt Con's gaze on her. She could easily retreat back to her little cottage and forget about the Dragon Kings. The hard part would be to stay and help. It would most likely incur the wrath of her queen, but that was nothing new.

Leather squeaked as Con leaned forward in his chair to rest his arms on his desk. "I doona think she has anything to say, Kellan. She came to rile us. Childish, but it worked. Now you can leave, Rhi. We actually have business to discuss."

Rhi laughed to hide her fury and tossed her long hair over her shoulder. "Business? That's a laugh. You're talking about MI5 and Denae. Don't think to treat me as if I'm a child."

"What do you know of Denae?" the mortal asked.

She turned her gaze to him, and once more his mouth went slack. Rhi stood and walked toward the human. His kind, hazel eyes never wavered. He wasn't bad looking. With a new haircut and something other than a gray suit, he might even be handsome.

"Rhi," Kellan warned in a low voice.

She stopped next to Kellan. "Who is the mortal?"

"I'm Henry North," he said. "And what do you mean, mortal?"

Rhi was impressed. Most humans couldn't think past their desires. Henry was different. He might want her, but his brain ruled him, not his cock. She liked him instantly. "Nice to meet you, Henry. Aren't you the least bit curious as to how I got in here?"

Henry frowned and looked around. "As a matter of fact, I am."

"I—"

"Rhi," Kellan said over her. "No' now."

She walked back to her seat and sat. Kellan was right. It wasn't time to tease. She needed to tell them what she knew. "For several weeks now I've felt a . . . disturbance."

"What kind of a disturbance?" Kiril asked.

Rhi shrugged, but couldn't hide the unease she felt. "I've tried to locate it, but it's everywhere and nowhere. I can't say it's one person."

"So it could be a group," Con said and looked at Henry. "MI5 perhaps?"

It didn't take a genius to realize Henry worked for the agency. Who exactly was this Denae Kellan was asking about? Did she work for MI5 as well?

Rhys ran a hand through his hair. "MI5 would have to get intel on us first."

"What did you do to piss off MI5, Con?" Rhi asked, making sure to put an innocent expression on her face.

Con's eyes narrowed into dangerous slits. "Nothing."

"Hmm. I doubt that. Regardless, nothing I looked at took me to MI5. It took me all over Scotland, into Wales, and England, however, just to name a few places."

Kellan moved until he was leaning back against a wall. "And no' to any one person?"

"No." Rhi shook her head slowly. "The odd thing is, if I didn't know better I'd say they were using . . . magic."

Henry's face drained of color. "Magic?"

"Later," Banan told him.

"Any distinct kind of magic?" Con asked her.

Rhi thought back over the times she'd tried to find the source. "No. There were times I swore I felt the Dark Ones, and other times I would've wagered my new boots it was dragon magic."

If it was possible, Henry grew paler, but he held it all together as his gaze took in everyone.

"How close are we to getting the new ID for Denae?" Kellan asked Rhys.

Rhys checked his phone. "In a matter of hours."

"It needs to be faster," Henry said. "You need to make sure there's no trace of her when MI5 comes looking."

Kiril stood. "Doona forget Matt."

"He needs to disappear as well," Henry said.

Kiril's smile was slow as his gaze landed on Rhi. "Sounds like fun."

She watched him walk from the room before she turned her attention back to Con whose gaze seemed to be glued to her. "You don't have to believe me," she told him.

"I doona," Con stated.

"You do so at your own peril. Whatever is out there is strong. Strong enough that I felt it."

"Which means you've been in this realm for a while."

Rhi lifted a brow, daring him to order her to leave. Because while the Kings might be powerful, and they might have won the war between their people, he couldn't make her leave.

"Who cares?" Rhys said. "Leave Rhi. We've a more pressing matter."

"That's right. Denae," she said. "I think I'd like to meet her."

Kellan didn't move but she noticed a muscle twitch in his jaw.

Fascinating.

It was Con who said, "No."

"So who is it that has a soft spot for this Denae?" Rhi asked. "Is it Kellan? Or is it Con?"

"Enough, Rhi," Banan said.

But she wasn't nearly through. It was too easy to irritate Con, and she was too good at it.

"I can handle her," Con said.

Rhi rolled her eyes. She turned her attention to Kellan,

because it was apparent that Kellan was either in charge of Denae's safety, or he really did feel something. "I agree with Henry. If Denae is mortal, she needs to get away from here. The quicker, the better. Whether it is MI5 or something else, Dreagan isn't safe right now."

"Denae's new identity is ready. I'm going to pick it up," Rhys said as he started for the door. "Shall we meet at the docks?"

"An hour, Rhys," Con called when Rhys hurried out of the office.

That same terrible—but powerful—magic tickled the edges of Rhi's awareness. She closed her eyes and tried to determine which direction it was coming from. What she did know was that it was getting closer.

Her eyes snapped open to find the men's gazes trained on her. She swallowed and once more turned to Kellan. "Get Denae out. Now."

"What did you feel?" Con demanded.

She looked at him and said, "Something bad is closing in."

Con took a deep breath and jerked his chin to Kellan. "Do as Rhi suggests. Banan, you and the others make sure all the mortals are away from Dreagan in less than an hour."

"And you?" Rhi couldn't help but ask.

"I'll be here to greet whoever dares to come."

She had seen him in battle firsthand. Constantine wasn't anyone she would willingly tangle with if there were another option. She almost felt sorry for whoever came knocking on Dreagan's door. Almost.

Despite the Fae and Kings despising each other, they actually agreed on their feelings for humans. They were untrustworthy and destroyed everything they got their hands on.

Well, most of them did, anyway. There were a few humans who were different.

"You're still here," Con said in his most condescending voice. "Why?"

Rhi said the first thing that popped into her mind. "Who says I ever came to help you? Did the thought never pop into your thick mind that I might be here to help Denae?"

That made Con frown—and worry. Which is exactly what she wanted. Score one for her!

Rhi walked out of the office, not surprised to find Kellan on her heels.

"Are you really here to help Denae?" he asked as they walked down the hall.

She shook her head. "I came because I wanted to alert all of you about what I felt. I probably should've come sooner. It's just . . ."

"I know," he said into her silence. "We could've been alerted to the fact MI5 had executed a secret mission on our land. And in my cave."

"Ah. So that's why you're awake." Then the realization about what he'd said settled in her mind. "They went to your cave? Why?"

"It's something we all want to know. Denae was set up by her partner and they fought. She killed him, but he managed to wound her."

"And you brought her to the manor." Rhi rubbed her temple. "MI5 doesn't have magic, Kell. How does any of this fit?"

"We doona know, but we want to make sure they doona succeed in whatever they're planning."

"And they'll come for Denae."

"Aye."

"What is the plan?"

Kellan stopped and glanced at a door down the hall. "She's requested a new identity so MI5 can no' track her. She also knows what we are."

Rhi's eyes grew large as she halted. "Con let you show her?"

"Con is the one who showed her."

She hooked her thumbs in her belt loops. "He's going to use Guy to wipe her memories, isn't he?"

"He is."

"Then why show her?"

Kellan rubbed his jaw. "All I got from him is that he thought she might be hiding something else and by seeing who we are it might frighten her enough to tell us."

"That man," Rhi said with a roll of her eyes.

"Even if MI5 ever finds her, she willna be able to tell them anything after Guy wipes her memories. It's for the best."

"Kell, you've been asleep for a long time, but do you really believe MI5 would find their operative after endless searching and believe that she doesn't remember anything?"

"There is no other option."

"There might be," she said. There was an abandoned house several miles away. Rhi could keep an eye on it, and as long as Denae stayed there she might live.

"You want to take responsibility?"

The surprise in his voice caused her to glower. "Are you saying I can't?"

"I'm saying you might get called to your realm. Who would watch Denae then?"

Rhi had to admit he was correct. "True."

"Why would you offer?" His voice was soft, too much understanding in the words to make her comfortable.

"Temporary insanity. I don't know. Forget I said anything. Let's just get her out of Dreagan."

Kellan walked her to the bedroom door, and when he opened it, Rhi found a beautiful woman with dark hair and a body that would make any man stand up and take notice.

"Denae," Kellan said. "This is Rhi. She's a friend."

Rhi's smile widened when she noticed how the mortal's eyes softened when she looked at Kellan.

But it was Kellan's determination not to look at Denae that made Rhi bite her tongue to keep from laughing.

Men!

CHAPTER
TWELVE

Denae could only stare in stunned silence at the most beautiful woman she had ever seen. Her black hair had a blue cast to it, but it was her silver eyes that seemed to swirl that held her.

"Hello," Rhi said as she walked into the room with a welcoming smile.

Denae blinked and glanced at Kellan to see if he was as awestruck as she was, but he simply leaned against the door frame looking as bored as ever. "Hi," she finally said.

"Are you ready to blow this joint?" Rhi asked.

Denae was so taken aback by her speech that she chuckled. "Who are you?"

"Well, since you know about the Dragon Kings, I think it's safe to tell you. I'm Fae."

She had some retort on the tip of her tongue, but something held Denae back. It could be the fact that she'd seen Con heal her, and then there was the big red dragon she'd witnessed.

But seriously. Could the day get any more surreal?

"A Fae?"

Rhi nodded and flipped her long hair over her shoulder.

"We've got a long way to go, cookie. I think we best get a move on before your friends at MI5 show up."

"We?" Kellan said as he pushed away from the door.

Rhi rolled her eyes and faced him. "Not you too, Kell."

His nostrils flared as he stared at her. "Nay, no' me, but I'd much rather you be at the dock scouting things out ahead of time."

"Hmm. You do have a point." Rhi looked at Denae and winked. "See you soon."

And just like that, she was gone. Denae stared at the spot Rhi had just been for several seconds before she lifted her gaze to Kellan.

"A Fae?"

"Aye," he said with a resigned sigh. "There's a history between the Kings and the Fae, and it isna a good one."

Denae finished tying the running shoes Cassie had brought up earlier. "And yet she's here, so it must not have been too bad."

"It was bad. There was a war."

"I'm noticing a recurring theme with you Dragon Kings." It had been said half in jest, but it fell flat.

Kellan's celadon eyes went hard. "They wanted to take over this realm. We were assigned to be protectors of the humans. Would you have preferred we gave this realm up to the Fae so you could all be slaves to their desires?"

Denae licked her lips. She knew nothing of the Fae, but according to Kellan they were dangerous. So dangerous he let one near her? "Then why is Rhi here if none of you like the Fae?"

"Rhi is . . . different. She was once a lover to a King. Now come. We must leave."

Denae was dying to know more, but she hurried out of the room after Kellan, grateful to leave it behind and see more of Dreagan. As soon as she stepped into the corridor to follow Kellan, she noticed the huge paintings lining the walls.

If she didn't know better she would think she was in a museum. Small lights were fitted over each painting to give just enough illumination so a person could take it all in.

Although they were in a hurry, she found her steps slowing to look at every picture. It wasn't until they were nearly to the stairs that her eyes landed upon a picture with a bronze dragon, the scales metallic even in the painting.

Denae saw the two horns extending backward from its forehead before Kellan grabbed her arm and pulled her after him.

"I wasn't done looking," she stated.

"Would you rather look at the paintings or live?"

Well, when he put it that way, of course she wanted to live. But the bronze dragon had been Kellan. She knew it. And she wanted another look.

Denae's hand landed on the banister, and as she walked down the stairs she got to see more of the manor—and more dragons. They were everywhere. Her favorites were the metal dragons extending from the wall where the dragon's claw held the lights.

It wasn't until she reached the bottom of the stairs that she saw the carved dragon newel post and paused. She ran her finger over the etched teeth of the dragon.

She turned her head to Kellan. "How can anyone walk into this place and not realize what all of you are?"

"People see what they want to see. Few pay that close attention. Then there is the fact that very few ever see the inside of the manor."

"I did."

His hand dropped from her arm and their fingers brushed, sending a jolt of longing and desire roaring through her. Her skin heated, making her all too aware of the very virile, very handsome man beside her.

"You were dying," he said as his gaze met hers.

"Con could've healed me in the cave. Why bring me here?"

Kellan didn't look away, but there was a subtle shift about him, as if he were trying to come up with a suitable answer.

"Don't," she said as he was about to answer. "If you're going to lie, I'd rather you not answer me at all."

"Have I lied to you yet?" he asked softly. Too softly.

Denae wanted to back away, but the steps and banister blocked her. Kellan's voice was mellow, but in his eyes she saw anger. "Not that I know of."

"Have I mistreated you?"

"No."

"Have you suffered here?"

"Just the opposite."

He took a step closer until their bodies brushed. "Then why do you think I would lie to you now?"

Denae was having a hard time concentrating with him so close. Especially when all she wanted to do was touch him, to run her hands over his chest and feel the heat of him, the strength of his muscles. To shove her fingers into the long, glorious length of his caramel-colored hair.

"I could've been questioned in the cave after Con healed me. I was brought here to make me feel safe, and so that I'd let my guard down. Y'all wanted me to trust you. So when I was killed, I wouldn't see it coming."

His face lowered to hers until their noses were almost touching. "I give you my word that we doona plan your death."

Denae found herself leaning into him, his magnetism, his unmistakable allure too great to resist. Her body was a riot of pulsing need, one that only Kellan could quench. If he wanted her.

Which he didn't.

Kellan hadn't intended to get so close to Denae. Her words angered him, but that was no excuse. He knew to keep his distance from her.

They stood with their bodies grazing, their faces so

close he could move just a fraction and kiss her. At the thought, Kellan lowered his eyes to her full lips and bit back a moan.

She had the most amazing lips, as if she had been crafted to bring men to their knees with that mouth alone.

He longed to taste her, to sample her lips at his leisure. A slow, wet kiss that went on and on as their passion built. But he wouldn't stop at her mouth. He wanted to pull her close and feel her tempting curves again, to run his fingers along her long throat and watch her silky skin rise with goose bumps.

"The car is waiting," Kellan said and hastily took a step back before he did something stupid and kissed her.

"Of course."

He put his hand on the small of her back and escorted her to the foyer, inwardly smiling all the while. Because he had seen her desire, the yearning reflected in her whisky-colored eyes.

A black Range Rover Sport waited for them outside. Kellan walked beside her. "There is a man inside, a friend to Dreagan. He works for MI5 and is here to help."

She stopped in her tracks and looked up at him with startled eyes. "No. He can't be trusted. No one from MI5 can be."

"We trust him," Kellan said as he faced her. "Henry is a good man. He risked a lot by getting to Dreagan as well as learning what he could of your mission."

He waited as Denae looked nervously from the SUV to the open field. She was alarmed and alert, as anyone in her position would be. If it came down to it, he'd forcefully put her in the vehicle, but he hoped he wouldn't have to.

"How do you know you can trust him?"

"He's proven himself. We've healed you and shown you who we are. Now we are trying to get you away from here so MI5 doesna catch you. Shall we debate this more or leave?"

Her wariness was something he recognized and understood. He didn't want to connect with her that way, but there was no denying what he saw.

"I don't want to die."

"I willna let you," he said and opened the back passenger door.

Once Denae had climbed in, he closed the door and walked around the other side to get in the backseat. He gave a nod to Banan and Henry.

Henry turned around in the seat and held out his hand to Denae. "Nice to see you alive. I'm Henry North."

"Henry," Denae said with a small, nervous smile. Whatever reservations she had vanished. Henry was known throughout MI5 as a stand-up guy, one that could be trusted implicitly. "I know that name. You're renowned throughout MI5."

He chuckled. "More like infamous, I'm sure."

"What are you doing here?" Denae asked as she glanced at Kellan.

Banan started the SUV and put it in drive as he said, "He's here in case we run into problems."

"He means MI5 operatives," Denae said. Her lips compressed tightly.

"I doubt I'm even a part of the company anymore since I left the office last night," Henry said as he sat forward and buckled his seat belt. "I found out the truth about your mission, Denae. Matt might have said he was to wound you to use you as bait, but they wanted you dead regardless."

Though Kellan knew she had learned to control her emotions and reactions, Henry's words still upset her. She was motionless except for her hand that rested on her leg where she was rubbing her thumbnail back and forth.

"My superiors know what happened," Henry continued. "They had big plans for you, but a few—namely those running your department—had other ideas."

"MI5 should do some housecleaning," Banan stated as he drove out of Dreagan over rough terrain, off-roading.

Henry chuckled. "They should, but they don't always do as expected. The satellite office in Inverness will have already sent their people here. Are you sure they won't know where we're going?"

Kellan grabbed the back of Henry's seat when Banan took them over terrain filled with large rocks. "They can try to follow us."

"I know Jane isna happy I'm no' with her, and if any of you tell her how much fun I'm having, I'll make you pay," Banan said, a wide smile on his face.

Denae put her hand on the window to prevent her head from slamming into it as the Range Rover crawled over the rocks. "There's nothing like danger to make a man smile."

"You've been in plenty of danger," Henry said as he glanced at her over his shoulder.

She laughed, the sound shooting straight to Kellan's cock and making him bite the inside of his mouth so as not to release a moan.

"Danger has become a way of life."

Her statement had Kellan wondering just how many times her life had been on the line, and why she continued to put it there. But as he looked at her, it wasn't the cowering female clutching his arm that he expected.

It was a woman who looked her enemies in the eye and figured out how to best them. She was capable, adept, skilled, and clever.

He might worry if he thought for an instant that he would give in to her. No matter how great the temptation was, he wouldn't bend. Not with all he had been through with the humans.

Kellan tried to find the hate that always came so easily when he thought of the mortals, and when he did, it seemed . . . less than before.

Which couldn't be right. Humans were liars, thieves, and murderers. They raped the land without a second thought to the future or consequences. They fought over land and thrones like vultures fighting over a carcass.

Why the humans lived and the dragons were gone was a question Kellan would never understand.

Suddenly, Denae's eyes turned to him and her smile died, the light going out of her beautiful whisky eyes. He didn't want to think them pretty, but he couldn't stop himself.

"What is it?" she whispered.

Kellan looked away, but her gaze lingered. "Nothing," he said.

"Liar."

"Look out!" Banan called as they descended over the hill.

Denae flew forward, her seat belt the only thing stopping her from crashing into Banan's seat. The SUV tilted precariously to the right, causing her body to be tossed right at Kellan.

He grabbed her without thinking and held her tight. Then he made the mistake of looking into her eyes.

CHAPTER THIRTEEN

Denae reached up without thought and touched Kellan's cheek. The surprise that flared in his eyes caused her body to smolder.

Before she could gather the courage to kiss him, Kellan sat her up and turned his head out his window. When she faced forward, her gaze clashed with Banan's as he looked at her through the rearview mirror.

A glance behind her showed the cluster of rocks that had caused the commotion as they sped across the land.

Denae didn't know what it was about Kellan that triggered her heart to beat faster or why she was drawn to him in ways she couldn't begin to discern. All she knew was that she wanted his arms around her, wanted his lips on hers.

She didn't understand why his appeal robbed her of thought and words, or why the fact his lips didn't curve upward made her want to do crazy things just to see if she could get him to crack a smile.

The ride continued in silence for the next hour as Banan took them over increasingly more dangerous terrain. Every once in a while either Kellan or Banan would look at the skies.

It didn't take her long to realize they were looking for dragons. Denae could only imagine how easily a dragon could take out a chopper or plane with a single swipe of a paw.

"We're almost to the road," Banan said.

Five minutes later he slammed on the breaks when they reached a small grove of trees, causing all of them to fly forward. The seat belt dug into her chest for the second time that day.

"What is it?" Henry asked.

Kellan didn't say a word as he opened his door and stepped out of the vehicle. It was when he closed the door softly behind him that Denae knew he was going after something in the trees.

She reached for her door handle when Banan clicked the locks, preventing her from getting out. "Unlock the door," she said.

"No' going to happen," Banan said.

"Then go help him."

Banan snorted. "If you think he needs help, then I doona think you understand who he is."

"Oh, I understand. What if he . . ." Denae trailed off as she recalled how the only way a King could be killed was by another Dragon King.

Banan met her gaze in the mirror again and nodded as realization dawned on her. "Exactly," he said.

"Exactly what?" Henry asked in his British accent. "I'm getting the feeling I'm left out of some important fact."

"Denae just remembered that Kellan can easily take care of himself," Banan said to his friend.

Henry inhaled deeply. "Riiiight."

Denae didn't have to wait long for Kellan to return. He walked back to the Range Rover as if he'd simply gone for a stroll. When he was once more seated beside her, she noticed the few drops of blood on his shirt.

"It's taken care of," he said.

Banan pressed the accelerator to get them moving again. Denae stared at Kellan for three miles until he finally looked at her.

"How did you know?" she asked.

He lifted one shoulder in a shrug. "You're easy to pick out."

She didn't know if the "you" meant MI5 or humans, and either way, it was meant as an insult. Though she couldn't blame him after what he had told her humans did to his dragons. If she were in his place, she would hate humans too.

It wasn't long before they reached a road and they were able to go faster. The scenery sped by as Denae stared out the window. A light smattering of rain fell while pale gray clouds cloaked everything in a somber mood.

They passed few cars on the narrow road, and at the rate of speed they were traveling it was a good thing. The farther away from Dreagan they got, the more worried Denae became.

Kellan might have given her his word, but what did she really know of him? He saw her fight in his cave, and he had taken her to the manor. He told her a bit about his bronze dragons, and even a bit of his past, but she knew nothing of him.

What kind of man was he? What made him laugh, what made him angry? What would spur him to protect someone? And what would make him leave?

He had walked into the trees and killed at least one operative without so much as breaking a sweat. Then again, he admitted to killing a man for raping and killing a girl. Was everything black and white to Kellan?

She glanced his way to find him watching her with his celadon eyes, a hint of anger showing. "Still doubting me?"

"Can you read minds?"

He lifted a brow. "Nay, but I can read you."

She had hurt him with her mistrust. Which was laughable. It wasn't as if he trusted her much. Then again, he was trying to help her. At least she assumed he was. This trust thing was beginning to wear her down. "Where are we going?"

"To the sea."

The fact he answered without hesitation relieved some of her distress. It also helped that Henry was there. He obviously trusted Banan a great deal.

Unless Henry was in on it.

Denae stopped that train of thought. If she let herself, she could come up with hundreds of different scenarios where people betrayed her.

What Matt and her department had done left a mental scar she wasn't sure she could ever overcome. It would be bad enough that she was going to be on the run for her life. How could she ever trust anyone again?

Every meal she ate that she didn't cook herself could be laced with poison. Every person a potential murderer. Every place a possible death trap.

There would be no nights of sleep. She would have to move every few days, making sure wherever she decided to lay her head was protected, as well as setting an alarm of some sort to let her know if someone was trying to get in.

That was not the life she wanted. It wasn't a life she could live.

"Stop," she told Banan. "Just stop and let me out. It might be better if MI5 killed me."

"They won't kill you," Henry said as he turned to look at her. "They'll torture you until they get the information out of you. Then they'll kill you and make it look like someone at Dreagan did it."

Denae closed her eyes and blew out a harsh breath. She knew that was exactly what MI5 would do, but she had never been on the receiving end of their attacks. If she let herself, she would begin to question every operation she went on. "I don't want to be on the run forever. That's not a life. That's merely living. I can never have a family, never trust anyone."

"It'll get easier."

She opened her eyes to glare at Henry. "No, it won't. I'll never be able to go home or even make friends. I'll wonder if everyone I meet is connected to MI5 and a potential enemy."

"It'll keep you on your toes," Banan said.

"It'll be hell."

Kellan asked, "You would rather die?"

She turned her head to him. "Isn't what I'm about to do pretty much what you've been doing? Only you get to stay in one place. What would you rather?"

"Your choice is life or death, Denae," he said. "Death is easy. Life is hard. But you have the ability to choose what kind of life you'll have."

The Range Rover slowed and turned. Denae looked out the window and saw the sea.

"We're here," Banan said.

She remained silent while they navigated through the docks until Banan stopped the SUV and turned off the engine. For a moment, no one moved.

Banan then unbuckled his seat belt and turned around. "Henry and I are going to go look around. Good luck, Denae."

She couldn't return his smile, but she gave him a nod. "Thanks."

Henry held out his hand to her and she saw the dagger encased in black leather. "Take this," he told her. "It's always good to have a hidden weapon."

Denae accepted the gift. "Thank you."

"Kellan is right. You have a choice now. Safe travels."

Her stomach was in knots by the time she and Kellan were left alone in the vehicle. She turned the knife over and over in her hand. "When will you wipe my memories?"

"Before you get on the boat."

"And if we're not alone? It's just the four of us against whoever is out there?"

"Aye," Kellan said. "No' that you need to worry. I'll be surprised if MI5 tracked us here. You'll be on the boat shortly with a new identity and leaving all of this behind."

"You make it sound easy."

"It is. Are you ready?"

Denae answered him by opening her door and stepping out. The smell of salt filled her nose as the wind brushed from the sea and over her. Gulls cried loudly while boats tied to the dock moaned against the waves.

Kellan waited for her at the front of the Range Rover. She walked to him, but she couldn't shake the feeling that something was going to go wrong.

"What is it?" he asked when she kept looking around.

"We got away too easy. Way too easy."

Kellan's brow puckered. "We planned for that."

"You don't understand. They'll have been watching."

"It's sixty thousand acres. They can no' watch it all."

She wanted to believe him, but that nagging feeling had saved her life before. She wasn't going to ignore it now. "When do I leave?"

"We need to meet Con and Rhys for your identity packet. Your boat leaves in half an hour."

She scanned the boats she could see, wondering which of them she would board that would take her far away from Kellan and his mesmerizing green eyes. "Where is it taking me?"

"There are several ports it'll stop at. You get to choose when you want to depart. Come," he said and directed her to a wooden building painted what was supposed to have been a cream, but so much paint had chipped away that it looked gray from the exposed boards.

Inside, it didn't get any better. Denae expected it to fall down around her. She sat on a wooden crate and looked at Kellan. The wind had whipped his long hair about, and the way he ran his fingers through it was one of the sexiest things she had ever seen.

She had never liked long hair on guys. Until she met Kellan. Now, she wanted to tangle her fingers in it and beg him never to cut it.

"How long did you watch me in the cave?"

He jerked his head at her, surprise evident in his gaze. "I saw you come out of the water."

"In other words, you saw it all."

"Aye."

"Are there no humans you like?"

He shrugged, but didn't deny it. "There have been few mortals I encountered that were worthy of living."

"It might have been better if you let me die in your cave. You could've remained, and I wouldn't be in this spot."

"You're no' angry with me?"

Oddly enough, she wasn't. "You had to make a decision based on protecting yourself and the other dragons. Why would I be mad? It's what I did every day for the past seven years."

"You're certainly different, Denae Lacroix."

She smiled then. "My father used to say the same thing."

"Do you want us to get word to your family?"

Denae glanced at her feet. "That won't be necessary. My immediate family is dead. It's just my extended family, and I haven't communicated with them for years. Is there a restroom around?" she asked before he could speak again.

Kellan pointed to a doorway behind her. "Through there and into the next building."

Denae hurried away, hating how memories of her family

would hit her when she least expected it. She hadn't meant to bring up her father, but Kellan saying her father's favorite words brought a tide of memories she couldn't hold back.

She followed Kellan's instructions and walked into the next building. The building was full of fishing nets and crates and other things she had no clue about.

After spotting a door up ahead, she walked around a set of crates stacked high and stopped in her tracks when she found four men with assault rifles trained on her. As chilling as that was, it was nothing compared to the four men flanking them.

They had long, black hair streaked silver and red eyes.

CHAPTER
FOURTEEN

Kellan stared at the door Denae had disappeared through and paced several lengths of the office before he stopped and stared at the door again.

He blew out a breath. How long did a female need in the restroom? She had been gone several minutes already.

"Kellan," he heard behind him.

He whirled around to find Rhi, her eyes wide and distress tightening her face. He was immediately on guard. "What is it?"

"The Dark are here. And they have Denae."

He was shocked at the fury that rose so swiftly within him. For a human. Yet, he was the one supposed to keep her safe. He had failed, and he didn't like that feeling one bit.

"Where is she?" he demanded.

Rhi's boot heels sounded loud in the building as she hurried to the back windows. "There."

Kellan followed her and let out a sigh of relief when he spotted Denae standing on a pier alone. Then confusion set in. "They didna take her?"

Rhi looked away from the windows. "The Dark Ones aren't alone, Kell. They joined forces with MI5."

Now he was truly flabbergasted. "The Fae and the humans? That can no' be."

"It's not all of MI5, just a few. I was keeping an eye on things when I saw Denae walk into the other building. I followed, keeping veiled, and watched her encounter the small group of Dark and the spies. She's bait again, Kell."

"For me." Of course. Why hadn't he realized that sooner? That's the only reason Denae was still in this realm and alive. The real question was whether Denae was in on the Dark Ones taking him, or if she was a victim.

"The Dark Ones want a Dragon King. MI5 wants Denae."

"Kellan!" Denae called halfheartedly. "Can you come out?"

Kellan looked back at Denae and noticed how her eyes went anywhere but at the building he was in. She was alone, but the Dark Fae and the spies would be hiding close enough to swoop in the moment she tried to run or he appeared.

In dragon form, he could fly down and get her, but it would be a big chance. For though few Kings liked to admit it, the Dark Fae's magic could prevent them from remaining in dragon form, which is when they were their strongest.

The Dark couldn't just prevent it. There were instances when their magic could hinder a King to make him almost as feeble as a human. It was why the Kings rarely fought alone against the Dark.

But Kellan had given his word to Denae. He couldn't remember the last time he had saved a human's life, but that didn't seem to matter as he stared at her standing so stoically.

"No," Rhi said in shock. "You aren't seriously considering going down there. You can't. I heard the Dark. They want you."

Kellan took in the entire scene, determining where his enemies would hide. "I'm going."

"You don't care that they've targeted you specifically?"

He shrugged and picked out the hiding places the mortals would use. "Of course I care. They want something, and I want to know what it is. I willna learn that standing here."

"It's the Dark, Kellan," she stated flatly.

"I know." He turned his head to her. After what had happened with Rhi and her Dragon King lover she could've turned her back on them, but she hadn't. It showed just how deep her love for the King had been. If she only knew the truth . . .

"Kellan!" Denae called again.

Rhi blew out a harsh breath. "You're a Dragon King. Do you know what the Dark Ones will do to you?"

The pitch of Rhi's voice went higher. The Dark might not be able to kill a King, but the long-term effects of suffering their torture could do untold damage.

They had managed to capture two Kings during the Fae Wars. Kellan remembered all too well having to kill one King after the Dark released him and he set out to destroy Dreagan.

The other . . . the Dark had tried to use during a battle. Seeing a King held by Dark Ones had been horrible, but nothing compared to the King begging his brethren to end his life. It was Con who reached him first and killed him.

"She's right," Con said from the doorway as he and Rhys walked in. "The Dark can no' capture another King."

Rhi backed away when Kellan met her eyes. "I can do this with your help," he told her. "The Dark Ones doona know you're here."

Kellan looked from Con to Rhys and back to Rhi. He couldn't begin to explain his driving need to save Denae, only that he had to. It was an odd feeling after spending so much time hoping for the demise of all mortals. "I took responsibility for her. Because I gave Denae my word that she wouldna die this day. Because . . . I have to do this for her."

Suddenly Rhi gave him a wink. "Just what I wanted to hear, stud."

"You can no' be serious," Con said as he stalked angrily to Kellan. "You'll never get free of the Dark Ones."

"Thanks for the confidence," Kellan said sarcastically.

Con closed his eyes and fisted his hands, as if he were searching for patience. When his black eyes opened, he pinned Kellan with a hard look. "I doona want to have to kill another King who has been in the hands of a Dark. I can no'. No' again."

"Kellan! You should see this!" Denae shouted while glaring at a stack of crates.

Kellan itched to answer Denae. He knew exactly how Con felt. It was strange to hear Con talk of saving a King over a human. It wasn't something he had ever done before. Then again, it wasn't every day that a Dark tried to capture a King.

Just what were the Dark up to? He had to know if she was part of the plot. He had to know if he was being betrayed yet again.

In all his thousands upon thousands of years, there had been just a handful of mortals he'd helped. There was something about Denae—and not just her beauty—that he associated with. How he wished he hadn't, but once that connection was there, it was there.

Walking away from her, however, wasn't something he would do. Not yet.

"I'm going to do this," Kellan told the group. "I doona plan on being taken by the Dark, but I can no' do this alone. Either you help me or leave."

Rhys grunted. "As if we would leave. What do you want us to do?"

"Get the four MI5 guys," Rhi said.

Rhys smiled, his eyes alight with anticipation. "I can handle them on my own."

Kellan saw Denae look at a stack of crates to her left nervously. A Dark Fae must be there. She wasn't afraid of humans, but she was smart enough to comprehend the Dark were something else entirely.

"There were a few of the Dark who were eyeing Denae," Rhi said cautiously as she glanced at Kellan. "I don't think they intend to let the humans have her as was originally planned."

"They can have any woman they want," Con said. "Why do they want Denae?"

"Because she was with us," Kellan stated.

Rhi nodded in agreement. "If they want a King, it's just like those jackasses to want a woman who spent time with one."

"But Denae and Kellan didna do anything," Rhys said.

"It doesn't matter." Rhi wrinkled her nose. "Their hatred for the Kings runs almost as deep as their hatred of the Light."

Kellan's mind sank into battle mode. Denae had a chance to live if the humans took her, but if the Dark took her, she was as good as dead. "It's time to stop talking and get Denae free. Then we make sure the Dark Ones can't get her."

"We need a plan," Rhys said. "One that involves Banan and Henry as well."

Con slid his hands into the pockets of his dress pants. "MI5 can no' get ahold of Denae. We didna get a chance to wipe her memories."

Kellan set his shoulders. "No matter what, she lives. You made that much clear when I carried her out of my mountain."

"Then I suggest you doona get taken by the Dark," Con said.

* * *

Denae tried to slow her pounding heart, but she couldn't remember ever being so scared. It wasn't the operatives sent by the agency—it was the others. Those four weren't human or mortal.

Their hair was so similar in color to Rhi's, except for the silver shot through the strands, but that was not what made her blood turn cold. It was their red eyes and the way they looked at her as if she were a meal to be sampled at leisure.

None of the eight—humans or others—had curbed their talk in front of her. She knew they wanted a Dragon King and Kellan in particular. And apparently the humans were supposed to take her after the others captured Kellan.

The way the red-eyed men smiled when they talked about the Dragon Kings made Denae nervous. Kellan had said the only way to kill a Dragon King was by another King, but he didn't say anything about torture.

She eyed the water behind her. The tide was moving out, and with her strong stroke, there was a chance she could get away. There was also a very good chance she would be shot while doing it.

Denae lifted her eyes to find one of the red-eyed men watching her with a wry smile on his face. She stopped herself from shivering at the blatant sexual desire in his gaze.

"I dare you," he said and glanced at the water.

He knew what she was thinking. How? She had barely given the water a glance. Denae looked away from the man and sent up a silent prayer that Kellan would walk away regardless of how many times they made her call out to him.

But she knew he wouldn't. She knew their secret, and they didn't want that in the hands of MI5. The water might be her only option. If she dove into the water, it would release Kellan from his vow.

She would have to be quick and time it perfectly. Two of the four operatives were closest to her with their rifles trained on her, waiting for her to make a move. The remaining two were stationed on the rooftops and had her in their scopes in case she made a run for it.

Of the four red-eyes, only one was near her. She had no idea where the others were, and that was what worried her. They could be anywhere.

She was preparing to jump into the water when the sound of a door opening reached her. Denae then spotted Kellan's tall, muscular form striding toward her as if he didn't have a care in the world.

The waves of his long, caramel-colored hair lifted in the breeze, and his eyes locked with hers. What stole her awareness was the half smile upon his lips, which made him appear as if he looked forward to whatever was about to happen.

It transformed his rugged, handsome face into one that left her breathless and needy. With his olive-green shirt hugging his wide shoulders and his jeans slung low on narrow hips, he was a gorgeous sight to behold.

As he drew closer, his brows raised a fraction, as if he were daring her to say something. Her lips parted to tell him not to get nearer, but then he was before her, his steely arms winding around her.

And his lips locked with hers.

Denae was so taken aback that she had her arms around his neck and was returning his kiss before she realized it.

He kissed skillfully, sinfully. It was sensual and carnal, stirring and salacious.

And she never wanted it to end.

Her breasts swelled as he crushed her to him. Desire pumped through her, pooling between her legs as her passion built. Just as quickly as the kiss began, Kellan ended it as he kissed down her jaw until his mouth was even with her ear.

"Trust me," he whispered.

Her eyes widened to tell him who was watching when he kissed her again. This time the kiss was savage as he plundered her mouth with consummate expertise.

She was falling under his spell again, even with danger lurking all around her. She was powerless to do anything else. Kellan had a hold over her she didn't understand.

Her eyes opened when his hands came up on either side of her face and he lifted his head. Reality came crashing down like a bucket of ice water when she didn't see any desire in his green eyes. They were as stony and lifeless as ever.

Gone was the small smile. The lips that had just kissed her with such abandon and tenderness were set in a hard line. There was a loud retort and something slammed into her thigh painfully. In the next moment, he was shoving her to the ground.

At the same instant, gunfire erupted around them, directed entirely at Kellan. Denae ducked even as Kellan sheltered her with his body.

"Stay down!" he yelled at her over the shooting.

With no firearm, Denae had no choice. That is, until she saw one of the agents go down, his gun falling from his lifeless fingers. She rolled; gritting her teeth as her leg pulsed with pain from the bullet lodged within, and came up with the weapon in her hand, sending several rounds at an operative on the rooftop.

With that agent dead, Denae turned to another only to have Kellan grab her and pull her behind a set of crates.

"Are you insane?" he asked angrily.

Now he was showing emotion? Now that she was in her element and able to defend herself? She wanted to roll her eyes. "I was trained for this, remember?"

"Those are Dark Fae out there with your people."

"My people?" she repeated and gave a snort as she looked at his shirt riddled with bullet holes and blood. "As if I would claim the ones putting bullets in you."

"You could be working with them. How do I know otherwise? Everything that happened in my cave could've been planned."

"Yep. You found me out. I set up my own betrayal, knowing you were in the cave and would take me back to the manor so Con, with the magic I knew he had, would heal me, only to get shot again." Denae rolled her eyes. "Get a grip."

He sighed loudly and looked around the crates as the bullets slowly exited his body and the wounds healed right before her eyes.

"How bad is your wound?"

"It won't kill me." Denae raised her eyes to his face. He thought she was part of the trap. As if. But that didn't upset her nearly as much as the kiss. The kiss that had shaken her to her core meant nothing to him. It had been a distraction for her as well as their enemies.

She felt used, manipulated. And it hurt.

She scooted around the other side of the crate and took aim at a second agent on the roof through her scope. In one shot, he was dead.

"I'm trying to keep you alive," Kellan stated as he moved her out of the way.

"The Dark Fae want you," she told him.

"I know. Rhi heard it all as she was following you to keep you from harm."

"So you knowingly walked into an ambush while thinking I'm a part of it?" Denae shook her head. "And here I thought you were smart."

"I am," he ground out.

Her retort died on her lips when the Dark Fae who had been eyeing her earlier rose up behind Kellan.

CHAPTER
FIFTEEN

Kellan saw Denae's widened eyes and knew there was someone behind him, and by the look of stark fear on her face, he knew what—a Dark.

If it wasn't for Denae, he would turn and battle the Fae, but there was the female to consider. Instead of fighting, he clasped her arms and pulled her on top of him as he dove to the side as a blast of dark magic came at them.

Kellan rolled them until he was on top of her. His body, already heated from their kisses, roared to life when nestled against her soft curves.

There was no time to think about it, however, with a battle going on around him. Kellan looked up and saw something slam into the Dark One from the back. Rhi appeared for just a moment as nothing but a shimmer as her magic gathered and she focused it on her enemy. It sent the Dark from the realm, leaving only three others to fight.

Rhi glanced at him just before she faded again. Kellan jumped to his feet and pulled Denae up with him. "Are you all right?"

She was nodding her head when her body jerked and she fell forward. Kellan grabbed her against him, his hand going around to her back and meeting something sticky and wet.

He dragged her to safety and pulled his hand away to see it covered in bright red blood. Kellan knelt with her in his arms and gently turned her onto her back, careful to keep his hand covering the wound to stanch the blood flow.

Her face was pale, her lips colorless.

"It's going to be all right," he said. "I promised you wouldna die today."

She smiled wanly. "Even you can't keep such a promise."

"When will you stop doubting me?" he whispered.

Her lids slid closed over her whisky-colored eyes. Even with the kernel of doubt that she was part of the ambush, Kellan called forth his dragon power and found the metal bullets within her. He focused all of his concentration on the metal and extracting them from her spine and her leg.

The bullet in her leg fell first, and then the one from her back. But that didn't stop the blood. Before he could call to Con, the King of Kings stood before them.

Kellan glanced up and saw Rhys, Banan, and even Henry surrounding them as they fended off the Dark. Con knelt beside Denae, and without a word, healed her.

The fear that had turned his blood to ice was new. It had been so long since he had felt that particular emotion and he would be happy never to feel it again.

Denae's eyes fluttered open, a frown marring her forehead. "There's no more pain."

"Because the injury is gone."

"How?"

Kellan spotted a Dark Fae coming for them, so he got them on their feet and running. He paused beside another set of crates and peered around the corner. "Con is the only one who can heal a wound, and he did just that."

"You did something, I know it. What was it?" she asked as he jerked her after him as they ran to another spot.

"My gift is finding metal."

There was a beat of silence before she said, "The bullets. Thank you."

Kellan glanced at her, surprised to hear such words. Then again, she constantly astounded him. There was steel beneath her delicate frame, extreme intelligence behind her sexy eyes, and gentleness within her.

Not to mention passion beyond his wildest dreams.

Their kisses had sent his already heated blood to boiling. If she could do that to him with just a kiss, what would it be like to fill her?

Kellan swallowed and looked away from her beguiling gaze. The agents from MI5 had been killed, leaving only three Dark Fae left to battle. Rhi took care of another one a moment later, and just like that, the other two disappeared.

"Are they gone?" Henry asked as he rose up from behind some crates.

Banan looked around at the devastation. "No' for long."

"And those things were . . . ?" Henry prompted.

Con looked down at his white dress shirt ruined by blood and dirt with distaste. "Those were Dark Fae."

"You met another Fae earlier," Kellan said as he and Denae came to stand with the others. "Rhi."

Henry's eyes softened at the mention of the Fae. "She's a beautiful woman."

"And off-limits. You doona want to get involved with her," Con said.

"I don't think I'd mind," Henry said with a chuckle.

Rhys walked up and said, "We need to get out of here before the authorities show up."

"Denae can no' return to Dreagan," Kellan said.

Banan nodded grimly. "Agreed. We're being followed."

"Speaking of that, where is Rhi?" Con asked.

Rhys threw up his hands in a gesture of puzzlement. "Around somewhere."

"Are we sure the Dark Fae are really gone?" Denae asked.

Kellan glanced at her, and only then realized he still had a grasp on her arm. He released his grip and then fisted his hand to hold in her warmth.

"Good question," Banan said. "One we can determine."

Rhi appeared beside Rhys. "No need. They're gone, but I wouldn't suggest hanging around. They're pissed off. They're also determined to have a Dragon King."

"A what?" Henry asked.

Kellan ignored him and looked at Rhi. "Why?"

"They're after something," she responded.

Con blew out a harsh breath. "Did they say what?"

Rhi twisted her lips as she shrugged. "I'll keep an ear out for anything. My queen is calling for me, and I'm sure she'll be on the edge of her seat to hear this story."

And then she was gone.

"That would make traveling easier," Denae said with a grin. "Kinda wish I could pop in and out of places."

Kellan didn't know of any mortal who could make a jest after almost losing their life. Denae constantly confounded him, making him rethink everything about humans—and that disturbed him.

But no more than his hunger for her did.

He hadn't intended to kiss her. His plan had been to get her to safety before the battle began, but as he approached, her beautiful eyes had filled with such longing and desire that it had undone him.

The first kiss had been a mistake. The second, disastrous.

Now all he could think about was her. Her taste was on his tongue, tantalizing him with her scent and sensuality. His hands itched to free her hair from the braid and feel the silky tresses through his fingers.

"But would you dislike me less if I was Fae instead of human since you hate both?" she asked Kellan.

"I doona hate Rhi."

A sad smile pulled at Denae's lips. "Of course not."

Without another word, she turned on her heel and walked back to the Range Rover.

Kellan watched the sway of her hips. It was mesmerizing, seductive, and she didn't even know it. Everything she did was tantalizing and tempting, enticing and provocative.

Made all the more so because she had no idea of her appeal. And if she ever did, there wouldn't be a man—mortal or immortal—who would be immune to her.

Kellan already had a difficult time keeping his hands off her, and now that he knew the taste of her kiss, he had one goal—claiming her body.

Henry came to stand beside him and scratched his chin. "There were few men in all of MI5 who didn't want her in their beds."

"You included?" Kellan asked, a hard note in his voice.

Henry met his gaze. "Me included. Despite being a spy, there is something pure and honest about her that draws people in. There aren't many who retain any virtues after being a spy. Denae is different."

Kellan thought over Henry's words. Denae was different.

"There's blood on her shirt. A lot of it. Is she injured?"

Banan came up beside Henry. "No' anymore. Kellan and Con took care of that."

Kellan said no more as he followed Denae. He wanted to be alone with his thoughts, but he should have known Con wouldn't allow that.

"What's your plan?" Con asked as he fell into step beside him.

Kellan kept his gaze on Denae as he shrugged. "I need to take her somewhere safe from both MI5 and the Dark."

"I know you, old friend. You suspect her of being a part of this."

"I did. I do."

"Which is it?" Con prodded.

Kellan shrugged. "I doona know. My hatred of the humans for what they did to us, as well as my Bronzes, could be clouding my judgment. She was shot, a wound that would've taken her life."

Con nodded. "That shot was meant for you, but I understand. It's difficult to ignore. The Dark are after you. What could they want?"

Kellan glanced at the King of Kings and shrugged. "Who knows with the Dark? I'd feel better if we found out though."

"Me as well. Perhaps I should put Ulrik on their radar."

"And if he's the one, as you believe, behind all of this, how will that look?"

"I honestly doona care."

"I understand his hatred of you, but you were the one who betrayed him."

Con halted, his jaw set as he glared. "He betrayed all of us. Never forget that. I did what was necessary for the survival of the dragons."

"You two were as close as brothers. He was your rival as King of Kings, and yet he didna fight you for that honor."

"I'm no' talking about this," Con stated with finality. "There is a place on the Isle of Raasay. I'd tell you how to get there, but you've no' driven before."

Kellan walked away before he punched Con. He had agreed with Con on how to handle the woman who had deceived Ulrik, but he had never understood Con's hatred of Ulrik. And it appeared he never would.

When Kellan reached the Range Rover, Denae was already in the backseat with her seat belt buckled. He opened his door and climbed in beside her.

"I guess my leaving the country under a false name is out of the question," she said.

Kellan closed his door. "Aye."

"If all the Dragon Kings are at Dreagan, wouldn't that be the safest place for me?"

"No' with your people still looking for you. We need to

draw them away." Her head turned and she pinned him with her eyes, causing his cock to stir once more. "As powerful as we are, the magic of a Dark Fae can . . . hinder us."

"How?" she pressed.

"We're strong in human form. In dragon form, we're even stronger. The Dark Fae can keep us from shifting into dragons."

Her nose wrinkled. "That sounds unfair. What can you do to the Dark Fae?"

"The same thing we did to the Fae, which is fight them. All Fae can be killed. They are no' immortal. They only live an exceptionally long time."

"As in how long?"

"Thousands of years."

Both of her brows rose. "Oh, is that all? I was thinking it was a really long time or something."

Her dry wit had him almost smiling. "If the Dark Fae dare to come to Dreagan, there will be another war. That would show the world who we are as well as exposing the Fae."

"Can't Rhi and her people help?"

"The Light loathe the Dark. They are constantly fighting each other, and that's why, for the most part, humans doona see much of either Fae."

"And if we do encounter them?"

"The Light, those like Rhi, you've probably seen and no' known. They're forbidden to take human lovers, but it happens all the time. The Dark, however, like to steal men and woman alike."

"And do what with them?"

"Young girls are their favorites. They terrorize and torture them, feeding off their innocence until nothing is left but a shell. Then they are used for sex."

"And the men?" she asked in a soft voice.

Kellan looked out the window to see Banan and Henry approaching. "The men are used for sex until their souls are depleted. The only way they can survive after that is by continuing to have sex with the Dark Ones."

"Can't they be rescued?"

"No. Once someone is slave to a Dark One, they're lost."

Denae looked out her window as Banan and Henry got into the vehicle. Once the SUV was started, Banan quickly drove them away from the docks.

"Why are the Dark Fae after you now?" she asked.

Kellan wished he knew.

"They despise us for putting them in a position to sign a treaty," Banan said.

"That doesn't make sense to go after just Kellan then," Denae said as she looked forward.

Kellan had to agree with her. "There's only one reason they would want me. As Keeper of the History, they want something from our past."

And Kellan had an idea of exactly what that was. If the Dark got their hands on it, he wasn't sure the Kings could save the humans, much less themselves.

"Rhys is going to meet us later so he can take you and Denae," Banan said into the growing silence.

Henry rested his elbow on the armrest between the seats. "I don't want to know where, so be sure not to mention it. Meanwhile, I'm going to contact my superiors and see if I can put a stop to the operatives coming after Denae."

It all sounded like a good plan, but Kellan knew how quickly good plans could blow up around them. It had happened less than an hour ago.

He found himself looking at Denae again. It was his job to keep her safe from threats of Dark Fae and MI5 alike. Why then was he looking forward to more time with her?

CHAPTER
SIXTEEN

Denae couldn't stop thinking about what Kellan had told her about the Dark Fae. The carnality in the Dark Fae's eyes as he watched her earlier made goose bumps rise all along her skin.

She had been close to evil. Evil she recognized, but didn't fully comprehend. Until now.

All her life, the only thing she had felt she needed to worry about was the bad guys she eventually worked to bring down. Now she had learned that there were Dragon Kings, Light Fae, and Dark Fae.

At least she wasn't the only one with a shell-shocked expression. Henry wasn't much better, and he didn't know of the Dragon Kings. But he suspected the men from Dreagan were something more than just humans. It was in Henry's hazel eyes when he looked at any of them.

The forty-five-minute ride to meet Rhys was made in silence. Denae's mind should probably have been on the attack and the Dark, but all she could think about was her sister.

Why had she told Kellan about Renee? No one at MI5 knew anything other than that her sister had drowned, and her parents had died shortly after.

What was it about Kellan that made her open up? Was it his virile magnetism? His irresistible eyes? His finely honed body?

His mind-blowing kisses?

She didn't want to trust him, but he had come into the middle of a trap for her. He had pulled the bullets from her wounds. He had even shielded her with his own body. How could she not trust him?

Her life had been dedicated to finding the bad men who stalked, threatened, raped, and killed women. The Dark and MI5 were now coming after her. She was no longer a part of MI5, which meant she had to fight for herself now.

She wasn't alone, at least not for the moment. There might come a time that the Dragon Kings cut ties with her, and she needed to prepare for that day. Until then, she would stand beside them and fight MI5.

Battling the Dark was another matter entirely. Nothing terrified her like the Dark. At least nothing in a very long time.

"Will the Dark continue to come after me?" she asked.

Kellan turned his head to her. "It depends on whether the Dark and MI5 continue working together."

"They frighten me," she whispered as she met his eyes. She felt like that girl who had buried her mother right after her sister, and then watched her father slowly die. That forlorn girl was reaching out to Kellan to steady the world spinning out of control. "The Dark make me feel alone and lost. I haven't felt that since I lost my family."

He started to respond when Banan pulled over behind a white Mercedes G-Class. Instead of words, Kellan laid his hand atop hers and gave it a squeeze before they exited.

Henry merely gave Kellan a nod after all four had gotten out of the Range Rover. Then he looked at Denae. "I'm going to clear your name in this."

"We both know my career at MI5 is over. I'm actually all right with that." Which came as a complete surprise.

She had dedicated her life there. "I just want them to let me go without any fuss."

"Then I'll see it done," Henry said with a smile.

Denae noticed that Kellan and Banan exchanged looks, but nothing more. Kellan's hand then rested on the small of her back as he walked her to the Mercedes SUV and Banan and Henry drove off.

Rhys leaned against the vehicle with one shoulder, his arms crossed over his chest. He flashed her a smile as they neared. "Ready for your next adventure?"

"Always," she replied. It was part lie. Normally she never shied away from anything, but all she wanted to do was curl up with a glass of wine and pretend the day hadn't happened.

What was happening to the girl who feared nothing? She glanced at Kellan. He could have let her bleed out in his cave, and despite her current situation, she was glad he hadn't. She had gotten to see a dragon.

And kissed Kellan.

Denae touched her lips as she recalled the heat and passion, the desire and need that had scorched her with the intensity of that kiss.

She took the backseat while Kellan sat in the front with Rhys. Except when Rhys slid behind the wheel, he didn't start the SUV.

Kellan looked at him. "What is it?"

"You know they can track us."

Denae assumed "they" were MI5.

Kellan ran a hand through his hair to get it out of his face. "She can no' swim that far."

"I wasna talking of swimming," Rhys said and gave Kellan a knowing look.

Kellan blinked and glanced at her over his shoulder. "We would have to wait for cover of darkness."

"No' necessarily. Look." Rhys pointed to the dark clouds approaching.

Denae looked from one to the other, realization dawning a second later. "You want to fly to wherever we're going?"

"It would be quicker. And safer," Rhys pointed out.

Denae snorted. "Safer for who? I can already see lightning flashes in those storm clouds. Y'all might be able to withstand a blast, but I can't."

"She has a point," Kellan said. His disappointment was palpable.

She squeezed the bridge of her nose with her thumb and forefinger. "Look. Why don't one of you fly in and the other drive?"

"Because I'm no' leaving you," Kellan said. He paused for half a second, and her heart missed a beat. Then he said tightly, "And I doona know how to drive."

"I do," she stated.

Rhys began to nod. "I like it. I can go in and take a look around before you two arrive. It'll also let me know if they have anything watching from the skies."

"It's settled then," Denae said.

"Nay, it's no'." Kellan's pale green eyes were narrowed in thought.

Rhys's grin was wide as he said, "You know it's the right thing to do."

Kellan faced forward without a word. Rhys chuckled and exited the vehicle. The back passenger door was opened by Rhys, who waited for her to get out before he closed it.

"Where are we going?"

"The Isle of Raasay. Go west toward Skye. The ferry will take you to the isle. I'll be overhead."

Denae glanced at the sky. "Out of sight, I presume."

"Of course."

Rhys then took off his shirt and shoes and tossed them into the back of the Mercedes. When he reached for the waist of his jeans, Denae hastily got into the driver's seat and adjusted everything to her.

As soon as the back hatch closed, Kellan said, "We can leave now."

Denae pushed the start button and the engine roared to life. She pulled out onto the road and started driving. In the time she had known Kellan, they had been alone for very little. Now, she had hours with him.

She glanced at him to see one hand fisted on his thigh and his gaze on the sky. "You would rather be up there flying, wouldn't you?"

"Aye."

Denae was a little surprised he answered so honestly. "Rhys could drive me, you know."

"I gave my word I would see you safe."

"You would be, just from a different vantage point." Out of the corner of her eye she saw him staring at her.

"I'll take to the skies soon."

"When was the last time you flew?"

His sigh was long. "Nearly thirteen centuries ago."

Denae was so shocked she swerved on the road as she looked at him. She straightened the SUV and blinked. "Are you kidding?"

"Nay."

They drove for two miles as she waited for him to elaborate. When he didn't, she asked, "Will you tell me why it's been so long?"

"I was asleep."

She really needed to stop being surprised at everything that came out of his mouth. There were supernatural beings on Earth, sharing their world with humans. Who knew what kind of code they lived by, or even how they lived?

"You must have been really tired." Was it her imagination, or had there been a ghost of a smile on his lips?

Kellan shifted in his seat. "When you're immortal, time stretches endlessly before you. Sometimes we grow weary of it all, but we have responsibilities as Dragon Kings. We either stay awake and get through each day, or we sleep."

"In dragon form, I suppose?"

"Of course. It's our natural form."

She smiled softly at him. "So you slept for thirteen hundred years. What sent you into the mountain?"

"The one I killed, because even after what he did, we are supposed to protect humans."

He cut his eyes to her, but she kept driving. She knew he disliked her kind, but his voice had fairly dripped with loathing.

"It wasn't just that one mortal. I had grown tired of them and their ways. I had never stopped hating them for what they did to my dragons. I was supposed to defend the mortals, and yet I wanted to wipe them from this realm."

She was silent, taking it all in.

"It was Con's right to end my life after I killed that human. He opted not to, and I chose to sleep rather than see another human."

"And then Matt and I showed up," she said and glanced at him. "I can't begin to know what it's like to lose dragons, but I do understand loss. I don't think I'd have blamed you had you let me die in your cave."

"I honestly doona know why I didna. Maybe it was the way you fought Matt."

The windshield wipers came on as rain began to drizzle upon them. Denae knew she shouldn't prod into Kellan's past, but she was curious about him.

She licked her lips, suddenly nervous to pry. "You mentioned being the Keeper of the History. What did you mean by that?"

"I was in charge of the history of the dragons," he said and tapped the window beside him as a bubble of rain ran down the side. "I wrote down every birth, every death, every disagreement, every battle. It plays in my mind, allowing me to write details without having to witness anything. I kept numbers of each dragon clan. Some events I was part of. Like when we discovered Ulrik's woman had betrayed him and we hunted her down."

Denae gripped the steering wheel tighter. He had glossed over that part before, but would she hear it all now? "You were important?"

"We all are, in our own way. Ulrik was no less important than me. It could've been me who had a human female betray me."

"What happened?" she asked.

"No one ever spoke with her, so the only one who knows the entire story is Ulrik."

Denae put on her blinker and followed the signs west toward Skye. "I thought you recorded the history."

"Not everyday lives. It's important events that come to me."

"Has anyone ever asked Ulrik about his woman?"

"That would be difficult. When we learned of the treachery, Con gathered all of us to track her down and kill her."

"What?" Denae squeaked. "You killed her without asking her if the charges were true or even hearing her side?"

Kellan leaned his head back and closed his eyes. "We saw her meeting with a group of dragon hunters and giving the location to a clan of small pink dragons that lived in the cliffs nearby. Those dragons were no bigger than eagles. They would've been slaughtered."

"I'm glad you stopped them, but why kill the woman? And was Ulrik with you?"

A muscle in Kellan's jaw tightened. "Con sent Ulrik away."

"That wasn't very noble."

"Con and Ulrik were as close as brothers," Kellan said and then opened his eyes. "He was trying to protect Ulrik."

"And how did that turn out?"

"When Ulrik returned and found his woman, he . . . he grew enraged. Nothing any of us said could calm him. Con finally told him what had occurred. I'll never forget the look of betrayal that shone in Ulrik's eyes."

Denae's heart pounded as she waited to hear the rest of the story. "What happened?"

"I'm no' sure who Ulrik was more angry at—us, because we killed his woman, or the humans because they turned against him. In the end, I doona think it mattered. He went after the humans, wiping out entire villages with his silver dragons."

"Is that what started the war?"

"It was the tipping point," Kellan said. He rubbed the back of his neck and looked out his window. "Sometimes it feels as if it just happened, that I'm still in the middle of that war."

Denae slowed the Mercedes as they came to an intersection. Once she pulled out, she glanced at Kellan. "How long did the war last?"

"Too long. Humans began to kill dragons, and dragons began to kill humans. As Kings, we had to keep the peace. It didna always work."

"Like when your dragons were killed?"

His voice was hoarse with emotion when he answered, "Aye."

"I'm sorry. What became of Ulrik?"

Kellan cleared his throat. "He wouldna listen to reason from anyone, no' even Con. Con had no choice but to strip Ulrik of his magic."

"Con can do that to one of you?"

"Only with the other Kings using their magic. Ulrik remains immortal, but the connection to his Silvers was terminated. No longer could he communicate with them, or any dragon, for that matter."

She frowned, confusion filling her. "He was one of you. He had suffered from a betrayal on two sides, and y'alls only thought was to strip him of his magic and keep him from his Silvers? That was stupid."

"As Kings, we were divided. I agreed with Con, because I didna see another way. Others tried to talk Con out of it, and even went to Ulrik again. Now, when I see where the war has brought us, I also think Con should've handled it differently."

"Where is Ulrik?"

"In Perth. He has an antiques shop and moves around every few decades so people willna notice he doesna age."

"Did you talk to him after he was stripped of his magic?"

Kellan was quiet for several minutes. "Nay, but I went to see him. He was broken. Without him to lead them, the Silvers attacked all humans. We had to round them up and send them away with the other dragons. We captured a few of the biggest, and keep them caged in the mountain. Our magic keeps them sleeping."

"I feel sorry for Ulrik. He lost his family and friends, and he lost his dragons."

"Con can be a coldhearted bastard."

Denae locked that piece of information away. If she had learned one thing from Kellan's tale, it was that Con would do anything to protect the peace—no matter who had to suffer.

CHAPTER
SEVENTEEN

Somewhere in Scotland . . .

He seethed. The plan had been perfect. How had the Dragon Kings gotten wind of the trap? It should have been a flawless capture of Kellan with the female as a bonus.

Although he wasn't so certain the Dark Ones would allow the female to go to MI5. She was a pretty thing. He almost regretted targeting her to die in the mission, but beauty was fleeting and there were a dozen other pretty females about.

His plan had been set in motion a thousand years before. It was laid out like a chess game with him controlling everything.

To his bitter disappointment, his plan had taken careful arranging and a millennia of preparation. Then he had to account for the modernization of the mortals and their ever-changing technological advancements.

If he'd had his way, his revenge would have happened before the dragons were sent out of this realm. Instead, he had been . . . incapacitated.

But no longer.

He turned off the A9 toward Perth. The Dark wanted

retribution against the Kings for the Fae Wars. He happened to want his own revenge. Rarely did one of his plans go wrong, except when the Kings were involved.

In London a year before, he'd wanted to see how far they would go. To his surprise, one of the Kings had found a mate. It had been . . . eons since something so remarkable had occurred with the group.

It had given him pause, but only for a little while. Soon, it became apparent just how far the Kings would go for their mates. Which would be their downfall.

He drove into Perth and pulled into a parking spot on the side of King's Street. Millennia after millennia had passed as he planned out his revenge.

His spider's web of influences, acquaintances, and networks took generation after generation to build. He was so rooted in some families now that they would do whatever he asked of them at any time.

Infiltrating MI5 had been just as easy.

However, his web wasn't contained to just Great Britain. It extended all over the world.

He had many names, many faces. No one knew he was the one controlling things. And no one lived who ever dared to refuse an order—or cross him.

The planning to take down the Dragon Kings had been meticulous, right down to waiting until now to form an alliance with the Dark Ones.

The Kings would never see him coming.

He laughed and reached for his mobile to dial a number. There was one ring before a male answered.

"Well?" he asked.

"It's just as you said, sir," the male answered in a British accent. "They got Denae away from the port quickly and met up with another vehicle."

Ah, but the Kings were predictable, even after all these years. They were supposed to protect the humans, and that's exactly what they were doing.

"Where are they taking her?"

There was a short pause before the man said, "The Merc is on route west, sir."

"West? Do you have eyes on them?"

"We do, both on the ground and in the air."

He smiled. "Good, good."

"When do we attack? MI5 is anxious to retrieve Denae and learn how she's been tortured and what those at Dreagan did to Matt."

"You will do nothing," he ordered harshly. "Do you understand me? You will stand down."

"Yes, sir."

"Call me as soon as they reach their destination. Is that understood?"

"Of course, sir."

He disconnected the phone. It wouldn't be MI5 who paid the human and Dragon King a visit.

Kellan didn't think they would ever reach Raasay. They had to wait over an hour just for the ferry, and then the ferry ride itself.

Once on Raasay, Kellan directed Denae north to the plot of land the Kings had claimed as their own two thousand years before. It was Kellan who had found it. He had known then that they might need places outside of Dreagan.

Con had agreed, and immediately the Kings set up places all around the world.

The last time Kellan had seen the place on Raasay it was nothing but a small cottage. It brought to mind once again how long he had been asleep and all he had missed with his brethren.

All because of his hatred.

He looked at Denae as she drove up the dirt road constricted on either side by thick forest as they climbed in elevation.

Kellan loved the shoreline of Raasay, but it was always

important to have a good lookout, which is why he had chosen the plot of land high up in the mountains.

"How much farther?" she asked.

"I'm no' sure. It's been awhile since I was here."

"What brought you to the isle?"

"I often stayed here in between exploring Skye and the other isles."

The SUV rocked violently as it rolled over a large rock protruding from the road. Denae winced. "Sorry. Didn't see that. I was too busy gawking at you."

"You always say whatever is on your mind."

"Not usually, but I've learned the only way I learn anything about you is to say what needs to be said."

"That was a statement before, no' a question."

She shrugged and gave him a quick look with her whisky-colored eyes. "Does that bother you?"

Oddly enough, it didn't. He was used to mortals being frightened of him even if they didn't know what he was, and yet, Denae was different in that regard as well. He found he . . . liked it. "You're no' afraid of me, are you?"

"I have a healthy respect for you," she stated. "Fear? That I reserve for the Dark Fae. Now they're the stuff of nightmares. But, no changing the subject. Back to your visits to Skye. Why there?"

Kellan pointed to a sign that said Private Property with a faint dragon on the right lower corner. "Turn here."

"Are you sure?"

"There's a dragon on the sign, of course I'm sure."

She turned and then brought the vehicle to a stop at the closed and locked gate. Kellan got out and walked to the gate. The lock wasn't a human one. There were no keys to use or numbers to punch. It was a lock that couldn't be blown up, sawed off, or cut.

The only way to open it was by being a Dragon King.

Kellan put his hand on the lock. As soon as it sensed his dragon magic, it unlocked with a click and the gate opened.

When he climbed back into the Mercedes, Denae stared at him. He motioned for her to proceed forward. She did so after hesitating for a minute.

"Have you ever heard of the *Book of Kells*?" he asked as they drove down the winding drive.

"Of course. I don't think there are many who haven't. Why?" Her eyes widened and her lips parted suddenly. "Kells? As in Kellan?"

Her shocked expression brought his lips up in a smile that he quickly hid. He wasn't ready for her to know just how deeply she affected him—not when he hadn't worked it all out himself. If only the desire didn't complicate matters he might figure it out. "That was me."

She laughed, the sound music to his ears. "You sound so humble. The *Book of Kells* is an important part of history. That's amazing. Did you ask them to name it after you?"

"Nay," he said, affronted that she would think he would do something like that. "They did it on their own. So it is still around?"

"Most certainly. There are disputing theories as to its origin. Many say Ireland."

He made a disgusted sound at the back of his throat. "That's the Fae's influence. They've always had a stronghold in Ireland, just as we do in Scotland."

"I have to ask, the book contains the gospels from the Bible. Why that? Why not something else?"

"It was important to humans." He hadn't cared about what was inside the book, but he had been impressed with the work the mortals had wanted to accomplish. It was the reason he had helped them to begin with. To have that book survive all these centuries was something he had never expected.

"And you don't believe?"

He thought back to that turbulent time when the humans were learning more and more about themselves. "It matters no' what I do or doona believe. Humans did."

"Did you begin the book?"

Kellan wanted to end the conversation before she saw how much he loved the written word and all it held, but he couldn't since he'd introduced the topic. Damn him for wanting to see if any of him had remained while he slept through time.

"It's all right," she said suddenly. "You don't have to tell me."

He briefly closed his eyes and wondered why he found Denae so easy to talk to. Had sleeping through time helped to heal his hatred? No. He was sure it hadn't. There was just something unique and exceptional about Denae.

"I urged them," he said. "I also did most of the drawings."

Her smile was genuine when she glanced at him. "Wow. Just . . . wow. Why wasn't it ever finished?"

Kellan caught sight of the stone house as it came into view. It was larger than the cottage he had built, but the pale stone and gray roof matched the surroundings nicely.

Denae stopped the car at the back of the house and shut off the engine. Being back on Raasay brought forth a ton of memories involving the *Book of Kells* and his trips to Iona visiting the monks.

He wasn't sure if the memories were good or bad. Nor did he quite know how he felt about being so close to where everything had fallen apart for him. Was that why Con had sent them here? Was Con pushing him to see if he would repeat history?

Kellan looked at Denae. He wanted to be in the vehicle on Raasay with her. The realization was like a punch in his stomach. Never did he think he would want to be so near a mortal.

But it wasn't just being near to her that he wanted. He hungered for her—all of her.

"I'd grown weary," he finally answered. "I assumed the monks would finish the book and illustrations."

"Was it so awful being around humans? They were monks. How bad could they be?"

Her eyes held a sadness he felt like a punch to his stomach. It hurt her how much he despised her kind, because she thought it also included her.

He could tell her she was excluded from his view, but to give her that information would be giving her a way into his mind. In the past he wouldn't have dared.

Things were different now. All because of a beautiful spy who emerged from the water in his cave.

Did she even know how she kept him tied in knots? Did she know how much he wanted to pull her into his arms and ravage her mouth for hours before exploring her body?

He looked away from the sorrow reflected in her eyes and wished he knew something to say to make her smile again. Instead, he opened the door and got out with Denae doing the same. With her by his side, they walked around the side of the house. As soon as he saw the view of the water with the sun setting, he remembered why he had chosen such a spot.

"This is the most beautiful thing I've ever seen," Denae said.

He faced her then, wanting her to know the truth. "The monks didna drive me away. I missed my dragons, I missed flying whenever I wanted. I missed hearing the roars. And answering them. Every time I looked at a human I saw my dead Bronzes.

"Each day it was a chore no' to lash out at them, to yell . . . to kill. And then, the man raped and killed the young girl. I didna even stop and think. I just reacted."

"I think I'd have done the same. The man gave you his word. He lied and killed."

Kellan looked to the skies. "The dragons are gone. Forever. You can no' possibly know what it means to lose something you love."

"Right, because you Kings have a monopoly on grief,

sorrow, and anger." Her words were clipped and full of annoyance.

He took a step toward her. "How would you feel if your family was sent away and you were left behind?"

She smiled wryly, the iciness of it slamming into him like a fist to his jaw. "Do you ever listen to me? Or is it just background noise you hear when I talk?"

"I doona know why you're getting defensive."

He was trying to calm her, but his words seemed to set her off instead. Her chin lifted and her shoulders squared, much as they had done when she was fighting Matt in his cave.

"You don't know . . ." She trailed off and pursed her lips together. "My family is gone, dead, you asshole. I'm all that remains."

Kellan couldn't believe he had forgotten that fact, but it still didn't measure up to him losing his dragons. It might be the same if the entire human race disappeared, leaving only her, but he didn't think mentioning that now would be in his best interest.

"Denae," he started.

She gave a shake of her head and turned on her heel to start back to the vehicle. "Don't even try it."

He glanced at the sunset and knew the peace he wanted to experience with Denae would have to wait. Kellan lengthened his strides to catch up with her.

She altered course and went to the back door, but it had the same lock as the gate. He reached around her and unlocked it.

"Denae . . ."

Without a glance, she pushed past him and walked into the lodge. Anger rose within him. He had promised to protect her, had even used his dragon magic to pull the bullets from her. How had she repaid him? By getting upset while he had been trying to explain his love of the dragons and how much he missed them. He had shared with her what he hadn't spoken about with a single individual. Just her.

Kellan knew he should go to the opposite side of the house. Instead, he followed her up the stairs and into one of the bedrooms.

She reached for the door as she passed it, but he caught it before it could slam in his face.

"What—" she started when she turned to find him there.

Kellan grabbed her by the shoulders and pushed her against the wall. Desire surged, rose like a tidal wave. It engulfed him, consumed him.

All the raw emotions he hadn't known how to sort through turned into a blinding, dazzling flame of yearning. And it was focused on one woman.

As soon as her lips parted, he knew he was lost. He took her mouth in an unrestrained, brutal kiss full of burning need and alluring desire.

CHAPTER
EIGHTEEN

Denae wanted to push him away. She wanted to turn her head. But she couldn't. Because she was getting what she had wanted since the first moment she'd laid eyes on Kellan—and let him into her head.

Her body melted against his, her lips eagerly parting for his kiss. His hard body trapped her against the wall while he deepened the kiss.

It was fevered, frenzied. He stole her breath the same time his kisses aroused and enthralled. Denae dug her fingers into his shoulders to remain upright.

Her world was spinning out of control, and at the center was Kellan—steady and solid.

Never had a kiss been such sweet seduction, such tantalizing persuasion . . . such enticing inducement. All that potent virility about Kellan was unleashed fully upon her. She was no match for his commanding potency, his masterful touch.

Her chest heaved when he lifted his head and his celadon gaze speared hers. No longer where his pale green eyes cold and devoid of emotion. They burned with desire, scorched her with the intensity of the need he let her see.

Chills raced over her skin, but it didn't frighten her. It only made her passion rise higher.

He confused and confounded her. He made her long for his touch, crave his kisses. He made her ache for something she didn't dare voice, something she thought could never be hers.

Denae couldn't keep her hands off him. She traced the hard line of his jaw and his square chin. And, finally, she gave into the need and slid her fingers into the cool strands of his long, caramel-colored hair.

There were no words between them.

There was no need.

Everything could be felt, sensed . . . and shared.

She instinctively knew the flare of attraction, of undeniable longing between them was rare and special. Whatever gripped them, held them was both wonderful and frightening.

Her stomach quivered in anticipation when his gaze dropped to her mouth. But he didn't kiss her again. Instead, he ran his fingers over her bare shoulder where her wide-necked shirt had fallen.

His caress was tender and possessive, gentle and sensual. Her eyes slid closed when his hand traveled across her chest and then down between her breasts to her waist.

A moan pulled from her as his lips found her neck. Denae turned her head to the side to give him access. While his lips worked their magic, his hands had taken her wrists and pinned them above her head.

Her lids lifted and she breathed in the scent of him—a heady combination of spices, rain, and danger. He held her wrists as he lifted his head and gave them a slight squeeze.

Then, slowly, he ran his hands down her arms to the hem of her oversized shirt. Denae's body was primed for him. She was about to yank the shirt off herself, but she kept her arms above her, impatiently waiting.

He didn't jerk off her shirt. That wasn't Kellan's style. He slid his hands beneath the hem and rested them on either side of her waist on top of her cami. With her oversized shirt gathered at his wrists, he leisurely ran his hands up her sides.

Denae sucked in a breath when he paused to rub his thumbs at the undersides of her breasts. A small smile played at his lips, but it was the darkening of his eyes that made her knees weak.

He continued upward, his hands sliding over her breasts in a frustratingly slow movement. Denae bit her lip and groaned when he passed over her nipples.

They were instantly hard, her breasts swelling and aching for more of his touch. He persisted in his unhurried removal of her outer shirt until his hands reached her shoulders, moving up her raised arms and past her hands.

Her shirt was casually dropped in a nearby chair. And his gaze lowered to her breasts, where he could see the outline of her turgid nipples.

She lowered her arms and gripped the wall with her hands as he moved one finger around her nipples, but never touching them, teasing her mercilessly.

Her breathing was harsh, even to her own ears. She was quickly becoming a puddle of need, and she hadn't even gotten to touch him as she longed to do.

With that in mind, Denae grabbed the hem of his shirt. Kellan's eyes crinkled at the corners as if daring her. She laid both hands flat on the warm skin of his waist. There was steel beneath her fingertips, and she wanted a good look at it.

Denae wasn't as slow in her removal of his shirt. She pushed it up to his shoulders and then over his head as quickly as she could. His shirt remained in her hand as she let her gaze wander over his chest and the impressive, unique dragon tattoo that met her.

She absently tossed his shirt as she glanced at his face.

He was watching her intently, waiting to see what she would do.

There was really only one thing to do. She reached out with her right hand and placed it over his heart, on the dragon's large head where its mouth sat open as if on a roar.

Her other hand flattened against the hard muscle of his chest while her right hand followed the rare mix of black and red ink over the tat. She frowned as she swore that the image moved beneath her hand.

Denae took in the whole of the tattoo. It was situated more on his left side, with only half the body of the dragon visible on Kellan's abdomen. The other half was inked on Kellan's left side.

However, it was the dragon's wings that were astounding. They were spread open wide with one covering the entire right side of his chest and the other extending onto his left arm so that when his arms were by his side, it looked to be a seamless image.

She had never seen anything so striking, so amazing before. Denae was torn between studying the tat more, or studying *him* more. It didn't take long for her to choose.

While her hands caressed him, she could feel every tremor, every twitch that went through his muscles. Just as she reached for the button of his jeans, he kissed her again and again, until she could barely remain standing.

Only then did he kneel before her and remove her shoes and socks. She couldn't take her eyes off him. No man—mortal or immortal—had ever shown her such care, such attention as Kellan.

She smoothed back a lock of his wavy hair that had fallen into his eyes. A smile pulled at her lips when he neatly set aside her shoes and socks before he looked up at her. The fire in his eyes hadn't diminished. In his gaze, she felt beautiful and . . . wanted.

It wasn't until that moment that she knew she had been

searching for just such a look in men's eyes before. Always she had come away feeling a little let down. But not now, not when she had Kellan.

Her breath caught in her chest when his fingers slid between her pants and her skin. With their gazes locked and the flames of desire growing with each heartbeat, he gradually pulled her yoga pants over her hips and down her legs until they pooled at her feet. He grasped one leg at a time and lifted her out of the pants, which joined their shirts on the chair.

When he straightened, she rose up on her toes and kissed him. His arms were like bands of steel as they came around her, locking her against him.

His arousal was pressed against her stomach, causing desire to pool between her legs. An urgency filled her, a hunger to have him inside her that instant.

But Kellan held her back.

She tore her mouth from his and gasped for air as she leaned back against the wall. When she opened her eyes, he had somehow taken off his boots without her knowing it.

Denae's hands shook when she grasped the waist of his jeans again. This time, he didn't stop her when she unbuttoned them. She pushed the opening wider and caught a glimpse of his rod. Somehow she wasn't surprised he didn't wear anything beneath his jeans. She found it sexy, a turn-on that had her pushing his jeans down.

Soon he was completely nude and she stood in her underwear and cami. He reached up and pulled out the band holding her braid. Using as much care as he had in undressing her, he loosened her hair until it hung about her shoulders.

With her heart pounding in her chest, his hand slid around her neck and dragged her to him for another fiery kiss.

No longer was he patient and calm in undressing her. Her cami was quickly removed, their kiss interrupted only when the shirt was pulled over her head.

The longer they kissed, the fiercer their passion became. He bent his legs and tightened his arms around her as he lifted her and walked them to the bed.

She expected to be tossed down. She should've known better. He gently lowered her onto the bed, never breaking their kiss.

Kellan couldn't remember ever being so consumed by a woman. He couldn't get enough of Denae's delightful lips, her sweet taste, and most assuredly her passionate responses.

She was all fire and softness in his arms. Her feminine curves pleasing, as was the toned muscle he could feel beneath her silky skin.

He rocked his hips against her, and moaned at the exquisite feel. His body demanded instant release, but he wanted to take his time with Denae and savor her. He wasn't sure why, nor did he want to look deeper into himself and find out.

Her short nails dug into his back as she opened her legs so he was cushioned against her core. Kellan could feel her heat and wetness through the thin panties.

Need, craving . . . hunger slammed into him. It rode him hard, urging him to rip off her panties and fill her again and again until she screamed in fulfillment.

He fisted a hand in the blanket and fought to rein in the insistent need. But it had been so very long since he'd felt a woman's sheath around him, felt her slick heat.

Kellan ended the kiss and rose up on his hands, his arms straightening until he loomed over her. She blinked up at him with half-closed eyes and kiss-swollen lips.

He looked down her body to see firm breasts, a perfect handful, and dark pink–tipped nipples. They were too much to resist.

Bending his arms, he flicked a tongue over one hard peak and heard Denae moan. He settled between her legs and latched onto one nipple with his lips while he teased the other with his fingers.

Her hips rubbed against him in time with his suckling, causing a sheen of sweat to break out over his skin as she fought giving in to his desires.

He moved from one breast to the other, teasing, fondling, and licking each nipple until small cries fell from Denae's lips.

Kellan kissed the valley between her breasts and moved down her stomach to her hips. He looked up and caught her gaze as he grasped her panties in each hand.

He knelt on the floor and slowly pulled the thin cotton over her flared hips until a thatch of dark curls could be seen. His brow rose as he noticed the curls had not only been trimmed but shaped into a narrow strip.

Such a thing hadn't existed the last time he had taken a female, and he found the sight . . . exciting and titillating. As he pulled her panties down her thighs he smelled her arousal and it caused his already aching cock to jump in expectation.

Kellan removed her panties and ran his hands back up her shapely legs, pushing them farther apart as he did. Then he gently tugged her to the edge of the bed so that her sex, which glistened with desire, was near his mouth.

He leaned close and licked her, causing a low moan to fill the room. That one taste wouldn't be nearly enough. He knew the taste of her kisses. He wanted to know the taste of her essence now.

Running his thumbs in a light caress at the juncture of her thighs, he found her clitoris and began to slowly roll his tongue around it.

Denae's hips bucked against him, her soft cries turning to shouts of pleasure as he licked and laved at her swollen clit. When she was writhing on the bed, her head thrashing from side to side, he slid a finger inside her.

She came apart with a scream.

CHAPTER
NINETEEN

Denae was sailing, floating, soaring on a cloud of incomparable bliss.

Radiant, luminous rapture took her.

Brilliant, gleaming euphoria seized her.

White-hot, incandescent ecstasy entranced her.

With her body still in the throes of her climax, she felt Kellan rise over her. She reached for him, needing to feel his weight atop her.

As soon as her hands met his skin, she opened her eyes. His face was breaths from hers, stark with raw, visceral need. She urged him to her and gasped when his cock grazed her swollen, sensitive flesh.

His jaw clenched when the thick head of his arousal found her entrance. Denae's back arched as he slowly slid inside her, filling her, stretching her. She bit her lip when he pulled out, only to plunge inside her once more—harder, deeper.

She was soon rocking against him, their bodies moving together in a dance as old as time. Sweat glistened over their skin as the rhythm increased.

Denae never let go of him. She was descending into a

chasm of desire she knew would change her forever. In the middle of the storm was Kellan.

He was all that held her steady, all that kept her anchored.

And she never wanted to relinquish her hold, as unsure and unsteady as it was.

The familiar ache settled low in her stomach, tightening, constricting as the passion built with each thrust of his hips, each plunge of his shaft.

Her legs wrapped around him. One of his hands slid beneath her buttocks and angled her hips higher. As soon as he did, he drove inside her, filling her deeper than before.

Denae cried out from the exquisite feel of him within her, as if she was finally complete, finally whole. Their gazes clashed, held as his hips pumped savagely, relentlessly.

And then he kissed her.

She wound her arms around his neck while his unyielding body filled her again and again, each stroke taking her closer and closer to another climax.

As if knowing she was close, Kellan ended the kiss and looked at her. Denae was unable to look away, even as her body stiffened and the orgasm began.

She shouted his name, her nails digging into his flesh as she was taken higher, swept further than before.

Kellan was enthralled as he watched the pleasure fill her eyes and face, felt her body clamping around his cock. There was no holding back his own climax, not after seeing—and feeling—her peak twice.

He couldn't look away from her whisky-colored eyes. He was trapped, caught within her beguiling gaze. And he quite liked it.

With his hips pumping rapidly, he gave in to the orgasm, joining Denae as his seed poured inside her. The attraction he'd tried to deny, the need he couldn't ignore was strengthened, deepened into a thick thread that bound them.

Their breaths were harsh, their bodies pulsing from their shared climax. With limbs still entwined, Kellan pulled out of her and rolled to the side. He was surprised to find he liked—and wanted—her beside him, against him.

Denae didn't know how long she lay on his chest drifting between that curious state of sleep and wakefulness when she felt his cock thicken against the leg she had thrown over him.

She grinned as she leaned up on her elbow to find his eyes open. Denae straddled him, rising up on her knees until her sex hovered over his arousal that jutted upward.

Approval flashed in his celadon eyes. Denae took hold of his large rod, loving the soft skin encased over hard steel. She ran her hands down his length several times while his gaze darkened and desire flared.

She held him and slowly lowered herself onto his shaft until she had taken all of his impressive length. Then she began to rock her hips.

A low, deep moan rumbled from his chest. Never before had she felt such decadence, such hedonism. She was needy, burning for him. All for Kellan.

His large hands massaged her breasts, tweaking her nipples until they were hard and swollen. She rotated her hips, her movements getting faster and faster the more their desire grew.

Suddenly, he sat up and wrapped an arm around her. She ran her hands over the thick sinew of his chest and shoulders, marveling in his gorgeous physique and the power she felt just beneath her palms.

He leaned her back over his arm, one hand on her hip to keep her moving. Then he clamped his lips over a nipple and drew it deep into his mouth.

Denae cried out, her desire causing her blood to heat through her like fire. Running his tongue back and forth over the tiny nub, he pushed her higher, daring her to follow him.

She was powerless to refuse. Her body was an instrument he knew how to play to perfection.

He moved to her other nipple and gently bit down on the turgid peak and then swirled his tongue around it. Another climax was coming, and no matter what Denae did, he refused to allow her to try and hold it off.

And then she no longer cared.

She screamed his name as another orgasm took her.

As soon as the tremors stopped, she found herself on her stomach with Kellan behind her. He lifted her hips and entered her in one smooth thrust.

Denae moaned, her fingers digging into the covers. His engorged cock pounded into her. With the blanket rubbing against her cheek, she moved back against him, wanting more—needing more.

Kellan ran his hands over her perfectly formed ass. Each time he took her, he thought it would be the last. But every time he filled her, he wanted more.

She looked completely delectable with her bum in the air rocking against him as he thrust. Her responsive body only fueled his already ravenous need.

That need, that devastating yearning to claim her besieged him. There was no holding back, no gentleness as he mercilessly pounded into her tight sheath. Her cries of pleasure only pushed him further until the climax hit.

He threw back his head and shouted as his fingers dug into her hips.

They fell sideways together and he tucked his body next to hers, surprised to find a small measure of satisfaction filling him, but he knew he wouldn't stay sated for long—not with someone like Denae in his arms.

Even as Kellan thought about rising and checking the

perimeter and perhaps taking to the skies as well, he was lulled into resting by the way Denae tucked his hand against her chest and he could feel her heart beating.

Denae woke to Kellan kissing her back, his tongue and lips teasing her skin, arousing her with his skilled mouth. She felt his erection pressing against her back.

There was no stopping the hot, wet rush of anticipation that filled her. He wanted more.

He wanted her.

Denae rubbed her hips against his swollen cock and moaned when one large hand cupped her breast to tease her nipples. She didn't recognize her body because it was no longer hers.

It was Kellan's.

She wanted his touch, needed to feel him inside her. Only then was she complete, only then did the world make sense.

Denae murmured his name when he lifted her leg and entered her. While his arousal thrust inside her, his hand skimmed down her belly until his fingers delved into her short curls. Then he thrummed his finger back and forth over her clitoris.

"Come," he whispered in her ear.

As if her body had been waiting for his command, she screamed as the climax barreled through her. His hips stopped moving, but not his fingers.

He dragged out the orgasm until she was begging him to stop.

Kellan didn't answer her. Instead, he pulled out of her and rolled her onto her back to take her lips in a savage, brutal kiss.

He had taken her to heights she hadn't known existed, and she wanted to pleasure him. Denae shifted her hand between them and grasped his cock.

It jumped at her touch, causing her to smile inwardly.

She pushed against his shoulder with her free hand until he rolled onto his back.

Denae followed and knelt between his legs as she pumped both hands up and down his impressive length. His moan, low and long, was all she needed to hear to spur her onward.

He sat up and kissed her before giving her head a slight push down. She had never liked taking a man in her mouth, but she couldn't wait to taste him.

Kellan closed his eyes and plunged his fingers into her silky mane at the first touch of her lips on his cock. She licked and kissed up his length until she came to the head, and then with a flick of her tongue to tease him first, she took him in her mouth.

His groan filled the room loudly.

She slid off the bed to kneel beside it, her hands and mouth learning him in expert fashion. Her amazing mouth sucked harder as he pushed her head down each time he thrust. And she took him deeper.

He was waiting for her to stiffen, to turn away, but she willingly pleasured him, even when he bumped the back of her throat.

Her mouth was too much. Already another orgasm was racing up, and he wanted to spill inside her and claim another part of her, to see his seed on her lips. But there was still so much he wanted to do to her this night.

Kellan tried to pull out of her mouth when he felt his climax rush up on him, but her lips were relentless as she sucked him harder.

He gave a shout when his seed burst from him in a force-ful climax that left him shaken to his core.

Denae continued to suck and lick him until he was dry. When she lifted her face to him, Kellan was struck with how he wanted her yet again.

He pulled her back onto the bed, except he kept his

distance this time. The fierceness that filled him for her was alarming. He had to put some space between them.

Except after he dozed for a bit, her hand touched his arm. In an instant, he was hard.

And it never entered his mind not to reach for her or give in to the desire.

As the hours passed through the night, again and again they came together. Sometimes he went to her, sometime she to him. But always they gave in to the overpowering, uncontrollable desire.

Which strengthened the growing connection between them.

CHAPTER
TWENTY

Rhys rode the air currents, basking in the joy of flying, but even that didn't stop him from keeping watch over Kellan and Denae.

He hadn't bothered to go into the lodge and check on them after they arrived. The attraction between them had been palpable, tangible . . . blatant.

The only problem would be if Kellan gave in. Rhys wasn't so sure his friend would as long as there was a buffer between him and Denae. Which is why Rhys remained in dragon form.

He circled the area twice, letting his keen eyesight rake the ground below for the tiniest movement. So far there was nothing but the usual nocturnal animals prowling.

There was a chance MI5 could track them. A tremor of unease ran through him.

The humans and Dark Ones had worked together. If they did it once, they could do it again. That in itself was cause for major concern. The Fae—Light or Dark—didn't align with humans.

Rhys wanted to roar his fury. The only way the Fae and humans would align was because there was someone else mediating. And he would bet a thousand years of flying that the someone was the same person he and Banan had nearly gotten to in London after Jane was kidnapped.

He glanced at the sky. Dawn was coming. Kellan and Denae had had long enough. It was time they got moving, because Rhys couldn't shake the thought that they had been found.

Kellan didn't know what woke him. He came awake instantly alert, with his eyes closed as he listened to the night around him.

There.

That was it.

Complete silence outside. No animals, no wind, just . . . silence.

His ears didn't pick up any sounds within the lodge, but that didn't mean the threat wasn't already inside. He opened his eyes and turned his head to Denae to find her looking at him.

"What is it?" she mouthed.

He motioned to the chair that held their clothes. "Hurry," he whispered.

She rolled off the bed with nary a sound and hastily got to her clothes. Kellan sat up and made his way to the window, careful to keep out of the fading moonlight. A glance outside showed nothing.

His gaze turned to Denae when he heard a soft brush. As soon as he did, she tossed his clothes to him. Kellan was hesitant to put them on.

If he needed to protect Denae, the best way was in dragon form. A King was more powerful in dragon form, and he could fly them away if necessary.

Kellan put on his jeans and looked to the sky for a glimpse of Rhys. The fact he couldn't see his friend in the cloudless sky was worrying.

Denae's head jerked around to the doorway. Kellan followed her gaze to see the low-lying smoke come pouring in. Except it wasn't smoke. It was the Dark Ones.

"Denae!" he shouted, but it was already too late.

Behind her four Dark appeared and grabbed her, her scream cut short as they disappeared. Kellan leaped over the bed to attack three more Dark who appeared, but no sooner had Kellan began to shift into dragon form than he was hit with dark magic.

And everything went black.

CHAPTER
TWENTY-ONE

Perth

As soon as his mobile phone rang he set aside the book he was reading and answered, "Yes?"

"It's done, sir. The two targets were taken by the Dark as you ordered."

He let out a long breath. "Ah, finally. Anyone else around?"

"Not that we see, sir."

He sat forward in his wingback chair. "You fools. They wouldna leave Kellan and the human alone!" He was so angry he didn't care that his fake cultured English accent dropped.

"We scouted the area. There is noth—"

The report was interrupted by the sound of a male scream. He gripped his mobile tightly, hearing it crack. There was no need to ask his lieutenant to finish the report. They were careless, and that carelessness would be their deaths.

"What is it?" He heard the muffled question of his lieutenant to someone else.

More screams sounded through the phone, growing closer and closer until there was nothing.

He remained on the phone, wondering if the Dragon King would pick it up. And just as he expected, the King did. Except he said nothing as he ended the call.

His book forgotten, he rose and hurried to dial another number that was answered immediately. "Get me a new phone number, and make sure it's sent out to all my generals."

"Aye, sir. Right now," came the female reply in her heavy French accent.

He walked out of the building to his car parked down the street. The home he'd purchased in Perth was one of his favorites, but it was dangerous to remain now. Besides, he had hundreds of others to choose from.

And with Kellan caught, one integral part of his plan had been achieved. The Kings' attention would be diverted to the Dark Fae, thereby leaving him to do as he wished.

With Perth in his rearview mirror, he smiled, anticipating the eventual toppling of the Dragon Kings.

There would be nothing to stop the Silvers from waking and annihilating every human on the planet—righting a wrong done long, long ago.

CHAPTER TWENTY-TWO

Rhys stood in the middle of the forest, blood coating his nude body as lifeless MI5 agents littered the ground. He didn't need to check the lodge.

Kellan and Denae were gone.

Rhys had seen the agents and quickly shifted into human form to take them out, but by the time he realized the Dark Ones were inside the lodge it was too late.

He needed to alert those at Dreagan, but he couldn't make himself move. Kellan was prisoner to the Darks. Rhys knew what that meant, knew they would likely never see Kellan again.

"All isn't lost," came the feminine voice behind him.

Rhys fisted his hands. "I'm no' in the mood for a visit, Rhi."

"You were watching from the skies. I was watching from here. I woke Kellan and Denae in time for them to get out of the house, but the Dark were too fast."

Rhys turned his head to find Rhi leaning against a tree, her arms wrapped about her while she looked vulnerable and a little ill. "Thank you for trying."

"No, don't thank me." She pushed away, a hard expression coming over her face, making her silver eyes almost glow with fury. "They should've gotten out. Why didn't they? I gave them enough time."

"Kellan," Rhys said. "He wouldna walk out on the chance there was someone waiting for him."

"He could've taken the humans!" She closed her eyes and took a deep breath. When her eyes opened, she was calmer, more focused. "I need to report to Usaeil. My queen will want to know this."

"You can no' tell her you were helping us. You know what they'll do to you," he warned.

She shrugged and let her gaze wander his naked form. "She already knows I helped the Kings, handsome. I haven't been reprimanded yet." She winked, her smile shaky, and then disappeared.

Rhys opened his mental link with the other Kings. *"Kellan and Denae have been taken by the Dark. I killed the group of MI5 agents here, but it wasna enough."*

"We're on the way," Con replied.

In dragon form, Con and the others could be there in half an hour. It was half an hour too long as far as Rhys was concerned.

"Rhi!" He yelled for the Fae. "Rhi! Rhhhiiiii!!"

"What?" she snapped when she appeared before him. "I was just about to go before my queen when your shouting deafened me."

He grinned, beyond happy that she had returned. "Ah, so you can still hear us if we call for you."

She stilled and glared at him with glittering silver eyes. "Don't push me, handsome."

"That link was supposed to be severed between us after the Fae Wars."

Rhi shrugged and crossed her arms over her chest. "If this was just a test, I need to go."

"Wait," he hastily said before she could disappear. "Take me to the Dark Ones."

"Are you insane?" she asked, her eyes wide. Then she

shook her head. "Never mind. I know you are. Don't be stupid, Rhys. I can't take you there. Bad things happen to you Dragon Kings when you step through a Fae doorway. It's why none of you do it."

"So you doona know where they are?"

"Of course I do. All Fae know where the Dark are."

"Which is?" he prompted.

She sighed and dropped her arms, her frustration palpable. "You know where."

"I know all Fae have an affinity for Ireland, but *where,* Rhi? I'm no' leaving Kellan or Denae to those monsters."

"You'll never get in," she said shakily. "They'll know you're there before you find Kellan."

Rhys took a menacing step toward her, letting her see the stark anger he had hidden until that point. "I've got magic of my own. Or have you forgotten?"

"How could I?" she asked tightly. Then she sighed, her shoulders slumping. "You might be able to fight the Dark, but you against an army of the Dark? You'd be chained next to Kellan in an instant."

"At least he wouldna be alone."

"He won't be. I'd already decided to go in after them."

Rhys blinked, completely taken aback. "Why? It's a Dragon King and a human."

"I owe a favor I never repaid."

His eyes widened as he realized what she was talking about, but before he could mention it, she was gone again. Once more leaving Rhys to stare at the empty lodge, a reminder of how he failed to protect his friend and the mortal.

CHAPTER
TWENTY-THREE

Denae's head felt heavy and foggy, as if she was reliving that New Year's Eve during her freshman year in college when she got roaring drunk. That one episode had been enough to ensure she never drank that heavily again.

What had happened?

She put her hands on either side of her head to try and stop the pounding. It wasn't until she rolled onto her back and her shirts began to get wet that she snapped open her eyes.

It was dark, only one small light reflecting off the wet bricks and stones, giving the entire place an eerie, sinister feel.

The place wasn't recognizable, and Denae began to grow fearful the longer she went without remembering. The last thing she could recall was Kellan pushing her against the wall and kissing her.

Kellan.

Just one thought of him, and their night together came back in Technicolor. Her body flushed, her breathing quickened as she remembered every touch, every kiss, every caress.

She pushed past their lovemaking to dredge up what

had happened next. Denae's hands fell from her head as it all came back to her—waking to the silence, hurrying to dress, and then the Dark.

Denae sat up and squinted through the darkness. There was a shape lying on the floor on the opposite side of the room from her. It was unmoving, a black splotch of something that she couldn't quite make out.

But she could hear breathing.

Blinking through the inkiness, she put her hands on the ground and felt the cool, wet stones beneath. She started crawling toward the shape when a howling rent the space around her.

Denae jerked to a stop and lifted her head to try and see. She couldn't even make out where the small shard of light bouncing off the wall was coming from, much less discern what that howling was.

The sound came again, fainter. It made her shiver. She loved scary movies, but after this little trek, she was going to have to reevaluate her choice of cinema if she ever wanted to sleep again.

Denae started crawling once more. She ignored the wetness seeping into her clothes and skin. The need to find Kellan was pressing and twofold—because she wanted to make sure he was all right, and because she didn't want to be alone against creatures she knew nothing about.

She crawled only a little farther before she realized the shape was a person. Denae moved faster, praying it was Kellan, or at least someone who could help her.

Where are you, Kellan?

Wasn't he supposed to protect her? Did he get taken with her? Or did the Dark Fae just grab her? Would Kellan come for her? Or was she just another human to him?

The questions beat at her like insistent waves pounding at her self-confidence. With each question, more strongly she felt as if she would never leave wherever she was.

Denae reached the person who was lying on their side

facing away from her. The darkness prevented her from making out any features of the form. She poked the arm, but nothing. That one touch had granted her one thing—it was a man.

Hope filled her. It also gave her the courage to peer over the arm at the face. Gently, she moved aside the long hair covering the man's face and saw enough by the dim light to know it was Kellan.

She rested her head on his shoulder and bit her lip to keep from crying. Denae hadn't comprehended just how scared she was until that moment; keeping it behind a mental wall so she could stay calm and cool under such pressure.

If she didn't have the training from MI5, she was sure she would be huddled in a corner crying.

That helpless, vulnerable, powerless feeling that assaulted her reminded her too much of when she'd tried in vain to reach her sister before Renee went beneath the waves, never to resurface.

She couldn't go through something like that again. A person could only take so much before they cracked. And she was nearing that precipice.

"Kellan," she whispered. She wanted to talk to him before anyone came, because she knew someone was going to come for them.

The Dark hadn't followed them across Scotland only to leave them alone.

"Kellan, please," she pleaded as she shook him.

Denae glanced around, wondering where the door was. She didn't know if she was aboveground, belowground, or what. All she knew was that she could barely see, she was cold and wet, and scared out of her wits.

Regardless of the training she'd received, nothing prepared her for being captured by the Dark Fae.

The sound of rusty hinges popping open filled the unnerving silence. She couldn't see anyone else, but Denae instinctively knew that someone was in the room with her.

She didn't have to guess who it was—a Dark. Her fingers tightened on Kellan's arm, silently begging him to wake and help her face whatever was coming.

Suddenly, Kellan's body jerked and he was instantly on his feet. Denae heard the sound of chains rattling and caught the glint of light off a link.

So they had chained Kellan. Why him and not her? As if she needed to ask that question. He was a Dragon King. She was nothing more than a feeble mortal.

She had to get his attention and let him know they weren't alone.

Kellan couldn't contain his ferocity, his wrath. The Dark had dared to come after him again. And they took Denae—someone under his protection, someone he . . . cared . . . for.

He felt something against his leg, and without looking, he instinctively knocked it away.

Out of the corner of his eye he saw a body go flying. Only after he heard the soft grunt that sounded like Denae did he look.

The darkness was no match for the eyes of a Dragon King, no matter what form he was in. Kellan's ire grew— this time at himself—when he recognized Denae.

She touched her jaw where he had knocked her away and looked at him. He wanted to tell her it would be all right, but he couldn't. Not when the Dark Ones were watching.

Kellan hadn't meant to hit her, but in the end, it may be to her benefit. If they didn't believe she had any meaning to him, they wouldn't use her against him.

That didn't mean she was safe from the vile ways of the Dark. The only way to free them both was for Kellan to shift into dragon form and fly them both to Dreagan.

It only took a thought for him to shift, but nothing happened. Kellan turned and heard the chain. He stilled, every fiber of his being refusing to believe what he knew was true.

Kellan tested his left arm again, but there was no denying the cut of the manacle into his wrist or the weight and sound of the chains. They were using their magic to prevent him from shifting.

No Dark Fae, no matter how powerful their magic, could kill a Dragon King. So what did they want him for? To use as a sexual toy? The female Dark Ones would soon learn he wouldn't fall for their unquenchable sexual appetites.

He wouldn't have before, but he certainly couldn't now after a night in Denae's arms. Kellan fought not to look at her. He knew he had hurt her when he hit her, and he hated himself for it.

The sound of water dripping from the old bricks and stones was incessant and irritating. He didn't need to ask where they were, he knew the Dark had brought them to Ireland.

It was just across the Irish Sea from Scotland, but it could be in another realm for all the good that did them. Every King knew the Fae had numerous doorways to their realm in Ireland, but none of the Kings had ever found one.

That wasn't true. There had been one King, one who had dared the wrath of both the Fae and his own brethren when he followed Rhi.

But there wasn't time to think on that now. Kellan needed to concentrate on keeping the Dark Ones focused on him and away from Denae. Because once they turned to her, there wasn't anything he could do as long as he was chained.

He noticed the small fissure of light coming from somewhere and bouncing against a wall weeping with water. There was a way out. The Fae always had a way out. Kellan just needed to figure out where that was, break free of the damn magical chains, and get Denae away before they got ahold of her.

All too clearly he remembered the Fae Wars when the Kings and Fae had waged war on Earth to see who would claim it. Hundreds of thousands of humans had been left as shells—alive but with no soul—by the time the Dark had been forced to leave.

The thought of Denae being one of those shells, the light gone from her whisky-colored eyes, her wit, her smile . . . her passion, sent him into a mindless rage.

With thousands of millennia of practice, Kellan reined in his fury and turned to where the Dark Fae stood watching. He glared at the three males.

All his intentions went out the door as soon as one of them focused on Denae. Kellan might be chained, but he still had magic. They didn't know that, of course. He could use it now or wait until he had an advantage. The smart move would be to wait, but then again, he didn't like the way one big male was staring at Denae.

"Kellan?"

It was Denae's voice—and the slight thread of fear he heard in it—that stopped him from doing something rash. He turned his head slightly to her, but never took his gaze off the males.

"Where are we?" she asked.

"Ireland."

She sighed forlornly. "Ireland? How did we get here?"

"They used magic."

"Of course they did."

He bit back a smile at her sarcasm. Denae would keep her wits about her and remain calm. She wasn't the fainting sort. And was he ever thankful for that.

"Why did they put us in here together?"

He asked himself that same question, and he didn't like

the answer. Neither would she when she learned she would be used by them to get him to answer whatever questions the Dark had, which is why he decided to keep it to himself for the time being. "They could have many reasons."

"I see." She shifted slightly. "Why are you chained?"

"They've used their magic to prevent me from shifting."

There was a long pause, and then she said, "What do I do?"

"Doona trust anything you see or hear from now on." Kellan knew the Dark Ones would find her greatest fear and use it against her in any way they could.

"So I shouldn't trust that I'm talking to you right now?"

"That's right. I'm just a figment of your imagination, created by the ugly fuckers who took us."

At his words, one of the Dark Fae bared his teeth and took a menacing step toward him. Kellan had gotten a reaction, just as he figured he would.

If it was just him that had been taken, Kellan would have eventually worked out their weaknesses and gotten free, but he didn't have forever, not as long as Denae was with him. He'd made a vow to her, and he didn't intend to break it.

"They are pretty ugly. And you say that men and women fall for the creatures?" Denae asked, conversing as if they were chatting over tea. "Those people must have low expectations."

Kellan barely choked back his laugh. He didn't imagine there was ever a human who had turned away a Fae— either Light or Dark.

She was trying to help him, but all her comment had done was turn all three males' focus on her.

At the rate she was going, Denae's soul wouldn't last the next few hours.

"Enough!" Kellan bellowed. "Show yourselves. Now."

At once, a bluish glow filled the chamber, allowing him

to see where the shadows fell, and allowing Denae time to see just where she was being kept.

"That will be the last order you ever give, Dragon King," one of the Dark Fae said as he held up a hand and magic rammed into Kellan's gut. "You're our toy now."

CHAPTER
TWENTY-FOUR

Denae watched with horror as Kellan doubled over from the vicious magic attack. His hair fell to cover his face, but not before she caught a glimpse of the feral fury that filled his features.

She shivered, because it was just a matter of time before Kellan got free. When he did — he was going to rip the Fae apart.

And she couldn't wait to see it.

Knowing she wasn't alone helped to calm some of her fears, but not nearly as much as she wanted. How she wished she had magic of her own to help Kellan, but she was simply a mortal. The only thing she had going for her was her training and her wits. It was going to take both to get her out alive.

With her jaw still aching from his hit, Denae remained silent, hoping the Fae would forget about her. Two of them were focused on Kellan. But the third, a tall male with long black hair streaked with silver, and white marks all over his bare chest that looked like tattoos, had his red gaze on her.

Denae divided her attention between Kellan and the

Dark Fae. Kellan straightened and lifted his chin, daring them to use magic again.

The three Dark were attractive, and she could understand why so many humans fell prey to them. They were tall, lithe with sculpted bodies, though they didn't compare to Kellan's muscular form.

The Dark Ones' hair was black just like Rhi's, but the difference were the streaks of silver that ran through it. One of the Fae, the one who had spoken to Kellan, had his hair cropped short, which only accentuated the silver in his hair and his red eyes.

The second Fae's hair hung to his chin with two thick silver streaks falling on either side of his face.

Denae didn't want to look at the third again. He was the same one who had been at the docks, the same one who had ogled her then, as he was now. His black hair hung down his back almost to his waist with the silver mingling among the black.

"You can no' kill me." Kellan's voice rang out in the room hard and commanding.

The lead Fae simply smiled. "It will make our fun last infinitely, Dragon."

"As long as you hold me. When I get free—"

"When?" he interrupted Kellan. He gave a snort and looked at his companions before his red gaze shifted back to Kellan. "That'll never happen. Or have you forgotten what happened to the two Kings we captured before?"

Undeterred, Kellan said, "*When* I get free, I'm going to take great pleasure in ripping each of you limb from limb."

"Not going to happen," the second Fae said with a sly smile. "We've got plans for you, Dragon."

Denae spotted the third Fae walking toward her. She hastily climbed to her feet and turned away. Every instinct told her to face the creature and never turn her back to it, but she wanted to ignore him, to show him his wiles wouldn't work on her. In order to do that, she had to look anywhere but him.

"You think you can ignore me?" he whispered in her ear, moving her hair so that his fingers skimmed her ear. "That's not possible."

"I'm doing it, aren't I?" she retorted.

There was a pregnant pause and then a soft chuckle. He molded himself to her back so she could feel his erection. "Our females use your males for sex, and we also like to take a mortal woman. But do you know why we lure pretty young things like you?"

"I don't care."

"Hope. Optimism. Aspirations. Those are the emotions I feel within you. We take those from mortals, because they are too good to resist. But do you know the emotion that is the most delicious?"

Denae held back a shudder, but she refused to cower. She might later, but not now, not when this had just begun.

"Love," he said. "It's like a beacon." He spun her around until she faced him, and then he gently ran the backs of his fingers down her cheek. "You are a lovely one, Denae Lacroix."

"Go away."

His shocked expression soon gave way to anger. "You dare tell me to go away? You are mortal. Your feeble mind and body will break under my onslaught."

Denae lifted her chin defiantly. "Never."

It was most likely a foolish move, but she was tired of being told she was inferior. Humans had been doing just fine, and she might not have magic or be immortal, but she refused to go down without a fight.

The Dark glanced at Kellan before he leaned into her and ran his tongue down the side of her ear. "I'll have you on your knees begging me to take you," he whispered in a dark, seductive tone.

That only made her angry. How dare he think he could make her do anything he wanted? It infuriated her to know that humans were nothing but playthings to the Fae. To the Dragon Kings, they were interlopers the Kings had to protect.

Damn them both.

She was going to save herself.

Denae stepped away from the Dark. She didn't bother to say anything, because it would only further irk him, but it was on the tip of her tongue to tell him to go fuck himself.

It was obviously the right move when the male smiled and grabbed her breast and gave it a squeeze. She felt nothing. Not an ounce of pleasure or need.

The male's lips peeled back in a snarl when she didn't respond to his touch. "What magic is this?"

"I have no magic," she stated with a voice as sweet and innocent as she could make it—all the while seething inside. "I'm a feeble mortal, remember?"

It was all Kellan could do to stand there and watch the Fae put his hands on Denae. He was more than shocked that she wasn't ripping off his clothes the first time he touched her.

The more he watched Denae, the more Kellan realized she really didn't desire the Dark Fae. How was that possible? There wasn't a human alive who had ever been able to reject a Fae—Light or Dark.

What made Denae special?

Whatever it was, it could end up costing her her life. The Fae wouldn't handle being refused well at all.

"Leave her for now, Emil," the first Fae said. "There will be plenty of time for you to play with her."

Kellan didn't know their game, but he was surprised the Fae were going to leave them. Something wasn't right. It settled like lead in his stomach, knotted and bulging.

Emil gave Denae one last look before he turned on his heel and walked back to the other two. Then all three simply vanished.

The only sound breaking the silence was the continuous dripping of water. Kellan wasn't sure they were really alone. It would be just like the Dark Ones to hang around and listen to his and Denae's conversation.

He couldn't chance it, no matter how much he wanted to go to Denae and see if she was all right. They couldn't talk of plans, couldn't speak of anything really.

Kellan yanked on his chain, despising anything that kept him from shifting into his true form. The rusted iron bit into his flesh, cutting him. Blood ran down his hands to his fingertips before dripping onto the floor.

"Don't."

He stilled and slowly turned his head to Denae. "What?"

"Don't hurt yourself just because you can't die."

"Does the sight of blood bother you?"

She rolled her eyes. "You know it doesn't."

Now that he was looking at her, he couldn't tear his gaze away. Her hair was mussed, her shirt hanging off her shoulder once more, and dirt smudged her check. And still he thought she was beautiful.

"Doona infuriate them," he cautioned her.

She lifted a dark brow. "So you want me to let him fondle me? I don't think so, bud."

"They'll get into your head."

"I'm sure they already have."

Kellan didn't like the note of uncertainty he detected in her voice. "What do you mean?"

"Nothing," she hedged. "What now? Are they still here? Are they still listening?"

"Probably."

"They're going to use me against you."

Kellan swallowed and stared into her whisky-colored eyes, hating the distance separating them, and the fact that sometimes she was too smart for her own good. He could still taste her on his tongue, still feel her skin beneath his palms, still hear her cries of pleasure ringing in his ears.

"They'll soon learn how little I mean to you."

He saw her forced smile and how it wobbled a bit. Just as he expected, she had figured things out. Her intelligence was surprising and welcomed.

"I mean, I'm human," she continued. "Everyone knows how the Dragon Kings hate humans. It's all well and good to use us for sex, because who else are you going to go to?"

"They may no' be able to kill me, but they can kill you."

"And I'm sure they will."

She said it with such calm certainty that a roar of refusal nearly made it past his lips. The thought of life leaving her body was repulsive to him. He didn't want her to die. Not now.

Not ever.

Kellan didn't know what was wrong with him. He hated humans. Or he had.

How could he feel different about Denae after a night in her arms? He had spent many nights with females, but not one had ever touched him so completely, so absolutely as Denae.

"Don't worry about me," she said and walked to stand beside him. There she inspected where the chain was bolted into the stone wall. "There are much more important things than one human life. Like what the Dark want with a Dragon King."

Kellan wanted to run his hands through her hair again.

He wanted to drag her against him and just hold her. He wanted to kiss her and promise her that he would get her out alive.

Instead, he only stared.

She turned her face to him and smiled. "In the war with the Fae, did you fight the Dark?"

"Aye."

"Did they take any of you?"

"Two."

"It didn't turn out good, did it?" she asked, a small frown marring her forehead.

He shrugged, thinking back so many eons ago. "Both Kings had to be killed. I did one, and Con the other."

"What did the Dark do to them?"

"I suspect I'll find out soon enough."

She cleared her throat. "Their magic prevents you from shifting. Did they use it during the war?"

"Of course."

"And how did you combat it?"

"There were too many of us Kings, and then there were the dragons."

She nodded, a thoughtful expression falling over her face. "Isn't it odd that they've waited until just now to capture one of you?"

"In a manner."

Her gaze sharpened on him. "You aren't surprised by their move. Which means this all goes back to the information MI5 got on Dreagan and my mission onto your land."

"It does."

"Someone wants to expose you. Someone who has aligned with the Dark, MI5, and God only knows who else to do it."

"That they have."

"And you aren't worried?" she asked in exasperation.

Kellan took a deep breath and said, "Nay."

"I'd call you a fool if I hadn't seen firsthand what you could do. How are you going to get free of here?"

It didn't go unnoticed by him that she didn't include herself in that statement. Kellan let it slide. For now.

"With pleasure."

CHAPTER
TWENTY-FIVE

Isle of Raasay

After a quick look in the lodge, Rhys walked back outside, his face to the sky. And in the fast-moving clouds he saw a sight he hadn't witnessed in thousands of millennia.

A group of dragons.

The Kings learned long ago how to deftly move within the clouds and stay hidden, but a dragon knew how to spot others.

Rhys caught a glimpse of gold scales. Constantine. The King of Kings was defying his own order and flying in daylight. If the situation wasn't so dire Rhys had every intention of ribbing him about it.

It was easy for a dragon to remain hidden in the clouds, but he would have to chance being seen when he landed. And there was no missing the large size of a Dragon King.

With no rain in sight, they were taking a huge risk in being seen—one that, to Rhys, was worth it after Kellan had been taken by the Dark Ones.

Con was the first to descend. He tucked his massive gold wings and dove like a missile to the ground. Right before he would have hit, he shifted, tucking his body into a tight ball and rolling until he stood, his face to the sky.

Rhys glanced over the view of the sea from the house and, thankfully, saw no boats on the water. By the time he turned back around, Guy and Kiril were already on the ground next to Con.

A blur of amber sped through the sky, and Rhys recognized their newest member of the Kings—Tristan. He had been born to them just a few years earlier, though they still weren't sure how. No new Dragon Kings had been made since the dragons were sent to another realm.

Tristan shifted into human form and landed with as much grace and control as Con. Then, as one, the four turned to Rhys and started walking to him.

Rhys lengthened his strides and tossed them the spare jeans kept in all houses owned by the Kings for such eventualities. "You all took a chance. A picture of any of you could be splashed on the front page of every newspaper in the morning."

"Tell me what happened," Con demanded and jerked on his jeans.

The fact Con didn't even give Rhys's statement a comment told him how upset Con was. Rhys gave a little shake of his head. "For hours there was nothing. I remained in the sky keeping watch."

"Obviously Kellan didna sense anything." Kiril pulled his pants over his hips and spotted the pile of dead MI5 agents.

Rhys glowered at Con. "Kellan did exactly what Con wanted him to do—he got close to Denae."

"By close, I suppose you mean they had sex," Tristan said as he finished putting on his jeans.

Guy had his jeans on, but didn't fasten them as he walked to the dead bodies. "Of course they had sex. The attraction was evident to everyone." He turned back to Rhys and stared at him with pale brown eyes. "Kellan was occupied, but that wouldna have stopped him from noticing if something was wrong."

"Because nothing was wrong," Rhys stated. "It wasna until dawn that I saw the first movement in the trees. I remained in the sky watching the house to see if they would dare to approach, but they kept their distance. I knew Kellan would be able to handle anything, so I attacked the humans. Only then did I see the magic from the windows."

"Fuck!" Con shouted and turned away.

They were all surprised at Con's show of emotion. He was the one who always kept his cool, the one who could order someone's death without hesitation.

Rhys let the soft breeze rush over his heated skin. He wished he was done explaining, but he had one more bit of news. "There's more. Rhi was here."

Constantine whirled around, his blond hair windblown and his black eyes hard as ice as he speared Rhys with a glare. "What?"

"I'm no' some lackey you can threaten in that soft tone of yours belying your fury," Rhys said as he took a threatening step toward Con.

Guy stepped between them, his hands out, looking first at Rhys and then Con. "He's right, Con. Rein it in, or Rhys willna be the only one beating the shit out of you."

Con pushed Guy's hand away, his nostrils flaring. "What did she want?"

"Rhi?" Tristan asked. "Is that the female Fae I keep hearing about who showed up at Dreagan?"

Kiril nodded. "Aye."

"Then she must be trying to help."

Con swiveled his head to the youngest King. "Help? That Fae has done nothing but tear Dragon Kings apart. She wouldna know the meaning of the word help."

"Then why did she wake Kellan and Denae before the Dark Ones arrived?" Rhys shouted.

Con laughed dryly. "You always believe everything she says."

"Fuck you too, Con," Rhys said.

Guy ignored Con and faced Rhys. "Where is Rhi now?"

Rhys turned away and raked a hand through his hair, frustration riding him hard. "I asked her to tell me where one of their doorways was so I could go after Kellan."

"You idiot," Kiril said, but there was no heat in his words. "I hope you didna plan to go alone."

Rhys rolled his eyes. "Sod off."

Guy cut his gaze to Kiril and looked back at Rhys. "And?"

"Rhi refused."

Con barked with laughter. "Of course she did. How silly of me to ever doubt her."

Rhys was finding it increasingly difficult not to land his fist on Con's jaw. "She said she would find Kellan and Denae and help them escape."

"She's putting her own life at risk," Kiril said softly.

Con folded his arms over his chest. "If you think that, then you doona remember the Fae."

"I remember them perfectly," Kiril stated harshly. "Perhaps it's you with the clouded vision."

Guy shoved his long hair out of his eyes and muttered curse words. "We're lucky Rhi was here and is still willing to help us. You know if we go into the Fae realm the war will begin all over again. The Fae—Light and Dark—will take it as a show of force. We doona want them aligning together again."

Rhys pulled the mobile from his back pocket. "One more thing. An agent was on the phone describing the scene to someone. We need to trace the number to see who it belongs to. It could be the arse who's trying to oust us."

"We wouldna get that lucky," Tristan said.

Kiril held out his hand for the mobile. "We might. Let me see it."

Rhys handed him the phone and Kiril walked to the house to the computers inside. Rhys looked back at Con. "We need to go to Ireland."

"Damn," Guy said.

"How long do we have?" Tristan asked.

Rhys exchanged a glance with Guy. "For Kellan there is no time limit, no' really. They'll torture him repeatedly, but they can no' kill him. He knows what happens to Kings at the hands of the Dark. He'll hold out as long as he can."

"It's Denae," Tristan said with a nod.

Rhys looked at the house, wondering what he might have done differently. "He gave Denae his promise to keep her alive."

"Promises are broken all the time."

Guy rubbed the back of his neck. "Kellan was still sleeping when you came to us, Tristan, so you doona know him. Kellan rarely gives anyone his word, and when he does, he willna break it."

"Then I suggest we get our arses to Ireland," Tristan stated bluntly, his dark brown eyes meeting Rhys's.

Rhys couldn't agree more. He would go with or without Con's agreement.

"If I go, the Fae will take it as a slight," Con said.

Rhys couldn't hold back the sarcasm as he said, "I doona know why. You're such a nice guy in war."

"You try being responsible for an entire race and let me see your decisions," Con said tightly as he took a step toward him.

Rhys didn't back down. He leaned forward, anger radiating. "I was responsible for my Yellows. But you convinced us to send them away."

"To keep them alive!"

"Aye! And look where we are now!"

They were nose to nose, the air crackling with tension. Rhys wouldn't back down. He hadn't always agreed with Con's decisions, but he had always backed him.

"Enough," Guy said evenly. "We need to band together, no' fraction apart. Kellan and Denae need us, and I for one willna let them down."

"I'm going to Ireland," Rhys stated before Con could utter a word.

"We need a plan," Con cautioned.

Rhys snorted and turned on his heel to walk to the lodge. "You come up with a plan then. I'm going to Ireland."

Guy waited until Rhys was in the lodge before he turned to Con. "I'm no' going to Ireland with him, but only because of Elena. But understand, Con, she's the only reason I'm no' going. For the moment."

"Do you think we should go en masse, then?" Con asked sardonically.

Guy swallowed and kept his irritation for what happened to Kellan from boiling over. "I think a few of us going has a better chance, but if that doesna work, then we go to the queen."

"Usaeil?" Con asked in disbelief. "Have you lost your mind?"

Guy's control snapped. He whirled on Con and pointed to the house. "One of us was taken. A human under his protection was taken. By the Dark. Do I need to say more?"

Con suddenly grinned. "Just make sure Kiril stays with Rhys and keeps control of Rhys's temper. Then get back to Elena quickly."

Guy blinked, taken aback.

"I'll be going with Rhys too," Tristan said.

Con sighed. "Aye, but no' yet. Let Rhys and Kiril go first and report back. I want everyone else filled in and ready if there is a battle."

Banan slammed on the brakes, causing Henry to huff out a breath as the seat belt cut into his sternum. "Bloody hell, Banan. That's the second time you've done that in a few hours," Henry said when the SUV came to a screeching halt.

Banan's knuckles were white as he gripped the steering wheel. Just as before, he stared off into space, his chest heaving and his jaw set.

Suddenly Banan turned to look at Henry. "Kellan and Denae were taken."

"By MI5?"

"Nay. The Dark. But MI5 was there."

Henry rubbed his eyes. "How were they found? And how the bloody hell do you know this?"

"Telepathic link."

He couldn't believe Banan had actually told him the truth. Henry long suspected that Banan wasn't completely human, and after the past day with him, he knew it for a fact now. "Will you tell me what you are?"

"Soon," Banan evaded. "MI5 are good, Henry, but no' that good."

"Could the Fae have found them and alerted the agents?"

Banan shook his head of short, dark hair. "Nay. The Fae can lose track of people just like anyone. They are no' all-knowing. The fact the Dark and MI5 are working together is cause for concern. I had hoped it was just a one-time thing, but it looks more and more like it wasna."

"When we do work with other agencies, it's just for one mission. There has to be a good reason for this."

"We need to find out."

Henry pulled out his mobile and dialed his boss before putting it on speaker. "I've already called in all my favors, but there might still be a chance."

The line rang six times before Stuart picked up and said, "You better have a damn good reason for calling me."

"When have I ever let you down?" Henry asked.

Stuart's sigh was loud. "Never."

"Have I asked for favors before yesterday?"

"Never."

"Am I fired?"

"Never," Stuart said. "You're too good for us to fire you. If we did, the CIA or someone else might recruit you."

Henry briefly closed his eyes and released a breath. "Stuart, I think someone is using MI5 to attack certain individuals."

"After your last phone call I did some digging. That entire section Lacroix worked under seems to be corrupt. We've got some housecleaning to do."

"I'm glad to hear it. Meanwhile, do you have the name of who is leading the section? And do you know who that section would be working with?"

"They aren't sanctioned to work with any other agency."

Henry could hear the shuffle of papers and then the sound of Stuart punching the keyboard. "We think the head of the section, Frank, is the one doing the corrupting."

"It goes beyond McCall. Be careful, Stuart. Whoever is pulling the strings has a long reach, and he's dangerous."

"And a fool he is to think he can run MI5."

Henry wished he was at the office. Stuart was a good man, but he was older and had been in the agency for a long time. He operated by a code few recognized anymore.

"Don't do anything alone. Have someone with you at all times, Stuart."

"I was running ops before you were a twinkle in your father's eye, son. Don't be telling me what to do."

Henry ran a hand down his face and glanced over when Banan's phone beeped. Banan then handed him his mobile. Henry quickly read the text. "One more thing, Stuart. I've got a number that needs to be traced."

"Give it to me."

Henry read off the number and listened as Stuart punched it in. A few minutes later Henry said, "It comes up blank. Are you sure it's the right number?"

"Yeah. Thanks, Stuart. Call me as soon as you know something."

Henry disconnected the call and shook his head as he handed the phone back to Banan. "Dead end on the number. What is it?"

"An MI5 agent dialed it and spoke with someone as Kellan and Denae were being attacked. Rhys heard the agent giving details to someone."

"Whoever it was got their number changed quickly enough. Whoever this bastard is, he's good."

"No' that good, no' against us."

Henry watched a car drive around them. "This goes back to when I helped you in London, doesn't it?"

"It does."

"If you want my help, I need to know all the facts. I can't keep trying to fill in the gaps."

"Fine. We're dragons."

Henry blew out a breath. "I need you to be honest, Banan. I want to help."

"I am being honest."

He looked at Banan to see his friend wasn't jesting. "A dragon?"

"Aye. I'll prove it later. Right now we need to get to Dreagan. Several are going to Ireland to try and find Kellan."

"How do they know Kellan and Denae are in Ireland?"

Banan eased back onto the road. "Because that's where the Fae are."

"Of course. Why didn't I think of that?" Henry sat back, wondering how he was ever going to look at the world the same again.

CHAPTER
TWENTY-SIX

Denae's stomach rumbled with hunger, but she wasn't going to ask for food. There was no telling what the Dark Ones would give her anyway.

"Drink the water," Kellan said.

She glanced at the water leaking down the wall and knew she needed to stay hydrated. Without water, she was dead. She cupped her hands and let the water fill up before she brought her hands to her lips.

Once she drank her fill, she wiped her mouth with the back of her arm and asked, "Are they still here?"

"Probably. Maybe. I doona know."

"You can't feel them or anything?"

Kellan shook his head and yanked on the chain, trying to pull it from the wall. "Nay."

She didn't know how much time had passed since the Fae had paid them a visit. It seemed endless, but at least they had left the lights on, or whatever it was that kept the room aglow.

Denae walked to the opposite side of the room from Kellan and sat against the wall. "We're never getting out of here, are we?"

When Kellan didn't answer, she looked at him to see him still pulling on the chain.

"A non-answer is as much of an answer as a verbal one."

"I willna lie to you," he said and gave another hard yank.

She leaned her head back. "Silence is the best you got? I'd rather have honesty."

"Stop thinking about it. Concentrate on staying alive."

"Why?" she asked. "What do I have to go home to? I have no job now, not after MI5 turned on me. I don't have any family. I don't even have a home to go to."

Melancholy suddenly overwhelmed her, sinking her into a pool of despair that was as thick and cloying as tar. Her life was going nowhere. She had achieved all she was ever going to, which wasn't much of anything.

She was alone. Her chest tightened with the swell of desolation. There were no friends who would mourn her. No coworkers, especially since they'd betrayed her. The only lover she had taken in years couldn't stand that she was human.

"I have nothing. I am nothing."

The misery was deep, the hopelessness profound.

The anguish bottomless.

She should just give up. What had she been thinking in rejecting the Dark Fae? He could give her a little pleasure, maybe even some happiness.

When she saw him again, she was going to throw herself at him and beg his forgiveness.

"Denae."

She turned her head away from Kellan. "Leave me alone. What do you care anyway? I'm just a human."

"Denae, they're in your head."

"What do you care? Give me one good reason."

"Just listen to m—"

She sighed over his words. "Just as I thought. You can't give me a reason, because you don't have one. You couldn't care less if I die in here, and I will die in here. You know it. You just don't have the balls to tell me."

"Denae, doona let them control you."

"*He's right,*" someone whispered in her ear. "*The Dark Ones are messing with your head. And you're seriously demented if you think the Dark are sexier than your Dragon King. Have you so quickly forgotten your explosive night together?*"

Denae lifted her head and frowned. She couldn't see anyone, but she recognized that voice. *Rhi.*

Was Rhi really there? Or was she hearing things as well?

"*Look at Kellan. He tries not to watch you, but he is. He can't let the Dark know how much he's worried for your safety. They* will *use you against him, Denae. Prepare for that, because it won't be pretty. It'll be harsh and might seriously mess you up mentally, but Kellan won't leave you.*"

Denae looked at Kellan to find him watching her with a bland expression. Or at least it appeared bland, but she saw the way his eyes never left her face, how his gaze pierced her as if trying to tell her something without words.

How could he want her though? She was human. She meant nothing.

Denae shook her head to try and clear it, but the depression wouldn't loosen its hold.

"You're strong," Kellan said. "You can push them out."

Could she? Did she dare? Denae squeezed her eyes closed and thought of Kellan, but every time an image of them together tried to appear, it was pushed aside.

"I can't."

"You can."

His insistence snapped her eyes open, and she saw his unchained hand by his side, one finger held out to her. He was stretched as far as his chain would allow, just ten feet separating them. But it felt like miles.

"You fought off Matt. Remember?"

Matt? Then she recalled her fight with Matt in Kellan's cave. Denae no longer wanted to be alone. She wanted comforting arms around her, and she knew exactly whose arms she wanted—Kellan's.

She tried to get to her feet, but it was like something was pushing down on her. It would be so easy to lay there and not fight, so easy to just . . . give up.

"Denae."

Kellan wouldn't stop saying her name until she moved again. She managed to get to her hands and knees and began to crawl toward him, but all too soon her hands felt as if they were caked in concrete. She collapsed.

It was just too much. She couldn't be strong anymore. She was never the strong one. That was Renee. How many times had her mother said those exact words?

"Fight, damn it."

The words were clipped, angry. Whispered. Denae lifted her head to see Kellan staring at her, as if willing her to move with his eyes.

A spark of something had her use her arms to pull herself to him, inch by agonizing inch. Until she could go no more. She collapsed, ready to do anything it took to make it all stop.

Strong fingers wrapped around her wrist and tugged her over the floor until she was nestled against a warm chest with thick arms wrapped around her.

"Fight, Denae," he whispered in her ear. "I can no' do it for you. Only you can take control of your mind."

Take control? Did he mean someone was in her mind? Surely not? This depression was something she'd battled when her sister died, and again when her mother faded away and then her father had a heart attack and left her. All within a four-year span.

"Who are you thinking about?"

"Renee," she answered automatically. "She was so beautiful."

Something caressed down her face. "The nightmares can no' touch you here."

The nightmares. Yes, she knew them all too well. "We were inseparable."

His arms tightened around her. "You're strong. Say it."

"No." She shook her head. She wasn't going to say anything that wasn't true.

"Say it," Kellan insisted and flicked his tongue over her ear.

Heat instantly spread through her body. Images of their night flashed in her head, pushing past the fog that had seeped into every crevice of her mind.

"Say it, Denae. Tell me you're strong."

"I'm strong." She had to force the words, they were so difficult to say, but once said, they pushed the last of the fog away.

And whatever had taken her mind was no longer there.

"Denae?"

"What just happened?" she asked as she began to shake from the coolness of the room and her wet clothes.

Kellan rubbed his hands up and down her arms. "They got into your mind. They'll do it again too."

"That was awful. Everything I felt was what I went through when Renee died."

"Which is what makes it so real."

Denae closed her eyes, thankful to be in his arms. If it hadn't been for Kellan, the Fae would have taken her. That thought iced the blood in her veins.

"Can you fight it now?" he asked in a low voice.

She shrugged. "I don't know."

"I may no' always be around. You need to keep them out at all times, but it willna be easy."

"The one who came to me earlier, Emil. He said they feed off of hope and other such emotions."

Kellan's chin rested on her shoulder. "They do. So doona think of happy thoughts to pull you out of their grip. No' only will they take full control of your mind, but they'll suck your spirit right out of you."

"If you're trying to scare me, you're doing a bang-up job."

His fingers lightly caressed her arm. "If you were no' afraid, I'd be worried."

She opened her eyes and blinked back tears as she comprehended what it meant that she was in his arms. "You've shown them they can use me against you."

"They can try."

His words were chilling.

CHAPTER
TWENTY-SEVEN

Kellan let Denae drift off to sleep without moving her. All too soon hell would descend upon them.

The light that eased her fears and allowed her to see into the darkest corners would disappear.

The illusion of safety she felt while in his arms would be shattered.

The compassion, the gentleness he'd dared to show her now would cease.

The Dark Ones would torment her endlessly while he watched.

No matter what the Fae wanted, he wouldn't give it to them, not as long as it involved information on Dreagan or anyone there.

Kellan woke from his thirteen hundred years of sleep with hatred for humans still churning within him. But one courageous, beautiful woman had beguiled him, captivated him.

Utterly charmed him.

While changing his mind about her, and perhaps about a few other mortals in the process.

He didn't regret their night together. Quite the opposite.

He wished he had more time with her, but even if both of them got out alive, she would be forever changed.

The purity she had somehow kept despite working as a spy would be gone, wiped away as if it had never existed.

The protection he'd promised her was worthless while they were in the hands of the Dark. Especially with him chained. He was powerful, immortal, and lethal, and yet he was helpless to do anything but hold the woman he couldn't get enough of.

Kellan lifted a lock of her coppery hair in his hand and ran his fingers along the cool, silky strands. He let her believe the Dark Ones could be watching at all times, because he never wanted her to let her guard down.

Which is exactly what she was doing by sleeping in his arms. She expected him to watch over her. And she wasn't wrong. She needed the rest, but it was the last time he would allow her to have it.

For both their sakes, he couldn't be found holding her.

Kellan had no idea if—or when—his brethren would find him. He wasn't counting on them. He would break free. Somehow. Doing it before they took Denae's soul would be the tricky part.

Getting away before they could get to him as they had the two other Kings also weighed heavily on his mind. Kings by nature were the strongest of the strong, the deadliest of the deadly.

To know that two of his brethren had been broken was more than troubling. It was distressing. He looked down at Denae and knew that when the Dark came, they wouldn't hold back any punches to either of them.

There was no way Kellan was going to be able to watch as the Dark touched her, and yet he would have to. It was the only chance she had—and it was a slim one at that.

He liked holding her, liked that she trusted him enough to sleep in such a place. Even if he hadn't given her the promise to keep her alive, he wouldn't leave her.

There was something altogether different about Denae that he'd never encountered in a mortal before. Kellan couldn't pinpoint exactly what it was, but it held him attuned to her in ways that kept him spinning, disoriented.

And reaching for her.

Already he'd held her too long. Thinking of pushing her away was becoming more and more difficult, until his body was demanding he claim her again—for all to see. To let the Dark know that they might try to take her, but she would be forever his, just as he would forever be imprinted upon her.

The impulse to brand her as his so no one would dare to touch her, much less look at her, was so strong that his hand was beneath her shirt before he realized it.

Kellan paused and clenched his teeth. If the Fae knew how much he wanted her, they would stop at nothing to destroy her.

And that could very well break him as nothing ever had.

Not seeing his Bronzes dead.

Not watching the dragons leave the realm.

Kellan closed his eyes and savored the feel of her in his arms. It was the last he would give himself and her, because he had to be cold and calculating to save her. He had to dredge up the loathing that had been his constant companion for centuries, even though he felt nothing close to hate for the beautiful, amazing woman beside him.

He pulled his hand away and allowed himself a quick brush of his lips over hers. Then he gave her a little shake. "Denae. Time to wake up."

Denae was instantly awake, though she remained still, her gaze on Kellan as she swore he had just kissed her. But there was no passion shining in his celadon gaze. Only the same coldness she had seen when she first met him.

"Are they back?" she whispered.

"No' yet. You need to get on the other side of the room.

They doona have to be in front of you to get inside your head, so be ready."

She sat up, grateful for the rest she had been given, but already missing his warmth and his arms. "Anything else I should be prepared for?"

"They can use illusions."

"Great," she mumbled as she climbed to her feet and walked to her side of the room. "Talk about an unfair advantage over someone who has no magic. Tell me again why everyone falls at their feet? They're freaking monsters, is what they are."

As she expected, there was no response from Kellan. Denae remained standing, stretching out her arms and back. She might not be in a physical fight with the Dark Fae, but it was going to take more than just her mind to keep her one step ahead of the assholes.

Plus she couldn't sit still and not look at Kellan.

"Few call them monsters. Only the Kings dare that," Kellan said. "And a few Light."

Denae rolled her eyes. "Speaking of the Light, where are they? Shouldn't they be here rescuing us?"

There was a loud snort from Kellan. "As if the Light would demean themselves to help a mortal."

"Or a Dragon King," she surmised. "I'm right, aren't I?"

"Aye."

"No one knows where we are." The full comprehension of their predicament settled on her like a ton of bricks. The betrayal made her feel like she had been run over by a semi. This was a whole new level of hell she could do without. "It might have been better if MI5 had me instead of these brutes."

"Brutes?" came a voice into the room as the sound of a latch being lifted shattered the quiet.

The door swung open and in walked two Dark Fae. Denae immediately recognized Emil. The bastard was once more eyeing her like a starving man being offered a four-course meal.

"I think brute is a bit harsh," replied the other Dark One.

Denae shifted her gaze to the one speaking. His hair was more liberally streaked with silver so that barely any black could be seen, and it hung midway down his back. The strands were pulled away from his face to fall in a braid down his back, giving her an ample view of the vicious scar that ran vertically from his forehead over his left eyebrow to the top of his cheek.

Somehow, whatever had cut him had grazed his eyelid as well. But it was the scar itself, something none of the other Dark Fae sported, that held her attention.

"Ah," the Dark One said with a small grin as he fingered the scar. "You're wondering how I came to have this."

"Not really. I'm just wondering why it's visible. None of the others have such a scar."

His smile tightened, his red eyes narrowing slightly. "True, but then I was fighting a Dragon King."

"Tell her all of it, Taraeth," Kellan demanded.

Taraeth cut a glance to Kellan. "You see none of the others with such a scar, little human, because the others who dared to take on the Kings were killed."

"You ran," Denae surmised easily enough.

He chuckled and walked around her. "I'm leader here. None of the others dare say that."

Denae found it difficult to remain still. If she thought Emil was exasperating with his obvious seduction, he was no match for Taraeth.

Waves of lust rolled off him. She felt them, and yet, oddly enough, her body didn't respond as she had been led to believe. She felt . . . nothing for either of the Dark.

The Dark leader halted when he faced her once more. "Tell me, little human. What are you doing with a Dragon King?"

"I trespassed on his property, and they took me prisoner."

Taraeth barked in laughter. "Oh, how wonderful. Did you trade the use of your body with this one," he pointed to Kellan, "in exchange for your freedom?"

"No. I was attracted to him."

Taraeth's red eyes raked her from head to foot and back again with blatant sexuality. "Wait until you have me between those long legs. You'll forget all about your dragon."

Denae couldn't hold back her grin. "Does this normally work on us?"

Taraeth's eyes narrowed into dangerous slits, his smile disappearing as anger took hold. He jerked his head to Emil who merely shrugged.

"I told you, sire."

Taraeth turned back to her. He loomed over her, his body brushing hers. The way he stared at her seemed as if he were trying to push his will onto her.

More of the sexual waves—as she began to think of them—came at her. She felt them, knew what it was, but there wasn't an ounce of stirring.

Denae moved her head to the side and sighed loudly. "Do you know the definition of personal space? Because you've invaded mine."

"You should be stripping your clothes off by now," Taraeth said in dismay as he leaned back.

Denae shrugged. "Nope. Not feeling it."

"I will have you," he vowed in a low voice. "I'll take you as many times as I want, all while Kellan watches."

"Are you so hard up for sex that you would force me when other humans fall at your feet?" Denae rolled her eyes. "I don't see the point. As for Kellan? We had one quick roll in the hay. A one-night stand, if you will. Y'all are making more of our involvement than it is."

Taraeth stepped back and looked at Kellan. Denae glanced at him to see Kellan casually sitting against the wall just as she had left him moments ago, both forearms resting on his bent knees. And he wasn't even looking at her.

"You really think you hold no meaning to him?" Tara-eth asked.

Denae swallowed, more hurt than she liked that he hadn't even cared enough to be watching her. She'd expected to meet his celadon gaze and gain courage. "I know I don't. He loathes humans. I woke him after centuries of sleep, and he was horny."

Emil started toward her. "You'll fall into bed with a dragon, but not us?"

Taraeth didn't utter a word, just held out his hand for Emil to stop, which the Dark did instantly. Taraeth turned his head first one way and then the other as he regarded her solemnly.

"You intrigue me, little human. I'm not convinced you hold no emotion for the dragon, but I'll keep you for my pleasure."

"No."

The word sprang from Denae, and once released, it bounced off the walls like a shot.

One of Taraeth's black brows lifted. "No?"

"No. I don't want you. I don't want any of you. Find another human who does."

Taraeth's smile was cunning as he said, "That's just it, little human. You pose a challenge. One I'm most eager to overcome."

Denae wanted to scream her aggravation. She had thought to use her nonchalance to their seduction as a means of getting free. Instead, she'd sealed her own doom.

With a smile still on his face, he turned to Kellan and sent three volleys of magic, pummeling him in the head until Kellan was knocked flat.

Denae remained still, fighting the urge to run to Kellan and help. Then she remembered he was immortal, a

Dragon King as old as time itself. He wasn't the one she needed to be worried about. It was herself.

Still, it was difficult to watch him being tortured. But it was just the beginning for the both of them.

Kellan sat up, his light green eyes glaring daggers of hate at Taraeth. Kellan climbed to his feet and jerked on the chain that held him.

"I see you're still afraid to fight a Dragon King. How do the others follow such a coward?" Kellan asked coolly, his voice belying the rage shooting from his eyes.

Taraeth slowly walked to him. "Because I hold the most power. Isn't that why Constantine is King of Kings, ruling all of you, while your precious dragons are gone?"

"Con doesna rule me."

"Where were the dragons sent?" Taraeth demanded.

"Somewhere you'll never find them."

In response, Taraeth's hands erupted in fire and he placed them on Kellan's shoulders. Denae bit the inside of her mouth while Kellan growled through clenched teeth as his skin burned.

The smell was awful, and she knew Kellan had to be in pain. But he never showed it.

Finally, Taraeth extinguished the flames on his hands, but let Kellan's skin smolder. Without a pause, a long curving blade was suddenly in Taraeth's hand. He plunged it into Kellan's gut and twisted it.

Kellan bent over, blood gushing from the wound and dripping from the corner of his mouth.

"The first King of Kings hid something because he feared it. You're Keeper of the History. You know what it is I seek. Tell me where it's hidden," Taraeth demanded.

Kellan lifted his head and smiled. "Fuck you."

Taraeth plunged a second sword he plucked out of thin air into Kellan. Again and again Taraeth stabbed Kellan with blades until Denae only saw blood and Kellan was on his knees, still defiant.

The questions continued, each time Taraeth asking where the secret item was hidden, and each time Kellan's response only infuriated Taraeth.

But if Denae thought she was only going to watch the torture, she was wrong. Emil came up behind her and grasped her arms in a tight, biting hold.

"Taraeth won't be the only one you feel inside you."

CHAPTER
TWENTY-EIGHT

Rhys kept a lookout while Kiril easily broke the doorknob off the back door of a shop in the heart of Cork. They slipped soundlessly inside and headed straight for the clothes. They couldn't just take anything.

They were going to have to infiltrate the Dark Fae in Cork, which meant dressing to impress.

"We'll find Kellan and Denae," Kiril whispered as he buttoned a pair of ripped designer jeans.

Rhys didn't bother answering. He pulled a pale blue shirt off the mannequin and quickly put it on. Next, he chose a pair of dark denim.

He glanced out the store window and shook his head. "This place is infested with Dark."

"I know," Kiril said as he looked over his shoulder from inspecting a rack of shirts. "It makes me ill. If something isna done, this is what could become of this realm."

Rhys couldn't stop thinking about why the Dark would want a Dragon King. It had to involve the dragons. That was the only explanation.

He was still mulling over that fact when he found the shoes and chose a pair of leather boots in his size. After he put them on, he straightened to find Kiril waiting for him.

Rhys looked over Kiril's burgundy shirt with a design of an eagle with its wings spread wide on the back in black velvet.

Kiril smiled. "I was trying to find one with a dragon."

"You could always just wear a sign."

"I already thought of that," he teased. The smile dropped. "Ready?"

Rhys cracked his knuckles. "Oh, aye. Let's find us some Dark Fae scum."

Rhi stayed as long as she could with Denae and Kellan. Only a handful of Fae could remain invisible for an extended period of time, and when they did, they became incredibly weak.

If they appeared in the midst of an enemy, they could be cut down like a piece of grass.

Rhi didn't want to go to Dreagan in the state she was in, but she had no other choice. They needed to know what was going on. Anytime she faced the Kings, she liked to be at her best. Right now, she was at her absolute worst.

Then she thought of Phelan and searched him out. The fact that the Warrior, an immortal Highlander who had a primeval god inside him, was half Fae helped her pinpoint him easily enough.

It wasn't until right before she materialized that she took notice of the surroundings and found herself at . . . Dreagan.

She was too weak to remain incorporeal any longer. Though, she did manage to make sure she was alone in the kitchen when she dropped the veil.

Her legs began to buckle as soon as she materialized. Rhi reached for the chair to hold herself up, but she only accomplished in knocking it over as she fell to the floor in a tangled heap.

Rhi lay on the cool tiles and closed her eyes. She had never used so much of her magic at one time before, and she was paying the price for it now.

"You must be the Fae everyone is talking about."

Rhi stiffened at the deep voice and turned her head to find deep brown eyes looking at her. His long, golden-streaked brown hair was pulled back in a queue and he wore jeans and a tight-fitting black shirt.

"And you're Tristan." She tried to smile, but wasn't sure she succeeded.

He squatted beside her, his head cocked to the side as he looked anxiously at her. "You look a bit green. Should I be worried?"

"I just need a minute." She really needed about ten years to sleep, but that wasn't going to happen.

The sound of footsteps approaching couldn't even get her up. She remained on her side, her cheek pressed into the tile.

"Rhi?"

She cringed at the sound of worry in Aisley's voice. Did she look that bad? Before she could answer, Phelan's wife was beside her.

"Rhi? What's wrong?" Aisley asked as she smoothed aside Rhi's hair from her face. "Phelan!"

Instantly, the sound of heavy footsteps approached. They stopped, pausing at the doorway, and Rhi knew Phelan was looking at Tristan.

Well, it was bound to happen soon enough. Con could only interfere with the Warriors and Tristan for so long. If only she felt good enough to rub it in Con's face, but even that was too much effort.

Rhi opened her eyes and turned her head once more to Tristan who still stared at her. She'd known this time would come, and part of her hadn't wanted to be near when it did. Still, it was past time. "Do you know Phelan, Tristan?"

Tristan glanced at Phelan, but shook his head as he turned back to her. "Nay. Do you need something to drink? To eat? You're pale as death."

"You might want to get that drink for yourself," she said and tried to sit up. "You're going to need it more than me."

Aisley hissed Phelan's name, and the next moment he was helping Rhi into a chair. Once she was at the table, Rhi dropped her head into her hands and wished she was returning with better news.

The quiet of the kitchen was broken by the sound of Aisley pulling out the chair next to Rhi and sitting. Phelan picked up the one she had toppled over and sank into it on Rhi's other side, his apprehension and annoyance palpable.

"Rhi?" Phelan urged in a tight tone.

She raised her head, and though he had spoken to her, Phelan's blue-gray eyes were focused on Tristan who walked back into the kitchen with glasses and a decanter. Rhi covered Phelan's hand and gave it a squeeze until he looked at her. "He doesn't know you. He remembers nothing."

"Nothing?" Phelan asked with a deep frown furrowing his forehead. "Does Ian know?"

"No. You're the first Warrior to see him."

Tristan set a glass of whisky in front of her, but held onto the decanter. "And *he* is in the room with you."

"Aye," Phelan said and cleared his throat. "When did you arrive at Dreagan?"

"About two years ago."

Phelan glanced at Aisley. "Are you a . . . Dragon King?"

"Aye," Tristan said with a lopsided smile. "The newest."

"Your color?"

"Amber."

Rhi watched Phelan squeeze the bridge of his nose with his thumb and forefinger. "The amber dragon. I've seen you fight in the battle with the selmyr."

"Aye, and I've seen you. What of it?" Tristan asked.

"Because you're tw-"

"That will come later," Con said over Phelan.

Rhi stiffened as she felt Con's black gaze. She grabbed

the whisky and drained it, hoping it would fortify her for the inevitable battle of words. The bastard had always known how to make her hackles rise.

"Did you find them?" Con inquired.

She nodded. "They're in Ireland, in an abandoned manor near Cork."

"Who?" Phelan asked.

Con sighed and leaned his hands on the back of one of the chairs. "Kellan and an American named Denae Lacroix."

Phelan's brows lifted. "Kellan? The Kellan I've heard so much about? When did he wake?"

"Denae woke him," Rhi explained. "She worked for MI5, and they sent her on a mission into his cave. To make a long story short, MI5 betrayed her, she killed her partner in a fight, and Con took her as prisoner to find out what MI5 knew."

Con scraped back the chair on the tile and sat, a dark look directed at her. Rhi rolled her eyes and noticed one of her nails was chipped. Damn. Time for a new manicure and color then.

"Before we could get Denae out of the country with a new name and wipe her memories of us, we were attacked," Con finished.

Phelan looked from Rhi to Con. "By who?"

"MI5." Rhi swallowed and lifted her gaze to Phelan. "And Dark Fae."

Phelan sat back in the chair and scrubbed his hands down his face. "Shite."

"Did they take Kellan and Denae then?" Aisley asked, a frown marring her forehead.

Con shook his head. "We bested them at the dock, but somehow they followed Kellan to Raasay and snatched them there."

"Hal and Laith have been filling me in on the Fae,"

Tristan said. "I still say we should go after them and get Kellan and Denae."

Rhi took the bottle of whisky from Tristan's hand and refilled her glass, trying not to notice how her hand shook. "It will violate the treaty if you do."

"They took one of us," Tristan argued.

Con waved the bottle to himself, and Rhi gave it a shove across the table. He rose and found more glasses that he set on the table and then filled, handing each person one.

"It was the Dark Ones who took them," Con said after he took a drink of his scotch. "The Light rarely pay them any heed."

"Not true," Rhi said angrily. "We've been fighting them forever, and we will go on fighting them for eternity. It is our way. Just as they'll never defeat us, we will never defeat them."

"And if you ever decide to join forces?" Aisley asked.

Rhi looked at Phelan's pretty wife and shrugged. "It was tried once before. The war with the Kings. That didn't go so well."

"Forget about the past," Con stated. "What are you doing here? I thought you were going to help free Denae and Kellan?"

She didn't want to fight, especially not now when she was so weary. She was too tired to trade barbs with Constantine, but she couldn't show him any weakness. He would pounce on it, and never let her forget.

"Does your hatred make you blind?" Phelan asked Con. "Can you no' see she's exhausted?"

Rhi sat up straighter and forced a bright smile. "I'm fine. I came to report what I've found."

"You told us where they are. Get back there and keep watch," Con ordered.

It was too much. She'd offered to help because of her love of a Dragon King, but she wasn't Con's lackey to be ordered around. Rhi tried to stand, but her legs still refused to hold her. Instead, she threw her glass at him.

He leaned to the side at the last second, and it fell to the floor behind him, the crystal shattering. She couldn't stop the wrath that filled her—nor did she want to.

"Rhi," Con said in a soft, quiet voice. "Calm down."

"Calm down?" she repeated in dismay. "I didn't have to warn you of approaching danger. I didn't have to stick around and warn Kellan and Denae the Dark Ones were coming. I didn't have to follow them into that nasty dwelling. I didn't have to return here and tell you anything. And each time what do you do? You demand more and order me about!"

Phelan took one of her hands. "Rhi."

"What?" she yelled and looked at him.

He glanced at the hand he held. "You're glowing."

Rhi looked down to see that indeed her skin radiated the bright white light held inside certain Light Fae—a light that could be used to make life . . . or take it away.

She closed her eyes and concentrated on pushing aside her rage. When Rhi was once more calm, she opened her eyes to find everyone watching her.

"What was that?" Phelan asked.

Con leaned across the table and poured more whisky into a new glass before giving it to Rhi. "It's something only a few Fae have. Simply put, Rhi could have leveled this manor and everyone inside."

"Or brought life to a dying realm," she added with a dark look to Con. Then she looked at Phelan, Aisley, and Tristan. "I let my anger get the better of me. For that, I apologize."

"No need," Aisley said with a reassuring smile on her face and in her fawn-colored eyes. "Were you about to talk about Denae and Kellan?"

Rhi sat back in the chair and pushed her long hair over her shoulder. She wanted a shower and new clothes after spending so much time with the Dark Ones. "The Dark are keeping them together. They know they can't kill Kellan, so their plan is to torture Denae until he talks."

"He willna do it," Con said sternly, his eyes full of anger and regret. "He willna betray us, no matter what vow he gave Denae. And that . . . that will destroy him."

Rhi nodded in agreement. "Yes. It will."

"How did you get past all the Dark Fae?" Tristan asked.

She picked at her chipped nail. "I had to stay veiled."

Con frowned. "Are you telling me you flitted in and out of that place hoping they wouldna see you?"

This she didn't want to tell him. This was her secret, one no one else knew. If she explained now, Con would always know.

And he would *never* forget. The bastard had the memory of a damned elephant.

"No," she said, hoping he would leave it.

She should've known better.

"You remained veiled for an extended period?" Con asked in disbelief, his jaw slack.

Rhi shifted in her chair. Damn Con for making her choose between lying and honesty. Of course he would remember how she loathed lying. She had gotten that from her mother's side, a trait every Fae prayed they didn't get.

"Rhi," Con pressed.

It was on the tip of her tongue to lie, but even as she tried, her skin began to burn. She silently cursed the trait and sent Con her worst glower.

He merely lifted a blond brow.

"Yes," she finally answered and banged her fist once on the table. "Damn you, Con. Why did you have to press?"

Aisley looked across the table to her husband. "Why not just lie?"

"Rhi can no'. No' without great pain," Con stated.

Rhi drained her glass and filled it again. "The Dark got into Denae's mind. She kept talking about her sister, Renee, who drowned, and how everyone always left her. She was sinking into a depression. I tried to help her, but ultimately it was Kellan who pulled her out of it."

"He did?" Phelan asked with a whistle. "That's impressive."

"That's only part of it." Rhi looked across the table at Con. "She's immune to Dark Fae seduction."

Con's face went blank for a moment as surprise set in. "How?"

"No' even the Dark know. They're as baffled as I am. I've never heard of such before."

Aisley said, "Well, that's a bit of good news, isn't it?"

"No," Con and Rhi said in unison.

Rhi swallowed hard and looked at the table. "Her . . . aversion . . . to them has drawn the attention of Taraeth. He considers Denae a challenge, and he won't rest until she is his."

"Why did you leave them, then?" Con asked, his words clipped and hard.

Rhi lifted her gaze to him, then her head swung to Phelan. "I came for you."

CHAPTER
TWENTY-NINE

Cork, Ireland

Rhys knew the moment he saw the pub *an Doras* that it was a pub for the Dark Fae. He and Kiril exchanged glances and crossed the busy street.

The streetlights were bright, the night deep. Music played loudly and the young and beautiful filled the pub. Rhys spotted the large Dark Fae guarding the door.

He stood facing the street, his hands clasped in front of him, his long, silver-streaked black hair pulled back in a braid.

"I'm going to ask him where he got those red contacts," he heard a young female ask, rushing to the Dark.

"Think he'll recognize us as Kings?" Kiril asked as both men slowed once they reached the sidewalk.

Rhys shrugged while watching the Dark zero in on the flirty female asking about his supposed contacts. "A possibility. I've got an idea, though."

Kiril raised a brow, but merely smiled when Rhys motioned to the four twentysomething girls standing around a streetlamp. "Oh, I like your thinking."

As one, the two changed directions and headed to the

women. The females saw them approaching, and each stood straighter, pushing out their breasts.

It was really too bad they were on business, because Rhys would like nothing more than to take two of the girls and pleasure away the night.

"Hello," said a female with deep red hair and sparkling green eyes. She had tried to cover her freckles with a ton of makeup.

Rhys stopped beside her. "I've always been partial to redheads, green hair, and freckles."

"Freckles?" she asked, her eyes glued to him.

Rhys nodded. "Freckles."

"What are you lasses doing this evening?" Kiril asked as he came up between two of the girls, giving each a wink.

A tall, leggy blonde looked Kiril up and down. "Scotsmen, aye? What would we want with you?"

Rhys laughed and tugged the redhead against him. "After a taste of a Scot, you'll never look elsewhere again."

A brunette smiled seductively. "That's quite a boast."

"I'm quite a man," Rhys said. "Why no' let us buy you lovely lasses a drink and we can . . . debate . . . this more."

"I'm game," Freckles said.

The others were quick to acquiesce. Even as the six of them made their way to the door of *an Doras,* Rhys knew there might be a chance he would have to use magic against the Dark Fae guarding it.

But just like any man being ruled by his cock, the Dark barely paid him or Kiril a glance with the four young females around them.

Once inside, Rhys had to fist his hands as he looked around at all the Dark Fae disappearing with the men and women of Cork behind hidden doors in the walls.

Some came out again, their souls all but gone.

Others were never heard from again.

Rhys glanced down at the females around him. There's

no way he could leave them in good conscience. At Kiril's grim look, he had come to the same conclusion.

"This place isna for you lasses," Kiril said over the music.

The women immediately took offense, all talking at once. Before Rhys could diffuse the situation, a Dark Fae with short hair and an expensive suit walked up.

"Is there trouble here?" he asked smoothly, eyeing Freckles.

Rhys held Freckles closer to him. "Nay." The less he said, the more he might get away without the Dark realizing he was Scottish.

The red eyes of the Dark lifted to him. "I was asking the ladies."

Freckles, as if sensing something was amiss, took the hand of the female closest to her. "Nothing's wrong. We just wanted to leave."

"Leave?" the Dark asked, his gaze narrowed on her. "Why would you want to leave?"

"They've had a long night," Rhys said as he stepped between Freckles and the Dark Fae.

Red eyes blazed, completely focused on Rhys. All the while, Kiril was quickly and silently getting the four mortals out of the pub.

"You're a Scot," the Dark said, his lips peeled back in displeasure, as if just saying the word was revolting.

"And you're Irish. I'm so glad we got that settled," Rhys said with a fake smile. "Now, tell me why all of you are wearing those red contacts."

It went against every instinct Rhys had not to kill the Dark, but he needed information—information about the Dark Ones, their plans, but more importantly where they might be keeping Kellan and Denae.

The Dark Fae rolled his eyes and turned on his heel to disappear in the crowd.

Kiril slapped him on the back. "Quick thinking."

"Are the females safe?"

"Aye. They're also verra afraid. I doona think they'll come near this place again."

"Good." Rhys scanned the bar until he found two stools. "Time to get to work."

Kiril rubbed his hands together. "With pleasure."

Denae couldn't move. Emil had used his magic to hold her against the wall, the cool, damp stones making her shiver.

There was an unnatural light to his red eyes, one that said it was his time to play—and he was going to take full advantage of it.

She wanted to look at Kellan and see how he'd fared with Taraeth, but she didn't dare. The second she did could be the second Emil slipped into her mind.

Kellan had told her to stay vigilant, and that's what she was going to do. No matter how much it killed her to do it.

There was a bellow of rage that erupted from Kellan. Out of the corner of her eye she saw him jump to his feet and lunge for Taraeth, the chain stopping him just short of the Dark leader.

There was a loud snap, and Denae winced because she knew that was Kellan's shoulder popping out of joint. And still he reached for Taraeth.

She couldn't see Taraeth's face, but she supposed it looked similar to Emil's, which was alight with glee and satisfaction. They thought they had won.

Perhaps they had.

For the moment.

But Denae had no doubt that one day Kellan would get free. When he did, he would leave nothing but destruction and death in his wake.

She didn't know much about the Dragon King, but she recognized the thread of danger, the layer of dark menace lurking just beneath the warm skin and thick muscle.

A scrap of recklessness he held firmly in check.

Until someone pushed him.

He was absolute power, total dominance.

Utter, breathtaking control.

Even in a rage and bloodied, he was magnificent. At that instant, Denae fully comprehended him as a Dragon King. He was protector, defender, and guardian of the realm.

He was also judge, jury, and executioner of any who dared to harm it.

"You look at me, but you think of him," Emil said as he leered at her. "I can't have that."

Denae swallowed and focused fully on the Fae before her. He was a nuisance, a pest who could do untold damage to her body and mind if she wasn't careful.

"Are you sure it's Kellan I'm thinking of?" she asked with a sly look.

Emil's lips peeled back as he reached for her shirt. In one yank, he ripped her oversized shirt in two, leaving it hanging precariously on her arms.

The only things separating her bare skin from the Fae were her cami and yoga pants. In mere seconds, even those were gone.

Denae was plastered against a wall, bare-assed and unable to defend herself against her would-be attacker. It was humiliating.

And infuriating.

Denae had never felt such rage, such sheer ferocity. It replaced the fear, leaving her cold and calculating. She let her gaze rake over the Dark Fae in contempt.

"How sad. You can't even make one insignificant human want you in the smallest way. Your two friends witnessed it before. I bet they're talking about you now. How quickly do rumors spread among your people, I wonder?"

The laughter and desire instantly faded from his eyes, replaced with evil intent. His hand wrapped around her throat and began to squeeze.

Behind them, she caught a glimpse of Taraeth looking

over his shoulder. His eyes glowed red right before he bellowed Emil's name.

"She is mine!" Taraeth shouted.

Emil's hand dropped and he stepped away from her, but in his gaze, he promised retribution.

If Denae thought she would be released to have control over her own body again, she was dead wrong. With Taraeth's attention now on her, he faced her and smiled wickedly.

"Ah, but I knew your body would please me, little human."

Denae might be afraid of Emil, but she was terrified of Taraeth. There was something about the Dark leader that made her want to huddle into a corner and cover her head with her hands.

He was the evil in the darkness, the malevolence lurking in the shadows waiting to snatch unsuspecting females. He was death in disguise as pleasure, but she saw him for who he truly was.

And it terrified her.

She wished her clothes were still on. Denae felt powerless and incapable, helpless and weak. Instantly she thought of her sister and how her eyes had pleaded with Denae to believe her about her stalker.

Denae's chest constricted as emotions tumbled upon her like an avalanche. Instantly, she shut off those memories and focused on herself.

There had to be a way for her to turn Taraeth off from her. Name-calling hadn't helped. Neither had her aversion to them. In fact, that had seemed to set them off. The only thing left for her to do was to pretend to give in.

Taraeth took three steps toward her, his red eyes raking her from head to toe and back again.

"Are you done with me already?" Kellan asked.

Taraeth stilled, his advance halted with Kellan's words. Denae had a reprieve, but she wasn't sure it was going to be much of one based on the eagerness in the Dark leader's eyes.

"Rest, Dragon. I'm going to take some enjoyment," Taraeth stated with a wide smile directed at her.

Denae wrinkled her face. "I think you might be disappointed."

So much for her pretending to give in. The thought of his hands on her made her physically ill, and the words tumbled from her lips before she could think better of them.

"Not in you." Taraeth let the swords in his hands disappear and cupped his engorged cock. "I think we're going to have a lot of fun, little human."

"You misunderstand me. You're going to be disappointed because I don't want you."

Taraeth was undeterred. "Maybe at first, but you won't be thinking that after I pleasure you."

Denae didn't have time to form another response as he quickly closed the distance between them and kissed her.

"What do you mean you came for me?" Phelan asked Rhi.

The Fae had dark circles under her eyes and her skin was pale. The lines of fatigue around her mouth were another indication that she had pushed herself to the limits.

"You're part Fae, Phelan," she explained. "You can find the doorways and get inside."

He turned his gaze to Aisley who looked at him with unblinking fawn-colored eyes. It was her silent way of telling him she would back him on whatever decision he made.

"I've never found a doorway before. How are you sure?" he asked.

Rhi's smile was small. "The doorways were closed in Scotland. There are one or two in England, but if you really want to find one, you must go to Ireland."

Phelan had never met Kellan or Denae, but the Dragon

Kings had come to his aid, as had the other Warriors and Druids from MacLeod Castle on several occasions. How could he turn them away now?

"What do I need to do?"

Rhi briefly closed her eyes, relief pouring from her in waves. "This isn't going to be easy, stud."

"When has battling evil Druids been easy?" He gave her a wink and held out his hand atop the table to Aisley. Once she had taken it, he linked their fingers. "I thought you said the Dark Ones were in an abandoned manor?"

Rhi licked her lips. "They are. In order to get in, you'll need to find the doorway."

"He'll walk into a slaughter," Tristan said.

Phelan looked at the newest Dragon King again. He still couldn't believe the face staring back at him. As much as he wanted to talk to Tristan about it, it would have to wait until this latest crisis had been averted.

Con drummed his fingers on the table. "Aye, he will. Is there another way, Rhi?"

"Yes," she said with a roll of her eyes. "As if I would send my prince into a death trap. Give me some credit."

Phelan coughed to cover his laugh while Aisley turned her head into her shoulder, her smile wide.

"Well?" Con asked, his voice laced with annoyance.

Rhi turned her silver eyes to Phelan. "The doorway you need will lead you to a maze of underground tunnels."

"Aren't the Dark Ones using it?" Aisley asked.

Rhi shook her head. "The tunnels yes, but not the doorway. I made the doorway before I came here."

Tristan crossed his arms over his chest and leaned against the wall. "What about these tunnels? You say the Dark use them?"

"Without the Fae, they would be nothing but underground tunnels shaped by water. However, the Dark Ones have allowed the wall between our realm and yours to . . ." She paused and shrugged. "It's all but gone."

Con let out a string of curses as he rose and began to pace. Phelan looked from the King of Kings to Rhi who was inspecting her nails.

"I gather there will be unsavory things in these tunnels?" Phelan asked.

Rhi gave a silent nod.

Con whirled on her. "How long have you known? Do you know what could happen if any of those creatures find their way to the surface? Or what about a mortal who decides to venture into those tunnels?"

As soon as Con began to yell, Rhi's eyes narrowed on him. She pushed her chair back and stood while leaning her hands on the table. "I just discovered it. I didn't even take the time to alert my queen on the matter, you asshat. I came here first, and yes, I know very well what could happen!"

Phelan looked at Aisley who gave him a small nod. He released her hand and stood. "The sooner I get there the better, but Rhi, you need to rest first."

"There isn't time," she protested and turned her head away.

"I'm going to need you at your best." He stared at her until she relented with a loud sigh.

Tristan pushed away from the wall. "I'm going with you."

"As am I," Aisley said.

Phelan walked around the table and drew his wife into his arms. "You know I want you with me, but no' this time, beauty. If those Dark Fae got ahold of you, the Phoenix, I doona know what I'd do."

"Phelan is right," Con agreed. "It's safer for you here, Aisley."

Aisley lifted her head from his chest and sighed. "Find Kellan and Denae, kill as many of the Dark as threatens you or them, and then return to me as quickly as you can."

"Always," he promised and placed a kiss upon her lips.

Con speared Rhi with a look. "How long do you need to . . . recover?"

"I am recovered."

"That's shite," Con said, distaste twisting his face. "I can see how puny you look. You wouldna stand a chance against a Dark Fae."

"Want to test the theory? How about I drop your high-handed ass into a bunch of them and see how long you last before I have to save you?"

"What is it between them?" Aisley asked Phelan in a whisper. "Just the war?"

Phelan tucked her long hair behind her ear and leaned close to say, "From what I've pieced together, Rhi was involved with one of the Kings."

Aisley's eyes widened. "Was it Con? He sure does hate her."

"No one will give me a name."

Con pushed his chair in calmly, his face a mask of cool indifference. "You're no' indestructible, Rhi. You might want to remember that when you have your prince and a Dragon King in those tunnels."

"Both Phelan and Tristan can take care of anything they encounter," she retorted just as calmly as he had spoken.

Tristan frowned. "If we'll be in the tunnels, where will you be?"

"With Denae and Kellan," Phelan surmised as he looked at her. "The place they're being kept doesna have access to the tunnels, does it?"

Rhi gave a slight shake of her head, sending her long black hair moving gently over her back. "No. I'm going to have to lead them to it."

"While staying veiled," Con added. He took a deep breath and slowly released it. "Can you do that again so soon?"

"I will."

"Can you?" he repeated more forcibly. "I'll no' have Usaeil blame me for your death."

Instead of answering him, Rhi turned to Phelan. "Give me fifteen minutes, and then we leave."

Before he could answer, she was gone. Con turned and walked out of the kitchen, and Tristan followed. Phelan used that precious time with Aisley.

"Are you sure about this?" she asked.

"I've never been to the Fae realm. I doona know what to expect, or what we might encounter, but I have to do it."

"I know. I'm just worried. If they can stop a Dragon King, what could they do to you?"

He looked down into her eyes and smiled. "I'm part Fae, remember? They'll soon learn who they're dealing with."

There were no more words as they kissed, the world fading away with the passion that rose. He took her lips again and again, deepening the kiss each time.

Then, all too soon, Rhi returned.

"I love you," Aisley said.

Phelan winked. "I love you too, beauty."

He followed Rhi out of the manor to where Con waited in the next valley. They had barely walked up when a dragon with scales the color of polished amber dove from the sky to land softly before them.

"He can carry you in his hand, or you can ride upon his neck," Con said. "Your choice."

"I'll ride," Phelan said as he walked to the dragon.

Tristan looked at him with his apple-green dragon eyes and held out a thick arm with five digits and long talons extending from them.

Phelan climbed upon the proffered arm and settled at the base of his long neck. He glanced back and saw the tail, which had a stinger on the end.

"How you could've started out a Warrior and become a Dragon King is a mystery. For now," he whispered.

Tristan swung his large head around and looked at Phelan before he snapped his wings open and closed.

"He's ready," Con said. "Are you?"

Phelan had barely given a nod before Rhi was gone. "How will Tristan know where to go?"

"He willna. You will," Con said with a smile.

Phelan gripped the scales when Tristan jumped into the air and climbed high above the clouds as night descended.

CHAPTER
THIRTY

It took every ounce of control, every iota of restraint for Kellan not to yank against the chain and try to reach Denae. The absolute fury that filled him, the sheer possessiveness that surged for Denae took him by surprise.

He couldn't stand to see her stripped naked and leered at by the Dark, but worse than that was Taraeth kissing her. Kellan's self-discipline was fast waning the longer he watched Taraeth with Denae.

Kellan had known this was coming, but he hadn't expected to be so . . . affected by it. When Denae had been left in the same room as him, it was obvious they assumed she meant more to him than she did.

At least that was Kellan's thinking.

Right up until Taraeth kissed her.

Then the only thing that remained was getting Taraeth away from Denae. And killing the Dark Fae leader slowly.

Kellan hid his frown when Denae opened one of her eyes and looked right at him. After the night they'd spent in each other's arms, he knew her passion. And there was nothing in her whisky-colored eyes now.

Even though she was returning Taraeth's kiss.

Kellan shifted his gaze to Emil and saw the Fae watching

him with open malice. Kellan lifted a brow before he turned and walked to the wall where he was chained, the sound of the metal against the stone echoing in the chamber.

He sat down and leaned back. His heated skin came in contact with the cool stone and it helped him rein in his wrath. For the moment.

It simmered, festered.

Smoldered.

Denae was his to protect, his to defend. His to . . . touch. Kellan wasn't the type to share, especially with a Fae. He understood the Fae's interest. Denae was unique, courageous, beautiful, and altogether tempting.

It was her daring, her pluck that originally caught Tara-eth's attention, but now that the Dark One had seen the treasures of Denae's body, there would be no stopping him.

Kellan concentrated on the breath leaving his lungs, and then filling them again. In and out, in and out. He felt his lungs expand as Denae returned Taraeth's kiss. His lungs compressed when the air left his body as he saw Taraeth grab Denae's ass.

"Is it difficult to watch?" Emil asked, a sneer causing his top lip to lift, show his teeth.

Kellan made himself look away from Denae to Emil. "I doona know. Is it? How badly does it sting to watch the human you want taken by Taraeth?"

"He's my leader."

Kellan thought of Constantine. He might be King of Kings, but Kellan wouldn't stand by and allow Con to have a woman he wanted. Nay, he would fight Con for him.

"Just another difference between us," Kellan said and faked a yawn. "We doona share our women, no' even with Con."

Emil's gaze swung to Taraeth. "Not even if Con demanded it?"

"No' even then."

While Emil glared at Taraeth, Kellan was trying not to

notice how Denae hadn't turned her face away from the Dark Fae. Had the legendary attraction of the Fae finally broken through whatever had kept her from initially falling at their feet?

Kellan still didn't understand why Denae had withstood their seduction. No other human had. Ever.

Taraeth ended the kiss and looked down at Denae as he tested the weight of her breast in his hand. "You kiss well, little human. I'm going to enjoy my time with you."

Denae's smile was wide as she gazed adoringly up at him. "Release your hold on my arms. Let me touch you," she begged.

Taraeth chuckled and squeezed her nipple. "All it took was one kiss and now you're mine."

Nay!

Kellan held back the bellow. Barely. Many times he had seen human females fall helplessly under the Fae's spell, but this time it cut deeper than any blade could.

After the fight Denae put up, Kellan had somehow expected her to continue resisting them. Had it really only taken one kiss? Was Denae now theirs to play with sexually and mentally until they destroyed her?

"I saw her first," Emil stated. "I want her, Taraeth."

Taraeth didn't pay him any heed. "You can have her when I'm finished. If I ever tire of this little human. I think I may keep her for eternity."

Kellan fisted his hand behind his back and imagined finding one of the Fae's many enemies and handing Taraeth over to them. Let him see how it felt to be kept as a prisoner and tortured for eternity.

"Taraeth," Emil began, his voice loud and hard.

Taraeth whirled on him, his red eyes glowing. "Dare you question my orders?"

"I want her," Emil continued while his anger grew.

Taraeth glanced back at Denae. "But she didn't want you. Remember? She turned you away."

"You as well."

Kellan smiled. It was so easy to divide the Dark Ones. If only the argument would evolve into a battle, and then perhaps Denae would be granted another reprieve.

When he looked to her, Denae's eyes were on him. She stood with her head held high while the two Dark Fae argued over who would get to use her body.

Her whisky-colored eyes were clear as she held his gaze coolly. It was then he realized she had been acting with Taraeth. She had done such a good job that she had even convinced him.

Then she winked at him.

Kellan wanted to return the wink, but suddenly the argument ended and both Dark Fae were looking at him. He stretched his legs out in front of him and crossed his ankles. "It's no' a good sign when one of your men question you, Taraeth. No' for someone who claims to have absolute control."

"You like to pretend you don't care for my little human, but I think you do," Taraeth said. "I think you care a great deal. You go out of your way to bring our attention back to you time and again. Tell me, Dragon, how does it feel to know that you might have taken her, but I'll be the one that remains in her mind?"

"You willna leave her a mind to have," Kellan said succinctly.

Taraeth turned back to Denae and began to play with her hair. "I think I might. She's exceptional, rare. She will please me greatly." His red eyes shifted to Kellan. "I'll wipe every memory of you from her until she believes she is a Dark Fae."

Apprehension settled in Kellan's gut. Once, so long ago it was just a distant memory, Kellan recalled the mention of a Fae wanting to turn a human. Kellan didn't know if it was successful or not, but the mere fact Taraeth brought it up didn't bode well for Denae.

"She would make an excellent queen," Taraeth said. "But that is on your shoulders, Dragon."

"How so?"

"You give me the answers I want, and I won't have to hurt her. The more I hurt her, the less likely she'll survive. I can't make her my queen if her mind is gone."

Denae was again looking at Taraeth as if he hung the moon just for her. Kellan knew Denae was strong, both mentally and physically, but under the onslaught of Dark magic? In the end, she was still mortal and weaker than a Fae. Could she stand against him?

"I willna tell you anything," Kellan stated.

No matter how much he wanted to protect her, he wouldn't betray his brethren. There was too much at stake. The very idea of the Dark Ones aligning with humans to capture him told Kellan something big was about to happen, and it hinged on knowledge that was hidden.

"Oh, but you will. One more chance. Tell me where it's hidden."

Kellan knew exactly what Taraeth was asking about. The very first King of Kings had found it and hidden it away. Not long after he was killed, so were the next three in quick succession until Constantine took over.

There were only two Dragon Kings who knew what the Dark searched for—he and Con. But Kellan had a suspicion the Dark—or whoever it was who aligned with them—wanted the Silvers who were caged and remained sleeping. The havoc those dragons could wreak upon the world would be catastrophic.

Keeping the Silvers sleeping was one of many reasons none of the Dragon Kings ever ventured far from Dreagan for any length of time.

"Nay," Kellan answered.

Taraeth put his hand on Denae's head, and she immediately went white, her body shaking as she began to scream and jerk weakly against the magic holding her in place.

"I can hurt her. Painfully," Taraeth said. Then he yawned and dusted off his boots.

Kellan ground his teeth together while he somehow remained where he was. Everything inside him bellowed to go to Denae and save her from the suffering he could only imagine she was enduring.

At that moment Kellan couldn't grasp how he had ever thought he could hate Denae. It seemed like centuries had passed since she had come into his life. He had changed so much, and yet the change had been so slow he hadn't recognized it until now.

To see her in such pain was worse than finding his Bronzes dead. It was unfathomable, immeasurable.

Kellan tried to swallow as he kept his gaze on her, hoping to give her strength any way he could. She had to endure it, because if she didn't, Kellan wasn't sure what he might do.

After another few seconds Taraeth lifted his hand and her screams stopped. "Or I can do this."

Kellan barely had time to register that Denae was no longer in pain before Taraeth slowly ran his hand across Denae's breasts, down her stomach to her sex. His hand stopped at the black curls, and a low moan fell from Denae's lips.

Her head fell back against the wall and her chest heaved. With her hips rocking forward slightly, her moans grew louder and louder until she screamed as a climax rocked through her.

Cold, deadly fury filled Kellan. Denae was his. And the Dark had dared to not just torture her, but to give her pleasure against her will.

Kellan was going to kill him. He would enjoy watching Taraeth die. Perhaps he would let Denae help and let her get revenge on the Dark who'd invaded her mind and body. It might help her heal.

He wouldn't even allow himself to think what might

happen if she didn't come out of everything herself. She was strong, a survivor. He kept repeating that silently to himself. It gave him hope—hope he hadn't known he even needed.

"That was beautiful," Taraeth told her as he nuzzled her ear. "That's the first of many, little human."

Kellan didn't know which was harder to watch—the torture or the pleasure. Both affected him in ways he wished he could ignore, but he couldn't. Both would haunt him long after he escaped the confines of the room.

"Are all the dragons gone from this realm?" Taraeth asked.

Kellan smiled coldly. "Of course no', you imbecile. You're looking at one."

"Not a King," Taraeth said harshly. "Your dragons. Are they gone?"

"Aye."

"All of them?" Taraeth pressed.

Kellan gave a single nod.

"How many Dragon Kings remain?"

"As if I would tell you."

"You told me of the dragons."

Kellan began to laugh. "Because that, you sodding fool, is common knowledge. There was no secret about that. We sent our dragons away to protect them."

"And what would you do if your dragons were no longer protected?"

Kellan tried to keep his smile in place, but he knew it fell. There was no anger, just a coldness that settled around him as it always did right before a battle. He was focused, intent.

And ready to kill.

"You'll never find them. However, if so much as one dragon is harmed, you'll know what it feels like to have every Dragon King hunting you and your Dark Ones, Taraeth."

His words didn't seem to faze Taraeth who used his magic to make Denae moan again. "The first time I made her peak with just magic. This time I'll make you watch as I put my mark on her and claim her body as mine, Dragon. Tell me where the object is being hidden."

"Keep him talking," a voice whispered in his ear, a voice he recognized.

Rhi.

"Help is coming, but you need to get him out so I can help free you and Denae," she continued.

Kellan glanced around him. He could feel Rhi's presence now that she had made herself known, but he wasn't sure how she was able to keep herself veiled for such a long time.

Denae moaned again, her eyes focused away from him. She was embarrassed, and trying to fight something she couldn't. Kellan had just thought he hated humans. Now he realized true revulsion—and it was focused solely on the Dark.

"You know the location," Taraeth said as he let his fingers slide into Denae's black curls. "You can stop this if you'll just tell me."

Kellan wasn't that stupid. Taraeth was going to take Denae no matter what he said. A glance at Emil showed the Dark's growing rage as he watched Taraeth taking the human he wanted.

"I'm no' so sure taking Denae in front of Emil is a good idea." Kellan didn't hide his smugness when Taraeth's gaze landed on him. Anyone looking at Emil could see his fury and the death he wished upon Taraeth.

Taraeth turned from Kellan to Emil. All thoughts of Denae were severed as Emil let out a low rumble and attacked. Taraeth blocked the first assault, but in a matter of seconds, magic was flying everywhere.

Kellan saw Denae make herself as small as she could while Taraeth quickly gained the upper hand and had his fingers around Emil's throat.

Taraeth was breathing heavily, his lips peeled back in a dangerous scowl. "I'll return after I deal with this," he promised and quickly disappeared.

For a beat of four seconds Kellan didn't move. Then Rhi materialized. "About damn time," he ground out.

CHAPTER
THIRTY-ONE

Denae wanted to stay inside the small room in her mind she had created, to forget she was in a place no human should ever be, being touched by a Dark Fae with evil intent.

Taraeth had barely touched her, but he had invaded her body, made her orgasm by his magic alone. She had been assaulted in a way that should never have happened. She knew how to defend herself, how to pick out predators. But no one had told her about the Fae or how they could gain control of her body and mind no matter how she fought it.

She felt minuscule, insignificant. Used. It was the most horrendous thing she had ever endured. It didn't help that her skin still sizzled from the ferocious orgasm Taraeth had forced on her. She wanted to scrub her skin raw to get his touch, his scent off her.

The thought that it might never happen made her retreat deeper into that little room in her mind.

"Denae," Rhi's voice said near her ear. "Taraeth is gone. You're free. Focus on Kellan and remember the special night you had in his arms."

She turned her head away. She didn't want to listen to Rhi, or face Kellan. A cry rose up within her as she realized he had witnessed her attack. She would really become the weak human now.

"Look at Kellan," Rhi whispered urgently. "Look at the anger in his eyes for what was done to you. Both of you are at the mercy of the Dark. Stay united."

Denae wasn't sure she could do as Rhi asked. It was too much. All of it was just too much.

Rhi let out a sigh. "Damn it. I need to go to Kellan. Please, Denae. This is killing him. He might never show it or say it, but you could see it in his eyes if you but looked."

Denae wanted to ignore the Light Fae, but she couldn't disregard her need for Kellan. Being in his arms had been the best thing of her life. Feeling his touch, tasting his kisses. It had been heaven on earth—something she hadn't thought existed.

She opened her eyes to find Rhi standing beside Kellan. He was speaking in low tones with Rhi, and she couldn't make out what they were saying.

Denae focused on Kellan's lips. He had full lips, lips a man like him could use as a weapon. She thought of his kisses and how she'd felt them all the way through her body into her essence and her soul.

The same couldn't be said for Taraeth. He was average, at best.

Denae inwardly snorted. So much for the seduction of the Fae. But the Dark still managed to win in the end.

Denae turned her head, the last vestiges of her control slipping away when she found herself still held by Fae magic. She couldn't cover herself, couldn't claw her way through the stones, or even cover her eyes in an attempt to hide the tears that threatened.

"You did well," Rhi said, beside her once again. "Concentrate on that. Not many could infuriate Taraeth the way you do. Bravo!"

Denae was thankful the Fae didn't try to get in her face.

Instead, Rhi stood on her other side and draped something over her as she talked nonstop and smiled often.

That kind gesture was too much for Denae. She closed her eyes and fought against the moisture that gathered in her eyes. The last time she cried was when she buried her father. Her heart had been ripped from her chest as she watched the third member of her family lowered into the ground in a four-year span. She'd sworn to never shed another tear again.

"Are you hurt?" Rhi asked gently.

Denae swallowed twice before she could find her voice. "No."

"I don't know how long we have," Rhi said. "Tristan and Phelan are coming, but I have to get both of you out of here."

"Denae."

She pressed her cheek farther into the cold stones when Kellan said her name in a soft voice too kind to come from someone like him. Was she that much of a mess? Did he know she was on the jagged edge and about to fall off?

"Look at me," he urged.

She wasn't sure if she could. Not after what Taraeth had done. It was worse than the moment of pain Taraeth had put her through.

Pain she could handle. And though she wasn't mindless with need for any of the Fae, Taraeth had still been able to manipulate her body into pleasure.

It was sick and dirty, and . . . wrong.

How many more times would Taraeth do that to her? Worse, when would he take her as he'd promised to do?

"Denae."

This time Kellan's voice was hard and demanding, almost daring her to face him.

Now that was the man she knew. Cold, shrewd, and cunning. This man she could understand. He was dedicated to the Kings, devoted to Dreagan, and single-minded with purpose for both.

She opened her eyes and slowly turned her head until she was looking at him. His celadon eyes were penetrating, pointed. He asked no questions, just stared. Then his head lowered slightly as if asking her without words if she was all right.

Denae took a deep breath and nodded. If she thought Kellan would pity her or show a hint of compassion, she was dead wrong. It was a good thing too, because she would have fallen apart if he had.

"Rhi, get this damn chain off me," he said through clenched teeth.

The petite Fae ran to him and wrapped both of her hands around the manacle surrounding his wrist. Beneath her hands, coming from around the iron, Denae could have sworn she saw a bright light. Yet, not even that could release the chain.

Instead of getting angry, Kellan merely gave Rhi a gentle shove aside. The next thing Denae knew, Kellan had raised his hand, palm forward, right at her.

She winced as if expecting a blow. Instead, her arms dropped to her sides and she was able to move away from the wall. Her gaze jerked to Kellan.

Rhi's silver eyes were large as she stared at him. "You can do magic while still being in their chains?"

"Aye," he said angrily. "I just can no' shift."

Denae took the man's button-down shirt Rhi had draped over her and put it on. It came to the top of her thighs, but at least she was covered.

She was in the process of buttoning it when she caught Kellan's scent. This was his shirt. Rhi had given her his shirt. Her eyes lifted to his to find him staring at her.

The shirt reminded her of tangled limbs, long kisses, cries of pleasure, and desire unlike she had ever known.

She inhaled his scent again and burrowed deeper into the shirt. It was her armor now.

Without words, without a touch, Kellan had given her the courage to stand tall once more. Denae took a step toward him. His gaze didn't leave hers, and it gave her the daring to walk to him.

He met her as far as his chain would allow. She was promptly dragged against his chest and his arms tightened around her. Denae closed her eyes and buried her head in his neck as she held onto him tightly.

Rhi had been right. Kellan wasn't one to show emotions, but if a person knew where to look, they could see or feel it. Like Denae did now. His arms shook, and his chest rose and fell rapidly. His hands gripped her firmly, as if he were afraid he'd never get to hold her again.

"It's almost over," Kellan whispered.

Before, his steely gaze and nod had let her stand tall. Now his touch and soothing words handed her the means to remember the trained professional she was.

One of Kellan's hands slid into her hair and held the base of her head. He was holding her as if she were precious, as if he was as affected by what had happened as she was.

At that moment, all the fear that had been building dissipated as if it never was. Because of Kellan, because he was strong and powerful, resilient and dangerous.

And because he cared.

"Follow Rhi. She'll lead you out," he said.

Denae leaned back to look at him. "What? You're coming with us. Just use your magic on the chains."

"I've tried. These were made to hold a Dragon King. The Dark magic used doesna recognize my magic, or even Rhi's. Only a Dark One can release me."

Denae couldn't believe what she was hearing. After all she had been through, it was Kellan who'd kept her holding it together. She wasn't going without him.

"Take her," he ordered Rhi. "Get as far from here as you can, and make sure they can no' get to her again."

Rhi's forehead furrowed as she looked away. "Kellan . . ."

"I'll withstand whatever they have in store for me," he said. "Without Denae, they have no leverage."

Denae waited to hear Rhi's next argument, but the Fae merely grabbed her hand and led her to the back wall where water dripped down.

"No," Denae said and tried to pull back, but the Fae was stronger than she looked.

Denae glanced back at Kellan. He stood solemnly, a glimmer of sadness in his pale green eyes just before Rhi yanked her through the wall.

She found herself standing on the edge of a stream that wound through semidark tunnels. The cold caused her to shiver, and while she rubbed her hands up and down her arms, Denae glowered at Rhi. "We can't leave him."

"We had no choice. If any of the Dark return and find you gone before we get out of these tunnels, you'll know the full extent of just what they can do to you. Without you there, Kellan can endure anything. You're a liability."

"Because he cares?" she asked carefully, not sure if she wanted it to be true or not.

Rhi sighed and shook her head. "He gave you a promise. Kellan will see it fulfilled regardless of what it costs him. He also made a vow to his brothers. Dreagan and all Dragon Kings are to be protected no matter what. The two oaths could tear him apart."

Denae should have known she didn't mean anything to Kellan. It was silly to be so upset, especially when he chose his people and his way of life. Their night together had meant something to her. It had changed her.

And regardless of how he felt, she didn't regret any of it.

"They'll torture him more," she said. "Will they use the females on him?"

Rhi looked first one way down the tunnel and then the other. "Probably. We need to go this way," she said and pointed to the left.

"No." Denae crossed her arms over her chest. "I'm not leaving unless Kellan is with us."

Rhi slapped her hand on her thigh. "Damn it, Denae. Don't be stupid. Being out here isn't exactly safe. This tunnel allows the Fae world to bleed into yours. There is danger everywhere, including behind that wall where Kellan is. He's trying to save you so that both of his promises will be kept. Don't let that be in vain."

Denae dropped her arms and looked at the wall they had just walked through. "There has to be a way to unlock his chains. Everything has a weakness. Locks can be picked, metal corroded."

"If you go back in there, I don't know if I'll be able to get you back out."

"Then don't."

Rhi rolled her eyes. "Really? After the episode with Taraeth you want to go back for more? There's a very real possibility you'll never have another chance at an escape. Trust me when I tell you that if Taraeth takes you, he'll never let you go."

"By take you mean if he has sex with me." It was enough to cause Denae to hesitate. The aftermath of her assault would be with her for many, many years.

She didn't want anywhere near Taraeth again.

As if sensing her uncertainty, Rhi said, "Yes. You've been strong so far, but you saw how easily he used your body against you. Think of that, but multiplied by a hundred. That's what it'll be like."

"If I can't resist him."

"The more you resist, the more he'll push until you go insane."

"He mentioned turning me into Fae to be his queen."

Rhi look aghast. "What? Are you sure that's what he said?"

"Yes, I'm sure. Can he do that?"

"It's just another reason to get you far from here."

"He'll still come for me, won't he?"

Rhi rubbed her temples, agitation causing her to stamp her right foot. "Yes, he will, damn it all. As long as you're somewhere he can find you."

"Which means what?"

The Fae turned her silver gaze to Denae and looked her squarely in the eye. "Anywhere that isn't with Light Fae or the Dragon Kings."

For several seconds Denae simply returned the stare as her mind went over everything piece by piece. She looked at it as she would a mission from MI5. "You're telling me that I can't live my life now? That I'll have to be at the mercy of your people or the Dragon Kings? Based on what I've heard, I don't think your people will take me in, and if I leave Kellan behind, I don't imagine the Kings will be pleased to see me."

"They'll protect you. For Kellan."

"Wow. That makes it all better." Her voice was heavily laced with sarcasm. "I don't want to go back in there. Taraeth and every one of the Dark Fae scare me to death. But I can't leave Kellan. He wouldn't leave me."

"He would if it meant the other Dragon Kings and Dreagan would be left alone."

Rhi's statement hurt, more so because Denae knew it to be true. But she was a highly trained operative with MI5. She had faced scary scenarios before. This—whatever was going on—was more important than anything she had ever been a part of.

"I'm just one human. I matter little in the grand scheme of things. The Dragon Kings are needed. Kellan is needed. Regardless of what he would do, I'm going in after him."

"You're a fool," Rhi said, but there was a grin on her face. "I liked you from the moment I met you, Denae Lacroix, and right now is exactly why. I wish every mortal was like you."

Denae laughed, the sound full of fear and anxiety. "I could be walking to my death."

"You won't die in pain at least."

After what Matt and MI5 had had in store for her, that was a plus. "I don't know if I can face Taraeth again."

"You will. You're strong, just as Kellan said. A survivor. Don't let him touch you. You're not you when you're with him. You're on a mission, and you're just playing a part."

That might work. It was a way for Denae to distance herself from her attacker, but she'd much rather kill him. "It'll take every ounce of my training to fake wanting Taraeth's touch."

"You'd better if he gets ahold of you, because if he suspects you're immune to his charms, he'll turn you over to the rest of the Dark."

That was enough to put things into perspective for Denae. She faced the wall and took a deep breath. "Do you have any advice for me?"

Rhi put her hands on Denae's shoulders as she stood behind her. "Pray hard, chick, and wish for luck. You're going to need it."

Denae had no chance to comment as she was shoved back through the wall.

CHAPTER
THIRTY-TWO

Kellan had sent Denae away knowing it was the right thing to do, but it bothered him that she had gone so easily. She was a warrior, one who would never leave someone behind.

But she had left him.

Granted, he and Rhi hadn't given her a choice, but he expected humans to think of themselves first, knowing he was immortal and could survive. Not to mention what she'd gone through at Taraeth's hands. It was only natural that she'd want to leave.

She had fought against MI5, battled against the Dark Ones, and outwitted Taraeth without him even knowing it. She was special.

At least Rhi, Phelan, and Tristan would get her away from Ireland and the Dark Ones so Taraeth could never get his hands on her.

Kellan wondered if Denae would still be alive when he finally managed to escape. Con and the others would make sure she was looked after and want for nothing. Neither MI5 nor the Dark Ones would ever get ahold of her again. Of that he was certain.

He leaned against the wall and looked to his memories

where he stored every minute he shared with Denae. He thought of her alluring body, her inviting mouth, and her enticing cries of pleasure. His hands remembered the silky feel of her hair, the soft-as-cream skin, and every curve and contour.

Amazingly, he found sadness filled him, sadness that she was gone from him. He should be happy to have her away from Taraeth, but all he could think of was holding her again.

There had been a moment after Taraeth left that he thought Denae had been broken, but the strong woman he knew had faced the world with a brave face.

He had seen the uncertainty in her whisky-colored gaze, and it had been all he could do to remain where he was. A part of him had been ripped away when he saw her held by their magic, naked and squeezing her eyes shut.

Kellan hadn't even realized he'd called her name until he saw her flinch. It had been a whisper, a breath of need that had passed his lips.

That's when he knew she needed strength and power. He'd hidden his rage and his shattered emotions and gave Denae what she wanted. Once in his arms, Kellan hadn't wanted to let her go.

She'd trembled, holding him as if he were a lifeline. If only the damn chains didn't prevent him from communicating with the other Kings via their link he would make sure Guy wiped her memories of anything to do with Taraeth so Denae wouldn't have to go through life suffering.

Kellan dropped his chin to his chest and closed his eyes. Even mentally he couldn't say farewell to Denae, not when her scent still clung to him.

As if his thoughts had conjured her, Denae stumbled through the wall, her wild whisky-colored eyes going right to him. She said not a word as she rushed to him and started pulling ineffectually on his chains.

"What are you doing here?" he demanded more roughly

than intended. Kellan was both angry and pleased to see her. Once more she shocked him by doing the exact opposite of what he expected.

She glanced up and gave him a stern look. "Don't act as if you aren't happy to see me. I saw your eyes light up."

"My eyes don't light up."

"Of course not," she said in a strained voice as she put a foot against the wall and pulled. "What was I thinking?"

Kellan grabbed her by the shoulders and jerked her in front of him. "What are you doing here?" he asked a second time.

"Someone has to save your ass."

He tried to push her away, but instead he dragged her closer, his gaze lowering to her mouth. He knew she tasted as heady as honeyed wine, knew her lips were as soft as down.

"Yes," she whispered breathlessly as her fingers delved into his hair at the back of his neck.

"What?"

"The question in your gaze."

He could hardly think with her so close. Her warm breath fanned his cheek before she placed a kiss on his jaw. It was so blatantly sexual that he fought not to take her right then, to sink into her wet heat. His shirt looked good on her, and it was all that separated him from her amazing body.

"What is the question?" he finally asked.

Their eyes met, clashed. Desire sparkled in her gaze. "You're wondering if we could chance making love. My answer was yes. I need you. I need to feel you inside me."

As if he could deny her that simple request. But he knew it went deeper than that. She wanted Taraeth's taste erased from her memory, just as he wanted to erase it.

His hand splayed on her back as he pressed her against him. Her curves, her softness only spurred his passion.

Then he lowered his head and took her lips in a seductive kiss that was both fierce and tender, savage and gentle.

Wild and untamed.

He wanted to shove up the shirt until his hand found her breast. But he held back. She hadn't been in control with Taraeth. To give her back what had been taken, he would let her take complete control.

His hands remained at her waist until she quickly unbuttoned the shirt and brought his hand to her breast. She moaned into his mouth, her nipple going hard in his palm. While he teased the turgid peak, she unfastened his jeans and jerked them down his legs.

The need driving them was too great to go slow, too overwhelming to put off. No matter the dangers.

He felt the need driving her, ruling her. Not once had Kellan ever given control to a female, but with each kiss, each touch that Denae decided upon he saw the uncertainty vanish and the self-assured woman return.

"What do you want?" he asked her.

"You. I want you right here, right now," she said between kisses.

He had to be inside her, had to feel her tight, slick walls envelop him.

Kellan smiled when she shoved down on his shoulders until he was sitting. She straddled him, a fierce, provocative look in her eyes. His hands landed on her hips as he held his breath while she rose up over his engorged cock.

It jerked, anxiously waiting to have her tight wetness surround him. She gasped and moaned, her head dropping back when she rubbed her sex against the head of his arousal.

She was oh, so wet, her chest heaving and her nipples hard. A woman flushed with desire and in control was a beautiful sight to behold.

"I need to feel you inside me."

Something profound shifted in his chest. What was it

about Denae that called to him time and again? What made her different from the other mortals? Every time he thought he had it figured out, she surprised him again.

Her head lifted and their gazes met. He waited for her to decide if this was really what she wanted. When a slow smile tilted up her lips, his balls tightened.

Then she gradually lowered herself onto his cock until he was fully sheathed. She moaned temptingly and her lips were swollen from his kisses, but it was her eyes glazed with pleasure and focused on him that stole his breath.

She began to rock her hips, the hunger pushing them ever onward. Her nails dug into his shoulders the harder she rode him. When she thrust a breast near his face, he eagerly took her turgid nipple into his mouth and suckled deeply.

The danger was an added element that sent them both careening toward a climax. His balls tightened when Denae whispered his name right as her body tightened around his rod. She stiffened with the force of her climax.

The instant her walls clamped around him, he welcomed his own orgasm as they traveled the road of pleasure together.

It took them, swept them into a paradise of light, the rapture, the ecstasy so forceful it shook Kellan to his very core.

They stayed as they were, breathing heavily, with Denae's head on his shoulder. Reluctantly, Kellan lifted her head and kissed her slowly, languidly.

He wasn't sure what had just happened to him, but he suspected it was profound. There wasn't time to think on it now, however.

When she lifted her eyes to him, Kellan knew that somehow, someway he was irrevocably tied to her. It should have terrified him, but all he felt was . . . a rightness he couldn't understand.

"You want to know why the Dark have no control over me?" Denae asked. "It's you. I was in your arms. I had you inside me. You're the one who kept me from falling under their spell."

He slid his fingers into her coppery locks and yanked her against him. He liked her in control, but now it was his turn. "I'm going to take you again and again until that bastard is wiped from your mind."

"He already has been. You let me do that," she said with a small smile.

Kellan watched as she rose up on her knees and then climbed to her feet. He stood and helped button his shirt until her beautiful body was covered once more. He hadn't expected her statement, and it did strange, amazing things to him. He cleared his throat to give himself time to gather his thoughts. "You shouldna have come back."

"Shut up and help me figure out how to free you."

He smiled despite himself. "There's no lock, you stubborn wench. It'll take magic."

She cut her eyes to him and then stuck out her tongue. "I refuse to leave you, so just keep an eye out for those jerks to return and let me work."

Kellan pulled up his jeans, not surprised to find he was already hard for her again.

Damn but she was beautiful.

Phelan dusted off his clothes and looked around the Irish countryside. It wasn't that different than Scotland, but it lacked a . . . wildness that Scotland possessed.

A sound in the brush behind him had Phelan turning around. He spotted Tristan walking through the small copse of trees with nothing but a pair of jeans on.

"Next time, warn me before you decide to dive to the ground and then toss me off," Phelan said.

Tristan shrugged coolly. "Stop your grumbling. I've never had anyone on my back before. Besides, you're immortal. What do you have to worry about?"

"You obviously doona have a woman in your life. You get to explain to Aisley when we get back."

"Explain what?" Tristan asked with a snort. "You heal, idiot."

Phelan ran a hand through his hair. "No' the point, Dragon."

"It's exactly the point." He cut Phelan a look. "Now, why no' stop your bitching and find the doorway. It's why you're here, is it no'?"

Phelan hadn't known Duncan before he was beheaded, but he had spent enough time around Ian to recognize the stubbornness of the Kerr family running through Tristan. Phelan held back from stating it, however, since the subject of where Tristan had come from seemed to be a tricky one.

Pushing that aside for now, Phelan concentrated on the area. In the darkness he let his enhanced eyesight look over the terrain as if it were daylight. He didn't spot anything on first glance, so he decided to walk around.

There was an abandoned manor over the next rise. Even up in the clouds Phelan had detected the thousands of Fae doorways throughout Ireland.

It wasn't until they were over Cork that he sensed the ones below, but there was one that stood out brighter, as if Rhi had put flashing lights around it.

He held back a laugh knowing that's probably exactly what Rhi had done. Leave it to her to do something outrageous.

"There," Phelan said and pointed to the right. "It's right there."

Tristan scratched his chin, in need of a shave. "Let's go then."

They walked side by side to the doorway. Phelan paused outside of it and looked at Tristan. "Can you see it?"

"Nay."

"How many Kings have gone through a Fae doorway?"

A muscle ticked in Tristan's jaw. "Three. Two taken by the Dark that were later killed."

"And the other?"

"He went in on his own."

Phelan knew he was trying to keep something from him. "Who was it?"

"That I doona know."

"But you know who he followed." When Tristan wouldn't meet his gaze, Phelan shook his head as he realized the answer. "It was Rhi."

Tristan let out a sigh. "Aye. The King followed Rhi."

"What happened to him?"

"That part of the story I doona know. I barely got the little information that I told you."

Phelan thought of Rhi and how much she hated interacting with the Kings. Yet, she was helping them now. Just what was the story between Rhi and her King lover? He faced the doorway and drew in a deep breath. "Guess you'll be the fourth King to go through one. Ready?"

"I'm ready to kill the Dark."

"Follow me," Phelan said as he stepped forward.

He took a step into the doorway and felt the magic shimmer around him. As soon as he was through, the damp foulness of the tunnels slammed into him.

Tristan was right behind him. He let out a muffled curse. "It reeks."

"Aye. Rhi said there were Fae animals walking about, so let's keep an eye out."

"Fine. Which way do you want to begin?" Tristan asked, looking first one way and then the other.

Phelan threw up his hands. "I doona know."

"You're part Fae, right? Can you no' sense them?"

"No," Phelan ground out. If only he could it would make things so much easier. "We can no' split up either."

"This is more your territory than mine, so I'll let you choose the way, Warrior. Just choose correctly."

"You certainly have the disposition of a Dragon King." One side of Tristan's mouth lifted in a grin. "Lead on."

Phelan choose to go right. They had walked for about two hundred yards when they reached a fork in the tunnels. Phelan once more chose to go to the right, and as soon as they did they encountered a body of water running down the middle of the tunnel.

There was a small path on the edge of the water they traversed. Phelan's foot slipped on a small rock and one foot fell into the water.

He glanced down to find his leg from the knee down fully submerged. He and Tristan exchanged a look. Just as Phelan was about to get out of the stream, Tristan's gaze sharpened.

"There's something in the water," Tristan whispered.

The ripples fanned out over the water as whatever was beneath raced toward them. Phelan called to his god. His skin turned gold and claws shot from his fingers. He raised his arm, ready to swipe at whatever rose from the water.

All of a sudden, a large snakelike creature with a head the size of a small dog rose up and aimed its open mouth and impressive fangs at Phelan.

He jerked his arm down, his claws severing the head. When he looked up, Tristan had jumped into the water and found a second head that he ripped off with his bare hands.

Tristan released the severed head and limp body and made his way back to Phelan. "Let's keep moving."

"No wonder Con was so worried. If any of these creatures make it to the surface, the mortals doona stand a chance," Phelan said as they started walking again.

"I'm still new to being a Dragon King, but learned more after Rhi's visit. The Dark Ones shouldna be allowed as much freedom on this realm as they have. It appears as though the Kings assumed the Light were taking care to keep the Dark Ones in check."

"It doesna appear as if that's true."

"Nay. And it's troubling."

"Verra. Just like the idea of the Dark Ones aligning with mortals, especially MI5. Who else have they aligned with?"

Tristan shrugged. "That's a question I'd like answered."

Phelan let the conversation lag as they wandered the tunnels looking for any sign of Rhi, Kellan, or Denae. "So you really doona remember anything from before you became a Dragon King?"

"Nay. Let me guess, you want to fill in the blanks?"

"Is it no' odd that you come into a group of men who happen to know us Warriors? One of who is your twin?"

"I have no twin." Tristan pushed past him when he paused. "I doona know nor care, Warrior, to answer any of your questions."

"What are you afraid of, Dragon? You afraid to learn what happened to you? That you really are Duncan Kerr?"

Tristan halted and swung around to Phelan. "My name is Tristan."

"What do you remember of your past before you became a King?" Phelan pressed.

There was a slight tightening around Tristan's mouth. "Nothing. You say I have a twin. I've no memory of that. For me, my existence began when I landed atop that mountain naked in the snow. I may look like this Duncan you speak of, but I'm no' him."

"Ian will find out sooner or later. What will you say to him when he walks up and you find yourself looking into a mirror?" Phelan didn't know what to make of Tristan. He was Duncan, of that much he was sure, but to have no memories of his past? That would hit Ian hard.

"I doona know."

"I didna know Duncan. I do, however, know Ian well.

He's a good man who has suffered from the loss of his twin. You may no' remember him, but he'll remember you. Do everyone a favor and doona be cruel to him. He's a good man."

Tristan's dark eyes narrowed. "You think I would be cruel?"

"Perhaps." Phelan was beginning to think he wouldn't. Tristan was so much like Ian in action and appearance, right down to their long hair, that it boggled his mind. "But if there is even a smidgen of the Kerr blood left in you, you'll do the decent thing."

"I make no promises, Warrior."

Phelan slapped him on the back and grinned. "That's all I can ask. Come, Dragon. Let's find your friends. Maybe we'll get lucky and find more creatures to kill."

"Now that sounds like fun," Tristan said as they fell into step together.

CHAPTER
THIRTY-THREE

Rhi lingered near Kellan and Denae. She knew it was suicidal, but for some reason she couldn't leave the dragon behind.

"Stupid, stupid dragon," she murmured as she walked the corridors outside the room they were being held in.

Rhi remained veiled. Though she thought to stay near the couple, it was the shouting coming from somewhere in the ruined manor that caught her attention.

Fae, by nature, were sexual creatures who could be benevolent, but normally weren't. They thought of their own interests first and foremost, which meant that most times humans were casualties.

It's one of many reasons the Dragon Kings had fought so hard to keep the Fae out of the realm. Rhi understood their arguments, but she would defend her people to her dying breath. No one was perfect, least of all the Dragon Kings.

As quarrelsome as the Light Fae were, it was nothing compared to the Dark Ones. The Dark were aggressive, belligerent, and confrontational. They searched out their quarry and thought out their torture, though the poor mortals never knew what hit them.

But when the Dark fought amongst themselves, it could

get downright vicious. Based on the shouts she heard, there was definitely about to be a fight.

Rhi had to know if it was Emil and Taraeth. For many centuries she had been waiting for Taraeth to be killed, but so far no one in his group had managed to take him down. A few tried, but Taraeth quickly killed them.

It didn't take long to find the group in what remained of some large room. Taraeth and Emil stood in the center while dozens upon dozens of Dark Fae circled around them hollering as they waited for the fight to begin.

Taraeth was the most powerful. He held his position only by taking down any opponent who dared to challenge him. And many had. The fact he had run away during the battle with the Dragon Kings and was scarred by one was a bane upon his existence. Despite that, he had managed to lead the Dark Ones ever since.

Rhi stilled when a Dark Fae came up behind her. She didn't turn around, didn't so much as breathe. She was veiled, but that didn't mean she was invisible to a Fae. If they concentrated hard enough, some could detect another Fae.

"I know you're here," he said.

Rhi inwardly cursed at how close he was behind her. If she hadn't been so intent on wishing Taraeth be taken down she wouldn't have been caught unawares.

The last thing she wanted was to be caught by the Dark. They might be unkind to mortals, but they were deadly to one of the Light. Her torture would last to infinity, and it would be horrendous.

"Why not come out and play?" he coaxed, his voice laced with an Irish accent.

Rhi slowly moved to her right until she was away from him. She then turned her head to look at him and felt her stomach fall to her feet like lead as she recognized him.

Balladyn.

"There is only one I know who can remain veiled so long. What are you doing here, Rhi?" he asked softly, his red eyes darting around to try and locate her. "These are dangerous times."

She swallowed and fought not to answer him. Balladyn had been one of her closest friends. He had been the only one who had helped her and her Dragon King lover. She thought he had died in a battle with the Dark Ones.

Now she knew the truth.

And it made her want to cry.

Balladyn, the stalwart one, the loyal one. Never would she have imagined him turning to the Dark.

"What happens, pet, when you're too weak to remain veiled?" he asked succinctly. He paused for a couple of seconds and swung out his arm.

He missed her by scant inches. And still she couldn't move. To know Balladyn was alive was a shock to her system. She had mourned him. How she wanted to hug him, then hit him for not letting her know he wasn't dead.

Suddenly his head turned to her and his red eyes blazed as he looked right at her. Rhi almost dropped her veil, but if she did, hundreds of other Dark would see her.

With one last look at her friend, she disappeared back to the tunnel. Only then did she allow the veil to drop as she braced her hands on the stone wall and hung her head.

"Oh, Balladyn."

Denae looked at the lock and sighed. Of course it wasn't a traditional lock she could pick. No, it had to be magical like the ones on Raasay.

"As I stated, only a Dark can unlock it," Kellan said.

She held up a finger to quiet him as she stared at the lock. "No. There has to be another way, and I'm going to find it."

"There is no other way with magic. It is what it is."

"I don't believe that." She couldn't believe that, because if she did, she would die there. And she refused to do that.

The chain rattled as Kellan reached for her. His hands

grabbed her arms as he made her face him. "I didna expect you to come back. Thank you for that."

"You expected me to leave you?"

"Aye. I'm immortal."

She shook her head as anger spiked. "So? Is that supposed to make it easier for me to walk away?"

"Aye."

One word. One simple word had the ability to make her see red. "You asinine, obtuse jackass. You lumped me in with every human you've ever known and thought the worst. I should leave you here just for thinking that, but I don't leave friends behind."

"Is that what I am?" he whispered casually as if the idea amused him.

"I don't spend a wonderful night in a man's arms and not have some kind of connection. I felt something, and though I know you didn't, I couldn't live with myself if I abandoned you. Regardless if you're immortal or not. It's just not right."

When he didn't say anything, Denae turned from him so that he no longer had ahold of her. She grabbed the chain with both hands. It was heavy, the links a half-inch thick. It would be difficult even if she had a bolt cutter.

What an idiot she was to think there might be something between her and Kellan. He hated humans, and although they had shared an amazing night, where she thought there might be some kind of connection between them, he felt nothing.

It was just her luck to finally find someone who affected her the way Kellan did, and he didn't want her. The unfairness of it all made her squeeze the chains to release some of her anger.

"I've never had a human call me friend."

Denae told herself not to look at him, but she couldn't stop herself. When she saw him staring at her with his celadon gaze warm and full of emotion, she wanted to wrap her arms around him and never let go.

"Don't look at me like that," she warned him.

He frowned. "Like what?"

"Like I've surprised you, like you might actually like me a little. It'll make my anger dissipate, and I'd like to hang on to it a bit longer."

Kellan suddenly smiled. "You constantly amaze me. I never know what you're going to say or do."

"Good. I'd hate to become a bore. Now be quiet so I can figure this out."

His hands covered both of hers. "The longer you remain, the higher your chances of being caught. Rhi risked her own life to help you."

Denae wouldn't let go of the chains. She gave them another hard squeeze. His hand squeezed with her, and Denae heard a crack.

Her eyes jerked to him. "Did you hear that?"

He nodded woodenly, surprise making his face go slack. "Let me try."

Denae released the chain and stepped back, but no matter how he tried to use his magic, nothing else happened. "My turn," she said and moved his hands out of the way.

She took the chain in the same spot as before and squeezed, but it was as if she were a flea trying to move the Great Wall of China.

"It's going to take both of us," they said in unison.

Kellan moved to the other side of the chain so they were facing each other and once more covered her hands with his. She gave him a nod as she tightened her grip and he used his magic.

There was another loud crack before several more smaller ones, and then the chain broke in half.

Denae covered her mouth to hide her laugh. "We did it."

He looked at the broken chain and quickly grabbed her hand. "We can celebrate later. We need to get out of here."

"Shift into a dragon."

He held up his wrist that still held the manacle. "No' possible."

Denae rolled her eyes and put her hand on the cuff. "Don't be stupid. Put your hand on mine. If we're going to get out of here, you need to be able to turn into a dragon."

There was a moment's pause before he covered her hand. The manacle took longer than the links. Denae's fingers began to cramp, but she refused to give up.

It felt like an eternity later when the manacle popped open and fell to the floor. Denae wiped the sweat from her brow and tugged Kellan to the wall.

He grabbed the fallen manacle and they ran through the wall, stopping once they were in the dark tunnel.

"Why did you bring that?" she asked and pointed to the manacle.

Kellan lifted the iron in his hand. "I want them to think I'm still hindered."

"I like the way you think. Now, which way?"

"Left."

She fell into step behind him, her feet splashing in the edge of the stream. An urgency pushed her hard, making her feel as if the hounds of Hell were nipping at her heels.

Denae crashed into Kellan's back when he came to a sudden halt. She looked around his shoulder and spotted what appeared to be a solid white moth the size of a Fiat with some type of glow about it perching on the side of the tunnel blocking their way.

It was stunning, an exact replica of the moths she would chase in the summers when she was a little girl. Except those moths could fit in the palm of a child's hand.

The giant moth moved its wings in one heedless flap that sent a gust of wind so strong it would have knocked Denae off her feet if Kellan hadn't been standing in front of her.

Denae took a step back and her foot slipped into the water, making a loud splash. The moth raised its head and looked right at them. Then it opened its mouth to show razor-sharp teeth.

It let out a roar with spittle flying. Denae was shoved to the ground by Kellan as he launched himself at the moth just as it pushed off the wall.

Denae couldn't take her eyes off Kellan as he advanced deftly, his body moving fluidly, nimbly as he dodged the moth's claws that tried to scratch him.

The darkness of the tunnels prevented her from seeing everything, but her eyesight was accustomed enough to witness Kellan's impressive attack.

He rushed the moth, then diverted toward the wall. Just as he reached it, he turned and dove, rolling to his feet behind the giant creature.

With the moth limited in its movement because of its size, Kellan cleverly kept out of its reach. He jumped on the moth's back and grabbed its head, giving it a hard jerk to the side.

The creature fell into the stream dead.

Kellan leapt off as it fell and landed on his feet near her. He held out his hand, one corner of his lips lifted in a smile.

"Shall we continue?"

Denae took his hand and stared at the huge moth as they walked past it. "That was impressive."

"I know."

She made a sound in the back of her throat. "Anyone ever told you that you're conceited?"

"Many times."

Denae wouldn't want to be in the tunnels with anyone else by her side. Kellan might be conceited, but with moves like he just displayed, he had every right to be.

CHAPTER
THIRTY-FOUR

Kellan's skin felt too tight, his irritation too great.

His fury too boundless.

He wanted to shift into dragon form, but it wasn't time. In order to have his retribution on the Dark Ones for taking Denae, he wanted as many gathered as he could before he shifted and wiped them out.

Denae tripped, and with his hand holding hers, he was able to keep her on her feet. She let out a string of curses that made him grin.

"You're smiling, aren't you?" she ground out as she came to a halt and gingerly touched her bare foot. "Laugh at the human because I can't see in the dark."

He frowned as he considered her words. "I could light the way."

"No," she said with a shake of her head, her copper brown hair sliding sensuously over her shoulders. "It would alert them we're here."

"If they listen closely enough, they'll hear us coming anyway."

"It's not smart to alert them to exactly where we are just because I'm hindered in my eyesight."

Normally, Kellan would have agreed. As he stared at

her, he found his way of thinking was changing when it came to humans—rapidly. And all because of Denae.

"The Dark Ones willna touch you again. Ever."

Kellan was shocked at the vehemence of his words. And the truth of them.

Denae's face softened as she put a hand on his cheek. Whatever she was going to say halted before it passed her lips. She dropped her arm and looked down the tunnel they were traveling.

"Is Rhi near?"

"I doona know," Kellan said as he fought against begging her to say the words she kept from him. "Why?"

"She could stay with me so you can go ahead. You'll move quicker without me slowing you down."

"Nay."

She rolled her eyes. "Oh, don't get mad. I'm trying to be practical. I do have some training in this, you know."

"No' training in dealing with Dark Fae."

"True," she grudgingly admitted.

He grabbed her hand again and started walking. "We've lingered long enough. We must keep moving."

She didn't argue as her strides lengthened to keep up with him. Not once did she complain of the grueling pace, the awful stench of the place, or the fact he didn't stop to rest. She kept pace with him while he did his best to keep them moving quietly and helping her not to stumble or run into anything.

They walked for another half hour before he paused as something evil and furious rushed through the tunnel that even she felt.

"What was that?" Denae asked as she shivered.

Kellan glanced down at her, wondering how it was she felt the Dark Fae magic. "They know we've gone. Taraeth will be combing the tunnels looking for us."

"Now is the time to shift into a dragon. You can get us both out."

He glanced above them. The tunnel was high, but he didn't know where they were. "There's a chance we're beneath a city. I could kill dozens of humans as I explode from the ground. And if it's during the day, they'll see me."

"And if it's just a field we're under?"

"I can no' know for certain. We've remained hidden all these millennia because we didna take such chances." Even when he wanted to do just that to get Denae away from the Dark.

Damn but it was hard not to give into his need and shift.

"Then we best get moving," Denae said and took off running.

Kellan caught up with her and jerked her away from an outcropping in the tunnel that she nearly ran into. They kept that pace as he moved them from one tunnel to the next.

"How do you know which way to go?" she asked breathlessly.

He couldn't tell her it was all by chance. Instead he said, "My magic."

A soft chuckle came from her. "Liar. You're just guessing."

There was a distant sound ahead that caused him to stop. He pulled her into his arms and whispered, "I am. Scared now?"

"I've been terrified since the moment I saw my first Fae on the docks."

She had hidden it well, which made him appreciate her even more. It would be almost impossible to get them out if she were hysterical.

"What is it?" she whispered.

He bent his head near her ear. "I hear something ahead at the bend."

She gave a nod to tell him she understood the danger and waited as he moved in front of her. It amazed Kellan how easily they worked as a team. She seemed to know exactly what he wanted or what he would do without any words spoken between them.

He released her hand and relaxed when he felt her fingers grab one of his belt loops. She didn't pull or tug while she walked behind him. It allowed his hands to be free and to keep her safe. The only drawback was they moved slowly.

The closer Kellan came to where he heard the sound, the more his muscles bunched, ready to fight. They moved step by step, soundlessly, stealthily.

Just before they reached the location, Kellan touched her hand. Instantly, she released him and stayed behind while he continued on to the slight bend in the tunnel.

Kellan fought to keep from shifting into dragon form. He hoped it was Dark Fae. He wanted to kill every one of them for the torture and groping Denae had endured at their hands.

He fisted his right hand and lunged around the corner at the same time two males came at him. One male grabbed him by the throat while the other had gold-colored skin.

"Kellan?" said the male who held his throat.

He narrowed his gaze and recognized Tristan. "Aye."

Tristan released him and stepped back. "We found them, Phelan."

Kellan looked past Tristan to the Warrior who stood staring. "Phelan. You're the one who is part Fae?"

Phelan gave a single nod. "Have you seen Rhi?"

"No' for a while. The Dark know Denae and I are in the tunnels. We can no' tarry."

Phelan turned and motioned for them to follow. "We can lead you back out."

"Wait," Kellan said as he pulled Denae to his side. "I'm no' just going to leave."

Tristan's smile was wide and sly. "I didna figure you would. I might no' have been around for the first war with the Fae, but I'll be a part of this one."

"Whatever," Phelan said. "Let's get moving."

"What about Rhi?" Denae asked. "Could the Dark Ones have her?"

Phelan shook his head. "Rhi is too smart for that. She's in the thick of danger, no doubt, but she'll get out once she knows all of us are free of the tunnels."

"How far until we get out?" Kellan asked.

Tristan shrugged. "Depending on how fast we move, we could be out in three quarters of an hour."

"Is the doorway away from any cities?"

"Aye," Tristan said with a grin. "It's situated in an open field."

Denae pushed her hair behind her ears. "What about now? Are we beneath a field?"

It was Phelan who shook his head. "We went in the direction of the nearest city."

"Damn," Denae muttered.

Kellan reached for her hand, knowing exactly how frustrated she felt. "Phelan, you take the lead. I'll follow with Denae behind me."

"And I'll bring up the rear," Tristan said.

Kellan nodded. "I want Denae protected no matter what."

Phelan rubbed his hands together, his long gold claws clicking as he did. "She will be. Now, let's get the fuck out of this nasty place."

Rhi returned to the room Kellan and Denae were being held in only to discover they were gone. She stared in shock at the broken chain.

It didn't matter how strong a Dragon King was, they couldn't break through a chain spelled by Dark Fae. But something—or someone—had been able to.

Rhi knelt beside the chain and reached out her arm to touch it when the sound of the door opening reached her. She had mere seconds to veil herself before she was seen.

Her power was running low. She wouldn't be able to stay veiled for long, but she had to learn as much as she could. She rose and backed away as Taraeth, his clothes torn and bloody, stopped at the doorway and gaped at the empty room.

"Where are they?" he bellowed.

The men behind him immediately turned and rushed out of the room, barking orders to get search parties together for the castle and tunnel.

Taraeth walked past the broken chain to the back wall. He watched it for several seconds before he murmured, "How did you get loose, Kellan? And more importantly, how did you know this was a doorway?"

Rhi fisted her hands. Taraeth had defeated yet another rival. Would no one ever take him down?

Suddenly Taraeth's head swung in her direction. "Who helped you, Kellan?" he asked.

Rhi's magic was wearing thin. She might hate Taraeth, but if her veil slipped, she wouldn't have much magic with which to fight him. She had no choice but to leave.

She appeared in the tunnels and dropped the veil. Her knees buckled, and she hit the ground hard. Rhi winced as a rock jabbed into her left knee.

Balladyn was alive. Taraeth had killed another rival after kidnapping a Dragon King and Kellan's woman. Not to mention MI5 had some alliance with the Dark Ones.

All of which Rhi needed to tell Usaeil. Rhi couldn't go to her queen yet. Kellan and Denae where somewhere in the tunnels, and she couldn't be sure if Phelan and Tristan had found them or not.

"A fine mess you've gotten yourself into," Rhi said.

She wearily climbed to her feet. How she hated feeling so powerless when her magic was drained.

"Not a good place to be weak, pet."

The soft Irish brogue, the endearment. Rhi didn't have to turn around to know Balladyn had found her.

"These are dangerous times," he said. "Too perilous for the likes of you."

"A lot has changed." Rhi slowly turned around and met Balladyn's red gaze. She hid her wince. Gone were the kind silver eyes she remembered. "For the both of us, it seems. I thought you died. I mourned you."

"You'd have been better off thinking I was dead." His gaze shifted and grew hard. "I know what happens to Light Fae who grow weak down here."

"So. You've come to take me to Taraeth." She was surprised, shocked right down to her now-ruined boots. Balladyn had been her dearest friend. What had happened to him?

Balladyn inhaled deeply. His long mane of black hair was cut to his chin and now sported streaks of silver. "Eventually. I've got something else in store for you."

The menace in his words made her blood ice. "Why am I so special?"

"As if you didn't know, pet."

Rhi licked her lips and hoped her magic was strong enough against one as powerful as Balladyn. "Oh, and what is that?"

"You should never have come here. I had hoped to track you, make you run and worry. You know how I always loved the thrill of the hunt."

She believed every word. In all the years she had known Balladyn, he had never said anything he didn't mean. The fact he was threatening her life told her he was well and truly a Dark One.

"War is coming, Balladyn. War with the Light and war with the Dragon Kings. Either way, I'll be fighting the Dark. Choose your side wisely. Don't make me kill you."

He smiled, but it didn't reach his red eyes. "Time for

words is over, Rhi, because the world as you know it is about to end."

She ducked just as he sent several blasts of magic to incapacitate her. With the last vestiges of her magic, she disappeared.

CHAPTER
THIRTY-FIVE

Denae wasn't sure if it was a rock or something else that sliced the bottom of her foot. She didn't say anything to Kellan or the others. What good would it have done? They needed to get out of the tunnels quickly, and she was still able to walk.

Phelan and Kellan stopped in front of her and knelt. Denae quickly followed suit only to have Kellan motion for her to remain as he and Phelan moved farther into the darkness.

"How badly are you bleeding?" Tristan whispered.

Denae sighed. Could she keep nothing from these men? "I'm all right."

"You're limping. It willna take Kellan long to notice that."

"I won't slow us down."

"Never said you would."

She glanced behind her, but she couldn't make out Tristan's face in the darkness. It felt weird being in the company of such men. Dragon Kings and Warriors.

They were protective in a way she had never experienced before. Unlike the mortal men who either thought she should know her place as a female or the ones who regarded her as an equal who could take care of herself, Kellan made her feel both shielded and capable.

He was archaic in his thinking of the fairer sex, but that hadn't stopped him from allowing her the ability to handle whatever came her way.

It was . . . refreshing and entirely too amazing. She leaned a shoulder against the tunnel wall and thought of Kellan. A Dragon King. A dragon and a King.

A gorgeous man who kissed as if there were no to-morrow and made love skillfully, adeptly. He could have let her die. Instead, he took her on a journey that opened her eyes to an entirely new world both beautiful and frightening.

How could she not want to know more about him?

How could she not crave to be in his arms?

How could she not fall for such a man?

Denae smothered a chuckle. Fall for Kellan. It was laughable. She hadn't just fallen for him, she'd tumbled, plunged headlong for all that was Kellan. Impulsively, recklessly.

She knew the type of man he was—honest, depend-able, and guarded. He hadn't wanted to like her, and she wasn't even sure if he did.

He'd enjoyed her body, and gave her pleasure unlike anything she'd thought was possible. But he was from an-other world that had no place for her in it. He protected only because he had given his word.

Once she was safe—well, she knew exactly where she would stand with him.

Not even knowing she would end up alone with only her memories could stop her heart from pitching headfirst into love.

A warm, large hand covered hers. Denae knew in-stantly it was Kellan.

"Ready?" he whispered.

She nodded, knowing he could see her.

"What is it?"

Denae scrunched up her face. "I want out of this place."

There was a beat of silence before he said, "Let's go."

She stood and again took hold of his belt loop. They walked for what seemed like hours, occasionally pausing to listen, while at other times they would run short distances.

Twice Kellan shoved her out of the way while he, Tristan, and Phelan fought whatever monster crossed their path. The tunnel had gotten so dark she could barely make out shapes, much less know what it was that they were fighting. And a part of her didn't want to know after seeing that giant moth.

All the while, she worried about Rhi. And she wasn't the only one. Phelan wasn't happy Rhi had yet to show up.

"She'll be fine," Kellan said. "Trust me."

"How do you know?" Phelan ground out.

Denae felt Kellan shrug. "I've known Rhi for a verra long time, Warrior. If any Fae is capable of outwitting a Dark One, it's Rhi. She isna in the Queen's Guard for nothing."

"Queen's Guard," Tristan repeated. "The Light queen needs a guard."

"Since the queen rarely leaves her palace, nay. It is more of an honorary position filled by the strongest, most lethal Light warriors, and Rhi earned her right to be there," Kellan explained.

"You didna see her at Dreagan," Phelan pointed out. "Tristan found her collapsed on the floor. She was pale and . . . weak."

Tristan mumbled, "Aye, she was."

Denae waited for Kellan's response, but seconds ticked by, making her think he wasn't going to give one.

"There is much you doona know of Rhi," he finally said.

"Who was the Dragon King she had an affair with?" Tristan asked.

They came to an instant stop, which caused Denae to run into Kellan's back. He didn't so much as tilt forward from the impact.

"Did the King leave her?" Phelan asked.

Deane realized his voice had gotten closer, and that meant he was most likely facing Kellan now.

"It was a long time ago," Kellan said.

"What happened?"

"Ask Rhi."

"I'm asking you."

"And I'm no' telling."

Denae rolled her eyes and moved around Kellan to stand between him and Phelan. She had to worm her way between them, and she gave Phelan a little shove so he had to step back. "Come on. It's not Kellan's story to tell. If you want to know, ask Rhi."

"Is it you?" Phelan asked Kellan as if he hadn't heard Denae.

"Nay. I wouldna say she was a friend, but she's the closest thing I have to a friend except for the other Kings," Kellan answered.

After a moment, Phelan turned and walked away. Denae was about to return to her spot behind Kellan when his hands fell on her shoulders and he turned her to face him.

"You thought to protect me from a Warrior?"

Was that a hint of laughter she heard in his voice? She hated that she couldn't see his face, but he could see every emotion that crossed hers. "Protect? As if. You're a Dragon King. I simply wanted to diffuse a situation that was quickly growing out of control. If you haven't noticed, Phelan is rather partial to Rhi. He thinks of her like a sister."

"I noticed," he said softly.

Denae swallowed, unsure of his gentle tone. His hands moved up her shoulders to her neck while his thumbs played with the edges of her lips.

Didn't he realize his touch was all it took to throw her off kilter? The tunnel, with all its horrid surprises and revolting smell, fell away. There was only Kellan.

"You would stand between a King and a Warrior?"

She was having a difficult time keeping her thoughts in line with his thumb tracing her lips. He closed the distance between them, and his heat surrounded her. Unable to resist, she rested her hands on his chest.

"No. Yes." She squeezed her eyes closed for a moment. "I don't know."

"Why?"

Why? What did he want to know again? He was so close she could rest her face on his shoulder. But it was his lips she wanted.

"Why would you stand between two immortals?" he asked.

Denae shrugged. "I didn't like him all up in your face."

"So you sought to protect me?"

When he said it like that, it sounded laughable. Denae parted her lips to tell him it wasn't like that at all when his mouth descended on hers in a fierce kiss.

He seized, he captured.

He dominated.

And she loved every second of it.

The kiss left her dazed and needy, and it ended entirely too soon. He kept his hands on either side of her face as if to keep her away. It was only then that she heard his harsh breaths.

"I want you," he whispered.

Denae smiled, because she knew that was as close to a profession of affection as she would ever get from Kellan.

And oddly, it was enough.

"Get me out of this tunnel and you can have me."

He snorted and dropped his hands. "Is that a promise?"

"You bet."

"I'll hold you to that," he said as he took her hand. "Tristan."

Denae heard the sound of footfalls and realized that Tristan had walked away sometime during their interaction, but she had been too preoccupied with Kellan to take notice.

Kellan was a dangerous distraction for sure. But one she was glad to have. He made life interesting and fun again. He made her want to embrace life and see where it would take her.

And none of that included running for the rest of her days from MI5.

She forgot all about her injured foot as they started hurrying through the tunnels. They came to fork after fork in the tunnel with Phelan softly calling out right or left each time.

And before Denae knew it, Kellan pulled her through the doorway.

She blinked against the bright sunlight and quickly raised her arm to shield her eyes. But Kellan kept her moving. Denae bit back a curse when her toe jabbed into a rock. Yet, it was the growing danger that kept her on her feet.

There was a small grove of trees that he brought her to and pushed her against one. "Phelan?"

"I doona see any of them," the Warrior answered, his gold skin shining in the sun.

Denae caught a glimpse of his fangs and wondered what else the Warrior could do. He was tall, his long, deep brown hair wild. His eyes, gold eyes from corner to corner, kept a constant look around them. His claws looked sharp enough to take her head, and she had the impression it was something he had done before.

Tristan looked at Kellan from his spot on their other side and shook his head. "No' yet."

"That gives us time to set up," Kellan said.

Phelan turned his gaze to Kellan. "We need a plan first."

"Plan?" Kellan chuckled, the sound icy. "The plan is to kill as many of them as we can while making sure Denae isna taken again."

"We're no' the only Kings in Ireland," Tristan suddenly said. He smiled widely. "Rhys and Kiril came looking for you."

"Call to them," Kellan said and then faced Denae. "It's going to be all right."

She grabbed ahold of him when he started to turn away. "It'll be all right when we're out of here. I just want one promise from you."

He seemed shocked she would ask for such a thing. "What promise?"

"That you don't let them take you again. No matter what."

His brow furrowed as his celadon eyes stared at her. "I doona give promises easily."

"I know."

"And if they take you?"

"Then they take me. This promise will trump your first one. You've gotten me out of there."

"But you are no' safe."

"I've never been safe, Kellan. Whether it's from the Fae, sickness, danger, or my enemies. Make me this promise. Please."

"Why?" he asked, all emotion erased from his face.

Denae could come up with some lie, but she wanted him to know the truth of how she felt. Even if it was for naught. "The thought of you in those chains again makes me ill. I don't know what they're searching for, but it can't be for anything good. You aren't meant to be a prisoner. You're powerful and incredible."

"You've no' seen me in dragon form."

"I don't have to. I see the man before me now."

CHAPTER
THIRTY-SIX

Kellan couldn't give Denae the promise she wanted, because he would do anything in order to keep her out of the Dark Fae's clutches.

The certainty, the irrefutable reality was that Denae was his. He should be surprised, but he wasn't. She had proven herself time and again. Yet, it was more than that.

There was a part of him that had recognized Denae as his the moment he opened his eyes and saw her in his cave. It was his hatred of humans that had kept him from acknowledging the truth as long as he had.

"Give me the promise," Denae urged again.

Kellan shook his head and tugged on her long, coppery brown hair. "I can no'."

"I'm just a human, remember?" she argued, her brow furrowed with frustration and a hint of worry. "I mean nothing."

He put his finger over her lips to silence her. "Doona ever say such things again. I can no' give you the promise you ask because you are yet unsafe. We might be out of those damn tunnels, but the Dark are about to attack. Anything can happen."

She gently moved his finger from her lips. "That's right. Anything can happen."

He looked for anything to change the subject and turn her mind away from the promise she sought. That's when he spotted the blood on the grass at her feet. "Are you injured?"

"It's just a cut on the bottom of my foot."

Fear, an emotion he hadn't experienced since he saw his Bronzes killed, swarmed him. A cut could kill a human. With the foul odors inside the tunnels, there was no telling what she had stepped on.

There was nothing he could do. For the first time he wished he had Con's power.

"It's just a cut," she said again. "I'm fine."

But the worry had already settled around him like a thick mist. He had just admitted to himself what she meant to him. To think that he might lose her . . . He couldn't even finish the thought.

As if sensing his worry, Denae said, "I've had worse, Kellan. Go kick some Dark Fae ass, then you can help me tend to my very minor wound."

Her saucy attitude made him smile. At least she had forgotten about the promise. He was still unsure about how minor the wound was, but she was a warrior. With a sigh, he relented. "With pleasure."

"What do I do?"

"Remain here. Phelan will be close, and hopefully Rhi as well. Tristan and I will keep the Dark occupied until Rhys and Kiril arrive."

She visibly swallowed and handed him the manacle they had taken from their prison. "I thought I had seen evil before, but I was wrong. The Dark Fae embodies evil in a way I didn't know existed."

"I'll wipe them from your mind." Kellan was already planning months alone with Denae, making love to her and learning everything there was about her.

Denae smiled then. "Go, since you won't give me my promise," she said and gave him a wink. "The others are waiting for you."

"They can bugger off," he said and jerked her against him for a quick, hard kiss.

As soon as she melted against him, Kellan was tempted to get her away and leave the others to the fight. Then he recalled how Taraeth had touched Denae.

His woman. Violated, tortured, all because the Dark searched for the one thing they couldn't have.

Kellan ended the kiss as his mind focused on killing one Dark Fae in particular.

"Good luck," Denae said before he turned on his heel and strode away.

Kellan stood beside Tristan as they opened their minds and called to any Dragon King nearby. If the Dark Fae wanted a war, they were going to get one.

Tristan jerked off his shirt and kicked off his boots. There was a smile of anticipation on his lips that Kellan understood all too well.

"You crave battle," he said.

Tristan chuckled. "In a way most wouldna understand."

"You just came to us, so doona get caught by those arses. I'd rather no' have Con in my face because you didna return to Dreagan."

"Ditto. Except it would be Denae in my face. Personally, I'd rather deal with Con than her."

Kellan grinned as he glanced at his woman. She was a force to be reckoned with. He took in a deep breath and felt the dragon within him stir, rouse.

He couldn't wait to feel the wind beneath him, to stretch his wings and soar upon the clouds. It had been so long. He wouldn't fly for pleasure, but a purpose a long time coming.

The Dark Fae had been a scourge upon the realms that had dared to travel to Earth. The mistake had been trusting that the Light Fae could keep the Dark in check and push them out of the realm of Earth.

With the Kings being intent to remain secret, the Light had stopped fighting the Dark.

And the Dark . . . they had grown into a powerful group.

Tristan glanced at him before he jerked off his jeans and leapt into the air, shifting into the form of an amber dragon as he did.

Kellan watched as Tristan's wings spread and caught on a current that propelled him up. There were few clouds to hide in, but then again, Kellan didn't plan on doing any hiding today.

He shifted his gaze to find Phelan concealed near Denae, his gaze focused on the doorway.

Denae had her whisky-colored eyes trained on him as he put the manacle over his wrist so it appeared as if it was still locked. The need to protect, to defend and secure what was his swallowed him like a tidal wave.

He didn't fight against the tide. He simply let it take him, accepting that somehow, someway a human had opened his eyes.

And taken his heart.

His gaze jerked to the doorway as Taraeth stepped through with his red eyes blazing.

"I figured you would've run," Taraeth said when he spotted Kellan in the field. "Do you miss your room already? Are you waiting for me to bring you back, perhaps?"

"I'm here to kill you," Kellan said.

"Kill?" Taraeth laughed as he looked around at his fellow Dark Fae that were steadily filling out around him. "You can try, but we all know our chains prevent a Dragon King from shifting. You're nothing but an immortal who can die over and over again at our leisure. Just as the last two Kings we had."

The Dark Ones laughed at Taraeth's words.

A pleased, confident look stole over Taraeth's face. "I'll

have you back in your prison with more chains added. Then, I'll find that pretty human of yours and take her repeatedly in front of you until she no longer remembers your name."

"You can try, but you willna succeed."

"And why is that?"

Kellan smiled just before he shifted.

He stood in the open field and roared his fury. His wings opened and flapped as a dozen Dark rushed him. The force of the air from his wings sent them tumbling back.

Just as they got to their feet Tristan suddenly appeared out of the sky and clamped his huge jaws around half of them. The other half tried to rush back to their comrades, but one swipe of Tristan's tail cut them in two.

"Kill them!" Taraeth bellowed.

Kellan kept his eyes on Taraeth even as he worried about Denae. The Dark Ones were too intent on him and Tristan. And Kellan was going to make sure they remained that way.

Kellan waited until the Dark were close before he jumped into the air only to swoop back down, his claws tearing through the Dark like a hot knife through butter.

He tucked his wings and spun before shooting up to the sky. As he did, he felt a blast of magic narrowly miss him.

It only made him angrier.

Rhi jumped to the field to discover a battle. She was glad she had remained veiled, especially with the Dark all around her.

She easily meandered through the thick throng of Dark Ones until she spotted Phelan in a grove of trees, his face a mask of fury for being kept out of the battle.

But that was because he was the last line of defense for Deane.

Rhi used her magic and appeared next to Phelan, dropping her veil as she did.

He glanced at her, his face still grim. "About bloody time. Where have you been?"

"Learning more than I wanted to."

His gaze jerked to her as he frowned. "Are you all right?"

"Yep." She plastered a bright smile on her face. "Remember, stud, I'm Fae."

"I'm just glad you're here. I was about to go back in that awful place to look for you."

She took in a deep breath. "Don't do anything stupid, stud. Aisley will skin you alive if you get yourself in trouble. How's Denae holding up?" she asked to change the subject.

"Pretty good. I heard her gasp when Kellan shifted, but she's not uttered a sound since then."

Rhi patted his shoulder before she turned and walked the short distance to where Denae stood against a forked tree with a base as wide as a small car.

"How ya holdin' up?" Rhi asked, using the best Southern accent she could muster.

Denae smiled as she glanced at her. "Close. You're too Southern and not enough Texas. I'll get you there though."

Rhi actually laughed. "I bet you will." She looked over to see the shape of a bronze dragon diving and soaring all around the Dark Ones. "Does he frighten you?"

"Yes. And exhilarates me. He twists me inside out, makes me forget my name, and turns my knees weak. He's simply . . . wonderful."

"Ugh," Rhi said and rolled her eyes. "Don't tell him that. Kellan is already conceited enough without him knowing you think of him as a god or something."

"I'm not stupid. I know I don't belong in his world."

Rhi couldn't look at her, because Denae spoke the truth. A few of the Kings might have found mates, but that was just a handful of them over thousands of millennia.

"Thanks for not trying to lie to me," Denae said.

Rhi looked down to find she had chipped another nail. She thought of Balladyn and the grief that had consumed her when she thought him killed.

The world as she'd known it for so long was already changing. There was a battle going on between the Dark Fae and Dragon Kings that hadn't happened in over fifty thousand years.

"You're part of this world now," Rhi said to Denae. "Whether you want it or not, you are. You've seen things, heard things, experienced things that no amount of time will erase. Do you think you can walk away and forget?"

Denae's eyes followed Kellan for several seconds before she looked at Rhi. "No. Never. I'll always remember."

"I don't know what the Dark have planned, but whatever it is isn't good. There has always been a line drawn between our world and yours. That line is fading fast."

"Can't you and the Light Fae do something?"

Rhi shrugged helplessly. "I'm not sure anymore. We've always had a difficult time battling the Dark, but they are different now. More powerful, almost."

"Has that happened before?"

"No. I don't believe in coincidences, and there've been too many recently. The Dark Ones' power growing, MI5's association with them, and someone trying to expose the Dragon Kings."

"I agree," Denae said and took a deep breath. "I suspect if we dug deep enough we would find one source connecting all three."

"It sounds like you want that job."

"I do have a history with MI5. With Henry helping me and getting me back inside headquarters, there's no end to what I might find."

"And the rest?" Rhi prompted.

"You mean the Dark Fae and the unknown person?"

Rhi nodded, her eyes tracking the Dark who were focused

on the Dragon Kings. "Con suspects the unknown person trying to expose them is Ulrik."

"Kellan told me of him. He certainly has motive to want to harm Con, but the rest?" Denae asked, her lips twisted. "I don't know enough about him."

"I don't think Ulrik would. He vowed revenge on Con, but only Con. It's been thousands upon thousands of years though. Ulrik's rage might have turned him insane."

"Then I'll look into him as well," Denae stated. "As for the Dark Fae, I figure I've got an ally who can help me there."

"Who?" Rhi asked with a frown.

"You."

Rhi slowly smiled. "Oh, you're good. It's no wonder Kellan fancies you."

"Get ready," Phelan said, growling low in his throat as two Dark Fae approached the grove.

Rhi walked past him. "Oh, let me," she told him.

She sent a blast of magic that beheaded one Dark Fae as she spun out of the trees and whipped out a long blade that pierced the heart of the second, ending his life instantly.

"I want one of those," Deane said in awe.

CHAPTER
THIRTY-SEVEN

Rhi wiped off the blade and held it by her side. "Kellan might not like it, but I think you're going to need a weapon."

Denae couldn't wait to get her hands on such a weapon. It wasn't in her to stand on the sidelines and watch. She had extensive training, and though she might not be immortal or able to do magic, she could take off a Dark Fae's head or pierce their heart.

The more she thought about leaving this new world she'd found, the more she knew she didn't want to. She might not be able to have Kellan, but she wouldn't walk away from the war that was obviously already here.

Denae would do her part and learn who was after the Dragon Kings. She would find why MI5 aligned themselves with the Dark. She would ferret out anyone and everyone who posed a threat to the Kings.

And she would stop them.

She now had a mission, something to fill her life, and she couldn't wait to get started.

"Kellan will never allow her to have such a weapon," Phelan said to Rhi.

Denae narrowed her eyes at the Warrior. "I make my own decisions, thank you very much."

"Good luck with that," he said with a snort. Then his gaze looked past them and grew hard.

Denae saw the Dark Ones getting closer and closer to the trees again. The two dead Fae had caught their attention.

Phelan didn't say a word as he shoved Rhi aside and used his incredible speed to kill four more Dark Fae.

Rhi let out a string of curses. She tossed her sword at Denae before she grabbed the two dead Dark by their hair and disappeared, them along with her.

Denae swung the sword around her, getting used to the weight of it. With her training and the sword, she could hold her own against the Dark.

A moment later Rhi reappeared and smiled as she saw Denae ready to fight. "Yep. Just what you needed," the Fae said with a wink as she caught hold of two more Dark and vanished again.

Denae was surprised at the lightness of the sword. The blade was narrow as it curved ever so slightly toward the end. The pommel was made of a dark wood with gold knot work etched into it. The blade itself had . . . a dragon.

Denae's heart missed a beat. A dragon that stood on its hind legs, wings outstretched with its head thrown back in a roar. Was it coincidence that Rhi had had a Dragon King lover and also had a dragon on her sword? It was an effective weapon, and one she would master.

In no time Rhi had removed the dead Fae and Phelan was once more within the copse of trees with them. It was obvious he wanted to be in the thick of things. She hated that he was there because of her.

"Go," she urged him. "Rhi is here, and I've got the sword."

Phelan grunted. "I gave Kellan my word, and I doona break my word. I'd kill anyone who vowed to protect my woman then left her undefended."

"I'm not unde—" she started, but Rhi stopped her with a hand on her arm. Denae rolled her eyes. She wasn't helpless. She wasn't.

Well, not entirely, not now that she had Rhi's sword.

Phelan raised a dark brow at her. "You know he's doing all this for you, do you no'?"

Denae looked through the thick tree limbs to the sky in search of Kellan, but he was impossible to see. "You're wrong. He's doing this because they took him prisoner."

"I hate to say it," Rhi said with a sigh, "but Phelan's right. Kellan could've taken you away as soon as you came through the doorway. The Kings would've returned en masse and decimated the Dark Ones."

"Instead, he remains. I gather something bad happened while you both were held," Phelan asked, his gaze never leaving the battle as he squatted in front of them.

Denae licked her lips and shifted from one foot to the other as she tried not to recall what Taraeth had done. "It could've been worse."

"The fact something happened at all is the point," Phelan continued. "No one touches my woman and gets away with it."

Denae opened her mouth to talk when she caught sight of the long bronze body of Kellan as he flew down the middle of the Dark Fae, scattering and killing as many as he could. Right behind him was Tristan who killed more. All the while both dodging magic thrown from the Dark.

Suddenly there were two other roars, distinctly dragons. Denae craned her head to see a yellow dragon and a burnt orange dragon.

"They're beautiful, aren't they?" Rhi asked.

Denae looked at her as she heard the longing in Rhi's voice. "Who was he?"

Rhi cut her eyes to her and replied innocently, "I don't know what you're talking about."

Denae let her lie. It was Rhi's right to keep that part of

herself secret and hidden. She nodded to the Light Fae. "They are beautiful and deadly and breathtaking."

"Yes. They most certainly are."

Denae glanced down at Phelan to find him watching Rhi intently before his gaze turned to her. There was a bond between the Warrior and Rhi, one of a brother and sister, which made Denae miss her own sister even more.

She put her hand on a tree, the bark biting into her palm, as Taraeth threw a bubble of magic at Kellan. He was as agile as a hawk in the way he avoided the first and second shots. The third hit him in one of his wings.

Denae's heart jumped into her throat as Kellan fell from the sky to land upon the earth, the impact shaking the ground beneath her feet.

The yellow dragon landed in front of Kellan's still form and breathed fire at any Dark who drew near. His fire managed to eradicate any magic hurled at them.

"Well," Rhi said with a soft whistle. "That's something I've not seen before."

Denae started toward Kellan only to have Phelan hold her back.

"Nay, lass," he said softly. "If you go to him now, everything the Kings have done today will be for naught as the Dark Fae will focus on you."

Denae realized that even though Kellan might have wanted a fight because Taraeth touched her, he participated in the battle to keep the Darks' attention off her.

She turned to Rhi. "Can you get me out of here?"

Rhi's silver eyes turned to her as she slowly shook her head. "I used too much of my magic today staying veiled and then carting off the Dark Ones so you could remain hidden."

Damn. That wasn't what she wanted to hear.

"He's not moving," Denae told Phelan as she stared at Kellan.

The Warrior's hold refused to loosen. "The only thing that can kill him is another Dragon King. There's no need to worry, lass."

As if waiting for Phelan's words, Kellan stirred and lifted his head before his dragon form got to his feet and stood side by side with the yellow one.

The amber dragon dropped out of the sky to stand beside Kellan, and the burnt orange dragon flew down to stand beside the yellow one.

The sight of all four dragons, their bodies immense, their scales shining in the sun, was surreal. She got her first good look at Kellan, and she was duly impressed.

His metallic bronze scales were the same vivid shade on his back as they were on his stomach. They gleamed as if polished, the sunlight winking off the scales.

His white eyes were like beams of light they were so pale in his large head. Two large horns extended backward from his forehead. What looked like a spiky membrane ran from the base of his skull down his back to the tip of his long tail.

He was stunning and terrifying all at the same time. And she couldn't get enough of him.

"There is bad blood between humans and Kings," Rhi said from Denae's other side.

Denae glanced at the Light Fae, wondering when she had moved.

"Kellan's hatred runs deep. Or maybe not anymore," Rhi said with a kind smile as she looked at Denae. "Tell him what you think of him in dragon form. It's important to them."

"And you know this how?" Phelan asked.

Rhi tucked a strand of black hair behind her ear. "Keep asking, stud. You might get an answer someday."

Denae took a step back farther into the grove of trees, and this time Phelan released his hold. She leaned against a tree with the sword still held in her right hand while she watched the four Dragon Kings being pelted with magic from the dwindling forces of Taraeth's army.

Oddly, Denae couldn't find Taraeth anywhere on the battlefield. She started to push away from the tree when a hand clamped over her mouth.

"Make a sound and I'll slit your throat were you stand," Taraeth whispered in her ear with his Irish accent.

Denae's heart pounded against her ribs like a drum. Fear, soul-gripping, heart-stopping fear, made her blood run like ice in her veins. Taraeth had her. Again.

She promised herself never to have such fear consume her again, and yet here she was. Denae had allowed herself to believe that she would never be in a Dark Fae's clutches again. As if tromping through the monster-infested, foul-smelling tunnels to get free wasn't enough.

"You're going to come with me," he said.

She shook her head as much as she could with his hand over her mouth and the tree behind her.

"If you want me to allow Kellan to live, you will."

Denae nearly laughed out loud. Taraeth made a mistake in threatening Kellan because of two things: Kellan was immortal, only to be killed by another Dragon King . . . and she had Rhi's sword.

Whatever distress and anxiety she had from being held by the Dark leader evaporated into nothing. He was just another asshole with a god complex. And she had the means to stop him as she had so many others.

She gave a quick nod of acceptance.

"I knew you were a smart girl. I'll make you happy, little human. Just you wait and see. I'm going to take my hand away. Not a sound, remember."

He waited for her to nod again.

Then he continued, "We'll go back through the doorway. All your troubles with MI5 will cease. There'll be nothing to worry your pretty head about. I'll take it all away."

Denae's eyes were on Kellan, praying he didn't look her way, as she slumped weakly against the tree. She had a good plan.

"Exactly," Taraeth whispered happily. "No more fighting the inevitable. Even had you made it away today, I'd have found you again. You're too tempting of a morsel, little human."

He slowly pulled his hand away from her mouth, and when she didn't make a sound, Taraeth reached for her. Denae whirled around, bringing the sword up to clutch it with both hands.

The world stilled, going into slow motion as she witnessed Taraeth's red eyes go wide as he spotted the sword. Denae swung the sword down in an arc, intending to take Taraeth's head so he would never bother her again.

In her anger, she forgot about his magic, so never saw it coming at her, hitting her in the chest. The pain was debilitating. The fingers of her left hand loosened on the sword, and Denae fought to keep the weapon in her right hand even as she felt herself pitching forward.

She squinted as the rays of the sun hit against an amulet Taraeth wore right into her eyes, blinding her for a moment.

Taraeth turned his body away as he raised his arm. The last of Denae's strength left her as her knees buckled. But she brought the sword down and saw it connect with Taraeth's arm.

As soon as the blade went through his arm, the world around her returned to normal in a deafening rush. She heard her name shouted behind her, and all she could think about was Kellan and how she'd failed to kill Taraeth.

Denae watched the sword fall from her grip and Taraeth vanish before her eyes. She pitched forward only to be caught in arms she knew all too well.

"I've got you," Kellan whispered.

She blinked up at him, but couldn't form any words.

"The pain will pass. Just breathe," he said as his arms tightened.

"That was a killing blow of magic," Rhi said. "She should be dead. That's the second time I've seen Denae do something no human should be able to."

Denae didn't care as long as she survived. With each beat of her heart she was feeling better. Kellan's big hand pushed aside her hair so he could see her face.

His pale green eyes held a wealth of worry. "I doona know how you did it, but you cut off Taraeth's arm."

"Just his arm?" Denae asked. "I was trying for his head."

CHAPTER
THIRTY-EIGHT

Kellan couldn't make himself let go of Denae. Even as the yacht Guy and Laith had driven to Cork cut its way through the Irish Sea back to Scotland.

Thunder rumbled over the roar of the motor and a second later, an impressive display of lightning lit the sky. The storms were a great way for the Kings to fly unnoticed, but for once Kellan wasn't thinking of taking flight.

He was thinking of the female in his arms.

"She's not going anywhere, you know?" Phelan said as he reclined on a chair with his arms spread along the back.

Kellan glanced at the Warrior opposite him, noting his irritated expression that hadn't softened since Rhi had refused to return with them. "Denae could've died with the magic Taraeth used against her."

"But she didna. Just as, for some reason, she didna succumb to the Dark Ones while you were being held. Just as she somehow helped break you from the magical chains."

Kellan squeezed Denae harder. She hadn't woken since she had fallen unconscious. He'd already searched her for any injuries, but there had been nothing. That was the only thing keeping him calm.

"She's special," Kellan finally said.

Phelan turned blue-gray eyes to him. "Everyone can see she means something to you."

"I didna want her to."

"That's normally how it works. I wasna prepared for Aisley, or the way I couldna stop thinking about her. I was obsessed with having her, holding her. I didna relent until she was mine."

Kellan merely nodded, because he understood all too well what Phelan was talking about. It was just one of the reasons he wasn't able to put Denae down on the couch next to him, or even in one of the many rooms on the yacht. He had to hold her against him, to feel her breath fanning him.

"What's going to happen once you return to Dreagan?"

Kellan shrugged. "I've no' thought that far ahead. I'm still trying to process all that's happened. What about you? What are you going to do now that you know Tristan is the twin to one of your friends?"

Phelan's gaze instantly swung to the narrow doorway leading out to the deck of the boat and Tristan, who stood at the railing with his back to them. "He says he has no memories of being Duncan."

"I doona believe he lies."

"Nor do I. It's just . . . it's hard. I never met Duncan, but I've fought alongside Ian. I heard the stories of Duncan and Ian while Deirdre held them in Cairn Toul Mountain. I know Ian. I know that Tristan is his twin."

"He just doesna have Duncan's memories."

"That'll kill Ian," Phelan said as he frowned and turned his head to Kellan. "Ian was lost after Duncan died. He'll be overjoyed to know Duncan is alive."

"But is he?" Kellan asked. "None of us can remember the last time a Dragon King was made. I doona know how Tristan became a King, but I do know that he is now ours. There might be a good reason all of his memories of his former life as Duncan Kerr have been wiped."

"So what do I tell Ian?"

"Perhaps nothing."

Phelan gave a quick shake of his head. "With the way the Kings and Warriors interact, how long do you think it'll be before Ian sees Tristan?"

"No' long."

"Precisely. Ian has to know."

Kellan liked Tristan. A lot. It wasn't just that he was a Dragon King. Tristan had proven himself as someone Kellan could trust. He would do whatever Tristan wanted regarding Ian. If Tristan didn't want to see his brother from another life, then Kellan would make sure Ian didn't interfere.

"We'll protect Tristan."

Phelan raised a dark brow, an eager light in his eyes. "And we'll back Ian."

"This should be interesting."

"Aye."

The boat began to slow, the motor no longer as loud as before. Rain pelted the top of the yacht. The ferocity of the rain proved that it was going to be a long storm.

Kellan didn't stand until the boat was docked and tied off. Before he could take the first step onto the deck, Con blocked the doorway, his blond hair dripping with water and his dark red dress shirt plastered to his chest.

"Is she all right?" Con asked as he nodded to Denae.

"She will be."

Con's black gaze shifted briefly to Phelan before he gave a slight nod and walked to stand next to Tristan in the rain.

"Why do I get the feeling he isna happy you've brought Denae back?" Phelan asked.

Kellan flattened his lips. He had gotten the same vibe from Con, and it didn't sit well at all. "I doona give a rat's arse what he thinks. I make my own decisions."

"Even living at Dreagan? I get the feeling Con makes the rules."

Kellan snorted. "He tries. We all tell him to go bugger himself if we doona agree."

"As would I."

Kellan stepped in front of Phelan before he could walk out. "Con is a good man. He'll have your back if you ever need it."

"Aye, I know."

"But he'll also turn on you quicker than you can blink if he feels it's justified."

Phelan's brow furrowed. "Can you give me an example?"

"Ulrik."

"I've heard that name before. He doesna happen to be the King of Silvers, does he?"

"Aye. How did you guess that?"

Phelan paused long enough for Kellan to know that Con had let something slip. Anger filled Kellan. "What did Con tell you about Ulrik?"

"He didna say Ulrik's name. He asked if we knew anything about a shop in Perth called The Silver Dragon."

"Shite," Kellan said and glanced down at Denae in his arms. "Be forewarned, Warrior, when it comes to Ulrik, the Kings have always been divided. We united the first time to stop the war with the humans, but if there was a choice now, none of you would want to be in the middle of that war."

"Point taken. As much as I want to hear more, I want to get back to Aisley. And I know you want to get Denae out of this weather."

Phelan was the first onto the deck. When Kellan turned to step outside he found Tristan already walking down the dock, mindless of the rain.

Guy laid a trench coat over Denae, making sure to cover her head. As Kellan followed Guy off the boat, he spotted Phelan running down the dock in the opposite direction from Tristan.

It wasn't until Kellan was in the Mercedes G-Class with Guy behind the wheel and Con in the front passenger seat that Tristan climbed into the backseat with him.

"She's still unconscious?" Guy asked.

Kellan nodded as he removed the coat. "Aye."

"I thought you said nothing was wrong with her," Con said as he shifted to look in the backseat.

Tristan crossed his ankle over a knee and slowly turned his head to Con. "She was hit with magic while wielding Rhi's sword and trying to take off a Dark Fae's head. She deserves to sleep as long as she needs."

Con looked from Tristan to Kellan. "You expect me to believe Denae survived Dark Fae magic?"

"I doona give a shite what you believe," Kellan said. "It's what happened when Taraeth tried to take her again."

"Taraeth." Con's frown grew. "Humans can no' survive the Dark Fae."

Kellan ignored Con. "Let's go, Guy."

There was a beat of silence before Guy started the engine, a smile on his face.

Not once did anyone mention Rhys or Kiril. Both had opted to return to Dreagan as dragons rather than by boat. Kellan had told Tristan to do the same, but the King of Ambers had refused.

It was obvious Con wasn't happy. Whether it was from the fact some Kings had gone to Ireland to look for him, that they had battled the Dark without waiting on Con, or that Denae was returning to Dreagan, Kellan didn't know nor care.

Everything had changed for the Dragon Kings the moment they sent their dragons away. The same rules that had governed the Kings for hundreds of thousands of years no longer applied.

They needed to find their own way, and it was only with

the hope that one day the dragons would be returned as well as keeping the Silvers contained that they remained together.

If it wasn't for the Silvers, Kellan fully believed the Kings would have scattered, not just across the earth, but across the realms.

Con kept the hope alive regarding their dragons, but Kellan knew the truth. Their dragons would never return. The humans were too many. There was no place for dragons on earth, and he was beginning to wonder if there was even a place for Dragon Kings.

Earth had been theirs for millions of years before humans came. The realm was supposed to have been shared, but that had gone to shit in a short time.

The pride of being a Dragon King no longer remained. They were hidden, the secret of their shifting kept tightly guarded. No one knew of their powers or immortality.

Not that he blamed Con and the others for the decisions they had made regarding Dreagan. The humans had always been too easy to riot, too effortless to frighten, and too dense to think for themselves.

They had a pack mentality that was too easy to put into play by a few humans who could rile them into a frenzy and get them to do whatever they wanted.

Even now, with all the technology and paranormal things being found and investigated, the humans wouldn't accept that there were Dragon Kings. They wouldn't accept one of the Warriors either.

The humans claimed to want to find beings with paranormal abilities, but it was just a statement. Some would run away screaming in fear, some would try to kill them, and still others would try and capture a Dragon King so they could "study" him. Which everyone knew meant dissecting.

Now Kellan comprehended there would be a few, a

very select few, like Denae, Cassie, Elena, and Jane who would accept the Dragon Kings for who they were.

He looked down at Denae to find her cheek resting against his shoulder. Kellan gently tucked her long, coppery brown hair behind her ear.

In the short time he had known her, she'd been stabbed, shot, accosted by the Dark Fae, and belted with a large amount of Dark Fae magic.

She'd taken it all without so much as a grumble. Denae was a trained fighter, with an intelligent, cunning mind. She was easy to smile, quick-witted, and deft with retorts from her sharp tongue.

Her body was amazingly taut, with all the wonderful, feminine curves he'd always enjoyed. She had the most stunning hair, and eyes that held him transfixed from the first moment he'd dared to look into the whisky-colored depths.

The question of what would happen once they reached Dreagan wouldn't be difficult to answer. He wanted Denae to remain. Kellan might not be ready to offer her forever, but he wasn't ready for her to leave yet.

He had the perfect argument as well. MI5 was still looking for her, and after cutting off Taraeth's arm, the Dark Ones would also be after her.

There was no safer place than on Dreagan.

Kellan was confident he could convince Denae to stay, and if words didn't work, he was prepared to use his hands, mouth, and body to change her mind.

Just thinking of sliding into her tight body again had him hard and aching.

He released a pent-up breath and raised his gaze to find Tristan watching him with a slight smile. Tristan gave him a nod of approval and turned to look out the window at the passing scenery.

Kellan ran a hand through his wet hair and began

planning the night ahead with Denae. It would be one without interruptions of any kind, one he vowed she would remember for the rest of her life.

Just as he knew he would.

CHAPTER
THIRTY-NINE

Rhi didn't go to her queen when the Kings departed Ireland. Instead, she went to her cottage. As soon as she entered the small house, she fell face-first onto the bed of black-and-pink lace and let the tears come that she had been holding back.

Tears for Balladyn, but also tears for herself.

She hadn't realized how difficult it would be to be around the Kings and not think of . . . *him.* Of their time together, and the wild love that had developed.

How many centuries had it been since she had last felt his arms around her?

How many since she had tasted his lips?

How many since she had felt cherished?

Loved?

Too damn many.

Rhi rolled onto her back but didn't bother to wipe the tears that now trailed into her hair by her temples. It was odd. She thought she was past the tears, but just being around the Kings seemed to trigger the past—no matter how she tried to bury it.

And Balladyn. She couldn't wrap her mind around the

fact he was now Dark. Her queen was going to be devastated. Not nearly as much as she was, however.

Balladyn had always been a part of her life, even when she was just a young girl. He'd been her brother's best friend and always around.

Then the Fae Wars had begun. Rhi could still recall standing with her mother as her father, her brother, and Balladyn gave one last wave as they headed off to war.

Balladyn was the only one to return.

Her mother had succumbed to grief a short time later, leaving Rhi all alone in the world. Balladyn had become her family, her mentor, and her friend. He'd helped her hold it all together, and in turn she'd helped him cope with the wars and coming home when her family hadn't.

Balladyn was there when her relationship with her Dragon King was put to the ultimate test. He was there to hold her as she cried until there were no more tears. He was there to comfort her when the world no longer made sense.

He was there when she'd wanted it all to end.

Balladyn had forced her to live again. She'd fought him every step of the way, and in turn, he'd pushed her harder. Until one day, she took that first step out into the world again.

It was no wonder that everyone thought she would die of grief when, during a skirmish with the Dark, she saw Balladyn fall.

She had wanted to retrieve his body, but the Dark Fae were too many. One of her greatest regrets was leaving him. Now she knew he hadn't died. He had been wounded. Had she only gone to get him he wouldn't be Dark now.

Rhi cringed when she felt the pull of her queen, a sign that Usaeil was calling her to court. Rhi rolled onto her side and curled up into a ball with her arms wrapped around her middle.

She wasn't ready to face anyone yet, not after enduring the Kings as well as being at Dreagan, which brought back too many long-buried memories.

She suddenly sat up and dashed away her tears. If she wallowed in the memories any longer they would take her. She would allow it one day, but not today.

"Not yet," she murmured.

Rhi stripped out of her dirty clothes and riffled through bags from designer shops until she found an outfit she wanted. She tore off the tags and put on the faded skinny jeans and black blouson shirt.

She grabbed her two bottles of nail polish: a lavender named Do you Lilac It?, and a deep eggplant color called Vant to Bite My Neck? She dropped them in her Louis Vuitton purse and teleported to a storage unit. She flipped on the lights and gazed at the Lamborghini she had wrapped in black cherry matte.

She might be a Light Fae, but there were times she liked to pretend to be human. It wasn't like she could just teleport into her favorite salon and not have someone notice in such a crowded place.

Sure she could teleport somewhere else and remain veiled until she knew no one was about, but it was just too damn much trouble.

Rhi started the Lambo and grinned at the rumbling, gritty sound of the engine. She gunned the engine, her smile deepening the louder the engine roared in the cramped unit.

"Damn, but I love this car."

She used her magic to unlock the garage door and roll it up. After putting the car in gear, she backed out of her spot, shutting and locking the unit door with magic once more, and drove out of the parking garage and into the crowded streets of Austin.

There wasn't anywhere in the realm of earth that she hadn't visited. There was something about the nail salon she'd found in the swanky Lake Travis area of Texas that fit her vibe. Which is why she kept returning.

Besides, walking in and being so welcomed by the girls, especially her nail tech, Jessie, could wipe away the bad memories she didn't—couldn't—face.

Rhi shut the door to her memories involving *him,* and let the Lambo's engine purr as she pulled into traffic.

Denae noticed the softness of the sheets first. Kellan had gotten them back to Dreagan. She'd never doubted he would. She opened her eyes, hoping to find him in the room, but she was disappointed.

She threw her arm over her eyes. Returning to Dreagan meant facing her future. How easy it had been to forget when she was trapped in Ireland with the Dark Ones.

No doubt MI5 had already cleared out her loft and put all of her belongings into storage somewhere she would never find. It was all right. The things that meant anything to her were safely ensconced back on South Padre Island.

Denae sighed and sat up. Her muscles were sore, but she didn't feel any lasting effects from Taraeth's blast of magic. She threw off the blanket and looked down to find she was still in Kellan's shirt. Despite all she had been through while wearing it, she could still smell him on it.

She took it off and neatly folded it only to hide it behind a pillow in the overstuffed chair. That way when she left Dreagan, she would bring a part of Kellan with her.

Denae walked into the bathroom and turned on the shower until the water was steaming hot. Her mother used to laugh at her, not understanding how it could be nearly a hundred degrees outside but she always had to take a hot shower.

As soon as she stepped into the shower and the water fell over her, Denae let out a sigh. She tilted her head back to wet her hair as she closed her eyes. For several minutes she stood there, enjoying the heat of the water before she washed her hair and body.

She was rinsing the last of the conditioner from her hair when she was hauled up against the shower wall by a muscular form. Kellan didn't give her time to acknowledge him before he was kissing her. He kiss was deep and thorough, calling her passion and desire easily.

Her body melted against his. She was insatiable when it came to him. He had woken a shameless wanton with his skilled touch and ravenous kisses.

His hands were suddenly everywhere, touching every part of her until she didn't know where he ended and she began. With greedy hands she touched his steely muscles and warm flesh. His moan of pleasure only inflamed her own desires.

"You were no' in the bed," he said between kisses down her neck.

"You weren't in the room when I woke."

"We doona need a bed."

She shook her head and then gasped as he bent and closed his lips around her nipple before suckling. "No, no bed ne . . . needed."

"Do you like that?" he asked, his voice husky from desire.

Her voice would no longer work. Denae simply nodded her head.

He began to kiss down her stomach, and she hastily pulled him back up for a kiss. She knew if she let him have his way with her it would be hours before she could think straight again, and she wanted her fun with him this time.

Denae shoved him back until he was against the wall, a teasing light in his celadon eyes. "What's this?"

"This," she said as she ran her hands down his chest until she wound a hand around his engorged rod, "is my turn."

His fingers flexed on her arms, but he didn't stop her.

Instead, he watched her, the hunger growing in his gaze until her knees nearly buckled from the passion running through her.

Denae knelt before him with the water beating upon her back. She looked at his impressive arousal, running both hands along his length. Then she looked up at him and slowly wrapped her lips around the head of his cock.

As she took him into her mouth, he let out a long, low moan. Denae squeezed her legs together and sucked him deeper, moving her head so he slid in and out of her mouth.

She had barely gotten into a rhythm before he had her on her feet and against the wall. He hooked an arm beneath her knee and filled her with one thrust.

"Your sweet mouth was about to make me come, and I needed to be inside you," he said with heaving breaths.

Whatever words Denae was going to say were lost as he began to move inside her. She clung to him, her nails digging into his shoulders as her head dropped back.

There was a hurried and frantic feel to their lovemaking. He swept her on a tide of unending, frenzied passion that took her breath and thought.

With each thrust he went deeper, harder. Try as she might to deny it, Denae felt the strings of their bond growing thicker, tighter.

It frightened her, this draw he had, and when she tried to pull away, he pinched her nipple, reminding her that she was his—even if it was just for the moment.

Denae couldn't deny him, not even when her heart was in jeopardy. She opened her body and her heart to him— whatever the consequences.

His fingers dug into her hips as he pounded inside her, the water slicing between them. The climax came with no warning, it was wild and intense, made only more so as Kellan continued to plunge inside her.

Denae was hanging onto Kellan, wondering how he

could remain standing. Her body hummed with satisfaction, but she should've known he would want more from her.

He withdrew and positioned her so that she was leaning forward with her ass in the air. He came up behind her and filled her.

Denae moaned, her hands spread on the wet glass as she rocked forward with every thrust. The feel of his balls grazing her thighs sent a flood of desire straight to her already sensitive sex.

Then he reached around and cupped her breasts, teasing and massaging her nipples. As if on cue, her body responded to his touch.

Her second orgasm was coming closer, her body on fire once more. One of Kellan's hands then found her clit. With one swirl of his finger, she was tumbling into another climax, this one stronger than the first.

She screamed his name, just as he gave a bellow and thrust deep and gave in to his orgasm.

For a long time they stayed as they were. Any minute the world would intrude, but each precious second was theirs. Kellan kissed the back of her neck and slowly pulled out of her.

Denae straightened and turned as he grabbed the soap and began to wash her. Laughter filled the bathroom as they washed each other, stopping for long kisses and teasing touches.

It was during one scorching kiss that a series of loud bangs could be heard from the bedroom door. A beat later someone shouted for Kellan.

He pulled back, a slight frown marring his features. "I have to go."

"I know," she said and made sure he accepted her forced and shaking smile. She wanted him to walk away without knowing that she was falling completely apart.

She waited, her heart in her throat, for him to say they

needed to talk, or even to ask her to stay awhile. Instead, he turned off the shower and handed her a towel.

Denae held the towel against her as he walked from the shower and into the bedroom.

Just as she knew in her heart he was walking out of her life.

CHAPTER
FORTY

Phelan walked into the cottage he shared with Aisley to find her sitting in the living room sharing a drink with Laura and Charon.

All three heads turned to him when he entered through the door. Charon, a fellow Warrior and a close friend, immediately frowned. Aisley was on her feet and walking to Phelan before the door shut behind him.

He welcomed her loving arms as she wrapped them around him. Phelan held her tightly, burying his head in her neck.

"You're home now," Aisley whispered.

They didn't keep secrets from each other. She knew why he had gone to Dreagan, and he had kept her as up to date on things as he could. What he hadn't wanted to tell her until he returned home was that Tristan was Duncan.

Such a secret weighed heavily upon him, and Phelan knew that as soon as he shared it with her, things were going to change for all the Warriors and Druids, but most especially those living in and around MacLeod Castle.

Aisley pulled back and ran her hands over his face, her worried gaze searching his. "You look like you could use a drink."

"Two or three, in fact," he said. He kissed her, reveling in the fact such a woman was really his.

She wasn't just a Druid, she was a Phoenix—able to regenerate after death with fire. Phelan had lost her once and thought he'd have to live the rest of his immortal life without her. But when they burned her body, she had returned to him. It was how everyone, including Aisley, learned of the rare heritage passed through her family.

At least when he ended the kiss and she pulled out of his arms, Aisley was smiling. With her in his life he could face anything—even something as awful as what was coming.

"We were getting a bit worried," Laura said as she greeted him.

Phelan smiled at the wife of his best friend and fellow Warrior, Charon. "I want a shower to scrub the stink of the Dark Fae off me, but not yet. There are things everyone needs to know."

"That sounds ominous," Charon said with a frown after they clasped hands and he resumed his seat on the sofa opposite Phelan. "I thought you were just going to Dreagan to chat with Con and the others."

Phelan looked at Aisley in the kitchen, who gave a shrug.

"I didn't know how long you would be, or what would happen," she explained. "Had I told Charon everything, he'd have been at Dreagan himself demanding to be standing alongside you."

Charon's frown deepened as he looked from Aisley to Phelan. "I'm getting pissed. What the bloody hell are you two talking about?"

Laura put her hand atop Charon's. "It looks like Phelan has gotten himself involved in something."

"I think you're right," he answered, continuing his hard stare at Phelan. "And I've got a feeling the Kings didna bother to mention how deep the shite was before Phelan stepped in it."

Aisley sank beside Phelan on the sofa and handed him the opened bottle of ale. He drank down three huge gulps before he set the bottle on the table between the sofas and met Charon's gaze. "I knew the shite was deep when I agreed. I wasna fooled into helping out."

Charon took in a deep breath and slowly let it out. "How bad is it?"

"Potentially devastating."

Phelan went on to tell them about Denae, MI5's involvement with the Dark, Denae and Kellan being taken by the Dark Ones, and Rhi helping to locate the Dragon King and human in Ireland. He described the Fae doorways, how the Dark Fae had taken over an abandoned manor and somehow opened the Fae world beneath with tunnels, and how Phelan and Tristan helped to get Kellan and Denae out of the tunnels.

He drained the last of his ale as he told of the battle and how the Kings, along with Denae, got back to Scotland.

"The Fae opened their world up into ours?" Aisley asked, her voice shaking.

Phelan took her hand in his. "No' yet. Rhi and the Kings are worried it might come to that. For now, it's confined to the tunnels beneath the manor."

"How bad is it?" Charon asked.

"Bad. Verra bad," Phelan said. "The creatures we encountered are huge and vicious. If the Fae world bleeds into ours, the humans willna know what to do."

Laura's intelligent eyes met his. "Are the Light Fae doing anything about the Dark? Or are they joined in this together?"

"This was all the Dark," Phelan said. "Rhi was right there beside us battling them. There wasn't much said, but I know the Kings are suspicious of the Dark Fae's alliance with MI5."

"And just who put that alliance into motion," Aisley guessed.

Phelan grinned. His wife had spent enough time in the midst of her evil cousin to know how villains thought. "They suspect it's Ulrik."

"That name again," Laura said with a shake of her head. "I have a feeling he's the one who came into the bar months ago. He looked lost, haunted. I wouldn't peg him to be evil."

"But evil has many faces," Charon said. "We learned that well enough."

Laura tucked her legs beneath her and twisted her lips in a grimace. "Truer words haven't been spoken."

"So," Aisley said. "Where does that leave things?"

Phelan leaned back and regarded the three people around him. They were his family. For centuries the Warriors had battled *droughs,* or evil Druids. Aisley's cousin, Jason, had been the last to be killed.

It would be easy to tell the Dragon Kings to fight their own battles. How many centuries had passed before the Kings had deigned to tell the Warriors of their existence? Not once did the Kings step in and help during the Warriors' war.

Not until it appeared that the war was bleeding into the humans' lives.

Just as things were about to now.

Phelan blew out a harsh breath. "The Kings are powerful. I saw just what kind of damage they can do to the Dark. I also saw how the Dark Ones could inhibit the Kings, all but preventing them from shifting into dragon form."

"Fuck," Charon mumbled.

Phelan couldn't have said it better. "I think we need to be ready in case they do call upon us for anything."

"I agree," Aisley stated.

Laura and Charon nodded together.

Phelan licked his lips. That was one burden off his shoulders. He would have to repeat it all again at MacLeod Castle for the other twelve Warriors and their Druid wives.

"There's something else," Aisley was quick to say.

Phelan ran a hand through his hair. "What I'm about to tell you three must remain between us for the time being. I'm no' sure what to do or how telling the others will impact things."

Charon finished off the last of his Dreagan whisky and set down the glass on the coffee table. "Well, you've certainly got my attention. What kind of secret did you learn?" he asked with a smile.

Phelan couldn't share that smile, not when he knew the chaos that was about to ensue.

"Just tell us. The anticipation is killing me," Aisley said with a grimace.

"I met a Dragon King today called Tristan."

Laura raised a brow. "All right. What is it about him that has you worried?"

Aisley's eyes widened as she realized what he was about to impart to the others.

Phelan cleared his throat. "As many times as we four have been to Dreagan, can you remember meeting him?"

Charon chuckled. "Every time we're there more Kings are around. I can no' keep up with them all. But the name doesna ring a bell."

"I don't either," Laura said. "Most of the Kings not mated tend to stay away from the manor."

It was as he'd expected. Some would be suspicious that Con had made sure to keep Tristan away from the Warriors. And they would be right.

"Do any of you recall seeing an amber dragon?"

"Yes," Aisley immediately answered. "Several times in the battles we had with Jason."

Charon's smile slipped a little. "I do as well."

"Count me as one who's seen him," Laura said.

Now came the hard part. Phelan wasn't sure how they would react. In hindsight, he could have handled things with Tristan better than he had.

"Phelan," Charon said in a low, dangerous voice.

He lifted his gaze to his closest friend to find the smile completely gone. Phelan swallowed, his throat tight. "There's a reason none of you have seen Tristan before. Aisley and I saw him this last time at Dreagan, but it was by accident."

"Why do you say accident?" Laura asked.

Aisley reached for Phelan's hand and said, "Because if you had, after one look you'd know who he is—or was."

"And that would be . . . ?" Charon urged.

Phelan let the silence stretch for several seconds before he said, "Duncan."

His revelation shocked the room into a silence that was deafening. Phelan suspected his face had been as incredulous as Charon's was now.

"Are you sure?" Laura asked.

Phelan lifted Aisley's hand to his lips, kissing the back of her hand. "Aye. I might never have met Duncan, but there's no denying he's Ian's identical twin."

"I don't understand," Laura said. "How is it that Duncan was a Warrior and killed, and then became a Dragon King?"

Phelan shrugged. "No' even the Kings can explain it. Apparently, there have been no new Kings for ages."

"And Duncan, I mean Tristan?" Laura asked. "Does he know he's Ian's brother?"

Phelan had known this question was coming, but even that didn't make forming the answer any easier. "Nay. Tristan claims he has no memories of a time before he woke at Dreagan after falling from the sky."

It didn't go unnoticed by Phelan that Charon had yet to utter a single sound. His friend was sitting still as stone, his face pale from shock.

Laura glanced at Charon and cleared her throat before she looked at Phelan. "I gather Con wasn't happy you saw Tristan."

"That's putting it mildly. But the Kings asked for my help with the Fae. It wasna until I arrived that we learned Kellan and Denae had been taken by the Dark. Then Rhi arrived so weak from being veiled for an extended time that she could barely sit up straight. That's when Tristan came in."

"Is Rhi all right now?" Aisley asked worriedly.

A special bond had formed between Aisley and Rhi, one Phelan encouraged. Rhi had not only helped him accept his Fae half, but she was also teaching Aisley about the Fae.

"She was the last time I saw her."

Charon suddenly stood. "I need to go for a walk."

Phelan and Aisley watched him stalk from the house, Laura quickly following.

"I knew he wouldna take the news well," Phelan said.

Aisley shifted until she was sitting on the edge of the sofa, her body facing him. "Now that we're alone you can tell me what it is about Rhi you're trying to keep from me."

"Beauty—" he began, but she quickly cut him off with a palm in the air.

"Don't even try it. Rhi is like a sister to me as well. Tell me what you know."

Phelan pulled Aisley into his arms until her back was resting against his chest. He wrapped his arms around her and set his chin atop her head. "Nothing more than we've already learned about her having an affair with a Dragon King. Things didna go . . . well for Rhi and the King."

"Anything more you've learned that makes you think the affair was with Con?"

"Nay. Kellan knows something, but he willna say. I doubt it's Con, beauty. They hate each other."

"There's a thin line between love and hate."

Phelan decided then and there that he would broach the subject with Rhi the next time he saw her. Hopefully, she'd be more willing to share information than any of the Dragon Kings had been.

CHAPTER
FORTY-ONE

Kellan stalked into Con's office, surprised to find it was just the two of them.

"I've shocked you. No' something that happens often," Con said as he screwed the cap onto his pen and set it aside before leaning back in his chair.

Kellan wasn't fooled by Con's laid-back attitude. "What was so important that it couldna wait until morning?"

"Denae."

Kellan's hackles instantly rose. It was Con's tone, the one he used when he thought he could order the rest of the Kings around. It hadn't worked in the past, and it sure as hell wasn't going to work now.

"She's no' your concern."

"I disagree. She's in my home."

Kellan held his breath for two heartbeats, the time it took him to rein in his fury. He didn't quite manage it, but it was enough that he was able to talk instead of wanting to beat Con's face in.

"Your home?" Kellan asked faintly. "I seem to recall putting as much blood and sweat into designing and building this place as any of the other Kings. This isna *your* home, Con. It's ours."

"I'm leader here—"

"That can change quick enough," Kellan said over him.

In all the years he had been King of the Bronzes, Kellan had been content to rule his dragons. But he knew that he—and any of the other Kings—had the right to challenge Con and rule.

At any time.

Con's black eyes hardened as he lifted his chin. "Is that a challenge?"

"That depends on your next words. I've stood behind you even when I didna agree with you. You're treading a fine line."

"I'm doing what I think is best."

"For you?" Kellan snorted. "You've always done what was best for you. When have you thought about any of us?"

"Every damn day!" Con bellowed as he came out of his chair to lean on his desk.

Kellan bit back a smile. It wasn't every day that someone managed to rile Con. Matter of fact, the King of Kings was known for his control. "Did I hit a nerve?"

A muscle ticked in Con's jaw as he straightened and ran a hand over his hair to make sure no strand was out of place. When he spoke again, he was once more calm and collected. "If Denae remains, MI5 will continue to come after us."

"They doona have to know she's here." Kellan had already thought about every argument Con could up with, and he had an answer for each of them as well.

"They'll know." Con resumed his seat and put his elbows on the arms of his leather chair before steepling his fingers. "MI5 is a thorn in our sides. As much as they can disrupt our lives, it's the Dark I'm more concerned with. She cut off Taraeth's arm."

Kellan leaned back against the door and folded his arms over his chest. "If any of us had done that, you would be patting us on the back. A mortal, one who had been touched and tortured by the Dark, does it and she's a liability. Odd that your mantra of 'protect the humans at all costs' doesna come into play now."

When Con merely glared at him, Kellan continued. "You convinced us to send our dragons to another realm so the humans could live. You stripped your best friend and rival of his powers to save the humans. When it comes to you, Con, you'll do whatever it takes to secure what you want."

"Are you saying I'm happy I had to do that to Ulrik?" Con asked with a heavy chill to his words.

"I'm saying you didna mind it. I'm saying you didna hesitate. I'm saying you saw an opportunity and took it."

"You know nothing," Con said between clenched teeth.

Kellan smirked as he dropped his hands and pushed away from the door. "I record the history of the Kings, remember? I know it all."

The conversation was interrupted by a knock on the door and Kellan's name said through the wood.

"This is over. Denae will stay as long as she wants. And if you force her away, I'll go with her."

"You can no'," Con said, a hint of surprise on his face.

Kellan put every ounce of anger into his words as he said, "Watch me."

He turned and yanked open the door to find Tristan. Kellan walked out of the office, not bothering to close the door behind him as he and Tristan walked away.

"What is it?" he asked the new King after they were some distance from Con's office.

"Rhys and Kiril have no' returned."

Kellan stopped and glanced down the hallway to Con's office. "Why no' tell Con?"

"Because Con didna want them to go to begin with. Banan is on his way back after dropping off Henry, and Guy is just staring at the Silvers."

The Silvers. Kellan hadn't gone to see the dragons since

he'd awoken. It was too hard to look at the magnificent creatures and not long to free them, to see them take to the skies with their roars—regardless that it would mean the end of the humans.

They were dragons, the essence of who the Kings were. The Silvers were the last link to the dragons the Kings had sent away so long ago.

"Leave Guy for now. He needs to be alone," Kellan said. "Where is Hal?"

"With Cassie dealing with some distributor issue in the Dreagan offices. I didna bother him. Laith, Ryder, and the others are busy as well." Tristan's dark eyes were ever watchful, catching every look, every gesture a person made.

Kellan motioned to Tristan and they began walking again. "Rhys and Kiril should've returned by now. Have you tried to call to them using your Dragon Voice?"

"Aye."

"Let's give it another try before we go looking for them." It was Kellan's worry about his friends that kept him from returning to Denae, but when he did get back to his room, he and Denae were going to have a long talk about the future.

What he was going to say he hadn't yet figured out. All he knew was that he wanted her with him.

Denae turned off the blow dryer to the sound of the bedroom door opening. "Con," she said when she looked out of the bathroom.

"I was wondering if we could talk."

She was immediately put on the defensive. Had Kellan sent Con? No. That wasn't like Kellan at all. He would take care of his own business, no matter how nasty it might turn out.

"About what?" she asked as she tucked her still-damp hair behind her ears.

"The girls found you clothes, I see."

She glanced down at the jeans and vintage Dr Pepper tee. "Yep. What do you want to talk about?"

"What are your plans?"

It wasn't like she could tell Con she'd been hoping she and Kellan would have this conversation first, or that she desperately wanted to stay with Kellan.

Instead, she told him what she'd already decided on. "I'm going to contact Henry and see about sneaking into MI5 so I can determine who made the union with the Dark Fae. Then, I'm going to erase myself from their database."

"Really?" Con asked with a raised blond brow.

"Really." The part about her finding out who was after the Dragon Kings was none of his business. She wasn't doing that for him. She was doing it for Kellan and their time together.

"I may have misjudged you, Denae."

She rolled her eyes. "I'm sure you have. Now, ask me what you really want to know."

"And what would that be?"

"When am I leaving?"

He stared at her quietly for several seconds before his wide lips softened into some semblance of a grin. "Is there somewhere I can drive you?"

Denae was glad he couldn't hear the frantic, anxiety-filled beat of her heart. It was costing her everything to leave. But there was work to be done, work only she could do.

For the Dragon Kings.

For the world as she knew it.

For . . . Kellan.

"I'm better on my own," she said. "Don't worry. I'll be outta here shortly. Oh, and one more thing. Are you going to wipe my mind like you first planned?"

Con took a deep breath and slowly released it. "If we did, the Dark would find you, and you would have no way of defending yourself."

"So, you're going to take the chance that I don't tell the world that you are Dragon Kings?" She knew she was pushing it, but she had to be sure.

"I am. I know you care for Kellan. If you let our secret out, you put him in danger."

She crossed her arms over her chest and studied Con. "That, I would never do. Now that you know, I won't have to tell you."

"Good luck to you, then." With a nod, he left with the door shutting softly behind him.

"Wow," she mumbled to herself as she dropped her arms. "Not even an offer to call if I need anything. You can be such as asshat, Con."

It was easy for Denae to focus her anger on Con. It was better than wallowing in self-pity because she was leaving Kellan. It wasn't as if he had asked her to stay, and that was only part of the reason she was barely holding onto her emotions.

She probably should've enlisted Con's help in getting out of the manor without running into Kellan. Or maybe that's exactly why Kellan had left her alone, to give her time to leave so he wouldn't have to run into her.

Denae sat on the edge of the chair and put on her hiking boots. MI5 had trained her well. She was resourceful and well equipped to get across the world with just the clothes on her back if she had to. Getting to London and MI5 head-quarters would be a cinch.

She stood and gave the room one more once-over. When she turned to the door, she spotted Rhi leaning against it staring at her nails that were polished a deep purple with lavender accents.

"Going somewhere?" Rhi asked and flicked her head so that her long hair slid from her shoulder onto her back.

Denae shrugged. "You look better."

"I just needed some downtime after using so much of my magic."

Denae knew enough about Rhi now to know the Light Fae hadn't just shown up. "How much did you hear of my conversation with Con?"

Rhi sighed dramatically and lowered her arm as she faced Denae. "I arrived while you were drying your hair. You didn't see me, and when Con showed up I didn't see a reason to alert him that I was around."

"Why did you come?"

A pang of sadness entered her silver eyes. "I wanted to see how you were. It was an incredibly brave and stupid thing you did going after Taraeth."

"He wanted to kidnap me," Denae said and shrugged. "He didn't give me any options."

"Oh, don't get me wrong," Rhi said with wide eyes. "I'm not at all upset the bastard is now missing an arm. He deserves that and so much more. It was stupid, Denae, because he'll hunt you through eternity now."

Denae sank into the chair and dropped her head into her hands. "Great. MI5 and Dark Fae. Anyone else want to hunt me?"

"If you leave without talking to Kellan, you can add him to the list."

Denae lifted her head and peered at Rhi. "How well do you know Kellan?"

"Better than any Fae, and in some instances better than some of the Kings. Why?"

"If he wanted me to stay, would he have asked?"

Rhi nodded. "Has he told you anything?"

"No. But I know with the Dark Fae and MI5 hunting me that if I remain here, it'll continue to put the Dragon Kings under a microscope until MI5 has a reason to invade as they want to."

"So you want to leave to protect him?"

"I don't want to leave. But I have to."

Rhi smiled brightly, her eyes twinkling. "I can help."

"You could get me out of here without Kellan seeing me?"

"I can take you anywhere you want to go. Even another realm if that's what you want."

Denae considered that for a moment. All of her family was gone. She didn't have any friends. Her only real connection was Kellan, and he was an immortal Dragon King.

"Maybe. First, I want to wipe any record of me from MI5 so I can forget about them. I want to make them think they're going crazy."

"Oh, girl. I can so help with that," Rhi said with a laugh. "Forget sneaking into MI5. I can take you exactly where you want to go in that building."

Denae smiled for the first time in hours. "I need the server room first. It's in the basement with multiple cameras and a half-dozen guards patrolling the hallway."

"So easy," Rhi said with a roll of her eyes. "Are you ready?"

Denae took Rhi's offered hand. "Yes."

CHAPTER
FORTY-TWO

Kellan spent the next thirty minutes walking the mountains trying to reach Rhys and Kiril by using their mental link. A great relief went through him when both Kings finally answered.

"Should Kiril still be in Ireland?" Tristan asked, having heard the answers through the link.

Kellan shrugged. "He's his own King. He can do whatever he wants. Kiril is tempting fate being so close to the Dark Fae, but maybe that's what he wants. You'd have to ask him to know for sure. Still, I agree that having a spy in Ireland is a good idea."

"What about Rhys?"

Kellan looked out over the mountains surrounding Dreagan. "Sixty thousand acres sounds like a lot of area to get lost in, but when you're a Dragon King and you can only be yourself on this land, it can feel as small as the tiniest island. Sometimes we need to be alone, surrounded by just the land and the air."

Tristan rubbed his jaw, the scrape of days' old whiskers drowned out by the whistle of the wind and the call of a golden eagle. "What do we do now? I doona like waiting for the Dark to make the next move."

"All the Kings know war is at our doorstep. We've been down this road so many times we all know our places."

"No' all," Tristan said softly.

Kellan clapped the King on the back and smiled. "Doona worry about your place. You've cemented your right to be here. Even had you no', the fact you have the tat on you, the sword, and can shift into dragon would be enough. You may no' know all of our history, but that doesna matter when defending our home."

"And what about my . . . life before?"

"You mean the fact you were a Warrior?"

Tristan gave a barely discernible nod.

"It just proves you know what loyalty and family are," Kellan said. "It also means you know battle."

"Ian, my supposed twin, is going to want to talk to me."

"Aye. It might be good for you to sit down with him."

"And tell him what?" Tristan said angrily. "That I recall nothing of him or my past? That I didna even know he existed until Phelan told me?"

"Maybe. Whatever you decide to tell him will be your decision. Ian lost a brother. Even if you doona remember your previous life, you could still find him to be a good friend. Twins have a bond only other twins truly understand. Was that bond broken when you became a King? I can no' answer that. Only meeting and talking with Ian will give you that answer."

Tristan's brows were furrowed as he looked down into a valley filled with sheep. "I'll think on it."

"Good. Let's return to the manor. I want to check on Denae. I've been gone awhile."

They started back down the mountain together. "What's going to happen to her?" Tristan asked.

"If she wants to live, she'll need to stay at Dreagan."

"Con doesna want that, does he?"

Kellan glanced at him and grunted. "For someone new to the Kings, you pick up things easily."

"I study people. It isna difficult to know their true feelings just by watching them. Take you holding Denae on the way back from Ireland. There were plenty of places you could've put her down, but you didna want to let go of her. You care for her, more than you even comprehend yet."

Kellan wasn't keen on how easily Tristan read him, but it might come in handy. "And Denae? What did you see about her?"

"She cares a great deal for you, but she doesna feel as if she belongs here. To her, you are a myth come to life. She fights her feelings for you, as if . . ."

When Tristan didn't keep talking, Kellan stopped and faced him. Unease rippled down his spine. "Finish."

Tristan looked away, and when his gaze returned to Kellan, he didn't hide his sorrow. "It's as if she's been silently saying good-bye."

Kellan stood there for a moment, Tristan's words like warning bells in his head. He turned on his heel and ran the rest of the way back to the manor. Even when he busted through the kitchen door, surprising Jane so she dropped her teacup, the relentless need to hold Denae in his arms didn't lessen.

He bounded up the stairs and ran down the hallway to his room. Kellan threw open the door, fully expecting to find Denae sitting there waiting for him.

But the room was empty.

Kellan didn't need to search the house or the grounds. He knew in his gut she was gone. How stupid of him to think she would wait around for him. That wasn't Denae.

She was used to being her own woman, making her own decisions. She was deadly in hand-to-hand combat, intelligent, and intuitive.

Even as something broke apart in his chest, fury raged. He knew who was responsible for Denae leaving. He'd warned Con. Now it was time to carry through with the threat.

Kellan turned and shoved past Tristan who had finally caught up. There was no time for talking. It was time for action. Kellan didn't slow until he stood in his cave once more.

His gaze went to where he first saw Denae. It seemed like a lifetime ago. She fit him as no one else had ever done. She understood him.

And he recognized her for what she was—his mate.

He might not have wanted to admit it, but he'd known. From the first, he'd known.

Like a fool he had fought it and tried to keep her at arm's length. When that hadn't worked, he still pretended as if it was just a dalliance, when it was so much more than that.

"Denae," he whispered, his chest aching where his heart was.

He would track her down. He would hold her once more, and then he would tell her what was in his heart.

But first, he would take his revenge out on Con.

Kellan walked to the back of his cave and put his hand against a small rock protruding from the wall. With a slight push of his dragon magic and a drop of his blood, small pebbles and dust rained around him.

The sound of rock sliding over rock filled the cave as a panel opened to reveal his sword. He reached for the leather-wrapped hilt, fit for single-handed combat.

Kellan pulled it from its hiding place. Some Kings liked to display their swords, but not him, not after what Con had done to Ulrik.

With an admiring eye, Kellan rested the straight blade on his left palm. Vines and leaves were engraved in the shoulder of the sword in a deep bronze before winding their way down the blade and mingling with a dragon.

It was a beautiful and deadly blade.

One made for the purpose of killing a Dragon King.

Kellan was prepared to take Con on in dragon form, but he would have his sword there as well.

The only way for a Dragon King to be killed is by another Dragon King in dragon form or with their swords. Kellan had both bases covered.

Sword in hand, he walked with long, sure strides to the manor.

Denae couldn't believe how easy Rhi made things. She had gotten Denae inside the server room in a blink, all the while deactivating the cameras.

"Get to work," Rhi said and disappeared again.

It wasn't until Denae got to the wall where the hidden keyboard and monitor were that she wondered if they had disabled her fingerprint recognition.

"Here goes nothing," she mumbled as she put her hand against the white glowing screen.

Green rays popped up and scrolled down her hand, and then back up before going side to side. Five pulsing circles appeared around each tip of her fingers. A moment later, there was a soft hiss as the silver panel in the wall moved and a large, flat-screen computer appeared.

There was a second hiss as another panel opened and the keyboard slid out.

"Well, I guess that answered that question. I suppose they figured I'd never get past security. That was their first mistake."

Denae's fingers flew over the keyboard, pulling up all her files—every report she'd filled out, every mission she'd ever been on, every mention of her name—and erased it all.

She replaced her name with another female name of an up-and-coming agent and made sure there was nothing MI5 could ever find of her again in their files.

It took her deleting everything three times, and then

ejecting the server disk to destroy later just to make sure. She held the small disk in her hand and marveled at how something so small could save—or destroy—her life.

"Ready?" Rhi asked as she appeared beside her.

"I am."

"That's all of it?" she asked, looking skeptically at the disk.

"Yep."

Rhi gave her a droll look. "Don't they have backups of their backups? Something done remotely in case someone decided to do exactly what you did?"

Denae palmed her head. "Damn. I forgot about them."

"How many are there?"

"Two that I know of."

Rhi nodded. "Who would know the locations?"

"Henry should. But my boss, Frank, for sure."

Rhi suddenly laughed. "I've not had this much fun in ages. I think it's time we screwed with Frank's head for a bit."

Before Rhi could zap them out of there, Denae jerked away. "Why hasn't anyone come in after the cameras were frozen?"

"Duh," Rhi said and held out her arms and pointed at herself. "I'm Fae. My magic can do wonderful, dangerous things."

Denae might be dying inside from leaving Kellan, but she wore a smile at the idea of getting back at the people who'd tried to kill her. "Let's find Frank."

Within five minutes they were in an executive office, the cameras once more frozen, and Frank sitting with a look of utter bewilderment and fear.

"Where are the remote locations for the backups of the server?" Denae asked.

Frank refused to look at her.

Rhi smiled and sat on the edge of his desk, one long, jean-clad leg crossed over the other. She put her hands next to her and leaned forward until their faces were inches apart. "Answer her."

"Never."

Rhi sighed. "Look, dickwad, I'm only going to say this once. Answer us and we leave you with a bit of sanity left in the pea-sized brain of yours. Force me to pull it out, and I'll make sure you're in a padded room for the rest of your life. And then I'll come to torment you just for the hell of it."

"As if you could," he said derisively.

Denae busted out laughing when, with a wave of her hand, Rhi had Frank hanging upside down in midair.

"All right, all right!" he screamed. "Just put me down."

Denae was ready with pen and paper as he gave her the locations and passwords to get in.

"Now, that wasn't so hard, was it?" Rhi asked him sweetly. "You should've thought twice about trying to kill Denae, but more than that, you made the worst decision of your life to mix with the Dark Fae."

Frank's eyes widened. "Ar . . . ar . . . are you a . . . a . . . a . . ."

Rhi dramatically rolled her eyes. "No, I'm a Light Fae. I don't take kindly to humans messing where they don't belong. And that means you. So, now that we have the locations, it's time to wipe your memory of anything to do with Denae."

"Wait!" he yelled.

But it was too late.

Denae waited a second before she stepped next to Rhi, who had her hand on Frank's forehead. "What if he lied about the locations, or left one out?"

"Already thought of that. I'm searching his mind now," Rhi said, her eyes closed and her face lined in concentration. A few minutes later she shook her head. "He told us the truth. Now, I'll just wipe his mind of your image and name, replacing it with the agent you used below."

"Will it really screw him up?"

Rhi opened her eyes and met Denae's gaze. "No. But I can. I'm willing, if that's what you want. He ordered you killed. And he's involved with the Dark. Not to mention he wants to know about the Dragon Kings."

"I do want to hurt him, but I won't. Let him live with his replaced memories. His comeuppance will arrive soon enough."

Rhi dropped her hand and moved around the desk. "Our next stop is Brazil. Rio is beautiful," she said right before they disappeared out of the office.

CHAPTER
FORTY-THREE

Kellan found Con in the mountain joined to the manor, the same mountain where the Silvers were imprisoned and kept sleeping.

He could hear the arguing coming from a back cavern as soon as he entered the mountain. Rhys's and Con's voices were the loudest of them all.

Kellan stalked into the cavern unseen, with everyone's eyes focused in the center of the room where Rhys and Con were nose to nose arguing. Kellan set aside his sword and stepped into the crowd of Dragon Kings.

Instantly, they parted, giving him a clear path to Con. Rhys spotted him, and there must have been something in his face, because Rhys took a step back from Con.

"You can no' just forget to check in," Con said to Rhys. "We have responsibilities here."

Rhys glowered with rage. "You're no' my father. Nor are you my keeper. I do my duties without having you keep tabs on me."

"The Dark could've captured you as they did Kellan. I couldna leave two Kings in their hold."

"But you could leave one?" Rhys asked, his face a mix of outrage and confusion.

Con's chest puffed out as he took a deep breath, his mint-green dress shirt constricting with the movement. "That's no' what I meant, and you know it."

Kellan was almost to them at this point. He didn't stop, didn't say a word as he approached and slammed his fist into Con's jaw.

Con, the hit unseen, staggered to the side. He touched his busted lip and slowly straightened before his head turned to Kellan. "Your rage is out of control."

The blow and pleasure at seeing Con bloodied only fueled his anger. "You have no idea. I warned you to stay out of my life. I told you I wouldna stand by and have you interfere, and you decided to ignore my threat."

He didn't give Con time to respond as he threw a left punch to Con's kidneys and ducked Con's wicked right aimed at his temple. Kellan straightened, and turned slightly to throw back his elbow twice into Con's nose. Blood spewed everywhere as the sound of crunching bone echoed in the cavern.

A broken bone wasn't going to keep Con down. He launched an attack at Kellan with fists swinging quick and deadly. Kellan managed to block some and duck another, but the rest landed just where Con wanted them.

Denae dusted off her hands and surveyed her handiwork. She and Rhi had made quick work of Rio before Rhi teleported them to Papua New Guinea.

"All done?" Rhi asked as she sauntered into the computer room.

"All done. I'm officially erased from MI5." Denae felt the tension ease out of her shoulders. "I'd never have been able to do this without your help."

Rhi rolled her eyes. "Oh, puh-leeze. You'd so have done it. It would've taken you longer, but you'd have made sure of it."

"Maybe."

"Maybe nothing. You've got skills, girl," Rhi said with a smile. That smile quickly turned into a wince.

"What is it?"

Rhi flicked her long black hair over her shoulder. "My queen has been calling me for some time. She's . . . well, she's pissed now and letting me know it. I've got to go, Denae, but before I do, I'll take you anywhere you want to go."

She wasn't ready to be alone. Without something to focus on, all she would think about would be Kellan. It would be so easy to have Rhi whisk her to some tropical island for some serious R&R, or even to another realm.

But in the end, nothing would change.

Her heart would still ache for Kellan, her body would still long for his touch.

There was only one place a person who was hurting as much as she was wanted to go.

"Home. I want to go to home."

Rhi's smile was kind and understanding. "Home it is then."

With one touch of Rhi's hand, Denae stood on the front lawn of her house on South Padre Island. She turned to thank Rhi, but the Fae was gone.

Leaving Denae with her past and her present threatening to swallow her whole.

Kellan lost count of the times he'd been hit. He also lost count of how many times he'd bloodied Con. Each time he managed it, it made his smile grow.

But that didn't put him any closer to getting Denae back. It was a start though.

He leveled a punishing hit in Con's abdomen, doubling him over before Kellan lifted his knee to slam it into Con's face. Kellan was getting ready to do it again when Con's arms wrapped around his middle and propelled him backward—right into the cavern wall.

Kellan bellowed in pain as something pierced his back.

He pounded both fists into Con's back as Con threw his right hook again and again into Kellan's side.

They were unceremoniously ripped apart. Guy had ahold of Con while Rhys grabbed Kellan. Between them was Banan who looked angrily from Con to Kellan.

"What the hell is going on?" Banan demanded.

Rhys released Kellan and shrugged. "Kellan wanted a fight. Who was I to stop him?"

Kellan was tired of talking. He wanted action. He wanted justice.

He wanted Denae.

Kellan shoved Banan out of the way and rammed his shoulder into Con's gut before Guy could release him. And they were back to beating the shit out of each other.

"Why?" Con rasped.

"You sent her away." Kellan finished the comment with an uppercut to Con's jaw.

Rhi appeared in the cavern sitting atop one large boulder, which gave her a great view of the fight between Kellan and Con. Her audience with her queen had been quick—a rarity to be sure. She was surprised to find Kellan involved in a brawl.

"I think I know who you want to win," Tristan said as he leaned against the boulder.

Rhi snorted. "You think so? You know me so well, Dragon?"

"You detest Con."

It was a fact. She shrugged. "I guess that does tip the scales in Kellan's favor."

"What are you doing here, Rhi?" Banan asked as he too walked up.

She would rather be back in her queen's chambers getting her ass chewed up one side and down the other than be in the midst of so many Dragon Kings on Dreagan. But Usaeil had given her a direct order.

Rhi couldn't exactly ignore it.

"What are they fighting over?" she asked instead.

Tristan cut her a look. "Do you really need to ask?"

"Denae," she said with a nod. "Con wanted her gone."

Neither King responded to her comment. What was there to say?

"He shouldn't have pushed Kellan," she said.

Banan sighed loudly. "Nay. I've already tried to break them apart once. I doona think this will end until one of them is dead."

"Kellan challenged Con?" she asked in shock. Her stomach had fallen to her feet in dread.

Tristan drummed on the boulder with his fingers. "No' exactly. He never outright challenged him."

"Did he bring his sword?"

Banan's face was grim as he motioned with his chin to a wall near the entrance where the sword rested. "Tristan told me what happened. Con overstepped. He didna do such a thing to me, Hal, or Guy. Why would he do it to Kellan?"

"Because he's a turd," she said, feeling a sense of dread she couldn't dispel.

"If someone doesna stop this, one of them will die," Banan said. "We lost so many Kings during the war when we were taking sides with Con or Ulrik. We doona have our dragons anymore, Rhi. We can no' lose any more Kings, not with a war coming with the Dark."

She knew he was right, but her hatred for Con was clouding her judgment. She could announce herself, which would most likely halt the fight—for a time at least.

But Con . . .

"Set aside your loathing this once," Banan said. "For Kellan, because I think you know where Denae is."

She pulled her gaze away from the bloody fight to Banan and stared into his eyes. "I do this for Kellan and Denae."

"Agreed."

Rhi swung her head to the other side and stared at Tristan until he gave a nod. "Of course. This conversation will go no further than the three of us."

She winked at the handsome King. "I like you, Tristan. Do me a favor and don't turn into an asswipe."

"I'll try my best," he said and winked in return.

Rhi swallowed and took a breath before she cleared her throat. Instantly, Con's black eyes jerked in her direction. He frowned, and with his attention diverted, he didn't see Kellan's fist coming.

She didn't bother to hide her smile as Con was knocked on his arse. Rhi began to clap loudly, the sound piercing in the cavern that had grown suddenly silent.

Kellan was leaning to the side as blood and sweat covered his face. His long hair blocked a portion of his face, and his clothes were torn and bloodied. With as fast as the Kings healed, neither of them sported any wounds.

"Well done, Kellan," she said and let out a loud whistle.

"Rhi," Banan whispered crossly.

She leaned to the left so he could hear her whispered words. "I said I'd do it for Kellan and Denae. I didn't say I was going to be nice about it."

Kellan's head swiveled to her and his celadon eyes narrowed. "Rhi."

That one word contained everything within Kellan. His fury, his worry, his sadness, his . . . hope.

Tears pricked her eyes. She remembered that feeling of hope. It had gotten her through so much. Up until it had been squelched out—emphatically and vigorously.

She remained atop the boulder as Kellan hurried to her. Con was close behind as he jumped to his feet.

"What are you doing here?" Con demanded before Kellan could talk.

"Go bugger yourself. Idjit," she said with a roll of her eyes.

Con's frowned deepened in confusion as he reached her. "What?"

Rhi ignored him and focused on Kellan. She wanted to tell him everything, but most needed to be said in private. His affection for Denae had grown into something amazing and wonderful. It didn't need to be sullied by Con.

She looked over Kellan's head to the other Kings in the cavern. "I'm here because my queen sent me. She is readying her army to fight the Dark. My queen wants the Dragon Kings to know that the Light Fae won't stand by and watch the Dark destroy this world."

"Well. That's good to know," Con said with a hint of sarcasm.

"The Kings need to be on alert," Kellan said to his brethren. "The Dark want one of us, and they will do anything they can to trap us."

Guy ran a hand down his face. "We need more intel. What we really need is a spy."

"Already in place," Rhys stated and then broke into a wide smile. "Why do you think Kiril remained behind in Ireland?"

Banan pushed away from the boulder. "I'll contact Henry again. We can also use the computers to track movement around the globe and alert us to anything odd."

"Which could be numerous," Tristan said. "Let's get started on that now."

As the Kings began to file out of the cavern, Rhi waited, hoping Con would also leave. She should've known better. In no time she was left alone with Kellan and Con.

"Why are you still here?" Con demanded.

She kept her focus on Kellan. "Denae is fine. I helped her erase any evidence that she was ever involved in MI5. They have no record of her, no picture, nothing. And I then wiped her boss's mind as well."

"Others will remember her," Con said.

Rhi shrugged as she glanced at him. "They'll think

they made her up or are remembering wrong. MI5, as an intelligence organization, keeps everything on computer records. To cut down on paper, all the reports are done electronically and stored on their servers."

"And you say she got it all?" Kellan asked.

"Everything in London. Then we had to go to their remote locations and destroy evidence there as well. Denae is quick, resourceful, and smart. MI5 made a wrong move wanting to get rid of her."

Kellan let his chin drop to his chest. Out of the corner of her eye, Rhi saw Con watching him. She wondered what was going through the King of Kings' mind. Did he realize how very much Kellan loved Denae?

Did he even care?

When Kellan lifted his head, some of the wildness had left his gaze. "Do you know where she is?"

"I do."

"Take me there."

Con reached out and grasped his shoulder. "Kellan—"

"Nay," Kellan said and jerked away. "I am still prepared to challenge you, Con. At this moment, I'm focused on Denae. If you want me to fight you to the death, I will. Just say the word."

"I didna send her away," Con said.

Rhi lifted a brow. "Didn't you? You went to her, asking her what she was going to do. You asked how you could help when she said she was going to leave. What you should've done is convince her to stay until Kellan had time to talk to her. But wait," she said with wide eyes and a sarcastic voice. "That's the point, isn't it? You didn't want them to talk. You wanted Denae gone. Regardless of what it did to Kellan."

Con held her gaze for several heartbeats. He then looked at Kellan. "Denae is a target. She might have taken care of MI5, but the Dark have her on their radar. They'll come for her."

"Let them try," Kellan stated calmly.

"If she agrees to return with you."

Kellan's smile was cold. "If she does, I want your word you'll accept her. Or I *will* challenge you."

Con gave a bow of his head and walked from the cavern.

Rhi slid off the boulder as Con's form turned the corner, leaving her alone with Kellan. "Let's go, sexy. I love happy endings."

CHAPTER
FORTY-FOUR

South Padre Island, Texas

Denae walked onto the porch with her tall glass of iced tea and sat on the swing. With one foot tucked beneath her, she idly rocked the swing with her other.

The air was hot and sticky with the humidity, but the breeze coming off the Gulf of Mexico helped to cool her. The AC was on inside, but the porch had always been a favorite of her parents. She recalled so many nights as a child when they would all come out onto the porch after dinner and stare at the stars.

Her parents would sit in the swing holding hands and smiling at each other as if they had been together months instead of years.

Denae and Renee would be on the floor playing with their dolls or cards. Those lazy nights had been her entire world, and she'd taken them for granted.

In one summer, her idyllic life had been torn to shreds.

Denae blinked against the wash of tears that threatened and drank deeply from her sweet tea. It was hard being back in the house. Every room she went into brought forth memories. Some good, some bad.

A buzzing sound drew her attention to her right. The crepe myrtle tree her mother had planted was in full bloom. The delicate limbs drooped with the weight of the bright pink flowers, and the bees, as well as the butterflies, were taking full advantage.

It made her smile. Her mother had loved working in her flower gardens. They had been her pride and joy. The crepe myrtle, she had told them, would offer shade and beauty when it grew.

"She was right," Denae said.

She sighed and turned her head forward. And nearly dropped her glass when her gaze landed on Kellan standing on the walkway, staring at her.

He wore black jeans slung low on his hips and a steel-gray shirt. His hair looked damp, as if he'd just gotten out of the shower.

Seeing him again made Denae realize how much she loved him. It had been the hardest thing of her life leaving Dreagan. What was he doing there? Didn't he realize she wouldn't be able to leave him again?

He took a step toward her, and that propelled Denae to stand. Her bare feet were silent as she walked to the steps.

She drank in the sight of him, the power, the virility, the sheer sexiness. She knew just how well those lips of his kissed, how gentle and coaxing his hands could be, and how mouth-watering his body was.

He put one foot on the bottom step and then slowly smiled.

"What are you doing here?" she asked, finally able to form words.

He looked around. "This is where you grew up?"

"Yeah," she said absently.

"It's nice. Needs a coat of paint."

Denae frowned, taking offense. "I know. I've had someone looking after the place while I've been gone."

"Why no' just sell it?" he asked, his celadon gaze landing on her once more.

"I was going to. I just couldn't let go. I had to make MI5 think I did, however, so I transferred the title into my aunt's name."

"Smart girl."

She shifted and finally stepped to the side. "Would you like to come in?"

Kellan climbed the steps onto the porch. His caramel-colored hair tempted her to run her fingers through it and drag his head down for a kiss.

Somehow, Denae managed to keep her hands to herself. She lifted her glass. "Would you like some sweet tea?"

"Nay, lass."

"A tour, then?"

"Nay."

Denae fiddled with her oversized cutoff denim shorts that hung precariously on her hips. Her red tank top suddenly felt too small and clung to her dampening skin.

That's what Kellan did to her. He sent her reeling, listing whenever he was near. She couldn't form a coherent thought or say a complete sentence because her mind—and body—were attuned to him.

"What do you want?"

"You." His voice was soft, low. His eyes were intense and watchful.

She melted on the spot. With one simple word she was ready to throw herself into his arms. Hell, who was she kidding? She'd been ready to do that the moment she spotted him.

"Why did you leave?" he asked.

Denae felt a drop of condensation from her glass drip onto her foot. "It was for the best. I have a plan."

"A plan you didna share with me."

He sounded offended, which made her raise her brows. "Why should I?"

"Because we're meant to be together. And you know it."

She shook her head slowly. "No. I don't know it. You're immortal. I'm not. You're a Dragon King. I'm . . . well, I'm a human. You know, the ones you despise."

"I did despise humans," he said as he closed the distance between them. "Until I met an American working for MI5 who snuck into my cave and woke me."

Kellan wasn't sure if anything he was saying was right. He'd never wooed a woman before, but he was willing to do anything to bring Denae back to Dreagan with him. Even if it meant he had to get on his knees and beg.

She looked delectable in her faded shorts and tank top. Her hair was down, the full length of it brushing the backs of her arms. She was the most beautiful thing he'd ever seen—or ever would see.

"I took care of MI5. I'll find a way to take care of Taraeth."

Kellan knew she was capable of a lot of things. Dealing with the Dark Fae, however, wasn't one of them. He wouldn't tell her that, not in so many words at least. She was a proud woman, and she had every right to be.

"The Dark are different than anything you've come up against before," Kellan said. "You got a taste of them in Ireland. The difference is, their attention was diverted between the two of us. Taraeth is going to be hunting just for you. You'll never see him coming."

"I'm not a fool," she said and glanced down. "Taraeth and all the Dark scare the hell out of me."

This was the in he'd been waiting for. He took her hand in his, and said, "Then let me help protect you."

In an instant, she jerked her hand away. "Is that what this is? Are you still deluded into thinking your promise holds? You saved me, Kellan. You got me away from MI5 and the Dark Ones. Your promise is fulfilled."

"Bloody hell, woman, you're maddening," he said and then let out a loud sigh. "I want to protect you because I love you. I want to make sure no one can ever harm you again, and if you are ever fool enough to get yourself in trouble, I'll be there to pull you out of it."

She blinked. "What did you say?"

"I said, I'll always be by your side."

"No. That first bit."

"That you're maddening?" he asked. He knew exactly which part she wanted him to repeat. He hadn't intended to blurt it out so casually. He'd wanted to do it with finesse, which had all gone out the window as soon as he'd laid eyes on her sitting on the swing.

The pulse at the base of her throat was erratic. "No. That middle bit."

"Oh. Where I said I love you?"

She nodded. "Yep. That one."

"I love you."

"You can't." She paused and swallowed. "You can't come here and say that."

He didn't think he'd ever understand women. She obviously liked hearing it, so why was she fighting it? "Explain it to me then."

"You don't like humans. You slept for centuries so you wouldn't have to be around us."

"I did," Kellan admitted. "I never counted on you, lass. You are strong, honorable, clever, shrewd, beautiful, and resilient. You doona ever quit, and you doona ever give up. So why give up on me?"

She turned her head away, but Kellan saw the tears gathering. He pulled her into his arms and held her as her shoulders began to shake.

There was so much about this woman that he didn't know, but he comprehended enough to understand that she was meant to be his. He knew he loved her, and if he realized nothing else, that would be enough.

Then it hit him that she might not love him. She'd enjoyed their lovemaking, but she'd never hinted at anything else.

"If you doona feel the same, I willna walk away. I will remain here and pursue you until I win you over."

Denae lifted her head, her lashes spiky with tears. "You would stay?"

"Aye. I need you, Denae."

"Con doesn't want me there."

"Con can go sod himself," Kellan said flatly. "We had a . . . chat . . . before I left. He'll welcome you."

"By 'chat,' you mean you had a fight."

Kellan glanced at the ceiling and shrugged. "You could say that."

"Why?"

"Because I thought he'd sent you away."

"Silly man," she said and touched his cheek. "How could you not know I left because I love you? I wanted to make sure MI5 would leave y'all alone, and I wanted to lead the Dark Fae away from you."

Kellan took her mouth in a scorching kiss, pouring all of his love, his desire, and his need for her into it. He wanted her to know through words and touch just how much he had to have her with him.

When he finally ended the kiss, her lips were swollen and he was backing her to the door of the house. He took her glass and set it on the arm of a chair before he opened the door and was hit with a blast of cold air.

Denae wrapped both arms around him and kicked the door closed as they entered the foyer.

"Will you come back with me to Dreagan?" he asked.

She nodded while jerking his shirt over his head. "Yes. Now, shut up and kiss me."

Kellan was smiling when their lips came together.

CHAPTER
FORTY-FIVE

Denae shouldn't have been surprised when Kellan rented a private jet to fly them back to Scotland. Not that she paid much attention to the inside on the eight-hour journey. If she wasn't sleeping, she was in Kellan's arms.

Once they arrived in Inverness, Tristan was there to pick them up and drive them back to Dreagan. Denae didn't know what to expect upon her arrival at Dreagan, but it wasn't Con waiting to greet her.

"I told you, he and I had an understanding," Kellan said as he held the Range Rover's door open as she climbed out.

Denae walked to Con with Kellan by her side. "I told you I would take care of MI5."

"So you did. With Rhi's help, I hear. But I'm beginning to think you'd have done it on your own," Con said.

"I would have."

One side of his mouth lifted in a grin. "Welcome to Dreagan."

And with that, he turned on his heel and walked away. Denae looked at Kellan who shrugged wordlessly.

"Let's get to our rooms before the women find out you're here," he said.

Denae started laughing when Cassie's voice could be heard shouting her name. Kellan grabbed her hand and raced her around the back of the house to enter through the kitchen. They ran up the stairs, not stopping until they were inside his room with the door locked.

He turned to look at her. "We've some talking to do."

"Didn't we do that on the plane ride over here?"

"I doona remember talking. I remember kissing, touching, and many orgasms, but no talking."

Denae bit her lip as he approached. "Ah, yes. You may be right. I thought we did all the talking needed back in Texas."

"There's something else I need to ask you," he said as he stopped in front of her and took her hands.

"I'm listening."

Kellan hesitated a moment. "I love you."

"And I love you." Denae rose up on her toes and kissed him. "We got that sorted already, remember?"

"Aye, but there is something else."

Her smile dropped as she glanced at the floor. "I don't know how long I'll have with you since I'm mortal, but I don't want to squander another second of it."

"What if you had forever with me?"

Her eyes jerked to his face where his celadon gaze watched her carefully. "Forever?"

"Forever. Eternity. We could have that."

"And the catch?"

"You agree to be my mate."

She frowned. "You mean like get married? I don't understand."

"It is like a human's marriage, but when a mortal agrees to become a Dragon King's mate, they are marked with a dragon eye and given immortality as long as their mate lives."

"So we could be together . . . always."

He nodded eagerly. "However, you're right. There is a

catch. There willna be any children. No mortal has ever been able to carry a fetus from us to term, if they get pregnant at all."

"But I'll be yours, and you'll be mine?"

"Aye, lass. Whether you agree to the ceremony or no', I'll always be yours."

A burst of pure joy filled Denae. Kellan was offering her more than she ever thought she could have. And by the way he was watching her, the silly man actually thought she might say no.

"Let me see," she said as she ran her hands up his arms. "You're offering me eons by your side where I don't age and have forever with your kisses and that gorgeous body for me to explore at my leisure? Hmm. My answer would be a definite yes."

His smile was tight. "Are you sure? You did hear me about no children, aye?"

"I heard you. We'll figure out something if the time ever comes where I feel the need to have a child, but I suspect you will always be enough for me."

She was jerked against his chest and held tightly in his grip. To her surprise, he was shaking. She would never question the depth of his love.

Denae ran her hand over his back. Despite the threat of the Dark Fae, she had never known such happiness.

Con stared at the papers on his desk without seeing them. Another of his Kings had fallen in love. He couldn't stop the apprehension that coiled tightly in his gut.

None of them should have ever felt love for the humans. Ever.

The Silvers moving two years ago, followed closely by Hal falling in love with Cassie, and then Guy for Elena, and Banan for Jane had all been forgotten.

They had then focused on helping the Warriors fight the evil Druids while continuing to remain secret from the world. But the threat that showed itself in London was poking them again.

And this time the enemy had enlisted the help of MI5 and the Dark Fae. It was only normal that everyone would forget about something like the Silvers moving.

Never mind that the Silvers hadn't moved for thousands upon thousands of years before that.

The Silvers were Ulrik's. Could he have found a way to contact his dragons again? That couldn't be possible. Con had taken all of Ulrik's magic, including his ability to communicate with the Silvers.

None of the Dragon Kings understood the lengths he had to go to while ensuring everything they had worked so hard to achieve remained secret. And it was better if they didn't.

Con looked at his mobile phone lying on the desk. Ulrik's number was programmed in. Not that he'd ever used it, but Con liked to be prepared for any eventuality.

"Why not just call him?"

He jerked at the silky voice belonging to Rhi. How he hated when she appeared in his office. He was missing the days the Light Fae had refused to show her face. Perhaps he should make it so that she couldn't just pop in at Dreagan whenever she wanted.

Con lifted his gaze to find her sitting in one of the chairs before his desk. "Who are you talking about?"

"Ulrik. Call him. You might be surprised."

Con had to call back the rage that flared within him. He stared into her silver eyes trying to see into her mind, to no avail. Damn Fae. "How do you know? Have you spoken with him?"

"No," she said and rolled her eyes. "You always think the worst. It's why you're losing the loyalty of your Kings."

This he didn't want to hear, especially from her. "What do you want, Rhi?"

"I took a sample of Denae's blood without her knowing it."

Now that got Con's attention. "Why?"

"I wanted to know if there was a reason she wasn't affected by the seduction of the Dark. Yes, Taraeth forced her to orgasm, but she fought him. Not once did she fall under any Dark Fae's spell."

"Kellan said the same thing, but I didna truly believe him. I thought him blinded by his feelings."

"He didn't lie. I saw it myself." Rhi licked her lips worriedly. "I wish I could say I found something in her blood proving she was part Fae or something."

"But there was nothing," Con finished.

Rhi shook her head of black hair. "Nothing. She's as mortal as they come."

"They why wasn't she affected?"

"I can only think of one reason—Kellan."

Con frowned as he leaned his arms on his desk. "Something Kellan did?"

"No. Their feelings for each other. Denae and Kellan made love before the Dark Fae grabbed them. I think it was during their time alone that the bonds of their growing love took root. I think that's what stopped the Dark from gaining a hold on Denae."

"I've seen women completely in love with their men forget they were ever married as soon as they encountered a Dark."

"True. But none of those men were ever Dragon Kings."

Con blinked and slowly sat back. "If the Dark have an advantage with their magic to prevent us from shifting to dragon, then it only makes sense a woman in love with a King might not be affected by the Dark's seduction."

"Exactly," Rhi said with a grin. "I wouldn't want to test my theory on Cassie, Elena, or Jane, but it's something to keep in mind."

Con regarded the Light Fae for several minutes. "You didna have to tell me any of this. Why did you?"

The seriousness fell from her face, replaced with the

disdain she kept for him. "Trust me, Con, you won't be the only one of the Kings I tell."

"Does your hate for me go that deep?"

"I could ask you the same question."

Just as countless times before, they were at a stalemate. "Thank you for the information, Rhi."

"Don't say I didn't ever do anything for you," she said right before she disappeared.

Con ran a hand down his face just as his door was thrown open. He lifted his gaze to find Kellan and Denae standing in the doorway.

"She's agreed to be my mate," Kellan said, a wide smile upon his lips as he gazed adoringly down at Denae.

Denae laughed up at him. "I did."

If Con tried to stop them, Kellan would challenge him. Con could either lose another King, or he could give in. It wasn't much of a decision to make. He had to keep his Kings united at all costs.

He rose to his feet. "Congratulations. When do you want the binding ceremony?"

"Tomorrow," Kellan said as he walked out of the office, the door shutting behind him.

Everything Con had been fighting against was coming to fruition. The hold the Kings had on this realm was slipping. Perhaps too quickly for him to alter the course they were rushing toward.

CHAPTER
FORTY-SIX

Kellan had never been so nervous. Or excited.

He was being bound to the most wonderful, beautiful woman, and he couldn't stand to wait another minute until she was officially his.

To his right was Con. There might be a smile on Con's face, but Kellan knew he wasn't happy about the mating. Not that Kellan cared. He was finally, truly happy—something he hadn't felt since the last time he had flown with his dragons around him.

Not all of the hate for humans was gone, but Denae had healed so much of him that it was just an annoyance now. Besides, how could he hate mortals when he was in love with one?

"Are you sure?" Con whispered.

Kellan caught a glimpse of Denae walking down the corridor of the mountain. Con had repeatedly asked him if it was the right decision to make Denae his mate. Kellan had one nerve left, and Con was firmly on it. "Ask me that one more time. I dare you."

He forgot all about Con and the other Dragon Kings that lined the cavern once he had focused on Denae. Her long coppery brown hair was down and fastened in large, thick curls.

Kellan smiled when he noticed the curve-hugging dress in a bronze color. The gown was strapless and floor length with a split up her right leg.

It was customary for Con to give the females a gift, a sort of welcome offering. Kellan was about to get angry until he saw a gleam of something through her hair. That's when Kellan saw the long dangly earrings with large-faceted, smoky-quartz stones.

Kellan glanced at Con to find him looking. Kellan gave him a small nod to show he approved of the gift.

And then, finally, Denae reached him.

Kellan took her hand and they shared a smile as he walked her into the cavern that was used solely for binding ceremonies. He watched her eyes look upon the walls where the light from the torches reflected. He inwardly beamed when he heard her soft gasp as she spotted the intricate etchings of dragons of all sizes on the walls.

He brought her to a stop as they faced Constantine who stared at them for long moments while the others fell into place.

"We lived through eons without finding our mates, and yet here we are in another binding ceremony with Kellan and Denae. Denae has proven she is worthy of being mated to a Dragon King by her fighting a Dark Fae—and taking his arm."

There was a loud cheer that made Kellan squeeze her hand. Denae beamed at him, her love shining in her eyes.

"Now, we will officially welcome Denae as mate to Kellan." Con's voice rang out in the cavern.

Kellan faced Denae and took both of her hands in his. It still boggled his mind that he had found Denae. What might have happened had she gone into another cave instead of his? He didn't even want to think of it.

"Kellan, do you bind yourself to the human, Denae Lacroix?" Con asked. "Do you vow to love her, protect her, and cherish her above all others?"

"Most definitely," he answered, causing Denae to flash him a bright smile.

"Denae," Con said. "Do you bind yourself to the Dragon King Kellan, lord of the Bronzes? Do you swear to love him, care for him, and cherish him above all others?"

"I dare anyone to try to stop me," she vowed.

Kellan wanted to kiss her right then, but he held her gaze instead. A second later, Denae's eyes widened and her left arm jerked as the tattoo only a mate of a Dragon King bears was seared upon her flesh.

Denae looked down at her arm. Kellan couldn't wait to run his fingers over the eye of the dragon and the flames surrounding it. The tat was about the size of Denae's fist and done in the same red and black ink as his own tat.

"The proof of your vows and your love. There's no turning back now," Con told them. He then raised his voice to the crowd. "Denae is officially marked as Kellan's!"

They were deafened by the cheers. Kellan pulled his mate into his arms. "There's no escaping me now."

"I never wanted to escape you," she whispered seductively.

Kellan sealed their binding with a kiss that left her clinging to him.

EPILOGUE

MacLeod Castle

Charon strode into the castle and paused long enough to find Ian sitting at the long table with his wife, Dani. Ignoring calls of hello, Charon hurried to him.

"I need to talk to you," Charon said as he stopped in front of Ian, the table separating them.

Ian's brown gaze landed on him, a frown marring his features. "What is it?"

"It's something private. Something you may want to hear without the others around."

Ian rose and pulled Dani up beside him. "She comes."

"Of course," Charon said as he turned and retraced his steps. He only got halfway to the door when Fallon MacLeod stepped in front of him. It was but a beat later that the two other MacLeod brothers, Lucan and Quinn, stood on either side of Fallon.

"What's going on?" Fallon asked.

Charon ran a hand down his face. The castle was the MacLeods', and had been opened by them for any Warrior and Druid. Because of that, Fallon was the unofficial leader of the group.

"Charon," Quinn urged.

Damn, but Charon didn't want to lie. He had done enough of that to Quinn while they had both been in Deirdre's control. But what he had to say was for Ian's ears first. Afterward, it was Ian's decision what he did.

Lucan put his hand on Charon's shoulder. "You look like you have no' slept in days. Is everything all right with Laura?"

"Aye," Charon said and looked at the torc Lucan wore. All three MacLeod brothers wore the ancient necklaces given to them by their parents. "Everything is fine with Laura."

"Then what is it?" Quinn asked.

Charon glanced over his shoulder to find Ian and Dani approaching. "I must tell Ian first. It'll be his decision after that."

Lucan's sea green eyes were filled with worry. "Is there anything we can do?"

"Be here for him," Charon said before he walked around the brothers and out the door.

It wasn't long before Dani and Ian met him in the bailey. Charon looked around the cobblestones beneath his feet. "Odd that this place used to be filled with horses and carriages and people. Now, it is used for the vehicles."

"You're scaring the hell out of me," Dani said. "Please, tell us what it is."

Now that Charon stood before Ian, he wasn't so sure he should share his news. Perhaps Phelan had been right, and it was something that should just happen.

Ian glanced overhead as thunder rolled. "Spit it out, Charon. What has you so upset?"

"Duncan isna dead."

Charon thought it might be better to just blurt it out, but as Ian's face lost all color, he was beginning to doubt everything.

"How can you say that?" Dani shouted to him as she stood in front of Ian and touched his face.

Charon rubbed the back of his neck. "Because it's the truth."

"How?" Ian asked, his voice harsh and croaky.

This was the part Charon didn't want to share. After becoming allies, things could splinter depending on how Ian took the news. "Phelan just found out and shared it with me."

"Wait. What?" Dani asked as she shifted to look at him. "You're not making any sense. If Phelan discovered it, why isn't he here?"

"Because he didna think I needed to know," Ian surmised.

Charon shook his head. "Phelan didna want to tell you the way I am, and since I'm making a complete muck of it, he was right."

"So, Phelan found out. How?" Ian's voice had gone hard, his eyes steely.

"He was helping the Dragon Kings. That's when he met Tristan."

"Who's Tristan?" Dani asked.

Charon briefly closed his eyes. "Duncan. It seems that Duncan was made into a Dragon King."

"He's alive?" Ian asked quietly, shock making his face go slack even as delight shone in his eyes. "My brother is alive? Why did the Kings no' tell me?"

"Because Tristan has no memories of his former life as your brother."

The excitement that had filled Ian's face crumbled with Charon's words. And he hated himself at that moment. He'd thought coming to Ian was the right thing to do. Now he knew it hadn't been.

"I want to see him," Ian said. "Does he know of me?"

"Phelan spoke with him at length. He does know of you now. And that's all I know."

Ian looked down at his wife. "I must go see him."

"I know. I'll be beside you the whole time," she vowed as she caressed his face.

Charon watched them walk back into the castle as the rain began to fall. He waited another few seconds before he got into his car and drove back to Ferness.

Cork, Ireland

Kiril opened the front double doors and stepped inside his new home with a smile. It needed a bit of sprucing up, but it would fit his needs perfectly. Especially the cellar.

He'd just stepped into the foyer when his mobile rang. Kiril answered without looking at the screen, since he knew it was one of the Dragon Kings.

"Hello?"

"Con blew up, just as you knew he would," Rhys said.

Kiril laughed. "It does him good to lose that infamous cool of his every now and again."

"What are you doing?"

"I just bought a house."

There was a pregnant pause. "You did what?"

"I bought a house," he said as he wandered the main floor. "Think about it, Rhys. We have houses all over the world, but no' a single one in Ireland."

"That's because of the Dark. Or do I need to remind you?"

"I refuse to live out of a hotel for however long I'm here. Besides, if things come about like we want, you know as well as I that we're going to need this place."

Rhys sighed through the phone. "You're right. I still doona like you there by yourself."

"I have to be by myself if I'm to spy on them."

"You going back to the pub?"

"Of course."

Rhys mumbled something Kiril couldn't make out. Then Rhys said, "Any potential problems?"

"There's one guy who has been staring. Of course, he could just want my body."

Rhys laughed, but both knew things could turn quickly from bad to worse.

"Call me before you go into the den of evil, and I want a call when you leave."

"Aye, Mum. If I've got the female, I'll text. Calling might be a bit difficult."

"You're walking into Hell and intentionally messing with demons." Rhys's growl rumbled through the connection. "I doona like it."

Gone was any jesting from Rhys's voice. Kiril stopped in the kitchen and leaned against a wall. "Someone has to do it. You were too noticeable the last time. It had to be me. I'll be fine. And if I'm taken, I'll get out. Kellan did."

Rhys grunted. "Be safe, jerk."

"You too, bitch."

Kiril disconnected the phone and laid it upon the counter. He *was* willingly walking into Hell, because someone had to do it. Con wouldn't have agreed to it on the chance a King could be taken.

He knew that was exactly what could happen, and if it would give him the information he needed to help the other Kings to discover who was after them, then Kiril would readily surrender himself to the Dark right at that moment.

There was a knock behind him as a male voice with a thick Irish accent said, "Mr. Kiril. Where would you like me to put your luggage?"

And so the deception began. Kiril pocketed his phone and put a smile on his face as he walked back to the front door. "The master bedroom, of course."

Read on for an excerpt from

FIRE RISING

Coming soon from Donna Grant and
St. Martin's Paperbacks!

In that place between waking and sleep, Sammi found herself thinking about Tristan and the dragon, until they became one and the same.

Tristan with his mysterious air around him, and the dragon, a creature of myth and legend come to life.

She thought of Tristan's soulful dark eyes and the dragon's alarm and concern—that same look had been in Tristan's gaze when she had tried to leave Dreagan and he stopped her.

Sammi's eyes flew open as realization hit her. She knew why the dragon's gaze had looked so familiar. It reminded her of Tristan.

Out of the corner of her eye, she thought she saw a flash of amber through the clouds. The sun had set behind a mountain peak casting the side of her mountain in shadows. She kept still as if asleep, and closed her eyes until they were slits so she could still see.

And then she waited.

Between dozing, she would wake thinking she heard the dragon getting closer and closer. This last time was different. She cracked open her eyes to see the dragon glide effortlessly down from the clouds heading straight for her.

Her breath locked in her lungs as she watched the dragon tuck his head and roll as the amber scales changed into sun-kissed bronze skin.

The man rolled as he hit the ground and came up on bent knees with his hands on the ground and his head still tucked, his long, light brown hair falling to hide his face. Slowly, almost warily, he lifted his head and his hair fell around his shoulders in disarray.

Sammi recognized him before he stood. She knew that hair, had longed to run her fingers through it. Then he straightened.

She drank in the sight of him from his wide shoulders corded with muscles to his narrow waist to his tight butt and long, muscular legs.

Her eyes jerked back up to his lower back where she saw what had to be a tattoo, but she couldn't make out what it was it was so long and narrow.

Then he turned to face her. Sammi had seen gorgeous men before, but not a one of them compared to Tristan in all his glory. He stood as opposing as a vengeful spirit and as commanding as a god. He was startlingly handsome, dazzlingly strong.

Mind-boggelingly virile.

The wind whistled about him, as if caressing his body as she longed to do. It pushed his hair away from his face. Sammi bit her lip as he closed his eyes and lifted his face to the sky as if being in human form pained him.

Her gaze lowered from his face to his chest and his impressive body, but it wasn't just the thick sinew that caught her attention—it was the tattoo that covered his entire chest.

The tat was done in an amazing mixture of red and black ink, making it neither red nor black, but a beautiful mix of both.

The tat itself was of a dragon. It stood on its hind legs with its wings spread wide. The tail wrapped from his waist around to his back. Her eyes drifted lower to his flaccid rod and long legs.

His eyes opened and looked at her before his narrowed gaze shifted to the mist. A muscle ticked in his jaw as if he were deciding on what to do.

The decision had already been made for Sammi. He had disappeared once. She didn't want him to leave again. When he took a step into the mist, she jumped to her feet.

His head whirled to face her, and all emotion fled from his face. He hesitated as if trying to decide to remain or go into the mist.

"I saw you," Sammi said, hoping it would keep him near. She wasn't sure why. She was both relieved she wasn't going insane, but a little scared knowing Tristan was a dragon.

A dragon!

Where she might have run from him earlier, she recalled all too well how he had calmed her where others never could. He had reached a place inside her that only her mother had ever been able to touch.

The fact he could do that was what kept her from being frightened. She did, however, have a healthy dose of anxiety to just what he might be able to do.

"You're dreaming."

A shiver raced over her skin at the sound of his voice. How she loved his voice. Sammi shook her head. "I'm not."

"You hit your head when you fell earlier. You're dreaming now, Sammi. You're shoulder hurts, and you have a concussion."

She smiled as she realized to what lengths he would go in order to make her believe she hadn't seen him shift from a dragon to a human. "I did fall, but I didn't hit my head. I was saved by a magnificent amber dragon. You."

His chest expanded as he took a deep breath, causing the dragon tattoo to puff out. "With your injuries, I can see how dreaming this would help you cope."

Irritation filled her. She knew she wasn't dreaming, just as she knew she hadn't hit her head. "Shift back into a dragon. Let me see you again."

"I can no'."

She took a step toward him. "I'm no' supposed to know, am I?"

Tristan glanced away.

That was answer enough. "You've been with me this whole time, haven't you? And don't you dare say I'm dreaming," she said before he could try that tactic again.

"Dammit, Sammi," he grumbled and ran a hand through his hair.

She let out a long breath. A kernel of doubt had begun to fester until then. "Your secret is safe with me."

"That's just it," he said. "It's no'. They're after you because of your connection to Dreagan."

"Dreagan?" she repeated and grasped that he meant her sister. "Jane."

"Aye. Jane."

"They want Jane?" she asked, more confused than ever.

"They want us."

Us, as in other dragons. Sammi's eyes widened. "Banan's a dragon, too?"

"We're Dragon Kings, actually," Tristan said and then frowned as he stiffened. "Shite!"

She opened her mouth to ask what was wrong when he closed the distance between them in two strides and grabbed her uninjured arm as he dragged her after him.

He wedged them both between two boulders, his body pressed against hers from shoulder to thigh. Sammi looked into his dark eyes and found him staring at her.

"What is it?"

He tucked a lock of hair behind her ear. "They've found you."

She tried to run, but he held her steady.

"Nay, Sammi. They willna find you. I promise."

But she couldn't listen. She had seen exactly what they could do. They killed indiscriminately, brutally. Viciously.

"Listen. Listen!" he repeated when she continued to struggle.

Sammi paused and heard the unmistakable sound of a helicopter. She glanced around his shoulder before jerking her gaze back to him. "Oh, my God."

"They shouldna be on our land. No one flies over Dreagan land but us," he ground out.

She blinked. "We're on Dreagan?"

"Aye. You left it to go to the village, but you returned when you ran to the mountains."

Sammi leaned her head back and winced as the sound of the copter grew closer and closer. "What do we do?"

"Nothing. They willna find you here."

She felt his hand alongside her face as his fingers slid into her hair. She forgot all about running with Tristan around. Her lips parted as she longed to kiss him, to run her hands over his sculpted body.

He was gorgeous, imposing. Irresistible, captivating. Seductive.

With a look or a word, she was putty in his hands. The world seemed to be at his beck and call just waiting for him to tell it what to do.

Sammi was completely and utterly enthralled with the man who was also a dragon. A dragon who had saved her life.

A dragon who made her heart race and her stomach flutter with anticipation and excitement.

"If they do find you, they willna live to hurt you," he vowed in that seductive timbre of his.

She calmed, because there was no way they could hurt Tristan—her dragon.